ELLIPSES...

DEZI GOLDEN

ELLIPSES...

DEZI GOLDEN

First printing: June 2022

ISBN: 978-1-7376566-9-2 Paperback

Visit www.dezigolden.com for autographed copies.

To those who believe in crossing soul paths, desire, passion, and healing forward...

This is for you...
and for P-

Chapter 1
PEG LAW

It was early October. Peg was, unsuccessfully, trying to calm her nervous stomach on yet another mundane Friday night in. She considered perhaps, that it was an evening perfect for a few "puff puffs" of the weed her daughter gifted her. Weed helped the anxiousness cease on occasion.

Pegasus Aine Law, as her father proudly named her, developed some strange sort of *swirly-esk* stomach issues in the last weeks upon returning to her hometown from Florida. She especially felt nauseous when it came to thinking of her horrendous divorce. Her face contorted, just the thought of Dereck made her queasy. She'd always had a stomach of steel prior to the 2021 year, but the subconscious fears surrounding his evil ways, seeped in, landing in her upper abdomen area, wreaking havoc on her digestive system as of late.

Her body, otherwise, was making her very happy. Down seventy pounds, and feeling more attractive, Peg noticed she could feel her *true self* was returning. Her true sexual prowess too. Leaving a mentally abusive spouse after twenty-two years created the space for her to think of her needs, her wants, and of course, her desires.

Stretching her legs out along the bed she thought of her Ayahuasca ceremony just fourteen days prior. She could still feel the earth medicine coursing through her veins and smiled. Deciding to put herself through the "ego death" and intense healing was, as expected, the best decision of her life. She hadn't surmised such a sexual awakening, or kundalini opening as it were, but she didn't much mind it at all. It felt as if her real self was once again emerging...*finally*.

She was informed that the Ayahuasca root and plant drink could affect her in many ways, sexually as well. It was the one least mentioned, but apparently how it wanted to heal her in her body. And ten years of therapy in just four short ceremony hours was incredibly profound, as promised. Peg remembered drinking the medicine the

Shaman handed her and feeling as if death was running down her esophagus. She wanted to choke and gag as she had imagined her father did while drowning all those years ago, but she fought it! Instead she relented, submitted to the process and instead pulled in a tantric breath asking for healing from her sexual sacral chakra. She allowed the death...and instead asked for self-love. She remembered slowly lying back on her mat, lying down on the soft pillow and snuggling under the blanket, ready to die. And...she did. The "old peg" did.

Peg crossed her legs, squeezing her lady bits, and reveled in the clitoral pleasures that shot up through her body as often happened now. Although the life-altering ceremony was long gone, the pleasures and healing still lingered within her body and cells. Her eyes gazed along the textured yellow paint of the ceiling and gave silent praise for the moment. Her stomach was easing and she exhaled realizing she was back. Driving two days from Florida, back to New Mexico, was not what she had planned on two weeks prior, but her new self, the loving self, demanded it. She knew she was ready to divorce and rid herself of a man, she now had to admit, was attracted to young girls and other men.

Peg huffed a small exhale, remembering the exhaustion of the last two weeks. Within an hour of driving into town, she moved in to her friend's kid's bedroom, and scheduled an appointment with the military JAG office to discuss divorcing her disabled, abusive ex-military husband. Being a military *spouse*, she had to seek counsel from those that understood military divorces and when a soldier goes... **wrong**. Her psychosis-riddled veteran spouse had decided to do some sort of drugs with friends in Colorado on a business trip and...was never quite the same after. Not that he wasn't already a horrible human by most standards, as Peg had learned, but getting dumber was definitely a result of his poor decisions, and she wanted nothing to do with what was coming down the road in his life.

Dereck had been diagnosed with Borderline Personality Disorder, Narcissistic Personality Disorder, and Histrionics Disorder in 2013 by a counselor he insisted Peg go to with him. She did, although the counselor fired him after a few weeks, stating, "I can't sit here and watch what you do to your wife." There was much wrong, but NOTHING trumped the Narcissistic Personality Disorder developed by his over-critical and under-loving parenting before the age of six. Peg knew he was not born fucked up, but he sure as hell developed into what she called a "Grade-A Asshole".

She tried *so* hard in the marriage. She tried so hard to love a man who could just...not *be a man.* Not even a human, but a false being. He was a wounded boy...and for that, she tried even harder to stick by him with her "love the boy, and the man will appear" philosophy. That doesn't work with a narcissist though. Peg proved to herself that no matter what, one cannot love enough for two people. And at forty-seven years old, she was back in town, no home, no business, and no more family. She was truly starting over, and although scary, it was way less frightening than continuing on in a pointless marriage pretending he was a good man and soldier. Peg knew she was the best part of their union, now she just wanted to be the best part of her new life and future.

Her shoulder-length blonde hair now flowed down the side of the bed as she moved to hang off of it. She watched the blades of the ceiling fan go around and around and around. It didn't help her stomach. With a deep breath, she inhaled healing energy, begging for a distraction to calm the heartbeat that moved to her abdomen.

Rolling to her side, she found herself feeling as if she'd been through a war. Parent, EMT, police officer, martial artist, foster parent, massage therapist, relationship coach, author, then retired to wind up back in Las Ramas looking to start all over again. He took their home, all the money, all the savings, all the retirement... so she'd struggle and have to come crawling back to him. *Never.* Peg knew she'd never go back.

Peg reminisced. All the years of school, her first husband, becoming a mother, divorcing, hitting bottom, coming back up, EMT school, riding the ambulance, saving lives, making a difference, passing the police exam, nine months of night police academy while working days on shift, training for her first of four black belts, unfortunately meeting Dereck, her martial arts instructor, years of turmoil trying to make a failing marriage work, being diagnosed with CPTSD, leaving law enforcement too early, years of failing karate businesses, trying to be a good parent, moving the whole family to New Mexico, fostering other people's children, becoming an author, massage school, being cheated on and separating, opening a healing arts center, becoming an instructor, helping an undeserving mother-in-law after she lost her husband, Covid, going to Florida to help Airbnb his mother's home only to be cheated on *again*, now back....her entire last thirty years flashed through her mind!

Peg squeezed her eyes tight willing the tears to stay away. She'd worked so hard to find the new self-love she'd been forcing forward in her life. *Don't cry, don't cry, you got this baby girl...don't cry.*

Her mind moved to the memories of her father. She smiled, the tears holding back. Peg never thought he would come through during her Ayahuasca hallucinations or tell her to return to Las Ramas, but she was so grateful he did.

Dead almost twenty-nine years, her father appeared to her so easily, as if he always knew he would see her again. He was relaxed, nonchalant, and almost matter-of-fact about how much he loved and admired her! He told her how proud he was of her. She cried deep tears of relief hearing him say how amazing she was, how she'd bravely survived her rough journey so far, and that she was always loved every day and more on the days she couldn't feel it.

When he told her that her journey was always going to go as it had, she eased into the thought and the survival of all the abuse. She purged her old self that night, in that beautiful yurt, with over a hundred other people. When leaving she was sure she was living her divine journey, as her father had mentioned, and that she must continue forward with the new knowledge. That she, was always living in the ways she was destined.

Peg's stomach churned again, making horrendous sounds into the quiet of the tiny bedroom. She remembered Dereck lived only one street over from her, in the house she half-owned and was now locked out of. Her overthinking was interrupted by the subtle ding of her phone app. The notification said:

Gunnar O'Clery
EMT? Never knew...awesome

Peg squinted to focus. Her eyebrows raised as she read the name and sentence. She looked closer, her heartbeat sliding slowly up from her gut to her chest. *Gunnar*

O'Clery? A smile formed across her lips. She couldn't believe it was *him*. She hadn't seen Gunnar in over ten years! She met him through Dereck. At a shake shop or at some pig roast fundraiser event...she couldn't quite recall. She could see Gunnar in her mind though and remembered how she'd felt shaking his hand for the first time. His eyes were kind, he was respectful, and very charismatic. She now regretted lowering her eyes as she would, to appease Dereck's fragile masculinity and make sure she wasn't obvious about her attraction. Dereck never deserved the faithfulness she gave. Peg then remembered how much her ex talked Gunnar up...as if he wanted to fuck him.

A small chortle came from her throat as all the memories flashed. She decided she would text back. She knew her brain was on the verge of a CPTSD relapse and Gunnar O'Clery was just the sexy distraction she needed to avert it.

Chapter 2
GUNNAR O'CLERY

Gunnar breezed into his office, slamming the door just enough to send the message that he was not to be disturbed. Not quite at a skeleton crew for the night shift, he knew he could get an hour or so to himself. His officers all had their orders and most of the previous night's fuckups were resolved.

A man of average height, yet over-sized muscle, he knew when he needed a break. Slumping down into his office chair, he pulled out his phone, realizing full well it could become the downfall of his night. At forty-seven years old he couldn't believe he had to be tied to it more than most teenagers. It saddened him that he had to rely on the tiny piece of technology so much. It was a necessary evil to do his job well but, the reality was, as a Lieutenant, it assisted in keeping him and his staff alive.

His arms, impressively built and artfully covered in tattoos, raised the phone up just high enough so he could lay his head back against the chair and rest. He opened the social media app to peruse for a bit in the hopes of easing his mood. After a few posts about politics, then one about a Sig Sauer firearm, he slowed when he saw her name. He stopped, noticing her bright smile beaming from the little round icon picture. Peg Law. *Fucking Pegasus Law.* He looked to see what she typed, a slight smile, forming at one corner of his mouth:

***

Peg Law

October 8, 2021

When I was an EMT, we used to mention this frequently, lol. Still so shocking that humans need to be reminded:

Just so you know, nothing ever accidentally goes in your butt.

Sincerely,
The ER Staff

***

Gunnar chuckled out loud, impressed yet again, by her sense of humor. He laughed louder realizing she'd seen some shit as an EMT, and remembered a conversation recently with his son about the same topic. He had no idea she had been an EMT, it intrigued him. Actually, he'd always kept an eye on Peg, there was... *something* about her. Something pulled at him whenever he saw her or her posts over the years. He moved his thumb up and clicked on the icon to message her:

EMT? Never knew...awesome

To his surprise, he could see the little green dot indicating she was logged on. Suddenly, the three dots started to move, and he smiled wider, knowing she was typing back.

Lol, those were the fun years. How ya been Gunnar?
You still the best shot around?

He was surprised she answered so quickly and even more shocked she remembered details about him. Leaning back, he hiked his legs up and crossed them on his desk. His knees ached from way too many squats at the gym but he ignored them, preferring instead, to answer her question. He could see her smile in his mind's eye, remembering her from all those years back.

Tired...busy...busy...how are you? Love your posts.
I can hold my own...2nd best this year...runner up at nationals.

The dots moved and waved again, she was typing back.

Thanks. I'm either loved or hated on this app lol.

Gunnar nodded, he too knew what it was like to be loved and hated. He liked her praise and was curious as to her whereabouts.

I love the humor...still in LR?

More bubbles, she was texting and engaged!

Ex? Gunnar frowned. Could she be talking about Dereck? Gunnar started typing again curious if she'd actually gotten away from the weirdo.

He...go off the deep end?

The bubbles started wavering again, and he waited thinking, *"There's no way she's single."* Could Dereck really have lost her? Could he really have fucked up his marriage to Peg? He watched and waited. Finally, a ding sounded as her message appeared.

Gunnar's eyebrows raised. Was she really free? And did she really just mention his kids? He instinctively responded, his thick Irish thumbs moving quickly then pressing send.

Well...if you need anything...I'm still here in LR...sorry to hear bout Dereck...

Her message came quickly, as they were typing at the same time. He thought it interesting that she used ellipses like he did. Not many do, but he figured, as an author, she was used to it.

He liked her quick response and started typing faster. Oddly, he wanted to tell her about his kids, give a little more personal information, and keep her sharing herself with him.

My kids are my shining light...had a horrible childhood...so I made promises...never let them follow my childhood kinda thing...
Beginning...was...rough...but had great times...many great lessons...
Yes still here...just a text away...
What are your books about??

He felt he could share with her, he wanted to! There was something about Peg's ways. He wondered how she'd respond to his childhood abuse and adoption. He wondered if she'd accept his meager start in life. As he typed, an overwhelming desire to share some things with her, deep things, engulfed him. He couldn't really understand why. She'd always seemed like the type he could talk to. His phone dinged with her reply.

That's the best way to handle a sucky childhood, make theirs better! Love that!!!

Only way I know...

Damn. Gunnar smiled, her answer was incredible. He wondered what she would think if he shared more about his parenting, his spouse, her secret lover, how his heart has been broken in ways he never thought possible...how he may never heal from it. He wondered if she could hear about all his years in law enforcement...or the fact that he'd love to fuck her now that she was unattached. He wondered much about Ms. Pegasus Law, Massage Healer and Author...now suddenly back in Las Ramas, New Mexico.

Gunnar adjusted his cock and himself in his chair, thoughts of her doing things to his body swarming through his active mind. He switched over to her personal page while she continued typing, the three dots wavering. He had to admit, he liked her attention.

A knock came at his office door. He looked up, only to see a supervising sergeant he had the deepest disdain for, and instead of waving him in, he waved him away, shouting "Busy!" Peg was more important and interesting than what Sgt. Dickhead wanted. He decided to entertain the thought of her a little longer.

Chapter 3
BULLY

She turned the key in the lock and took a last glance through the window of her counseling practice to make sure she'd turned off all the lights. There in the reflection of the glass she noticed his chubby frame and short stature. A cold chill ran down her spine and she sighed knowing this day would come. As she turned she was mindful of her concealed gun under her skirt and shifted her client folders and purse to her left arm as she was right handed. Her eyes met his and she tried to offer a small smile.

Josephine Adeyo was a small woman, tan, tattooed and hot tempered when she had to be. On the later side of fifty-six, she was more fit than most grandmothers which she attributed to overworking and under drinking. If anyone made her want to drink it was clients like Dereck Law which is why she fired him eight years ago. She'd heard his wife returned to town recently to divorce him and knew in the back of her mind she would see him. She'd just wished it wasn't so soon. Jutting her chin forward she began to walk to her vehicle, hating that he had positioned himself in front of his truck parked next to hers.

With an air of confidence she sighed and calmed herself to appear she was on her way to her next patient, "Dereck Law, how are you?"

"I need your help." His voice was deeper than she remembered. His wife once mentioned how he would apply his "ken doll" voice, when addressing women, thinking that it made him desirable to them. She found that very amusing. Peg was humorous when she would describe her husband. Humorous and very accurate. Deep down she'd celebrated when she found out Peg finally left his lying, cheating, narcissistic ass.

"What's the problem? I'm headed to the Urgent Care to start my shift."

"I need you to help me get my wife to understand some things." Dereck's hands lifted, open and surrendering, his face sad. Josephine slowed her stride, then stopped to keep him at a safe distance and her body in full view of the cameras on the building. She did not trust him.

She shook her head, "That's not something I can do bud. I haven't seen Peg in years. Hell, I haven't seen you since what? The last gun show in town?"

Dereck exhaled almost annoyed. He could have sworn Peg and she were friends and met for drinks on occasion.

"You haven't seen her or hung out? You two don't text or talk or whatever?"

"No." She lied, but he didn't exactly ask about them sharing memes on social media or commenting on posts.

"So you two aren't friends?"

Josephine walked to her car door and unlocked it, "Derek I've got to get going. You know full well that I can't disclose much about clients, including former clients."

"So she is a client then?"

"Not since I fired you and she no longer needed sessions."

"Yeah, about that-"

She threw her items across into the passenger side and put one foot in sure she could reach her firearm if he started to close their distance. Dereck was one of her least favorite past clients, a true douchebag in her opinion.

"I don't have time to get into all that. The past is in the past for a reason...and you and I know why I fired you that day and asked you to leave my office. Truth be told Dereck, many of us could not understand how such a decent, gorgeous woman, stayed with you. I know this may piss you off, but Peg wasn't wrong, she isn't wrong now. She is one of the more integrous humans I know...even with all that threesome shit you put her through."

"Now wait a fuckin' minute ma'am-"

"I don't have a minute Law, and although I haven't seen you both in years, my diagnosis of you still stands. Borderline Personality Disorder, Histrionics Disorder, and mother-fucking Narcissistic Personality Disorder. You deny it still but it's a diagnosis for a reason. And another thing! Who are you to go around telling people in this town that I'm not a real counselor and can't diagnose!?"

Dereck could feel his blood begin to boil but there was something so satisfying about her anger so he went for it, "You can't."

Josephine moved her foot out and almost jumped out of her car but then remembered this is his game.

"You know what? You better hope, YOU BETTER HOPE, that woman doesn't subpoena me for anything in the courts that you drag her through. I'll be there in a heartbeat to prove how my PhD says I absolutely can diagnose. What's your uh, what is it up to now, ninth or oh tenth fucking degree in martial arts you've granted yourself say you can do? Abuse young girls?"

Dereck stepped towards her wanting to snap her neck, "Watch yourself, Dr. Adeyo."

"You just answered any questions I might have had about you...and on camera no less." Josephine pointed to the security cameras on the outside of the building. "Don't say another word. Get in your truck and leave. I will not stand for your bullying tactics. That may have worked in the past but everyone's got your number now Dereck Law. Now leave or I'll have you arrested for harassment."

Dereck squinted, looking at her with disdain, his lips pursed as he stepped back. She smirked, unhappy with her lose temper but knew it was necessary. She slammed her door shut and started her engine watching him leave. She knew it had been years since she offered Peg the beer out...and it was time to make sure she made good on the offer. Peg needed to be warned about him.

Dereck pulled out of the parking lot and out onto Blintz Road away from the bitch. His heart pounded in his chest creating pressure and that familiar pain he hated. There was something lovely about pissing her off but then again, she was another person on "Team Peg" he wasn't expecting. He really needed allies and he was sure he'd be able to convince Dr. Josephine Adeyo of the lies, that it was Peg who needed help after all these years, that she had left the state, abandoned him, and embezzled his mother's money.

"Fuuuuuuuuuuuuck!" He shouted into the quiet of the truck. "Now what the fuck do I do!?" He slammed his hand on the steering wheel then accelerated.

Gunnar leaned farther back in his chair switching over from her profile back to their messages. He wanted to know more. He continued their texting:

October 8, 9:56PM
(Continued Texting)

21

Only way I know...

Marriage was a sham. Should've never been...from what I've found out but we all have our lessons. My books are mostly about crime and erotica...shit I saw in my two short years in law enforcement lol. Gave me plenty of crime to write about. Oh...and tantra. Nothing healed my shitty childhood like tantric energetic healing and interdependence.

Sham???
You sell audio books??

I don't have audio just yet. Could never get enough funds together for audio...we had an arsenal of guns we had to buy first, so my author dreams are still waiting. Perhaps divorce IS the way for my goals to flourish lol.

What is Tantra???

Tantra means "interweaving" it's...our energy within...a 5,000 yr old spiritual practice in which all aspects of earthly life, including sex, can be a path to healing. The essence of the practice is going into everything as completely, and consciously as possible...Mind and body are equally important and using the sexual chakra of our bodies to manifest healing. It's the bond that procreates life so...pretty powerful stuff. Incredible for healing CPTSD and childhood wounds.

You still married? I believe you were years ago when I last saw you...

I am...rough...rough marriage...but we have kids...
CPTSD? Arsenal??

Marriage is definitely an institution!
*Complex-Post Traumatic Stress Disorder (CPTSD). So PTSD can be from an accident, war, more of a singular moment incident that scars the neuro-plasticity in the brain the sufferer has to try and heal. BUT... CPTSD is where a child learns to live in survival and constant cortisol production from **multiple incidents** or lifestyle. There's no "off" switch for the cortisol so we go for careers that are adrenaline-based (EMT, Law Enforcement, ER, etc.) to distract and cope but, the body has a hard time when not in **fight-flight-freeze-fawn mode**. Our brains go towards trauma because it's familiar. Sucks. Kind of like staying in a toxic relationship because the person is just like our difficult (narcissistic) parent.*
Sucks donkey dick. Lol

Well HI!!!...thats me...I am more comfortable in gun battle...than brushing my daughter's hair...

Yes, I sensed that about you. But that's how you cope. You're trying to survive the rough beginnings, right?

I am...have been...is there...was Dereck...well was there just Dereck?

I stayed for the kids, and then one by one, we all moved out. My babies are like, "Mom, you deserve so much love. Please move on." Lol. Sad when even your kids are desperate for you to break free. Just Dereck...

Sorry...if I'm probing??

I essentially married my mother (Dereck is just like her) without even realizing the familiar wounding I gravitated towards. As a child we "developed" in it and our brain understands, all too well, the heightened moments. Not doing that again, lol. Now comes old age and the job of healing more wounds. I'm glad you can see the lessons. That's what the healing is...getting to the "a-ha's" right?

Well...healing looks good on you...I look forward to your posts...you are funny-

Ha! Thanks.

Libra vibes????????
I'm Scorpio

Oh myyyy, male scorpios are very...

Yes?

Confident...Determined.
Ambitious...

...in bed...too.

I can be...but humble to know I have to simply work hard...harder than most.

Gotta be sure to let those feelings/traumas out
Or they...stack!!

...very.....ambitious...
I do...I love unconditional...Kinda a scorpio...Irish thing

Ambition can be a great distraction...helps to have the drive for success but also pushes the pain aside to be felt another time. It's all good. We survive how we can...

That's me...but I will always take time...to enjoy something some would think is simple... everyday simple

Yes! I like that!!! It's all about the simple things. Life can be so...extra?

Yup...love sunsets...I do enjoy a day...make the best of it...usually my answer is "yes"...

Gratitude daily brings on more of that! Love the weather here compared to Florida. No other sunsets can match NM.

Or rain storms...

Right? Oh yum, the scents and the warm winds of the storms. Love it!

Right...how are your kiddos??

Doing great actually. Thanx for asking.
My firstborn, Jaeden, is 28 and just moved to NJ (to get away from Dereck but also for remote work near DC Hqtrs) He's an analyst for the Feds. Jersey girl here, with family on the east coast, so he went back to our family home there.
*My daughter, Zena works at **The Boneyard Brewery** and is figuring out being 20 with a straight-A brain but, also a hate for the educational system. She's my defiant hippie gal that dislikes her father's concepts. Heart of gold tho. Can't complain. My kids are amazing souls that never once got in trouble.*
I really lucked out with them.
You have two or three babies?

3...ages 22...19...and 10...

Oh shit! You go, Dad!!

What happened with Dereck...if I may ask? I always kept distance...seemed...well not sure...but cautious...flags were there

*I went to FL to help out with his mother's house while he transitioned her into Alzheimer's Assisted Living care. I also needed a break from him and a peaceful place to write and publish my novels. His Puerto Rican family got wind of him putting his mother in assisted living and turned him in for **elder abuse**. He loves a fight, so they all went at it in court. I stayed happily away.*

*Through the distance...I felt free and happy so I stayed a year. A soldier/black belt student of ours (we owned martial art studios in the early 2000s) had to come back to the states because Biden pulled the soldiers out. Dereck started pressuring me to go back to Las Ramas to do a threesome when the soldier returned. He's like a son to me so it was a **no**.*

3 some??? With a friend?

Yes, more like a 30 yr old son. I refused naturally, and I began losing respect for Dereck, more than in previous years. He doesn't let up and has a weird bisexual side always wanting two men with me (called a Devil's Threesome). When I refused again, he went forward in and replaced me in the threesome with a former massage client gal I thought was a friend. Long story short, he was "uninvited" to the threesome with them (that he coordinated lol) and the soldier called me, saying "your man is losing it" kind of vibes. "This is what he's doing behind your back while you're in FL"

?......

I put up with so much from him in 23 years it just killed whatever love I had left (Ayahuasca helped too). I just can't respect him. Then...sooooooo much truth starting coming out. It was as if people were coming forward, and out of the woodwork, to tell me how awful my ex is and they felt guilty, keeping his indiscretions from me. Some went as far back as when we were dating...apparently I was faithful to someone who was actually a covert narcissistic hoe and chronic cheater, lol. I now wish I had left the marriage sooner.

Ohhhhh...well...don't lose faith...you are a beautiful lady...truly...so threesome was his needs... not too see you happy?

My happiness was never something more important than his need for power. I believe the truth comes out at the right time.

Sure, I didn't want to believe he could be such a piece of shit but now I know things I can't unlearn about him.

Never would have seen that...but seems as such...so is he now a super jealous kind of guy?

Yep. He has a weird fetish for controlling the man and woman (in the threesome dynamic) and I guess... watching? Threesomes are great for a select few that are successful at them. Not when one person wants to be the puppet master and manipulate and pull the strings of the others. Jealousy and anger are his fuel, yes. I don't want any part of all that. Not my thing.

Never done one don't know...I'm sorry...never knew...red flags with him for years though...

He'd tell you an entirely different take on everything and that's fine. We all have our perception. Red flags? Oh...my yes.

It's funny how that happens...
He wanted to coordinate trainings...I just...really didn't believe much of what was being said

I'm glad you went with your gut. Wish...I had. Honestly, I'd just love it to all go away and be in the rearview.

...seems as you have...bet guys are breaking your door down...you are...genuine...hard to find in this world

Not really much on the "guys" stuff. Real seems too much for most.

Too much??? Hmmmm???

I can't do fake anymore. I had to fake it to make it for so long in a useless marriage, my body is like NOPE!

Good...a position of control...very powerful...very sexy.

IDK about sexy...or about this hookup culture. My friends are like, "Girl you gotta go through your hoe-phase for a while." But, being married to a hoe-cheater makes that seem like an assault against my being lol.

You don't seem like a shallow hook up...too much investment with someone to walk off... nope...not you...at all

Thank you. I'm not willing to self-abuse again. Life is too awesome to deal with...assholes lol.

Exactly...I know where you have been...just saying...connecting is too serious to walk off...even in college...hook up...wasn't me...

I likey! Connection is my jam. That's my tantra honestly. Delaying gratification and feeling hours of bliss with someone really heals the mind in unexplainable ways...to me, anyway.

College can be an issue lol. I feel bad for how some hook-up these days then try not to feel anything about it.

Healing...and trust...can't lose

Truth!

See...I can learn

Ahhh...yes, you are teachable!! Lol, I vow to always be a student of life...and err teachable!

Do you? How?

Just opening up to the lessons. Not sinking into victimhood but rather being open to changing what doesn't work.

Like getting away from trying to love a person who loathes themselves. He said every time he looks at me he feels shame and regret. Instead of making it right, he's made me a target. Soo... Ya can't love enough for two people. Gotta love you first so your cup overflows and then everyone gets the best of you. See...teachable! Lol.

Shame??? Regret???
Bull...just bull...
If your smile...is yours the world will know...and want to know why...thats why I messaged you...your smile...is infectious...in a good way...
Sorry if I am going too far-

*You're fine. Not too far at all. Just connecting with convo. Keeps me sane. Not easy losing an entire life suddenly and living in my girlfriend's kid's room. Thank you for the "smile" compliment. I've been told the same by others but then some say I'm **intimidating** as hell. Weird. If it makes me smile...I want to be around it. Life is too short for more sadness. There's gotta be balance at some point right?*

Didn't lose a life...great kids who learned direction from??? Life lived...never regret...

True. I should remember that first lol! Was feeling sorry for myself today because he got a locksmith to change the locks and I can't get into my home. JAG office says the judge will not look favorably on that. I was always reminded of how much more his guns were important, than me. Power is his first love. So he locked up all our guns...and me...out.

Guns???
Just metal and plastic

Right? They can't keep ya warm at night.

Yup...yup...I know...I have many...many...very nice guns...sponsored pro shooter

Oh my. Then you do know. Well, material possessions are fun...for a time.

Well, I hope you can find a way to stay warm tonight...I look forward to your posts...makes me reflect, smile, and laugh...

Thanx. Glad you like. Great talk. Be well, my friend.

You too.
Nite.

***

<u>**_Peg's Journal Entry 10/8/21:_**</u>

So, the most interesting, fucking thing happened tonight. I was lying on my bed, with another damn anxiety stomach issue, when a message came through on my phone from Gunnar O'Clery!!! Fucking Sgt. Gunnar O'Clery? I haven't seen Gunnar, since probably 2012, before Dereck got caught cheating with that hag and we separated for five years. Not gonna lie, I remember my body reacted almost electrically, when Gunnar shook my hand and I thought he was incredibly charismatic. Rugged, funny, and genuine, totally my type but...ugh, married. I'd dismissed my feelings of course, always the faithful wife to an asshole, but I've never forgotten Gunnar. There was just something about him. Quietly, I watched him over the years in town and recently on social media. Dereck would talk about him to his students and neighbors as if he and Gunnar were actually friends. I always thought that was so weird, but Dereck always idolized the people he wanted to be.

Bill liked Gunnar, had respect for him from what I could pick up in his comments. I mostly remember Gunnar would talk with Bill at the shake shop and Dereck was more of a tag-along.

Anyway, we had a really nice text chat tonight. I thoroughly enjoyed our back and forth. I may have overshared, ugh, I really wish I wouldn't do that. Who wants to hear all my drama? And... flirted a bit. Didn't even know I could still flirt. It's been so long.

*I find it slightly humorous that I met Gunnar through Dereck. He would blow a gasket if he ever found out Gunnar texted me. I'm curious to know if Dereck ever approached Gunnar to be a part of one of his grand threesome ideas. He always used me as bait to entice men **he** actually wanted. The things I'm finding out about Dereck are appalling now, but I'm free, and that's all that matters.*

A favorite part of our conversation was how he adores his kids. I always have such admiration for great fathers, I feel it has a lot to do with the rough beginnings. I'd love to know more about him and his children. It's so nice to see there are good dads out there, as Dereck was...not.

I sense a deep CPTSD connection between us. It's crazy to be able to talk and commiserate with someone dealing with the same survival life tactics. Makes me feel less alone in the world. I wonder if he feels the need to use sex to regulate his mind as I do...

I enjoy how curious he is and asks questions. I, of course, overshare because it's been weeks of not venting and rarely am I ever asked how I feel. Poor guy had to read all my rantings.

He was super curious about Dereck and mentioned he was cautious with him, that he felt red flags. I admire that he senses things in people...and listens to his gut.

He also asked about my kids, which warmed my heart. Rarely does anyone remember I have adult children, let alone ask about them. I was a fucking badass mom, and foster mom at one

29

point, and it's so easy to forget that now that they are all grown and out on their own. I miss them so much.

The uncomfortable part was his curiosity about the threesome, then again, who wouldn't be curious. It's what ultimately lead to the demise of my marriage, so it's something I'll need to learn to explain more. It had been the deal-breaker years back and then came around again to actually dissipate the marriage. Wow, I wonder what life would be like if I'd left the first time...or even the first time he cheated. I was one first-class dummy, but that's in the past. I don't want to "dummy" my way through life anymore, thinking that's what love is. Time for me to have patience and learn what this love stuff is all about.

He did say how guys must be knocking my door down, which was flattering, but I had to explain I'm really not like that. I wonder if he will pick up on how much of an introvert I am. He kind of complimented me also by admitting he liked my smile. That felt nice...

One part that really got me from the first few texts is the ellipses. **I've never texted with anyone else who uses them like I do!!!!!!!!!!!** What's that about? And when his name came over my phone in bold black letters, I felt compelled to answer. Why would I want to text with him...and share so much so soon? How was it we could connect so easily?

What's super interesting is my father and "Momma Aya" both mentioned, during my Ayahuasca ceremony, that I would need to come back to Las Ramas and patiently await what they were sending me. I believe it went something like, "Wait until you see what's coming. He's coming to you, and there is nothing to be done or reject, you must endure this connection. You deserve..." Could Gunnar be the **"he"** they were referring to? I remember nodding my head in obedience, and then Dad said, "There will be nothing you can do to escape this. You've completed your karmic debt to the other, now you deserve all you've asked for. Do not turn him away." Dad even motioned to my guides and angels to come to me and lead me. Now here I am, and this hot, older (my age, I hope) sexy warrior contacts me? Even his name (Gunnar) means warrior!! What is this madness that I welcome so easily into my new, crazy life??

I thought Dad may have been talking about Angelo, who'd been pursuing me hard while I was still in Florida. When I returned, all we'd done is smoke weed together, and I massaged him but never crossed a line. I didn't even let him kiss me. He's too young, and sexually, he'd need to be taught too much. Not interested.

Life is definitely interesting to say the least. I **thoroughly** enjoyed tonight.

Chapter 4

DREAM WELL

Gunnar reached for his phone, his morning erection stronger somehow and lingering longer than expected. Her words from the other night were still in his mind, her smile imprinted behind his eyes. He picked up his phone from the nightstand. She was online despite the early hour. His dick hitched. She had some sort of effect on his body. He was sure he'd overstepped a few nights ago and should say something...yet he was curious to dive deeper and know more. He moved his thumbs over the letters and pressed send:

October 11, 2021 8:13AM

Sorry bout all the questions the other night...Some were personal. Hope you are well.

(nothing)

***

Josephine pressed call and listened to the ringing over and over. Aileen wasn't going to pick up, she never picked up. The message followed with a brief "I'm not available, you know what to do." Josephine huffed a small laugh and shook her head.

"Yo biotch, it's Jo. I know you're probably busy munching carpet, you sick fuck, but I need to talk to you about something. Call me back."

She hung up smiling. She'd known Aileen Lauden since first grade. Aileen was her oldest, best friend, a huge woman, lesbian and retired FBI. Josephine knew, not only could Aileen help her with the Dereck Law encounter, she could advise her as well since Dereck and Peg were Aileen's neighbors over in the Dey Pradu development on the east side of town.

She sat back against her chair pinching the bridge of her nose to try and will away the headache that had been lingering. It was the sort of almost-headache that started behind the eyes and wrapped around to the face trying to take over but not exactly committing. Admittedly, she hadn't slept well since Dereck Law had visited her in the parking lot. Something was off about him. She still felt he was an unattractive, fat hispanic man with a wide nose and large monkey-type top lip. He appeared as if he might have been attractive at one time in his life but not at all since she'd met him. Peg was way out of his league and deserved better. Everyone knew it too. He really fucked up because from what she could see from Peg's social media posts, the woman was never going back to him. He seemed to think he could convince her otherwise.

Josephine closed her eyes remembering how she met the Laws. It was Peg who called. Her voice was velvety, melodious even, with a sadness behind it. She'd inquired about couples counseling due to infidelity. Josephine could tell it wasn't Peg who'd done the cheating, but rather she'd been blamed for it, hence the call for the counseling. She hated when men got caught being unfaithful and made their wives feel like it was something they weren't doing or that they weren't good enough. She actually enjoyed helping Peg understand that Dereck's cheating was never about her and every bit about him and his toxic shame issues. Diagnosing him was easy too. He was a horrible narcissist, which Peg already knew deep down and had mentioned in their first session, but just like most, he'd not been diagnosed. Josephine remembers the day she blew up at him in her office and announced that the session would be his last because she couldn't "sit here and watch what you do to your wife anymore". He was appalled and stormed out. It was amazing. She even continued to counsel Peg and remembers helping her understand that she would leave him one day...when she felt strong enough to sever the trauma bond. She wanted to jump for joy when she'd heard they were getting divorced. Now she needed to speak to Aileen because she just couldn't shake that Dereck wasn't safe. Something was very wrong with the guy, like a psychosis in his gaze. Very wrong.

P eg walked into her room and over to her cell phone still charging on her bedside table. She sat on the edge of the bed and looked over the notifications. There was a message from Gunnar O'Clery she had somehow missed days earlier. She actually thought he'd forgotten about her but it seemed he was apologizing. She smiled, liking that he had thought about their texts and that he was wishing her well. Quite a few friends had done the same lately. It seemed that word was getting out that she and Dereck were done. For her it had already been months of freedom which she was so proud of...like escaping a prison with invisible walls.

She decided to lay back against her pillow and see if he was available to chat. He did intrigue her.

10/14/21 7:19PM

Actually, many are curious and asking me about Dereck. I guess that's natural.

Yeah...I was just reading some of your posts...

Oh geez, lol. How's the busy work week been for you?

Great points of view...seems like you are getting better...work is very busy...way under-staffed...

Oh my. No bueno with skeleton crew...

70 cops short...long hours...

Ohhhhh no...

Very bad right now...officers very very burned out...

Thats so sad...

How long you staying in NM?

As long as I can afford to. My home is here, but he changed the locks. I'm a massage instructor, reiki master, and author, but I had retired, so getting back into everything isn't a bad idea. I'm hopeful life manifests for me here. I could open my healing arts center again in my home as I still have my LLC. He's kinda smokin' me out by transferring all our money into a new acct so I can't live on it. I'm hoping to stay but may end up back home in NJ where I was born (living with sister). Praying for divine intervention at this point lol.
How are you coping with the stress at work?

I work out...shoot...just try to relax...

Yezzzzz…

Sometimes works…some days no…

Yup. I get it. Some days I kick ass at the gym or heal people on my massage table. Other days I'm a mess and can't write a damn chapter. Just gotta keep keepin' on, right? I'm guessing you're working night shift?

Swing shift…what gym…pics look amazing btw…

Thank you! Filters are my friend lol. Planet Fitness. I spoil myself with the hydro-massage machine after my workouts because…well, massage therapists are picky about fascia and muscle. The hydro is as close to a man's deep strength as I can find lol…
You workout at the station?

No…gym on Valley/Boutz…usually when I wake up…

Oh wow, that's discipline! When you wake up? Great job.
Gets the day in check!

I try…some days it really sucks…

I hear that…Those are the days we really need it tho…

Exactly…they have sauna there…

Ohhhh nice…Infrared detoxes the thyroid. Ahhhhh….

Relaxes…helps me focus…

It really does. Great job taking care of you!
You happen to know your Briggs Myers personality test score?

I know I have taken it…can't remember…

Ah…

You??

INFJ…

A fuckin' feeler... But, it makes for good Tantra love-making lol...

In cop terms?

Didn't help me much in law enforcement. Too empathic...left due to CPTSD diagnosis...and catching my Sgt in his pickup truck in the woods with someone who was NOT his wife (oops) I resigned in 2001 after only two years in (NJ) due to pregnancy.

Wow...
I think I'm ENFP

Nice! Now I know why we get along...

You did cop work too?

For a short while. Dereck kinda ruined it for me. My coworkers hated him. He got me in trouble and written up for calling during my shifts too much. Lesson learned. Never date your covert malignant narcissistic martial art instructor lol. Damn those red flags I ignored. He was the activator of my CPTSD. I learned years too late that he secretly resented me for being a cop because he couldn't pass the tests. His dad was a cop, and I was (very briefly), but Dereck never got that far...so indirectly he made me suffer lol. I just thought he was competitive. Deep down though it's caused a lot of contention. Now I understand so much more.
You ever been secretly hated by someone who professed they loved you?

I think I certainly have...

Brutal...I'm sorry you experienced that...

Very...very...sucks when you are all in emotionally...
I knew Dereck's dad...seemed like a good man...

I think he tried to be...He wasn't loved well and had a hard time moving forward in life. He adopted Dereck but didn't know how to nurture him unless it was over-criticism and under-emotion. Perfect formula for narcissistic personality disorder creation (Dereck has it along with Borderline Personality Disorder) Bill followed rules but could never get Dereck to...sad...

That is sad...adopted??? I'm adopted!

Are you??? What's the story behind it...positive, I hope?

I am...it's a happily ever after story...

Irish, yes? Cuz...ya kinda look Irish...I love those happily ever after stories...

Massachusetts Irish kid...

Me too! Well...

From MA??

My Portuguese family is from Fall River, MA!
My Irish/Scottish family is from Browns Mills, NJ lol...I'm a mutt, but it feels right so...

We are all mutts somehow some way...how long have you been separated?

So, you were born and raised in MA?

Born yes...raised in Albuquerque...

Nice! Separated first time 2012-2017. This time for good...since April 2021...

Ahhh...I see...you dating at least?

Not yet...I'm not the dating type. I'd like to heal and be balanced for something real if that makes sense...
Dereck is just like my mother, and I don't ever want to gravitate towards what gave me CPTSD originally.
I connect too deeply for superficial dating lol...sucks...

He seems like a master manipulator...

You got it!

Yeah superficial stuff...kinda like comfort food...

Lol...

Corn dogs at state fair sound good...until you eat it...

36

Right??!!! Lol

How do you deal with stress...

As an INFJ, I have weird vices.

I write tantra and erotica within my suspense and crime novels. I have an energetic tantra practice that helped me survive a fraudulent man and terribly dis-connective sex. It did give me a healthy interdependence and self love, but it fucks me up for going forward and dating. Once you're raw and real, your body doesn't gravitate toward fake...

Huh? Ohhh...that...got ya...

He thought I was this amazing goddess but because he's a closeted bisexual, he kept talking me up with other men then pressuring me to do threesomes. When I would refuse, he'd try in different ways to manipulate me. I refused so much that he replaced me with a woman here in Ramas, who was a former massage client and friend (I thought). I didn't go down (Dereck was uninvited to the threesome after the two met and fell for each), but the guy (soldier I know) came to me and wanted me to know what Dereck was doing behind my back. I was in FL renting his mother's house out for him, and he thanked me by being a shady fucker. Even went out on dates with others. What's more, I later found out about some criminal stuff (can't prove yet), so I ended the marriage in April. I'm so much happier now...but he's punishing me of course. Oh well, it'll make a great book to be published I guess. It's all such bullshit drama. I want to be free of this crap and just love forward. Adulting wasn't supposed to be this hard. I want to go back to naps and spankings...lol

Well...you seem quite awesome...
Spankings??? Wow...

Spankings (joke)...You ever just crave real? Like despise all the fake crap? Fake people?

Every...day...

I knew you'd say that...

Why...

Law enforcement...that work made me deeply desire truth...It's so much easier to be real yet everyone is walking around putting on aires...I want an easy button Gunnar! Lol...

37

Yes...it is the search...seems harder to find...

Getting worse...I feel bad for our kiddos...

Yeah...they have a crazy world to roam...

Somehow, they're doing it though...we must have loved them up right somehow...can't go wrong if the love is at least real right?

Genuine truth there...we did good...

Mine kept my ass straight...I always tell them they saved my life...

Amazing feeling to know that huh...

Sure is! The only real complaint I hear now is, "Ya think ya could have divorced sooner ma?" You know, we stay for the kids, but they don't see that as desirable later lol...

Well...here you are with a beautiful smile...
Yeah...they know...

Thank you...I am smiling more now...nothing tastes as good as freedom feels...

I can tell...like your smile pics...frisky posts...

Frisky? I swear my kids knew shit before I did...I joke that they'll choose who I'll date next.

Like radar...

Right...and gaydar...I'm not good with...they know tho...

Your little flirty posts...subtle...but sexy...even dick pic one...

Ohhh you mean my posts from my weird sense of humor? Lol...

Love the sense of humor...

So glad you get my twisted mind...thats from the EMT days that rolled into "copville" law enforcement...

Was very funny...I giggled out loud...

What makes you giggle exactly?

The funny memes...like a shy girl...blended with a very sexy tone...I like how you add a spin to them...

Thanx, you're awesome...I only get away with it around masculine energy...

Well...I'm masculine...and I love it...general flirty fun...with an "I will ravage you" undertone...

Ravage is a favorited word of mine...I use it in my novels...

I'm certain...

Yep...YOU are definitely masculine, but I sense a nice balance with some feminine energy as well...cuz, well you love your babies...

They are my center...and stars...

I can tell...
That's the "reals" I like...

Other favorite words...

Uh...bliss, ecstasy, pleasure, rapture...

What's your definition of those...

Soul stuff...nothing better...raw, real energy...

Describe...tell me...

Hmmmm...

The synergy of connection is intriguing...

Like burying his manhood in her womb...surrendering to being engulfed and taken...Feeling her squeeze...and letting her take him as her god...into her goddessness....

...and in return for her?

Her? She surrenders...but...when she chooses...

Wow...
Heart kinda racing...

Heart racing? Is that a good feeling?

Very good...

I have a lot of useless crap rolling around in my head lol...

I am interested in it...

My novels have spiced up a few marriages here and there. For instance teaching men to match their woman's breathing can help them climax at the same time as she. Most don't know that but, it damn works!

Hmmm...I can't even reference how she is breathing...

Really? Can't hear how she's breathing? Or there is no connection? Are you more visual, auditory, or kinesthetic?

Not sure...100% kinesthetic...

Uh, I should know that, top shooter and all. So, you can feel your way around in the dark...nice!

I can...

That's hot!

You like? Do you find your way?

Damn...you went right to the front of the line Jedi! Lol...

Very spontaneous...

Lol...uh but yes, every time. Even with the wrong guy...ugh, I wasted years Gunnar...Oh well, can't spend time looking in the rearview lol...

Good view on that...

So, I guess I'm a dreamer huh?

...and that makes you hot...

You're very kind...

Nope...and you during your dreams...where does your mind go...

Oddly...during dreams? Reverse cowgirl...so...

Oddly??? Why's that...thats hotttttt!

Kinda is, huh?
I like strong hands on my hips while I smash...lol...

Lots of stimulation...lots...that would be an amazing view...

For me it's legs, feet, and curling toes lol...but feels yummmm...

I bet...

But by candlelight I'll take it...everything looks better by low lighting...like filters!

Does your skin become sensitive to touch...breath...

Yes...it "blushes" (Irish gal) sensitive to sensual kisses too...

Love foreplay?

(Later)

Too much???

Nooo...I love prolonged gratification...Sorry, had to hit the treadmill and weights before getting fondled by the hydro-massage bed...not been sleeping well so needed to workout...

Lucky hydro-bed...
Prolonged gratification...do tell??

Ok...so let me drop some ancient knowledge on ya here...

Please...

Tantra...like massage, is an ancient art and medicine for healing (5,000 years old). The idea was to come (and cum) together to create universal energy within each other. Creates life, balance, pleasure, wards off disease, heals, etc., and is the natural human connection (which we all seriously lack these days) You really want to learn this? Lol...

I do...

So, in tantra, we learn that men are more powerful when they delay ejaculation and the spilling of their "seed"

Delay??

Yes, men win wars, have better focus, love intensely... when they hold their ejaculation...they can fuck daily but hold their seed until say...the weekend when they can let go and fully recoup and sleep to rest. Now women, they require multiple orgasms daily (I recommend 3 a day to my clients lol). So basically, a man's body and need for power melds perfectly with a woman's needs. We're taught the opposite though (religious bastards). Men are told to have as many orgasms as possible while women are shamed for having theirs.

Wow...
Hell yes...so you self-satisfy 3 x a day...

I try yes...but in public I have to reserve myself to just using breath lol...

Toys??

You're not focusing O'Clery! Lol...Toys are meh...I prefer a warm, rigid
man-pole personally...Sooooo....

Ok...please continue...

Soooo...the powers-that-be figured out they could control the masses by preaching how sex is a sin (even though we all come from sex and its super healing) and fast forward to the Victorian era bullshit where religion got involved and told women to not worry about orgasm (because they'd become too powerful) and men could have as many orgasms as possible with whoever (hence rendering them powerless)...then porn was invented in the 1500s to control even more...so everyone is fucked...still lol...women are slut-shamed and feel they shouldn't self-pleasure...and men are encouraged to sleep with as many as they can to be a "man"...

sad

Nothing more sexy than watching a woman satisfy herself...

You think? Well, nowadays there is a lot of sexual dysfunction due to the desensitized result of focusing
on the end result orgasm...instead of connection...

No dysfunction here...

I'm at a place in my life where connection is hard to find...

If it's only physical...then there is no connection...
Connection = the stars and the moon...

Hmmm...I agree!
So...long story short, those who practice tantra get the healing effects. I love it for the balancing of
oxytocin, serotonin, and dopamine. Keeps ya young!

Yup...yup...

I really like connection...slow and sultry like...I feel unsatisfied if there's not enough time to build and
connect...

So what are ya gonna do?

Fuck if I know...just tryin' to make it through ovulation today...I swear, even a park bench looks sexy lol...

Ovulation make you horny?

Oh gawwwd yes. Worshipfully so...

Now what...

It's three days of hell..then it turns into regular yearning the rest of the weeks...

Wow...not helping...with these messages...

Lol...no...

Well...
Kinda sorta sorry...

Ever had multiple?

Orgasm??? Yes...often...

I mean...sometimes a quickie in the linen closet is needed...but when there's time...multiple are...very nice...

I like to be in tune...
And thorough...love touch...love scent...

Good man!

And you...what makes you explode...

Kissing and thrusting...in unison...scent, strong arms, crushing weight holding me down...penetration... exhaled breath slow in my ear, sexy words...

1 to 10...good kisser?

Been told a 12...but who knows...just flattering maybe...

Are you a multi-cummer?

Multi-orgasmic? Yep, praise be-jeezus...don't forget to eat your dates to raise your sperm count lol...

Noted. You like lots of sperm???

I don't mind a mess, but I am a Libra so...we like groomed and clean. When were you born?

November 73...
Groomed? Are you?

I'm a month older?! Oh shit...a youngin'...Groomed? Tastefully yes...Scorpio or Sag?

(Scorpio emoji)

No wonder we get along so well...

Why? Tastefully??

Tastefully...so nothing peeks out the sides of the thong or bathing suit bottoms...

Mmmmmmmmmmm...hot...hot...hot...

I mean sure we can all grow our winter fur if we try...

Wow...
So what is tantra and oral like?

Oral tantra is more intense because of the prolonged pleasure...feathers...fingertips...long shaft licking and rim sucking focus...Its also something to go back to when both are too close to climax. The goal of tantra is not the ecstasy ending, but rather the prolonged ecstasy over the hours. Taking breaks for massage, suckling necks, caressing tushes... Its not easy to find a slow-handed lover these days. It's more our age and understanding how to relax in life that can bring about mind-blowing connection.

Amazing...sounds like...after your hydro-massage...ovulation...messages...you must be...well... you know...

Already in bed? Yep, lol...I'm hoping for sleep tonight...I like that you pay attention to detail...

Are you...gonna???

A lady never tells...

When a man does finish...where do you like that...
For tantra...

Spilling inside of course...I love the pulsing and thrusting while I squeeze tight...hugging...kissing...but all areas can be explored no? You?

Inside...feels amazing...more intimate...slowly withdraw...
Whats off limits for you?

Off limits? Hmmmmm....

Boundaries?

Anything that would cause pain...with CPTSD I have the responsibility of healing with sex and pleasure... not relapsing with pain. Physically I can withstand a lot but no one told my brain that lol...

I don't do the pain stuff...

Ahhhh...
Damn...liking you even more now...

Damn???

When will you no longer be married...lol

I'm blushing...
Do you...squirt...

I've been known to...yes. Depends on the buildup...many women can squirt after 18 minutes of proper foreplay lol...Do you squirt lol!!

Wow...so hot...

Are you working? I don't want to bug ya...

I am...you are not...trying not to drive around with a boner...

Lol...
Me too...

How do you sleep...I'm thinking...t-shirt only...

No sorry...silk tank top...silk animal-print bottoms...
Honestly...I keep enough on in case I have to jump up from banging on the door with this PI...did I tell
you Dereck has some idiot PI after me?

PI...why??

....trying to serve me divorce papers...I already had him served, but Dereck is an asshole that has to win,
so he has this dummy following me. I already won by getting out of the marriage so...
Do you sleep naked? I'm thinking so...

I do...
Do you like to be woken up...

Oh my...yes...
Sleepy sex is so hot...best way to wake...especially from behind...if sleeping on your side...

Mmmm...wake up with mouth and tongue...

Oh myyyyy yes....

Slight fingers massaging...you...

Any massaging is good in my world...

You know what I meant...

Yep...

So what's the best technique to massage with fingers....

Hmmm...two inside curved in a "c" pattern to arouse the g-spot which activates the "squirting" glands...a whole palm caressing, down the neck, breasts, tummy...to my mound is sensual...induces arching...the back of the neck, down the spine to the "gluteal cleft" (tush)...light fingertips along ass then take a handful... sensual but firm. Where do you need touch and massage...as a guy?

I like...neck...shoulders...really like shoulders...down chest to stomach...legs...

Basically...all lol! Love massage...it's all good!

Touch is sensual...scent is intoxicating...eye contact...mmmm...

Yes...sir........

I'm a simple kinda guy...

Hmmm...I can't hear that...male Scorpios are NEVER simple, and I like that...they can't do boredom...I do, however, feel you understand connections and touch very well...

I do...I crave it...

I sense that...

If we ever had a first date...how would it end?
Hypothetically...

Respectfully...classy women don't give too much away, right? I would want to feel your embrace though... and how warm your lips could be for me...but, you're still married, and I worked with married cops, remember? Not a profession that encourages connection and faithfulness, unfortunately...

I understand...

Besides...what do you want with a chubby gal? Lol...

Physical characteristics don't mean shit to me...
I always liked your smile...your energy...I don't see you as chubby...at all...

Thanx...had no idea you noticed my smile so much. Did you think I was nuts to be married to Dereck? I often wonder what people think of it?

I just thought he was kinda weird...I certainly noticed your smile...

Show me yours?
Smile...
(Smiling pic sent)

(Sent two pics)
Wow...beautiful...

Oh yummmm....
Thats your "kinda" smile...I like your pursed lips, but I bet I could get a full-on smile...Got dimples?
I like how you've built your biceps...great work!!

Huge...Irish dimples...

Love them!! My Irish dimples are...lower lol...
I can see why you need shoulder massage now...

Lower???

Dimples? Yeah, lower...on my ass lol..
I have one big Irish face dimple near my smile...on the right...

I find you to be a beautiful insightful lady...

Thanx...I like your active mind!

My mind...never...stops...
Learning...reflecting...affirming...

Thats good!! The great Tony Robbins says, "Once you stop growing, you die." I vow...to always be
teachable!

What you gonna learn next...

How to be free...self-love has been a wonderful journey...taking what I want without hurting anyone has
been super liberating.

I'm unlearning too. Turning my survival in interdependence. Enjoying each breath...healing...I am so excited for my future. But...I do struggle here and there...

Struggle?
You love...loving?

I do love loving...as a woman I am in fear most days though. I'm a strong motherfucker but, I fear for my safety and have a strong need for ease and security now that I'm alone. It's messing with my stomach lately... and my sleep. No matter how much I show up for myself and say, "Peg you've survived 100% of your life so far, you've got this!" I still have bad days...today was rough...but you're helping!
So, what accomplishment has made you feel the most validated so far? What's Gunnar's personal favorite?

I have boxes full of trophies...national, world, dozens of state champ crap...been all over the world...best thing for me by far...is that my kids adore me...believe in me as I believe in them... know they will never grow up like I did...had a rough start...but making it work...
You have tremendous strength...fear is ok...failure is ok...giving up is not...

Love that you referenced your children!
I agree, giving up is not ok unless giving your heart to the wrong person/people...I am learning the importance of the option to divorce...it's good to have options!

Lesson come from struggle...

Damn-skippy!!

We talked and had paperwork ready to file once...we separated for about a year...

Oh my...how was that for you?

Confusing...couldn't be without my kiddos everyday...
Your song is on the radio...

My song?

Nine Inch Nails...Closer...

Fuckin love NIN!!!

See...your song...rhythmic...

Yummyyyyy....

So on a scale of 1 to 10...rate how good a kisser you are...

We went over this...I've only been complimented but you know how others flatter. I can tell you a kiss can get me really "going" if passionate and connective. I looooove kissing...everywhere... Favorite type of kiss?

Gentle...accepting...leaning into more passion...then deeper more passionate...lots of touching...closed eyes...to open eyes...slight nibbling...smell your hair...smell your skin...kiss you everywhere...

Best lyric in Closer is, "You get me closer to God." That's what tantra does! Oh hells yes, kisses that start off passionate, relaxed lips, slow tongue, trailing down to the neck, inhaling scent...

Yup...yup...end by licking...kissing...well...you know...

Nibbling at pecs, erect nipples, ribs, tummy...no ending...

Yes...lick until you absolutely cum all over...move back up...keep kissing deep...but sharing now...

Kissing properly has been known to induce climax. I do recover and go in for more. I've been able to "crash over the top" seven times in one evening but it was a full moon and during ovulation so there were forces at work lol...

Wow...so hot...do you take a man in your mouth after he's been in you??

Of course...I mean I'm not into women, but I'd like to think I taste good...will you kiss your woman after she's swallowed you?

Yes...and lick her after I cum inside...yes on kiss...if earned it should be shared...

Ahhhh, you understand the "reals"...nice!!!

Reals???

*What really **IS** vs. what society says should be "yuck". Sex is beautiful, making love...ecstasy...*

Very...will you swallow? Share kissing?

Of course. Intimate...when my needs are met, I give my everything...not easy to find...

Very...very...very sensual...everything???

Many women will when their needs are met...and it's really not hard to meet those needs when understood they're mostly above the neck lol. Just a sensual gal I guess...I can become addicted to pleasure though. It heals me in a way I can't articulate.

Damn...wow...
Can I ask a personal question?

Oh well...now that we're getting personal (laughing emoji)

Are you...wet???
Throbbing?

Uhhh...more moist...with aching...my body wants an egg fertilized lol...It's like a yearning to be filled and stretched. Kinda make sense?
Are you wet and throbbing?

Stretched??? Are you a size queen?
Tip...very wet...

Ahhhh....precum...yesss...
Size queen? Nah...

Yesss??? Nah?

Doc says I'm smaller..."tilted uterus" too...makes for a more snug fit I hear...lol...
You know about precum?

Precum??? Tell me...

In my books, I write about it..."his pearl of precum" or "his slick drop of precum"...hot!!!

Mmmm...so...are you horny...

I'm sufficiently aroused...I thrive on attention...this is new for me...but nice...I didn't think I had "flirt game" it's been 23 years of a shitty marriage...I hope I'm doing well...

Very nice...you've got game...any prospects...to help you...

One younger guy, but I don't want to cross that line. We're better off friends. I'm not looking to be hurt and sadly, I get too connected when I use my body to communicate my wants and give pleasure...

Young guy...send dick pics yet??

No dick pics. That would have turned me off...

Yeah...I sense that about you...
Why would Dereck just think you would jump into threesomes...was it something from the past...

He says he goes wild seeing me pleasured, but honestly, he loves dudes...

You guys...were like swingers for him to watch? Or was it a bridge...for him...

Him...he's a narcissist so...he would say it was all for me and there's nothing sexier than seeing me pleased, but that's all bullshit. The guy never invested one moment in anyone unless it benefited him. Worst... husband...ever...

Our conversation ok??

I'm enjoying how your mind flows yes...never knew you thought so deep...it's lovely...

Yeah...I can be kinda cerebral...when needed...
So...only moist...not wet?

Wet happens when it happens...kissing would help...

That sucks...I keep looking at your pics...imagining how you kiss...

10/15/21 12:00AM

I like to kiss...a lot...

Dereck still thinking you belong to him???

Hope not...because that will never be again...I have no love anymore in my heart for him...

I am sorry if I have been forward...I am normally kinda shy...

There is no way I would believe you are shy! Male Scorpios are NEVER shy...in bed either...we might make them speechless but...not shy lol...

Well...ok...
You ever been with a male scorpio?

Is this making your shift smoother to get through? I hope it is...you the OIC on shift? Male Scorpio? Yes, once...a cop...in 1998.

I am...
Did he live up to the scorpio name?

Uhhh...I have much respect for male Scorpios...Females? Nope, fuck their attitudes...you ever been with a Libra? Air signs are known to breathe life into others...

No Libras...never heard anyone say that...
So...your egg is needing sperm?

Lol...
Our bodies want sperm when we ovulate yes...I actually wish it was always this way...it's a hunger I can't explain...always the most riveting orgasms too...like one after another...I can't have babies but I sure as fuck like to try!!
No Libra ever??? Hmmm....

No...no libra ever...

Ok...now I'm hard...and wet...

Really?? What part got ya?

Hunger...orgasms...sure as fuck try part...
Hot!

Oh wow, so nice to know my honesty and vulnerability is attractive...

Very...most sexy thing ever...

Refreshing to just have straight talk...
Real is definitely a turn on...

Are you???

Hells yeah...it's new for me through texting...nice...

Me too...very...

I like...how your body follows your mind...

Tell me more bout that...

What do you want to know?

What's your exact thought right now?

Riding...
While caressing my clit...double the pleasure...gazing down with desire...wanting to bring that...s l o w l
y...strong hands on my hips, warm, guiding in penetration...torturous thrusts...

Mmmmm...yes...
more...please....
Are you...rubbing...yourself?

A lady never tells...

Rub your index finger in small circles...
On your clit...

Small circles?

Circles for now...then place clit between index and middle finger...rub a little...harder...
stimulate both sides...

Mmmmm...the hood...sooooo lovely...hoping you're parked?

Very...sensitive...
I am...
Make your finger motions feel your pussy lips...

Mmmmm...

Now...gently slide middle finger inside...slowly...gentle...gently lift upward...stimulate g-spot...

Whoa...slowing up a bit...needing to relax movements...

Rub...now more direct on clit...deliberate...imagine the tip of my big cock...warm...near...
precum...rubbing your clit...nipples erect...
Wanna tease you with my precum...tip only slides in entry...then I pull out...kiss your neck...
collar...nipples...tummy...tongue finds clit...you look down at me as I taste you...your hands
reach down...spreading yourself...exploring you...

Sliding...sinking your cock in...stretching and opening me...snug around you...my breath hitching,
feeling as if you've reached all the way up to my throat...and taken my breath away...

Strong hands on your hips...pushing in deeper...pulling you...harder...our thrusts in unison...

Burrowing deep within where its...warm and wet...

So wet...warm...deep...sooooooo deep...clit grinding...your 1st orgasm starts like a wave...can't
stop it...

Tongue plunging in your mouth...to explore and taste your sweetness...strong orgasm...takes o v e r...

Our sweetness...

I'm soaked, may be oozing a bit now down...

You squeeze me deep...I feel your cum dripping down my shaft...on my legs...you moan...kiss me deep...bite my lower lip...eye contact...

I do like nibbling...and eye contact...

You talk...tell me how much you are cumming...feeling me in you sooo deep...

I bite your neck just a bit...I can't speak when I cum, my whole body wreathes and convulses...

You gently slide off my cock...you work your way down...you slowly start to caress my cock... you bite my nipples...nibble, I writhe in pleasure for you...

I may need to suck gently...

I'm okay with that...

I want to taste you...feel your rim beneath my velvety tongue...encircle it...gently flutter and suck...

Mmmm...getting too close...turn you on your stomach...prop yourself up with a pillow...grab my cock...guide me in you from behind...slow...and deep...stretching you...slow, long, deep thrusts...pick up the pace...you moan...push your ass back towards me...

I love the feeling as you burrow in deep, your head gliding along my g-spot then filling me fully...

Rhythm...pace...rhythm...you begin to cum again...squeezing me hard as I fuck you from behind...

I would definitely push back towards you...wanting to meet you to squeeze you tight...arching towards you to cum fully and harder...

You relax...take me into you entirely...

Need to breathe...get ready again...

....and you cum again...I can see your glaze all over my cock...slowly...I slide out...

> You...run your palm down along my spine...to help reset my erratic breathing...

You turn and lay me down on my back...kiss me passionately...deep...tongues...lips...skin pressing skin...

> Dripping all over you now...I like you on your back...

You start to take me slowly in your mouth...your cum tastes amazing on my stiff cock...
You play with my balls as your tongue flicks the tip of my dick...sucking and stroking me...

> I take each ball in my mouth ever so gently...allll pleasure. So, you'd like to finish orally huh?

Not yet...

> Are you opposed to me climbing up and holding your hands to the bed?

Not at all...anything to please and pleasure you...

> I move down again and take you in my mouth...sucking and licking...I want you to cum...

You feel me get close...start to writhe for you...
I tell you...baby, I'm gonna cum for you...

> I know you are...

You keep me in your mouth...
You feel my hot thick load release and squirt into your mouth...you keep sucking each...and every drop...

> You feel me swallowing...

After...you keep me hard by...moving up and straddling my still hard cock...you move onto me...feeling me plunge deep in you...
I fill you...you lean down...pressing your lips to mine...you kiss me deep...your cum mixed with mine...on our lips...ecstasy shared...

I need those lips...pheromones...aromas in perfection!

So turned on...by kissing...sharing cum...we start to cum again...together

Now...thats hot...

You feel me cum with you...at the same time we're throbbing...pleasure deep...you feel and know...I have come deep for you...in your pussy...

...and I take it...and you with me...over the cliff...

You grind...milking every last drop...
You slide off...basking in candlelight...your legs open to me...your pussy spread...I can see my seed dripping from you...you rub your swollen lips to feel my cum...I lay watching you...

Oh wow...yezzzzz, very fevered and swollen...

I gently begin to kiss your thighs...your stomach...eventually kissing your swollen, engorged clit...two fingers slide gently inside your pussy...

Makes my back arch up toward you...

I push down on your pubic bone...two fingers caressing your g-spot...
You feel fluid building...I kiss your clit...my fingers moving in rhythm...beginning your orgasm...I keep kissing...licking...enjoying...you feel yourself begin to gush and squirt!

I...have to grab...onto the earth!

After...you pull me up to your lips...you kiss and taste your sweetness on me...your pussy still pulsating...dripping...

I moan into your mouth...you steal my breath...

We lay down...your head on my chest...silence...but our breathing...within minutes we are breathing in rhythm...laying in each other's cum..we feel satisfied...

Ohhhh...hells yeah...

How's...your pussy feeling?

Swollen...fevered...soooo happy...shyness now...

Imagine if this texting turned to touch...

I am...and my mind and body...doesn't know it didn't happen...mmmm...

Ohhhh my...if it were real...bout 5am...wake you up with my fingers...6am...share a shower... warm water running over our bodies...kissing...talking bout how amazing we are...together...

Wow...it's good to be the OIC on shift...a hot shared shower would be divine...I'd want you to stay though...

I'm home from shift now...stay??

Good connection...not common...I'd want to sleep in your arms and regain strength...

I would like that...then watch you wake...brush your hair...do makeup...dress...flirt with you...

Maybe go once more...real gentle...

I would like that...smell your hair...run fingers gently along your lower back...top of your ass...

Kissing...inhaling your fresh scent...from shower...

Quiet times after...amazing...

I'd caress your cock and massage it with light fingertips strokes...send tingling sensations on your shaft skin...I like the quiet...unspoken times reveal much...

I know you would...are your nipples sensitive??

They're an erogenous zone for me yes...I like sucking on them...with a fevered, hot mouth...

Nibbling?? Light kissing...

I like an ice cube sometimes...

Wow...what else do you like...

Nibbling works...light is best as pleasure is my favorite...

Do you like ass...touching...

Very much...did I tell you I wrote a book in a weekend where there's an ice cube sex scene on a yacht? Also a cold grape from the fridge...I created the scene from an experience I had in my twenties...

Tell me...

*Lol...grapes fit perfectly inside the vulva area atop the hood skin on the clit...
As for anal...I like it slow...*

Wow...more please...
You like anal????

Cold grape, hot tongue, oral play...amaaaazing...food sex is fun. I do enjoy anal, yes...

Wow...really?

Yes, with the right man, gentle, anal play can be lovely...not something I would allow with my control freak narcissist of a husband though. Respect is a huge turn on for me...and honesty...I'll give anything for honesty after so many years with a liar lol...

Wow...

Surprised?

Kinda yes...you are so sexy...

Really?

Yes...
Why really?

When a woman's needs are met, she'll give you the world. Just interesting I can surprise you...

You are...irresistible...

Are you an anal-virgin?

Yes...tried in college...didn't work well...not really in the know...

Great job trying...I love that! It only works with trust and ease...

Hypothetical...if I were there next to you...would you kiss me?

Of course...

To start?
Could I caress...your beautiful breasts?

I'd require it lol...feeling your touch...on my "twins" would be lovely...

Would you let me rub your clit?

If you promise...to touch it gently like a diamond at the apex of my...pleasure center...

Yes...I would...

Then I'd even guide your hand there...I love to be touched there...

Damn...what am I gonna do with you...

Sadly...we'll just have to be satisfied with our tiny emotional sexting affair tonight...

I'm glad to help in a little way...

Same...if I saw you now, I'd blush...I miss intimacy so much...feel like I need a fuckin' joint now lol...

I do understand...
Why??

Celebrate...that...was hot! I'm tired of being celibate for sure...

Glad I could warm you up...

Same...so easily too...

Yes...so would you...
Be able to do a PG massage with me?

PG?

If...I were on your table...could you?

I don't mix sex with my paid profession, so yes, it would be PG...but unforgettable...for both of us, I'm sure...

I know...
I truly enjoyed this evening...

Best evening for me since being back in Ramas...If I wasn't locked out of my house I could heal you on my massage table tomorrow...we'll see what unfolds...

I would like that...
Going to sleep...goodnight beautiful sexy lady...

Dream well...sweet prince (waving emoji)

***

<u>**Peg's Journal Entry 10/15/21:**</u>

So, I thought he'd just disappeared after my over-sharing and drama, who wouldn't, but Gunnar got a hold of me again this morning, and by evening, we were sexting! I can't even remember if I've ever had phone sex, let alone such luscious sexting. It was so fucking hot, I didn't want it to stop. Where did this creature come from and how did he end up crossing my path?!

Sadly, he seems to still be married even after a year of separation and divorce paperwork some years back. Says he couldn't really live without his kids, so I have a feeling he's staying in it as I did. WORST marriages ever are continued for the kids, I did it too, and they let me know how I shouldn't have. I guess children don't want to think they are the reason two people stayed miserable together. I get it but really wish he were free. Want him...

Perhaps we sexted because...well, it was so easy and hot...but more so because it was safe? Again, who the fuck am I??? Married men were never my thing...nor was cheating, even though Dereck deserved it. Why was I so faithful to him?

Kind of an awesome way to start a Monday! I learned more about him and that he works the swing shift but is short-staffed! I remember working on a skeleton crew, really wears on the adrenals. I feel bad that he has so much responsibility, but he's super fucking sharp, his mind seems to go a mile a minute. Intelligence is quite a turn-on for me.

He mentioned that he uses a sauna at his gym. Heat is super relaxing for CPTSD stress and calming anxiety. I wonder if he's ever been to the hot springs here in New Mexico. Best kind of sauna, in my opinion, natural, steamy, just the right temperature. Yummmmm...

It's so nice to talk and connect with someone who has similar interests. I enjoy that his mind is as twisted and dark as mine. I'm curious to learn more about him. So far, I enjoy our CPTSD mind connections.

At one point I asked him if he'd ever felt hated by someone who professed to love him and he simply responded, "I think I certainly have...". Wow. I know that pain, sad he does as well. Felt for him. Nothing worse than knowing someone hates you.

I love that he was born in MA and is Irish! It's like there's some strange unknown connection there lol, as my family is from Fall River, MA, and many of my childhood memories are from times spent in Massachusetts.

I haven't seen him in person for years but, wow do I want to now! He mentioned my smile and my posts...I seem to attract a lot of male attention with my fucked-up sense of humor. Not particularly interested in any others though. It's nice to have his attention. It's like...he gets me.

I love that he brought his kids up again and says they are his "center...and stars..." Nothing sexier to me then a man who loves his babies! I think it's because my father was so loving and Dereck was such a shit dad. My heart opened to Gunnar when he admitted his biggest accomplishment was that his kids adore him, that they believe in him as he does them. How he's committed to giving them a better childhood than he had. Reminded me of my father's whole purpose...and what a man truly is. Very attractive.

I shared a bit in how I write in my books, and he commented that his heart was racing. Love that! I sense he'd be really amazing at tantra. Then...the sexting...began...and ohhhhh myyyyyyy.

I
Can't
Believe

Me...with him

Who am I...again? This new life has really taken a hold of me. I honestly do wish I'd done Ayahuasca years ago...in my twenties! Then again, if I were this openly sexual back then, I would have gotten myself in trouble for sure. I mean, guys had commented, and Dereck always mentioned how "amazing" I was in bed but this...I don't know what this is...how does something so new feel so good? How is it I can talk with another about what I like and prefer, and it seems to be what they like as well?

***

Chapter 5

GETTING INTENSE

Peg awoke feeling completely satisfied orgasmically but yearning for external, physical touch. Gunnar's touch. Their connection was extraordinary and strangely familiar? She stared up at the ceiling, remembering the intense sexting the night before. Lt. Gunnar O'Clery was exactly her type, and she had no idea how.

She rolled to her side, hugging herself, feeling the intense awakening happening within her new, now seventy-pound thinner voluptuous body. All the naughty words they shared, the incredible visuals still swarming in her mind. She enjoyed how sexual and raw he was, *like her*. Her body reacted so easily to their back-and-forth banter. Her arousal was burning again, deep down in a place she'd closed off trying to survive her ex and his demon energy. Gunnar was certainly igniting something within her, and it was fearsome.

Inhaling deep to dismiss the nerves, she threw the covers off and sat up. Her muscular legs swung off the bed, and she stared at the floor realizing how desperately she needed intimacy from him. Her CPTSD mind needed regulating through connection and sex. She wondered if her desires had manifested this, err...him into her life. Perhaps since Ayahuasca, she was *attracting* powerfully and didn't even know it. Life had, in the last few weeks, been quite intense.

Standing up, she walked towards the bedroom door to go shower, wishing he were not still semi-married...or whatever *"rough"* meant. She wished she weren't either, but, most of all she wished he wasn't so damn compatible with everything she wanted and couldn't have. She spent years not getting what she craved. And...was quite tired of it.

Gunnar put his truck in park and grabbed his gym bag from the seat. He looked at his phone one last time before putting it in his pocket. No message from her yet, the little green dot indicating she was online was missing.

He got out of the truck and slammed the door, frowning slightly. His cock throbbed for her still, her answers to his questions still fresh in his mind. How she described herself, answering like he would, how they yearned for the same things, how she might kiss... He couldn't get the woman out of his head! He needed the workout to compartmentalize the visuals she created in his mind. He enjoyed their graphic sexting, his body wanted her, he just didn't know how to make it happen. Peg Law was a respectable, fiery woman. Her reputation in town was stellar, her choice in husband not so much. He had to admit, her strive to get away from the asshole was sexy as hell. Truth is, he liked her. And that was rare. But more importantly, he wanted her, and that...was "rough".

Opening the gym door he entered, the smell of sweat and determination hitting him. He waved to the employees and headed to the opposite side wanting to be alone with his thoughts...of wanting to be alone...*with her*.

Aileen heard her best friend pick up in the middle of a conversation, with what sounded like a staff member since she was offering instruction. Her voice finally moved closer to the phone as she said, "Hold on, I'm headed to my office."

"Oh okay."

Aileen heard more movement and the door shut.

"Hey girl, ugh sorry about that. My office manager is on vacation so..."

"Oh wow, fun times." Aileen slumped down on the couch to hike her swollen tankles up.

Josephine sighed, "So, ya finally decided to call me back. Guess you came up for air you sassy lil' minx you."

"Ha! I wish my life were that exciting."

"What, no girlfriend?"

"Nah, Jasmine decided to go strictly dickly."

Josephine tried not to laugh, "Oh wow, I'm sorry."

"Eh, it's fine. I don't have the energy for a younger girlfriend anyway. I'm too old."

"Stop that, you are not. You just need high intelligence Aileen. You were too bored around Jasmine."

Aileen giggled, "You're right Dr. Adeyo. I'll leave it in your hands to find my next victim."

"Oh fuck no. I'm not touching your love life!"

"Oh okay, so just sit back and analyze then." Aileen teased.

"Exactly, but speaking of victim..."

Aileen smiled, "What your hubby do now?"

"Not Mark, more like your neighbor uh...Dereck Law."

"Oh that fucker?"

Josephine huffed a laugh at her reaction, "Yeah, so he showed up outside my office some days ago talking about he needed my help."

"Oh? Why, because he's a smacked-ass that lost the best thing he ever had by cheating on her non-fucking-stop."

Josephine nodded on the other end of the phone, "Yes, so you know about them?"

Aileen did, "Well, I think we were all waiting for it." She chortled.

"Well, he's a bully...and it didn't go over well."

"There's no way I'd see you helping him Jo. You actually fired him as a client remember?"

"I did, and no I wouldn't ever help him hurt that poor woman or defend him, he acts innocent but he knows exactly what he does."

Aileen switched her feet, "What did he expect from you?"

"We didn't get that far. He pissed me off so bad. We got nasty quick. He even threatened me and called me a bitch." Josephine felt her blood beginning to boil. "He has one of those faces I want to smack!"

"He's so fucking annoying...more like punch. He needs to be punched square in his mouth."

"I thought I might have to pull my gun on him but as narcissists go, once he realized he was on camera he was ready to leave."

Aileen raised her eyebrows, "Wow Jo Jo, that could have gone sideways quick. I'm glad you're okay. I might be able to help."

"That's why I called...wonderin' if you know anything about him?"

"Well, I could. I mean I know what you've shared over the years and what I've monitored just in the neighborhood here. But I could get more in depth if you know what I mean." Aileen sucked at her teeth thinking about how she could hack into Dereck Law's life so easily.

"I don't want to ask but I just got a bad feeling about him. He's much worse than years back. There's...there's like a darkness in his eyes you know?" Josephine thought back to how she couldn't even see his pupils. His eyes were evil. Like Onyx and demon-like.

"No, let me see what I can get going. I do know he travels a lot for some job he has so he's not always around...could be a good thing. You feel like he may come after you Jo?"

Josephine had thought of it but she knows he's more of a coward and fraud then anything. "Not so much, he seems to have a focus on Peg right now."

"Do we know where she's at or..."

"No I don't actually. I hope she's happy though. I do know she's back in Ramas. One of my patients here is infatuated with the woman and mentioned how nice the town is now that she returned."

Aileen pursed her lips, "Oh my, how sweet. I'll find out...but this may take some time."

"No worries. Law seems to be in panic mode so he's at the beginnings of whatever he's concocting." Josephine sounded annoyed.

"Well, I'll keep on eye on him. In the meantime, watch out, he's not my favorite neighbor. Weird guy."

"Oh, I believe you. Heard he's super weird around young girls...friend in the foster agency told me."

Aileen's stomach felt queasy, "Oh you've got to be kidding me."

"I wish I was."

Chapter 6

FEEL

Rodrigo Pena had been a chaplain since his mid-forties. At sixty-three, and a recent widower, he felt he needed distraction and to do his counseling craft more than ever. Being busy helped with the loneliness of losing his wife to cancer.

He pulled into the parking spot he always used and checked his beard in the rearview mirror. He didn't see Gunnar's truck yet. He rather enjoyed their breakfast meetings over the years. If it weren't for Gunnar O'Clery, he'd not be as well known in the community as he was. Gunnar was the kind of cop that everyone wanted to know. Rod felt lucky to actually call him a friend. He'd counseled him lightly, here and there over the years, through some pretty intense career challenges from shootings, to child abuse cases, to even death threats. The man had nerves of steel on the outside, an intensely protected heart inside, and a deep compassion for children and the elderly. Underneath it all, he just wanted to be loved as most everyone does. Rod did. He'd never told Gunnar but he hoped he knew, he loved him like the son he'd never had.

Music blared from the truck as Gunnar pulled into the spot next to him. He waved, his cap low, his sunglasses covering his tired eyes. As he turned off his engine the parking lot got quiet enough to hear sirens in the distant. Rod walked around as Gunnar closed the door and extended his hand to shake his.

"Sounds like the town has awoke early." Rod gave him his crocked smile.

Gunnar nodded and took his hand, "Yeah, looks like Station three is on a small dumpster fire over off 17th."

"Oh wow."

"They'll be fine. How are you sir?"

Rod watched his eyes as he removed his sunglasses. Gunnar looked different somehow. Tired but different.

"I'm here."

"Well that's a start. What are we feeling today? Huevos rancheros or chorizo?" Gunnar opened the diner door for Rod and waved him in as he'd done for years. Rod noticed he stood a bit taller in his gait, he was a beast of a man, in a muscular pitfall sort of way, but today his energy seemed somehow lighter. There was a calm happiness about him.

Rod turned back slightly, "I think today I'll try steak and eggs. I'm feeling a shift."

"Oh wow. Sounds great."

After Gunnar made a quick round through the restaurant shaking hands and showing respect to those he knew, he joined Rod in their back booth, his eyes towards the door. He looked peaceful. Rod noticed his lips were less pursed and spread more into a smile showing his deep Irish dimples.

As Lucy brought there beverages and took their order, Rod noticed he checked his phone more than usual. He rested his shoulders and sat back against the booth readying himself.

"Okay you, spill it."

Gunnar clicked his screen shut and placed his phone facedown, "Spill what?"

Rod smirked, "I thought we were going to talk about the officer-involved-shooting but there are obviously more pressing matters by the looks of that half-smile."

Gunnar tried to frown but was unsuccessful, instead he smiled fully and Rod realized how long it had been since he'd seen Gunnar fully express happiness.

"My officer is doing better than I thought, totally justified so he'll be good. The week turned out better than it started."

"Hmmmm...."

"How are you?"

Rod shook his head, "No, we're not going to talk about me. Besides, nothing has changed. I'm still old, still heartbroken. I'm liking what I see here. What's going on son?"

Gunnar shook his head and everted his eyes down, folding the corner of his napkin under his index finger. "It's personal...not work stuff."

"That's quite alright. My loyalty extends to every part of your life. Is everything okay? Family?"

Gunnar lifted his gaze, his eyes soft. "Well, you know how years ago I told you my...well, my wife had a lover I found out about?"

"Yes. That was the worst I'd seen you Gunnar." Rod frowned a bit not quite understanding his good mood with such a tough memory.

"It was rough. And you know I've been staying...well, for the kids?"

"Things getting better?"

"No...well, not with my wife. I-"

Rod canted his head, confused. "Oh?"

Gunnar sat back against the booth and sipped water from his glass. He breathed a bit, not quite sure how to express what he was feeling. He exhaled, "I crossed paths with someone...from years back. She's just returned to town, going through it. Divorcing. I don't know...there's some sort of intense...connection?"

Rod knew not to judge. The man had been through hell and his training taught him judgement never solved anything. "Tell me about the...connection?"

"I can't really...explain it."

"Well, have you...have you fucked her?"

Gunnar smiled slightly, "I'd like nothing more." His eyes told Rod that was the truth. It was written all over his face.

"Oh?"

"I can't explain it...I feel...things."

Rod knew him. The man put everyone's needs before his own. The times he has done for himself or been "greedy", he's suffered with guilt he ends up overworking to get away from. He actually wished Gunnar could get satisfaction from his marriage but he just never quite respected his wife after her infidelity. They both haven't been angels, and staying for the kids never works. In this instance, Rod always felt Gunnar's loyalty caused more harm than good.

"You're allowed to feel things. How far has it gone?"

"Just...intense texting for about two weeks. She...uh, she intrigues me."

Rod lifts an eyebrow, "I bet."

"She understands...things."

"Sometimes that happens Gunnar. Validation, acceptance, compassion, understanding...it can change things. That's what makes a difference."

Gunnar nodded, a smile widening. He could see her smile in his mind...her lips sucking his nipple...grazing down his stomach...

"What are you thinking?" Rod could see Gunnar was thinking too much.

"Honestly, I don't really know. I don't think I've ever felt this...with anyone. And you know as much as I try not to think about feelings...I kind of want to when it comes to her."

Rod studied him and for the first time in a long time, hoped his friend would continue feeling...even if it was wrong. If anyone deserved love it was Gunnar O'Clery.

Peg looked down at the notification on her phone. It was a positive meme, and it made her smile. She hadn't heard from him in a few days and decided to reach out. She wasn't sure if she should, but something inside was pulling at her. She smiled, remembering the incredible orgasms she had the night before as she pleasured herself to the thoughts of all he could do to her. She typed and pushed send.

October 17, 2021 11:11 AM

Meme Sent by Peg:
TAKE TIME OUT TODAY TO TAG SOMEONE THAT YOU KNOW IS WORKING HARD AND TELL THEM YOU'RE PROUD OF THEM. WETHER THEY'RE WORKING HARD TO BE A BETTER PERSON, RUN A BUSINESS, OR CHASE A DREAM, TELL THEM THEY'RE DOING A GREAT JOB. YOU NEVER KNOW WHO MAY NEED TO HEAR THOSE WORDS TO KEEP GOING.

Thank you...how are you?

Well...how are things?

Doing great...just relaxing...

Atta boy! Same here...Sunday "laxin'" lol.

(Later)

My phone just notified me I can touch someone with words...made me chuckle...

Mmmm...I can be touched...

Sometimes it's all we've got, right?

So turned on from the other night...still now...

Really?

Yup...yup...

Any particular part cum to mind? (laughing emoji)

Initial insertion...so seductive...

Mmmm...it is!

What ya doing...

In my room...you?

Just relaxing...got back from the gym...

Oh good...feel better?

I do...great...great workout...

Very nice...

You laying down??

Slightly...on my chaise lounge trying to shake off some anxiety lol...damn brain of mine...

Ohhhhh...I will let you relax...

It's a vibration chair that keeps me levelheaded lol...

Ohhhhhhh my....

Oh ok...rest up...

Don't wanna bother...

Lol...you don't ...

Mmmm...ok...so insertion....

Yummmm...

Tell me...how is it different? For a guy its...total "I am allowed?" type...like she wants and desires this...

Oh I see...for me it's warmth, rigidness, opening me, burrowing, and sinking in and filling up...creating a tingling full body sensation. Makes my breath hitch...like I can feel it up into my throat and then into my mind...like, "He wants me!"...to possess me...bliss...

Mmmm...and cumming inside???

Cumming? I love the pumping...squeezing...rocking my hips...the slick gliding...

Yes?????

The vulnerability of release is hot...squeezing and clenching to make it better...more intense...I love the emotion and feeling of being free...

Hot sticky emotion...

Mmmm...that too!

Do you leave cum inside??

Yes...it's intimate, tends to linger for a few days...

Same for anal? Not so experienced here...

Anal? It lingers until potty time...not as much fun as vaginal but fine with me...it takes a lot to phase me... there's nothing about sex that I don't like lol...

Mmmm...so hot....

***

It's Sunday, so I ventured out to write here at Veteran's Park. I needed nature and time to reflect on things in my life. I'm seeing the value of endings, which if allowed, bring on needed beginnings.

As I look over at the pillars of the large white pavilion I see where I stood eleven years ago and married the worst man I could have chosen. I said vows I know now I didn't mean, for they were for a man I didn't know. Now that I think of it, it was more for a house we were building together that my sister said I could be thrown out of if we weren't "married". I have to laugh at how I am now locked out of that very house and wishing I hadn't ever entered into this sham of a union. For ten fucking years, I said no to each and every proposal and suggestion to marry him. Then, in the span of a few weeks after moving to New Mexico, I end up marrying him and suffering through the absolute worst years of my life.

Finding out recently, that even before we were pregnant, he manipulated a sixteen-year-old to blow him in the gym parking lot of one of our martial art gyms, was an incredible relapse into toxic shame. My ego was hit hard, but in all truth, his crimes have nothing to do with the person I am. How was it I was married to a fucking pedophile all those years? I even gave him a daughter, and look what he did to someone else's. I found out he even had that teen beat up in a sparring match in the gym, by Dean, to bully her, so she didn't ever tell. He showed her a lil of what would happen to her if she did talk. She's a woman now and could come forward at any time. I have a gut feeling now that if she did speak up, she wouldn't be the only one. I want to be out of this marriage and states away from him. He's gotten away with it for so many years. Dereck got a wife he didn't deserve, kids, a home, and a life he wasn't worthy of, all after traumatizing and possibly destroying a young girl's self-worth. What a disgrace.

I must admit, I feel relief knowing I never have to be in a life with him again, never have to deal with his nasty micro-penis creepy talk, never have to sleep in the same bed with his dark-narcissistic cloud looming over me...trying to destroy all that's good in me. I am free of being with a fraud, and that makes me VERY proud I put an end to things! I was a sucker...but I am forgiving me for standing by a false person, he is no man in my eyes. The lesson? I can't love someone into being a good person...oh, and I actually DON'T have enough love in me for two. Now I have enough time to love me...and everyone will now get the best of Peg!

I know I won't quite EVER accept all he's done but I no longer have to stand in judgment. Not my job nor do I want to judge him. He has to live with it. Perhaps this was all he was referring to when he said to me, "My past is coming back to haunt me." There might be more coming that I don't know about. Lordy, I can't even imagine what it would be like if he landed in jail! I don't think I would be hardly surprised. Ohhhh, the kids...I don't even want to think about how they would need to heal from finding out about their father's horrible choices.

The more interesting part of my life is, of course, Gunnar O'Clery. I'm intrigued, impressed, terrified...but, most of all aroused! I see how just our sexting helps regulate my stress and helps keep my triggers and symptoms away. I know he deals with his trauma in similar ways, sex being a priority as his conversations have revealed. I'm beginning to look forward to the times he messages me and when he has time to text about his life. A most compelling human...

Chapter 7
MORE SEXTING

Gunnar wanted to get a hold of her since he couldn't really text much from home the evening before. He hates that he had to push her aside while being the "family man" but, it's how he's had to compartmentalize himself in his own mind. Wanting Peg was not something he had planned, she just sort of happened...she was; however, incredibly intriguing!

***

October 18, 2021 8:05 AM

Holding up ok?

Yes...you holding up okay?

I'm great.

Yay! That's the way to live.
Hope everything is "hangin" well?

No complaints from me

Niiiiiiceeee!

What you doing??

Hangin' in my room.
Got a meeting with the lawyer at 3:30pm. What are you up to?

79

Ohhhh....just relaxing...

Ohhhhhh...
What's that look like?

Lying in bed...
You?

My relaxation is often that as well. Guilty...

Sounds fun...

He heee...

Have you thought about our messages from the other night?

They were incredibly intense, no?

Very...very...

I'm curious...
What stands out most for you?

Your openness...how you like pleasure...how you connect

Hmmmmm....
Are you often ignored?

No....I don't really know...but was great to hear those things...

Ah, I see.
It seems like you command respect in your day to day but perhaps the truth is a deeper connection is needed? I totally get that...I just want real at this point lol.

Like you said...honest discussion is amazing...I so enjoyed it...

Not gonna lie, I re-read them at Veteran's Park yesterday and had a difficult time with squirming in my seat at the picnic table I was journaling at. Sultry...

Wet again??

It's a thing...

Mmmmmmmmmmmmm....I had naughty dreams too...

Do tell...

Woke up with you after amazing sex filled night. Laying naked...you just rolled over and took me in your mouth...felt me grow hard in your mouth...you kept going until I came...you walked to the bathroom...looked back at me as you started shower...said...you know where I am if you want more...then stepped in shower...

You had more to give?
Nice visuals...

Yes...multi-cummer...

Ahhh...you did mention that...

After shower...you had a chair in room...sat me down...started to use yourself to show me how to touch you...you discussed every touch...every emotion...how to maximize your pleasure... As you were fingering yourself...you started to cum...I saw the changes in you...

That's quite the "surrendering" visual...

You pull me onto the bed...on your back...you guide me inside...feet against my chest...you start rocking against me as I drive in deep...

Ah, a favored position?

Your fingers playing with clit...you being stretched...slow...deep
That's my dream!

I kinda...really like how you dream!

(20 mins later)

Sorry, had to take a call…Just became a great aunt!

Congrats…was very vivid…realistic dream…

Realistic as in you could feel it in your sleep?

Yes…woke up…hard…tip of cock…covered in precum…

Oooooooh how lovely…

Touch yourself today?

If this keeps up, I'll have no choice.

Wow…is pussy warm…throbbing…

I feel like I need to hop in my truck and find a bumpy road, lol.
Aching these days…

I bet…

Throbbing comes from the warmth of touch.
Aching comes from no connection (sad face emoji).
Kissing somehow kicks off aching and throbbing lol.

Yes…deep…slow kissing…

Please…

Skin contact too…

Please and thank you…

Smell hair…smell skin…

Strong hands along my jaw and neck…pulling my lips in.
Hmmm…your scent.

Yes…fingertips rubbing neck…hairline…

82

Down the spine...

Wow...the next man that gets to kiss you is in for a real treat...

It's been soooo long...

Well...that guy better be ready...lucky dude...

We could discuss later. Massage therapist to client. Lol...

Done

Let me know if the owner of "The Gym" needs a resident massage therapist on site. Gotta pay for this ridiculous divorce and get my own place to heal...and such...

Will ask...

You'd get free healing of course. I don't do that often but...

Sounds great...love too...

Well, everyone in town knows I'm super professional when people are under my hands on the table for healing. I've never crossed the line (as an instructor you know there are higher ethics involved) but you would challenge me, I'm sure. Although I'd enjoy healing you as I could, I'd have to keep freagin' forcing my mind away from the visuals. But alas...I am strong so...lol. Wouldn't be able to have you as a paying client...

So...you would want...to touch me

Yes, why would I not? It's one of my love languages.

So hot...your restraint tested

True. But I do like a challenge.
I've done well so far...thank goodness for dreaming huh?

Yes...will be great to watch your struggle

Really?

To be restrained...yes...never in general

I don't think I'd be the one struggling the most (happy face emoji)

So true...very much know that

I really need a casita or space to open up a shop... Just, if you hear anything. I'd be forever in your debt kind sir...

I can check around

You're lovely (happy face emoji)

Maybe downtown mallish?

That's a second choice. I'd like to get away from "him" being able to harass me. Slept with my gun last night...ugh.

What gun?

*My lil' 22, he left me.
With him rolling back into town from the FL house I was taking care of (with Airbnb) and starting his texting, I realized he knows my whereabouts.
He was pissed that I'd been in Ramas since Sept, and he thought I was there. I don't want this one near me as he's not who he used to be. You know?*

Tell me something good that's going on for you these days.

Life is good...I am chatting with you...and you are intriguing

*You make me feel good deep down.
Can't remember the last time I was allowed to freely feel good.
I appreciate you...*

Empowered...

I do feel my mojo returning lol.

It's there...find little pieces here...there...

Thank youuuuu...I certainly am now! Selfie for a selfie?

Yup...yup...pg? PG13?

PG13 Monday "get through" yes!

You first...

Never shared this one with anyone. Was encouraged to do it after Dr. found tumors and she said, "Girl, you need to empower yourself with that body." So it's a secret pic for me and you.
(Pic on tummy on bed, high heels on legs crossed, lingerie on)

So...very...very...sexy...beautiful...empowered
Tumors?

6 benign now. They started to dissipate after I left him (funny) and I started acupuncture sessions but he cut off all money so I had to stop the sessions. I may be able to continue with a friend here if I barter bodywork. Lost 70lbs pounds with 25 to go. My friends all tell me that I lost 290lbs (him) and it's all downhill from here lol.
And your selfie?

Working on it...

This is like the words, "Don't cum yet..." when you're right at the cliff.
You're goooood at teasing. Lol

...or cum...and cum again...

Even more desirable...

I've been wondering how you'll taste...

Your mind is really neat...

Why?

Just what you wonder, how you can express that...the way you process...

Bad??

Oh my noooooooooo.
It's nice to know there is someone out there that wonders and processes like me lol.

Ok....mmmmmmmmmm
Work on pic...not so good at it...running around

Don't worry about it. I'm sure you'll deliver when you can.

I always keep my word.

I like that!

Me too....

It doesn't take much to make me happy. We should all just drop whatever and spend time together...fishing!
lol

Or a hike...or drive...or shooting...dinner...late movies...

Uhhhhh, yes please.

Kind...of...super simple dude...

I've always wanted to lay in the bed of my truck and see how amazing the stars are from that angle.
Simple is best. I'd forego any club scene for a lil bonfire and guitar lol.

Little glass of moonshine...little blanket...music...dancing

Fuck yeah.
Apple pie moonshine is my favorite. Makes for a wet apple pie inside...

Bare feet...soft touch...nerves everywhere...first kiss...

Wet pie inside???

French kisses.
Like that huh? Sorry, my mind is savage sometimes.

Yep...slow...sensual...deliberate
Like savage

Sensual is one of my most favorite words.
You're speaking my language.

Sensual has no routine...but a definite direction

Follow what's natural...

Have stretchy pants on?

Yep. My kitty and jeans are soaked but I'm on my fascia vibration chaise lounge
trying to calm my lady bits lol.

Soaked???? Why?

Why? Our flirting is intense!
Trying to drink a detox smoothie before I see this Mona Martine-Salo lawyer. My stomach is in knots, but you
seem to help that lately.

Hope you can relax...p.s. she is a bad ass lawyer.

Oh nice!
Hope too...

Wish...I could help more...long journey for ya

Really? I heard she might help me because she doesn't like when military spouses are shut out and abused. I
don't mind a journey...if it ends in my peace.

Right...

Mmmmmm...hot...so...hot...if I could...ginger ale 'n Jameson...ginger to settle tummy...warm bath ready...lavender candles...little epsom salt...warm towels...

All of that is soooo needed. Damn, you are woke boy!

Ginger ale...settle tummy...lavender calms you...warm bath escapes...warm towels are a "hug" of necessity.

Ever have Jack Daniels Honey Whiskey and ginger ale? Makes my hands want to touch and heal. I don't partake often but when I do...

No...but will try now...

All of that is true! Where'd you learn about lavender and Epsom salt?

I have lots of broken parts on me...couldn't find parts for me in a junkyard

Aw, I didn't know (sad face emoji)

All earned...wouldn't change a thing...

I mean I would eventually find them if you were on my table. Earned? Good one. Like our stretch marks. Worth every moment of that baby's life.

So very much

Ok, I'm headed out hoping I won't be followed. Wish me luck. Ttyl cutie.

Good luck.

(Later)
10/18/21 5:11 PM

New experience. Sitting at a lawyer's conference table (as she's a half-hour late) in "wet" stretchy jeans is humorous…

Mmmmmm…..

You wouldn't have just been driving on Valley would ya?

I am not…what ya doin

Was at a friend's new shop. She wanted to give me a protection candle for my bday. What youuuuuu doin?

Just hanging out with kiddo…just her and I out and about…

Awww, how neat. Gotta get that Daddy time. Gonna head to High Desert Brewery. Gotta peeeee. Lol. Enjoy!

You too…

Got a friend I need to thank for serving the divorce papers for me. Had a very good meeting with that lawyer. Gotta come up with 5 grand, but it should all be returned. Today has been a good day!

Glad to hear…nice awesome beer finish it off

Oh my, yes. Just one. Gonna buy you one someday.

We will…for sure

Ooof, got a swirl in my stomach with that. Might be dangerous.

Why danger???

Don't knoooooooooooowwwwwww.

Hmmmmmmmmm

I can maintain my distance....
I mean I'd be greedy with a hug...

But????

Gonna change the subject lol.

Alone??
Best beers are alone...

Yes of course. I go out every day alone. Lol. I am freeeeeee.
Are they? Yeah, you may be right lol.
I like it here. The drunks all leave me alone and the waitresses are nice.
Plus, it's hidden.

True

I don't like people much unless I can feel them on my massage table. You can tell a lot from people's energy. I much prefer dogs. Dogs are more human than humans.

Love the hounds

Sooooo smooshie and lovey. Horses are a close second but basically I'll introduce myself to the hounds before the humans. I like you even more now!

How so?

You get the unconditional K9 thang.

I do...K9 handler most of my career

Love it! Mmmmm "handler" lol.

That's me
How's that beer??

Half gone...I'm milking it. Enjoying the weather and the dogs and kitten walking around.

First thing on your mind...

Was thinkin' of the sunset over at the levee. You?
Spent so many evenings there trying to "think" and get out of the abuse. Now, I can sit and enjoy each breath,
talking to you and appreciating my day.
Life is magical when we have an attitude of gratitude.

Great day?

Yes! Things are looking up. It pays to be honest. He's done some very bad things to me and she (lawyer) feels a
judge will be appalled but I like how I conducted myself despite it all. How's the daddy-daughter date time?

Great evening...just listening to her talk...

I love those kinds of nights. My kids amaze me with how their minds work...

Had great day...you seem down a little...understanding that though

Really? I'm trying not to be down.

**Yeah...little...you have every right...but not who you are...you will conceal with beautiful
smile...beautiful eyes...charm...and wit...**

It might be fear coming through more than I want.

It's ok...new world...big decision...big change...better you

I don't think others really get the psychosis of a soldier with a brain injury. The lawyer was like, "Uh, has
anyone noticed he's doing really borderline personality shit?" It's alarming and hard to hide out here so I can
feel safe. I'm trying tho...

Brain injury? I negotiated a Marine with a gun for 6 hours one night...had TBI...

TBI is tragic. I'm so glad you could! You're kinda awesome.
Are you former military?

**No...but I have been on several contracts to teach very high level guys...DOE stuff...
The negotiation didn't work well...at all.**

Oh, it didn't? 6 hours was a good try tho, no?

No...he came at us with gun...didn't go well for him

Well...you gave him those 6 hours. Guess he chose suicide by cop?

Yes...with family watching...
I spent tons and tons of time at VA as a kid...

I feel deeply for those with trauma and all of you who serve for civilians. I think it's why I tried so hard in a failing marriage. When he finally admitted he wasn't a ranger and had been lying for years, I slowly lost more and more respect.
How did that affect you...the family watching?
VA as a kid? Ah, had father/gf veterans in the family?

Family...it sucked...not much in this job bothered me...that did...but...gotta move on...let it be in the rearview...thats why windshield is so much bigger...whats in front is more important

Truth!

Yes...I was adopted...stepdad had a spinal cord injury...paraplegic...spent all summer in VA... learned lots

Oh, that's intense.

Was...but...I grew up around heroes...I learned from every interaction

It's important to have that...heroes...

My gf...uncles Vietnam...stepdad Korea...cops...I had all alpha guys

Ohhhh...

At DOE...only cop there...all guys were seals...CIA...that stuff. How's beer?

Driving home. The beer feels good. Makes my lips warm.

Bet your lips are hot...love to gently caress your thighs as you drive...

> *Ya know...that would be hella nice! Been such a long time.*

Gentle subtle strokes...barely noticed but couldn't mistake it kind...then gentle...kisses... tongue flicks...along your neck...

> *Could be a hazard to traffic. I'm weak these days.*

No...great focus...at lights...stop signs...great deep...deep passion kissing...light touching... outside clothes

> *I do focus well when it comes to passion. It's my fav...*

I can tell

> *Best stuff ever invented.*

...and lube...
Just kidding

> *Never needed it much lol. I'm hoping that stays after menopause.*
> *I've been very happy with this body.*

Wow...way hot

> *It is kinda, right?*

So very...nothing makes a man feel wanted...more than that!!!

We have to have gratitude for the areas we are blessed in! Anal requires lubrication tho...Oh shit! So TMI!! My apologies...

Been able??????

Been able to slick things up properly. When I'm cherished, I'll definitely show want! It's all about needs being met.

Wow...without lube???

I...soak.
Or just burrow down a few strokes then switch up...

Soak? Mmmmmm...thats my turn-on...

It is?

Yes...so sexxxxxxxxy...

Well, you definitely have the banter for it.
It's crazy how the right convo can get things going.

Mmmmm...would love to watch you self-pleasure...just watch...learn...

Really? I like to teach too.

Totally...watch you please yourself...study...see how you work...what are the triggers to your pleasure...

You ever done thumbs down to help "her"?

Explain?

Welp, when we women ride and slide down on you, it creates all kinds of sensations, and for me, makes me want to grind and rock...

Thumbs Down??

But if you place your palm on my abdomen with your thumb down and...do circular motions on the hood of my clit while looking up at me...

Wow...squirter?

Been known to. I end up with my hands in my hair or holding my head as I increase the rhythm...because of the clitoral stimulation and...

Wow...how do you cum hardest...riding on top?

Vaginal stimulation plus clitoral...so it's like having two orgasms in one!
Cum hardest? Ironically, in missionary with deep kissing and my legs wrapped around pulling you in deeper.
There's something about being ravished and consumed so closely that makes me come the hardest.

Like you were struck by lighting...hard...like please stop...I can't do this anymore sensitive hard...

Yessss...makes it hard to walk...I may beg for rest...

...and I will let you...do you cum from anal?

Anal? Yes...e v e r y time. Anal is a whole different world.

How different...

Full body orgasm...It's important to be in sync with anal and try to release together because

Because?

Once you cum and the pleasure ceases...
Your body wants that big dick out of there lol!

Ohhhhh...but you cum from anal?

Yep.
Everyone can cum from anal if they relax enough...

Are you a size queen??

?...

You like big cocks??

Think so...been told I'm a bit tight? I mean our bodies acclimate (women), but when I'm at the gym...I pull
tantric energy from my Kegels with each rep...I want to keep things tight...

Wow...

Probably why I like gym-gasms so much lol.
Anyway, I try to work my tantra energy into my workouts to keep myself "fit"...

Mmmmmmm...so damn hot...
How wet is your tight pussy now?

Now? Uhhhh, I'm thinking a second shower is needed today. Lol

Wow...soaked?

Gloopy kind of soaked! It's been a tough day body-wise. Lol.

Built for sex...built for passion...sex is a bi-product. Gloopy?

I like how you think! Yeah, like thick. I know I'm done ovulating but no one told my crotch lol.
Soooo....
I have this group of women I go on cruises with every year. We have this saying about men- To describe chemistry...It goes, "The type we can't even be in the same room with, too dangerous."

Am...I...danger zone material?

I do believe so. My nose would make a beeline for your pheromones, I think. Even at a bar or party. I must stay awayyyyyy. I mean I felt something the times I'd been around you but just brushed it off as me being unsatisfied in my marriage.
After all this...talking with you all this time...though...

Me too...
Exactly...

I mean, I actually thought I had no flirt game...
Which is really not flirting because that can involve a lot of fake shit, but I've been VERY honest and descriptive, so I can't even call it flirting.

Ohhhhhhh hell no...you are the real deal...

Perhaps it's more intense because there's a screen and miles in between us...

No. It's real...nice try...

I hear we all get gutsy with a phone to hide behind lol...

Is that what you're doing...5G boldness...

Perhaps...
I have no fn clue...
Something feels damn good though...

Nor I...but damn you have my mind working

Same

Did you touch yourself today??

Not yet. I'm not in bed yet.
You?

Twice

Holy fuck
Nice...

Yup...cum everywhere orgasms

You did seem to sleep in a bit for a Monday?
Really??

Right...told you of my dream...made use of visual

You did share that. Nice dream. I'm honored to have been involved.

You were...
...very

Did you ever tell me your favorite position?

Whatever makes you pleased...

Noooooo, it's all good but you've got to have one that does you in faster or is a secret favorite. Nice try...

But tonight...I would like to gently finger you...building pleasure...building tension...as you cum...you bite my chest

I do bite...but lovingly...
Pleasure over pain always...

I also...
Love...love...love...to kiss and lick...
Pussy...

Oh myyyyyyy.....

Love it...

I enjoy oral. For both. I think it's lovely to be able to cause so much pleasure with our mouths...and then our bodies...
And then out mouths...lol
How do you feel about breasts being wrapped around your...

Mmmm...yes...
Tonight...I would tease you...

Tease?

Love to feel your breasts...

You like begging?
Teasing...can be torturous...
There's only so much one can take before saying pleasssssssssssse...

Yes...
Kiss all around legs...stomach...tongue gently passes over clit...as if by accident...light fingering gentle...take a minute...breath on clit...light breaths...small little tongue touches...

Very niiiiiiice....

Then you push your wet pussy to my face...two fingers in you...massage g-spot...tongue working hard along hood...along clit...

Ohhhh my myyyyy...

Push down on pubic bone with hand...rub g-spot...as you cum...you squirt...I slide down... finish your orgasm in my mouth...savor your flavor...

You're killin' me, Scorpio.

How??

I've been celibate too long.

You finish cummin...you pull me onto you...you guide me inside...

Ya got me walkin' funny...ugh, I love the initial entry! Takes my breath away every damn time...

Stretched...you push hips up...feel me deep...your nails dig my back...pulling me in deeper... Love...love...love...the first thrust into a dripping wet pussy...

Right? Makes me gasp!

Me too...thats the most sexual moment...it all comes together...one single gesture...

Magic...
Tingling...sparks fly...

Yes...I hold my breath...

You do?

Best when missionary too...

It is! I'd steal your exhale in a deep kiss. Explore your mouth with my tongue.

Yes...slow...entry...until balls deep...

Looooove balls deep!

Feel the tingle in balls...as I go in you completely...your back arches...

I love to arch my back!!! Especially in doggie!

Rub my fingers along ribs...lower back...caress the curves of your ass...

Pleaseeeeeee.....

Even slide finger in your ass...

Maybeeee...

You would reach back...push my finger deeper...
Feel my pulsating...hot cum...deep...deep...keep going...

Ohhhhhh...ummmmm....

Ummmmmmm???

(15 mins later)

Sorry, my roomie came in my room to check in and wish me a Happy Birthday. I think she needed a healing conversation. Had to put my "intimacy coach" hat on. My apologies...

Today your bday????

Tomorrow. She's early.

Ahhhh...how's roomie?

She's cracking me up. She wants to get pregnant (surrogate) and I'm like "Yeah bitch, let's pretend to try! It's way more fun." Lol...

She wants a kiddo?

She has her 8 yr old, had one surrogate for a couple in Canada...wants one more by surrogate before done.

Where she find dads?

Couples inseminate.

Then give embryos?

Yep. They have to attach. Lots of hormones and shots. I prefer the natural wayyyyyyyy...

Had friend ask me to be the guy few years back...had contract from their lawyer all drawn up...

Seriously???

Yes...said no...I could never not be a part of something I couldn't kiss goodnight to...

Oh, my heart...

Felt selfish of me...but...just the Irish kid in me

At what point did you say no when they said you'd not be able to be in your child's life?

In contract from lawyer...from beginning...said no thank you...

Wow. I can understand that. Sounds like they really wanted your seed my friend...

They did...lesbians...one said I was the only man she thought maybe she could...you know...
Wow...that's quite an honor...
(Sent pic of feet in tub)

You in bath...

Yep...Epsom salt...

Mmmmmm...will you rub...your pussy?

Mostly after, in bed, I prefer a bed...Plus the relaxation comes in after climbing in bed. My safe space...

Mmmmm...I soooo wish I was there...sit with feet in water...not talk...just listen...

Damn, you had a lesbian want you? That's some power!
I do like how you listen...

I guess...never knew...I like to listen

Savage...
It's hot how you pick up on detail. I was ignored for sooo many years...

Easy to listen...no expectations to outcomes...just smile...nod...always look in eyes...like Mr. Miyagi said...

Ahhhhh, Mr. Miyagi...

Posture allows you to know intention...

Roomie said something quite interesting...
She says, "Ya know Peg, it's crazy how people cross your path. Doesn't matter if they're across the country, married, or gay. If they're supposed to be with you it will happen."

What did you take from that...

She was speaking of her own journey and how things are unfolding from what I taught her 7 years back in our women's group every Friday night.

Teacher learns from student moment...priceless...

Yes!!
She was one of my clients (coaching and massage) that owed me thousands in coaching, so she gave me a place to crash (I still pay her rent tho, just how I roll), and now she's uncovering many manifestations still. She checks in with me so we can compare notes.

Notes?? On??

Life developments. Don't worry, I would never share about my personal passions. I don't like humans THAT much lol...

I'm not worried...how's bath??? How's skin feel?

Very nice. On my bed now. She just left and went to her room.

No more bath?

Done. Contacts out, just climbing under the sheets. It's warmmmmmm....

I bet...what ya wearing tonight?

Silk-

Top only tonight...please...

Top only?

Yes...top only...

But I'll be cold. No one to hold me and keep my temp regulated so I sleep through the night...

For a bit...top only...

Okay...

You lying under the blankets...

Yesssssss.....

Rub...gently...1 finger...slow...slowly...right along the lips of vagina...slow...no insert... Slowly...now two...rub outside...push down...pressure...on lips...as you slowly start to get wet... now slide middle finger inside...upward circles on g-spot...now run that wet finger in circles... around swollen clit...

Slightly more pressure from finger...enough to make you push up with hips...

More aggressive circles...around clit...every 5 or 6 rubs along clit...you slide 1 finger deep...

Think how the tip of my cock...soaked...in precum...soaked in your saliva...feels...rubbing along your swollen lips...hips pushing up...legs open more...head comes off pillow to meet my gaze...
The tip is so swollen...your wetness running down legs...you grab base of cock...you rub me on clit...from tip to balls you glaze my shaft...
You position your hips...you push your pussy up to my cock...you feel the tip inside...
Your hands move to your breasts...you are pinching your nipples...
I gently push slowly...slowly...in...but stop...

I slide out...kiss my way down...gently kiss your clit...slide one finger in...kiss your clit...you reach down...spread yourself wide...

Breath...tongue...vibration from moans...make you moan...I slide a 2nd finger in you...keep fingering you as I now rhythmically lick and suck clit...you moan...
You are about to cum in my mouth...I slide 1 finger gently in ass...this sensation makes you begin cumming...

As your orgasm slowly subsides...I kiss my way up to your lips...
You open your legs entirely...push hip to me...tip rubbing swollen lips...tip rubs clit...
Tip...slides in...
Shaft passes deeply in...

Need...time...

You reposition hips...push back...feel balls against you...buried completely...
Time?? Too much??

Just need a sec...
My body took over...

Go with it...

I can't fight...
It...

Meaning?

Imagining us...

Are you touching yourself?

Just need a sec to...

Mmmmmm...

Heart...
My heart is racing...

Good thing??

Fuckin' A
There was more. Had another...so strong...
Holy hell...

Wish I were there...to watch...observe...
Two orgasms?

Yes...need a sec...
Uh wow...

105

I should go…

Wish I could take over…
I do something wrong???

Nooooooooo…

Go??

I'm…
In my feels too much. Orgasm is sacred to me…

Too much?

Feeling vulnerable…

About?
If anyone needed release…was you…

Lol…you make me smile…

I'm sorry…didn't consider your day fully…hope you can rest…

Need spooning…
Whispers…

That would be great…
Slight touching…along hip…curve of your beautiful ass…

Yes please…
May I arch into you?

Absolutely…

Place your palms on my breasts…

Yes…my knees behind yours…

106

Feel your chest along my back...
Your breath on my skin...

Yes...our scent...

Tell me something in my ear...

You are the most sensual, sexy woman I have ever tasted...your scent is intoxicating...your touch is felt in my whole body...

That...is...

Thank you for trusting me...your pleasure was immense...I would whisper...that it turns me on to know my cum...is in you...

Makes me want to give...
More...
Thats so hot!!!

As we spoon...my cock would grow hard...I would slide in you from behind...hand works down to clit...

Omgggggggg...

Leave hard cock in you...manually stimulate you...with fingers...

I'd have to reach ups and grab your head to hold on...feel you nibble my neck...

Mmmmm...after buildup...mutual orgasms...
Mmmm....love nibbles...

I'm so spent but I'll find a way...
Might make me moan loud...

Did you finger your pussy???

I'm on my side doing so...

Fingering now???

Slow...I'm exhausted, but 3 a day keeps...

Willing to answer my question from earlier??

Which one?

How do you taste...lick fingers...describe...

F bb C x
Dripped my phone...
*dropped

Pretty hot there...

Damn, I'm a left-handed shooter but an even better left-handed texter...
Taste...sweet yet

Mmmmm....
Yet??

Lol...with a hint of

Yes??

Aromatic musk, like perfume...but...
Warm?
Glazy. Clear and slick....

Mmmmm...yes...I bet...could my hard cock...slide right in?

Sooooo....easily yesssssss...

If I were there...would you let me...

Damn. I'm pretty uh...
Let you?

108

Slide inside...

> *I'd take you...*
> *Or beg at this point...*

Mmmmmmm...many...many orgasms...sticky night...
How would you beg???

> *By biting your lip...*

What would you say...

> *May I...*
> *I usually beg without words...*
> *How do you feel about your ears being ...*

Mmmmm...you wouldn't need to beg...
My ears are super sensitive...

> *If I trailed down your neck sucking and nibbling, would you hear my begging?*

Yes...I would...I would...your hand on my hard cock

> *If I massaged your chest and swirled my tongue around your nipple until you begged me to suck it...would you hear my begging?*
> *If I trailed down your abs to your pleasure trail, would you understand my silent begging?*

Yes...I sooooo would...

> *If I took you full in my mouth would you understand...me?*

Yes...
I would...
If I were there now...would you...beg me?

> *Only until you told me to stop...*
> *Damn*

My heart is beating out of my chest again. I'm having difficulties regulating my cortisol tonight...

That would never happen...I would never stop you...
Heartbeat??

My body and mind are...

Are?

Ummm...

Ummm??

Fighting each other...I think?

Over??

Not quite sure yet...

Conflict?

Yes...

Overstimulated?
I'm sorry...I should let you rest...

No, I have a visual of you and all the pleasures that come with you...idk

Too much??

But...
I likey...
Soooooo much....

I'm glad...

Perhaps it's the mental piece, it's soooo good. But the body piece...?

Our puzzle pieces do fit...

Things do seem to be fitting...
At least during sexting...lol

Very
What ya doing tomorrow...

Getting older lol...

I heard...plans...
BTW...Happy Birthday!

Thannnnnnk youuuuuu...

Plans?

None. Didn't even think about it...

Me either...off all day...nothing till 4:30...
Rough day today...amazing day for you tomorrow...

Hope so...

Know so...hope you rest a little...
Hope you are relaxed...

Can't remember the last time I had a memorable birthday. When do they start getting fun again? 50? Lol.
I am relaxing. Got my heart to calm...Breathing is everything lol.

Wish I were there...gnite...

Night...same...
Hope you liked my selfie...still dreaming of mine...

Will get one to ya...loved your pic...sexy to leave imagination running...

111

For you only. I have more but they're super racey…

Super racey???

Yeah, tough to have up on here. The hackers are probably already rubbing one out to our epic connection…
they don't deserve all the goods lol…

Description?

(Pic of legs in heels/cropped)

**Ohhhhh….myyyyyyy…sooooo needed that…
No panties in that pic??**

It's a one-piece thong lace outfit but I cropped most out…

My…my…my…myyyyyy…..

(Sexy pic of whole body/eyes looking towards camera)
Okay…gotta goooooo…

**Oohhhhhhhh…my…leaving me like that…
Amazing…absolutely gorgeous…**

I think you are…yes…

Mmmmmm…..

Night…

Night…Happy Birthday beautiful lady…

Happy Birthday to meeee. Best day ever.

Yes…it will be…

***

I think I've just experienced the most exhilarating sexting ever...

Sooooo exhausted, in a pleasant and satisfied manner. My body is begging me to meet him in person, my mind is cautious. W...T...F...?

***

10/19/21 9:29 AM

Happy Birthday...again...

You're so sweet! Thank youuuuuu....

What ya doing

Shaving my legs lol...you?

10/19/21 6:59 PM

Hi

Hi!
(Sent meme of pussy dripping as a waterfall into the land)
My Ayahuasca friends just sent me this beautiful art. Thought you'd enjoy...

That you???

Ahhhhh, you got jokes tonight!

Jokey...jokes...

Humor heals...

Chapter 8

IN PERSON

Josephine got off the phone with her husband and decided to take his advice. She did see that Peg Law was back in Las Ramas and that her profile said she was single. Mark told her it was time to have that beer with Peg. It had been since 2014 since she counseled Peg and Dereck. She'd messaged with her and ran into her once at a gun show but that was just short cordial comments. It was time to really talk. She couldn't shake the eery feeling she got from Dereck when he approached her. She wanted to catch up with Peg and see if she could help in any way.

Looking through her contacts she was shocked she still had Peg's number. She had Dereck's as well but that's not what she wanted. She called and left a message hoping Peg would get back to her, or at the very least text her. The topic was more serious so a dinner, or a few beers out, seemed more appropriate than a few messages. She wanted more of a sense as to where Peg was emotionally with her new life.

Dereck boarded the plane already pre-annoyed as sweat poured from his temples. He hated planes, hated the small seats, hated the smell of recycled air, and definitely hated the people. If anything made him want to take a bunch of people out it was the whole flying bullshit process. He managed to make it through the TSA baggage check without getting into an argument, but that was only because the agent who scanned him was a blonde. He had imagined bending her over the conveyor belt and having his way with her. It calmed him.

The only thing calming him now was knowing he'd be in Colorado in a few hours and hanging out with his boss by evening. He hoped Trent's wife had one of those awesome gummies for him so he could forget about Peg for a few days.

Gunnar awoke, *she* still on his mind. It'd been two days, work took over, but not enough to erase all they'd sexted. *She was amazing.* He stood slowly, his hips stiff, his cock also. He wondered if he'd hear from her, or better yet, feel her lips around his rim someday. Pegasus Law was beginning to weigh heavily upon his mind.

Reaching in, to turn on the shower, he remembered how she's answered about his cumming inside her. Could she really be in agreement? Her views and style seemed *very* compatible with what he'd always wanted. He smiled, hoping... *yearning*.... He had no idea when he'd get to touch her, but damn did he want to. And the way things were unfolding, he wondered to himself if he'd actually wished her into his life!

He stepped in, the heat of the water washing over his head and down his large frame. He imagined the warmth being her, pressed snug up against his body. Her soft skin under his hands, her voice in his ear.

Sliding his hand down his stomach, he found his hard cock and slid it into his hand. Leaning forward to place his other hand on the wall then lay his head against it, he squeezed his eyes shut and began stroking, seeing her gasp and grab for him in his mind. Using thought and the energy of his self-pleasuring, he imagined them making love to each other, and decided he very much...wanted her...he *must have her.*

Peg was up and showered, ready to go. Her nervous energy had her mind spinning and her body wanting...*him*. He'd disappeared for two days so she decided she needed to get out of her tiny room and get the day going. She couldn't get him off her mind though. Before she chickened out, she clicked on his name and typed away, pushing send, then put her phone in her pocket. Picking up her keys and the bag of laundry, she headed towards the front door not sure if her life would change this day...but certainly hoping so...

October 21, 2021

Have to head to the laundromat...be great to "bump" into you. Might have a hug or two saved up for you...

Where at?

Load-n-Bundles...leaving in 20...

Ok...

If not, I'll surely save my hugs...

I will be there

Really?

(18 minutes later)

Almost there...
Side note, I am not "filtered" in person lol...

Do you have a filter...for your soul...character??? Hmmmm...

Oops...did I butt dial you?

You here?

Yep, round back...

(First meeting after 10 years)

***

<u>Peg's Journal Entry 10/21/21:</u>

So, I thought today was going to be just another Thursday, but I woke with a need to see him. It's been weeks of sexting and playing back and forth. I dug deep for my "brave" and told him I'd like to "bump" into him for a hug. HE ACTUALLY SHOWED UP!

I was so nervous to see him after all we shared recently, and it had been over ten years since I've seen him in person! As soon as I recognized him come around his truck and walk towards me, I wanted to be in his arms...and I wanted him inside me!! WTF?? He hugged me immediately, and it was as if our bodies melded together. His warm, enchanting voice was in my ear, his huge arms around me. He smelled fresh, and oddly, it was as if I remembered his scent. Like he was familiar...

home almost. My body reacted without my control. I was wet before he even released his embrace. He asked if I'd want to talk in his truck. I could tell he was already aroused, and his vehicle would be much more comfortable than a parking lot with people and cameras about.

As soon as we were in the truck, our hands intertwined, our body language facing in towards each other. He commented on liking my leggings and even touched them.

We stumbled through a conversation about our kids, a shooting he was involved in at the laundromat where he had no choice but to put the guy down, he mentioned how I'd brought him back to a place where he had PTSD flashbacks. I felt bad, but he said it was now on good terms and about us meeting, so a new memory was replacing the old. He joked about my tattoos and mentioned how he liked my outfit. I like how he pays attention to detail-his mind fascinates me, as the cogwheels in it are always turning.

We were both so nervous that somehow, we just ended up falling into each others lips and the kissing was amazing! My hand went right to his crotch while his found my breasts. I CANNOT believe his girth and length! He made no mention of how well-endowed he is.

I whispered, "Oh my god..." and he moaned in my mouth, obviously enjoying my touch. I kissed down his neck and somehow he took my hand, opened his gym pants, and suddenly his warm, rock-hard shaft was in my palm so I could slowly stroke him while matching the pace of our kissing. He found the front of my pants and slid so easily down into my vulva, once he realized how wet he made me, he slid his fingers inside causing my body to arch towards his hand while his tongue teased my mouth. It was exhilarating and a bit naughty, it felt great to be like a teenager again, but better to finally feel him in the flesh after so many weeks of having to be satisfied with just my imagination!

Things started to increase in pace, and I pulled away and tried to compose myself. He was whispering and so satisfying that I weakened and kissed him again and again, our hands roaming and caressing! I nibbled at his lips, taunted his tongue. He reached towards me again, gently teasing my body with his strong hands.

Things started to get out of hand again, and before long, I found myself wanting to climb into his lap and straddle him. I released from his kiss again and said, "I have to go." It's not truly what I desired, but I know I didn't want to fuck him in the parking lot of the laundromat with so many people around. He reluctantly released me from his grasp, and I kissed him one last time before opening the door and leaving. I don't think I've ever wanted a man so badly. What...the actual fuck, Peg?

Chapter 9

GREEN LIGHTS

eg's hands were shaking as she tried to load the washer with clothes. Her heart pounded, her body swirling with hormones that reached all the way down to her damp crotch, dripping with want for him. She didn't think he would feel so...*familiar?* She bent down to pick up a sock, and as she stood, a young twenty-something college student with an fraternity t-shirt on was handing her a pair of her teal lace thongs.

"You uh dropped these ma'am." His voice was low, his mouth pursed in a half-smirk.

Peg exhaled, her shoulders dropping more from relief than edginess, "Oh wow...uh, thank you?"

She took them and shoved them in the dryer. She huffed nervously, more so from just making out with Gunnar than embarrassment. He truly had her coming undone. She wanted him all the more now that she'd felt his touch.

"You're welcome." He turned and disappeared around the other side of the aisle leaving Peg to her moment.

Smiling, Peg shook her head slightly wanting to laugh at how her day had progressed. Her thoughts were again on Gunnar. His hug engulfing her entire body, his scent, his smile, how he walked her to his truck, his hands on hers so naturally, their conversation, falling into each others' kiss, her hand on his erection, his hand down her thong, his gentle circling caresses on her clit, fingers inside her, on her breasts, her lips on his neck, his tongue in her mouth...

Her body ached and yearned as she filled the machine with detergent. She couldn't deny how she wanted him to fill and stretch her. Her eyes shut tight, she tried to reset her vision so she could concentrate. How could she want him so badly? How did it feel so familiar? Does that even happen with people? She'd never, EVER been touched like that in her life. She'd met him years back but only shook his hand. How was it that this felt...*comfortable* somehow? As nervous as she was, Peg couldn't deny that he calmed her too.

She closed the lid and locked the door to the washer then stumbled on shaky legs over to the picnic table to sit and collect her thoughts. He'd already texted her.

***

Gunnar did not want her to go. He looked after her as she walked towards the glass doors and disappeared into the laundromat. He put his truck in reverse, his cock throbbing, still wanting her hands on him...her mouth. He drove out of the parking lot and away from the woman he would have just fucked right in the front seat of his vehicle if she hadn't stopped them.

He wanted to feel her mouth engulf him in the way that she'd slowly kissed him, teasing and tantalizing him with her warm tongue. He couldn't deny he desired her! He wanted her to explore his shaft and tip of his dick with her velvety softness. She was way more disciplined than he. He really liked how she kissed, how she gently groped and stroked his cock beneath his clothing. Peg was more than what he expected and he wanted her in every way now. Reaching in and feeling how wet she was for him was the biggest fucking turn-on in years! Her lips, her heat, clit, soft, inviting smooth vulva begging to be entered. His dick pulsed just thinking of her...

He had no idea how to even go workout or start a twelve-hour shift with her on his mind. He hoped she wasn't scared off...or worse, convinced they should never be, because one thing he was certain of, he wanted Pegasus Law more than anything. He picked up his phone to text her.

October 21, 2021
(five minutes after leaving)

W

O

W

I have no words...

Legs are shaking...I'm still hard...

120

I can't really walk well...lol. WTF?
Nice "bumping" into you SGT. I hope you have a lovely day...

I want to kiss you again...

I like how you kiss...

We kiss...

We...kiss...
So much more in it
I like your scent...
I'm a bit...soaked...

You have so much more self control

Lol...
That was not me controlling things...

Very much...yes...you were...

I know for sure I can't be "in the same room" with you now. Holy fuck.

You thought about...it?
Your taste...lingers...mmm

You tasted??

My fingers...your neck...your lips...your breath...

Took my breath away...

You ok? Seriously?

Yes, but I feel like I need the gym, soooo exhausted. Gonna go nap then get fondled by the hydro-massage bed lol...You ok?
Some dude just handed me my thong I dropped on the floor. I am a bit distracted...

I am...I am...
Mmmm...thong...

(LATER)

Ex is harassing me via text. Ugh-

Ok...
Can I help?

I don't know...this is new for me. Thank you for caring.

Might wanna delete our messages...he might hack...won't help your process...

Ok...

But...God I want you...

You...just calmed me...
Again...

Mmmmmmm....

How was your workout?

Distracted...hmmmmmmm...

Oh nooooo...

It's fine...my heart rate was up long enough...earlier

I did relax nicely after melding our energy closer...

Mmmm...I thought you were gonna...for a small second...take me in your mouth

Uhhhh, was a thought. I'd need more space and time...oral is very special...at least to me-

Ohhhhhh...very much so...you kissing...sooooo...good

122

I like our kissing...very much...

Mmmm...was a great morning...

Agree...you working? Don't want to bug ya...

You sure...you were ok with it? Heading in...

Mmm...so ok with our morning!

You...are...simply amazing...and complex...and...amazing!

You're amazing as well...nice to feel such passion. Sorry about the complex stuff, I can usually tuck that away better...lol

It's great too...

Balance...lol

(Later)

Still doing ok??

Awww you're sweet. Thank you for asking. Got a nervous tummy. You holding up?

I am...

Yayyy...I like to know you are...

You get a nap?

No...had to deal with bullshit on the phone. Would have rather dreamed...

Sooooooon...

(Later)

123

Peg sent a meme:
When He's already given you multiple orgasms and says: "I'm not done with you."

Sooo true...how are you?

Doing well! You holding up ok?

Doing great...keeping busy...wanting you...it's a good night...so far

Mmmm...tried to workout. Was great but things just seem to be building off of earlier...

In a good way???

Yezzz....

Mmmm....you had me on fire today...

It was intense...

Very...your nipples...mmmmmm....

I like how you...touch me...

I truly enjoyed...will I touch you again??

Please?

When??

Idk (sad face emoji)

Mmmm...just say when...

Mmmm...you say...

Now!!!

Whaaaat??? Thought you were working?

I am...greedy tho...want you...

Ohhhhhhhh.....

We get a lunch break...

I think I'm greedy as well...but, I don't really like quickies...I like to take my time...

I know...tomorrow??

Had a checkup recently?

Yes...
Bloodwork...less than a month ago...

I have as well, September...all clear...

All good...BP was a little high...high cholesterol

Uh oh...how about from other lovers? Everything good? I haven't been with another...kinda of a one man gal...this is scary...

Ummm...me too...

I uh...don't do "detached" real well...if I give...I really GIVE Gunnar...

Detached??

Uh...I don't compartmentalize as well as you do...have a hard time with being "emotionless"?

Nor I...

Once we do this...once we "share" energy...it can't be undone...unfelt...

I agree...

I need healing...your kind of...healing...

Tell me more about that...

My body...I'm feeling a "green lights" feeling...I guess you're doing everything right...

Ahhh...do you want more?

I do...but I can't do trauma...I'm afraid to take what I want...I want healing, not hurt in my life at this point...you know?

I do...
I honestly don't know why this feels...right?

It's scary how right this feels...I didn't expect you to show up today and see me...that was huge...

I didn't expect the offer...I couldn't say no...

Really happy you didn't...

Couldn't...who kissed who????

Not sure who kissed who now that I think of it...
I could tell my roomie you're stopping by for shoulder release massage...you could come check on my safety Sgt...if I provide my address?

That's great...shoulder is sore...

She's headed to bed...and my door locks...
How long is your lunch break?

Couple hours...

Really?????????????????

New shift out...we are back up...way slow...just radio monitor mode...

Mmmm...what lovely words you speak...

We can just hang out...finish our chat...no pressure

We can...as long as you don't mind my small bed...to heal your shoulder on...

I'm ok with that...

Her house is messy...but my room isn't...wanna come over and play?
Slowly...

Yes...

Positive?

Yes...

2307 Cinta Deringo Ave off of Renner Street...on the other side...of Ramas...

When??

When can you get here?
No need to ring the doorbell, I'll come open the door, might...want to park down the street since I'm being followed by my idiot ex...

In a few...ok...

O...m...g...

(13 minutes later)

Ok...I'm here...

Mmmmmmmmmmmmmmmmmmmmm.....

Chapter 10
THE FIRST TIME

Peg was nervous but more excited! He texted, "I'm here." And instinctively she sauntered swiftly and quietly towards the hallway and to the front door as if he were a magnet for her body. She was careful to unlock it and open it silently, so as not to wake her roommate and daughter.

For a moment, there was nothing, he wasn't there, only the glow of the streetlights on the pavement beyond her truck in the driveway could be seen. The cool night air was seeping through the glass door, and she reached to unlock it, her wetness profound as his silhouette appeared abruptly! His posture was cautious, as officers are taught, but he approached her, his uniform blending into the night.

His eyes pierced looking into hers, then his gaze traveled down her body, a slight smile at the corner of his mouth. His hand reached for the door handle, and he breezed into the front foyer swiftly, careful not to make a sound.

"Hi." he whispered.

Peg stepped to close the door, her eyes meeting his again, her hand gliding up around his ear to pull his neck so his mouth was on hers. He met her lips with hunger, a small moan escaping. She exhaled somehow knowing that what they were doing would change her in a way to where she'd never be the same woman again. She knew whatever this was could be wrong in so many ways for others but somehow it felt completely right for them!

Gunnar placed a hand around her waist and stepped forward, still kissing her but making it clear he wanted to move towards her room. She broke the kiss to lead him.

"This way." She told him in a whisper and nodded her head for him to follow. His eyes scanned the dark hallway and living room as his training demanded. She could see he was naturally cautious, like a sixth sense. She turned left and into her room, hearing his heavy footsteps and duty belt equipment following as quietly as possible.

Once in the dimly lit room, he stepped passed her and pivoted, just as she was about to lock the door. His hands were immediately on her, revealing his desire.

She turned to meet his lips again, this time with more hunger. Her pussy pulsed, aching for all that he had to offer. She moaned into his mouth and kissed him deeper, praising him for making the time to follow through with his promise. Gunnar didn't know it yet, but Peg's top needs were words of affirmation and quality time. Not only did he say he would be there, but he took the time to follow through, and she was honored and very much wanted to reward him for that.

Her hand slid down and grasped his already hard cock beneath his uniform pants. She remembered feeling him earlier in the day in his truck, but somehow, he seemed even larger and more engorged for her. He moaned in her mouth, his tongue exploring, his response arousing her already wet center. He pushed away grabbing at her silk tank, pulling it off over her head to reveal her aching breasts. Gunnar exhaled, moaning hungrily, and placed his hands on her, cupping her, his touch strong but gentle. Peg's eyes blinked slow at the feeling of ecstasy his warmth sent through her. She looked up at him, her knees weak with want for him to touch all of her. It had been so long since she'd been touched, and even longer since she'd felt this much desire. The low chatter of radio communication reminded them both that he was still clothed.

Gunnar stepped back, gazing at her body and beginning to pull at his gun belt, laying it gently across the room near the wall. Peg watched how he unfastened his bulletproof vest and removed it over his head to lay it down next to the belt. She felt nervous and exposed moving around the room preparing the bed, wondering what would happen first, excited he wanted her.

Gunnar continued to disrobe, shoes, shirt, pants, placing everything to the side while whispering how beautiful he thought she was. Peg smiled excitedly, reaching to help him with each layer. Her eyes widened as he revealed more and more skin. She had no idea how beautiful he was underneath his uniform! Being in bodywork the last fifteen years, she'd seen many bodies, but Gunnar's was by far her favorite. She smiled, thinking how she might be biased since he was about to share his with her.

Her gaze trailed down his thick neck to his broad chest, his pecs were beautifully sculpted and moved into tight, washboard abs and then to a tiny waist, maybe thirty-two inches if that. She liked his overbuilt lats and incredibly large biceps. Her body responded suddenly with aching and wanting as his erect cock moved toward her. Gunnar walked to her to embrace her and remove her last piece of clothing to the floor. Feeling his arms around her and the warmth of his strong hold solidified that she wanted nothing more than this moment. Gunnar had to have her and was amazed that he was even in her room eleven hours after kissing her for the first time!

Before she knew it, he was laying back on her bed, pulling her to him, his engorged cock wanting her.

"Come here, baby...."

Explosions were going off in Peg's brain as her body tingled all over. She couldn't remember ever wanting a man so badly. This being only the second time she'd seen him in over ten years, made everything so new and exciting. His body rippled with taut muscle, she had no idea he would feel so good under her hands. His chest huge as he pulled her close, his hands played along and down her body.

"You look so beautiful in this low lighting..."

He watched her smile at him then lower her face making her way towards his crotch. She placed her mouth softly over his glazed head, precum warm on her tongue.

"Ohhhhh myyyyy baby..."

She moaned, liking how he tasted. Peg noticed her mouth was a bit snug for his large size as she lubricated him and slowly began moving her lips and tongue down farther over his shaft. He was bigger than expected, but she liked it. Gunnar sucked air between his teeth at the pleasure of finally feeling her mouth on him. His cock hitched strong, she reached her palm around it moving him deeper in her mouth. Wetting her lips and then him more and more. Peg liked to go slow, and she wanted him to feel everything inch by inch.

"Oh my gosh, babyyyy..."

Gunnar whispered into the air of the room. Peg liked hearing she was pleasing him. She went very, VERY slow, wanting their time together to be something they'd never forget. She moaned sucking him, expressing how enjoyable it was to have him in her mouth for the first time. Gunnar caressed his hands down her shoulders and arms, his breath hitching in his throat here and there as he tried to hold off exploding in her warm, inviting mouth.

"Fuck...that feels so good..."

"Mmmmmm...." Peg hummed in agreement, her palm beginning to twist slowly around the base of his cock as her tongue taunted his tip. She got him close again, so he reached down to pull her up to his lips kissing her deep and moaning into her mouth, tasting her after she'd sucked and tasted him.

"Here, baby..."

Gunnar stood up, laying her down on the bed, and opened her legs. Pleased with the alluring sight, he groaned then opened her vulva and lips with his warm hands. He leaned down, driving his tongue into her, causing her to gasp. His mouth was soft, gentle...his tongue craving her.

He knelt on the floor, his mouth fully on her, and began using his tongue and lips to send her into another world. Peg arched into him, his oral play something she'd missed despite never having had him before. It was as if he knew her body already! His mouth continued its exploration, his tongue moving a bit faster, flicking as he kept in time with her rocking hips and heightened arousal. Peg was impressed he knew exactly where to keep his mouth and tongue, committed to her pleasure. She decided, Gunnar O'Clery, knew what he was doing!

"Holy fuck..." Peg whispered.

His hands traveled up to hold her hips, his mouth holding her down to the bed. A familiar fire erupted within Peg, and her breathing began to hitch. She reached up with one hand to cover her mouth while her other grasped at the comforter on the bed! Gunnar picked up the pace and groaned, loving how she was responding. Peg couldn't take it any longer and stopped trying to control her body from doing what it wanted. What he wanted! She knew she was very orgasmic, and since he was wanting her to, she allowed her body to succumb to his control. Peg whimpered beneath the hand over her mouth, her breathing becoming louder through her nose. Gunnar increased his tongue movements and pressed in causing her to crash into her first explosive orgasm with him *ever*....

Peg whimpered, her hand coming off her mouth as she grabbed at his shoulder, "Gunnar!" His name reverberated abruptly in the quiet of the room and sounded like heaven to him. He released from her, standing up to watch and see how he'd made her surrender to him so quickly.

"Beautiful..." he whispered, running his fingertips along her breast and tummy.

His Adonis body was hovering over her, he looked as if he wanted to do everything all at once. Peg recovered, her breath returning slightly. She moved quickly and stood up, turning him to lie on his back, elongating the full length of the bed. Gunnar did so willingly, not quite sure what was going to happen but trusting her as their oral introductions went satisfyingly well.

"Here. My turn." Peg smiled, loving how he looked stretched out in her tiny twin bed. Gunnar stared at her body, his hands open hoping she'd press against him.

"Okay..." he whispered, a smile pressed on his lips as he watched her climb up on top of him. "Oh myyyyyy..." He was not expecting her to want to take him so soon, but he wasn't about to complain. Her allure very sexy.

Peg took his hands in hers and put them over his head, her mouth coming down onto his to taste her on his lips. She kissed him deeply, rocking her hips up and down to lubricate his shaft with her dripping slickness. She released from his lips and looked into his eyes in the dimly lit room, "Are you sure?"

"Yes." Gunnar quickly answered.

"Are you positive?" She reached to the side of his head making sure the second sentence met his ear. "Once we do this, we can never go back." She wanted to make certain he was as sure and she was. Consent was important.

"I am..." Gunnar pressed his large cock into her moistness showing her his answer and how much he wanted her. Both were decidedly greedy and crossing a line. He was very certain. She was *very* certain.

Peg looked up and placed his hands so they were grasping around the wrung of the bed frame. She wanted him to hold onto the bed. She brought her arms down to the sides of his overly built chest and lifted her hips up so she could slide down on top of his fevered, erect penis. She looked at him as she tried to open to him, he was very large, and his tip entered but reached her tightness and slowed. Gunnar opened his mouth to gasp. She slowly sunk down over him, he stretching her open, the bliss something they both hadn't expected.

"Fuck..." Peg moved up and then sunk down deeper, her body finally relenting to his girth. The pleasure and initial penetration was something neither would ever forget.

She was worried she would be a bit small for him, and although the very first entrance proved it true, neither seemed to notice over their unified gasps. Peg sunk slowly down fully on him, opening to him, letting her slickness surround him, Meanwhile, he was burrowing himself into her, making sure they both felt they had come home. The pleasure was incredible...indescribable even.

Peg whimpered a melodious exhale of surrender and relief that was music to Gunnar's ears. He moaned and removed his hands from the bed to bring them down and cradle her hips pulling her so he could sink deeper.

"Oh my god, you are so tight...your pussy is so tight, baby..." He couldn't believe the feel of her and wanted more and more as she glided so expertly farther down and squeezed him as he reached the apex of her cervix. It was as if her body was made just for him, and he could feel her deep inside suckling at the tip of his cock.

"Youuuuu...feel so damn good. Oh my god, I didn't think..." Peg lost her words at the sheer, unapologetic pleasure coursing all through her body. She hadn't felt a man like this...ever.

"Think?" He looked up at her, wanting her to finish her sentence.

"...didn't think...it would be like *this...feel this...oh my god...*" Peg couldn't explain herself. "First-time Sex" was never this good. Not that she'd been with a lot of men. She never experienced such pleasure the first time with any other. Gunnar continued filling and stretching her so completely, the bliss came with each slow, sultry thrust.

"...uh...your..." Gunnar was lost in the movements of her body and hips.

Peg kissed his mouth then pushed her hands and lifted herself up to sit upright on him, his cock filling her even more and causing them both to lose themselves in the pleasure. The thrilling sensation made her begin to rock her hips on him a bit deeper, her hands finding her hair, her lungs opening for more air as her chest opened revealing her full breasts above him.

He looked up at her, "Oh myyyyy, yes..." Gunnar liked how she picked up the pace, she trying to match his breath. His warm, strong hands trailed up from her hips to her nipples, "Where...do you want me to..."

"Where you choose...I want you to cum where you want to." Peg brought her hands down and ran her palms down his chest, caressing his hard nipples. She smiled at him giving him permission.

"I can cum inside you?" He searched her face, not quite sure of what she meant by *where he wants to.*

She smiled wider, "Of course." She taunted him by picking up her rhythm, wanting to make sure he understood her decision. His eyebrows raised slightly, shocked at how she wanted him. Peg thought it odd that he would ask if he could cum inside her. She could sense he'd been instructed not to with someone, somewhere along in life, scolded maybe, or even shamed. Placing a hand on his chest and one on his thigh behind her, she picked up the pace as if he were her stallion to be tamed. Gunnar sucked air in through his teeth again and grabbed at her hips.

"Can we slow it down a little, baby...I don't..." He let her know he was getting too close and gently pulled her to the side, laying her down on the bed beneath him.

Peg was impressed not only with his gorgeous body, but how swiftly he could maneuver his...and *hers*... She opened to him wanting to feel him close. Missionary was her favorite position to feel him deep in her pussy and on her amazingly, sensitive clit.

Gunnar wrapped his arms around her, and she responded by grabbing at his lats. His mouth came crashing down on her as his cock drove deep and far as her body could allow. She moaned into his mouth, the ecstasy more than she could handle. Gunnar removed his mouth from hers, driving into her again and wanting to hear her. He liked hearing her breathless whimpers, enjoying every breath he could take away. Her voice was soon becoming his favorite.

He thrust again and Peg brought a hand to her mouth to cover the sounds she'd not made with any other man before. She felt as if he was taking over her entire body and there was nothing she could, or wanted to do, to stop it. His body was the perfect fit for her. His weight crushing her in the most magnificent way.

She took both her hands and grabbed at his back again, then down to his muscular tush, pulling him in, wanting him deeper and deeper despite how his large size was stretching her. He moved his lips to meet hers again, his lower half burrowing slowly over and over, getting her closer to another blissful orgasm.

"Oh babyyyy..." Gunnar purred. "You...are...soooo..."

Peg was nearing her climax. He sensed it and pulled out of her, sliding down her body to finish her again with his mouth! She was confused but arched instinctively towards his hungry mouth. He wanted to taste her again as she came, and he, told her so as he moved to slide his tongue in her, around her, and even into her ass. Peg gasped, she didn't know what to feel as every part of her body was tingling. He then moved his tongue up to her clit again and began flicking and sucking it faster and faster, Peg arched up and unexpectedly crashed over into another glorious orgasm! She wanted to cry his name again but instead covered her mouth as her eyes rolled up and back into her head. Her body pumped and convulsed and almost bucked. She fell into exhausted bliss and Gunnar released, standing to look down at her soaked and swollen pussy.

"Oh my god, you are beautiful..." He couldn't believe how sexual she was. Everything texted between them was slowly coming to fruition. "You have no idea how amazing you look in the lighting in here...and spread open before me..." His strong fingers gently slid into her slickness, her fevered softness gripping him as if wanting more. He watched, letting her catch her breath, then guided her hand standing her up, her legs shaking. He walked her over to her long white chaise lounger chair and laid her down on it with her legs open. He climbed swiftly on top and slid into her slick and easy. Gunnar thrust deep, Peg gasping at the pressure of his large cock in her at a seated, upright position. He continued over and over, teasing and tantalizing her until her breath labored a bit.

He then stood up, again pulling her upright by her hand. She followed trying to walk, her legs still weak from cumming and his glorious weight pressing on the length of her body. He turned them and Peg took over pushing him down. His hands came open wanting to catch her, but instead, she wrapped her mouth around his cock and took him deep into her throat. She loved the taste of them together.

"Ohhhhh baby...the...way *you*..."

"Mmmmmm..." she moaned, sucking him *slow* and up and down his shaft. He had a magnificent dick, and Peg made sure to show him just how much she liked it.

Gunnar lifted his head to watch her in the romantic glow of the room. He moved her hair to the side, "That feels...so good...do you like the taste of us?" Peg smiled and nodded.

"Would you want to swallow me?" Gunnar's head lowered and then lifted again to see her answer.

"Um hmmm...." Peg agreed, her mouth and lips moving along his length then to his tip. She swirled her tongue around in circles to make sure he understood her agreement.

Gunnar's head hit the pillow again, "Oh, my god...I've never..." His words hitched and he brought his hands down to her and pulled her up to him wanting to kiss her deeply. He was getting close in her mouth but stopped her before she could bring him to the edge.

He moaned in her mouth, kissing her again and again, his tongue searching her fevered mouth, tasting her mixed with his precum. She was breathtaking. Never had he had a woman like this.

Peg released and caught her breath realizing that she'd had two orgasms and he'd still hadn't had one...he was still holding off. She was impressed with his control.

She stood up turning him on the bed and positioning him lengthwise again, his head on her pillow. Since he almost came when she was on top of him before, she wanted to ride him again. She thought about straddling him in reverse-cowgirl but realized they hadn't talked of it yet and it might be too impersonal to be facing away from him as he came for the first time ever with her. She decided to bring that up another time and instead straddled facing him again, looking down at his face full of want and desire for her.

He reached for her. It'd been so long since someone wanted her...even saw her naked. He seemed to really want to, and she liked that. She decided she was going to give him a ride he'd never forget. She sunk down over him again, his girth making her breath rush through her teeth. She started her deep, sultry hip rocking and Gunnar's chest muscles bulged as he gripped her hips, one of his hands slid slowly up her stomach to her breast, he squeezed it just enough to send surges of pleasure through her! She picked up her pace then causing him to increase his breathing as he tried to mutter something, but he was losing his words. Peg increased even faster trying to match his breath, then humped him deeper, squeezing him inside her faster, and faster, and faster...

The room fell silent, Gunnar clenched his whole body as his grip on her hips was strong and fierce! He began to pump and pulse inside her. Peg looked down at his silent, serene look and felt so much elation while feeling him pump and spill his cum inside her. She thought how he looked so hot finally letting go, as if it'd been years since he allowed himself to feel such bliss. It pleased her to be able to pleasure him so. His face turning to a smile, he brought one hand up to hold his forehead then let his arm fall to the pillow.

"Are...you okay?" she whispered placing a hand on his heart. It concerned her slightly that he internalized his orgasm and went quiet, holding his breath. He did look incredibly serene and had a look of disbelief mixed with a dimpled smile.

He nodded, "Just...numb...my face and feet...numb..." Gunnar smiled wider and let out a chortle.

Peg leaned to get off of him and give him some time, but he moved to his side and pulled her to him to lay down, her ass up against his crotch. He wrapped his strong arm around her and she like how safe it felt, his breath on her neck, the warmth of him cradling her back. He was still hard surprisingly, and not getting soft. Gunnar pushed his cock slick and dripping between her tush and thighs, then pushed his tip inside a vulva, pulling her to him.

"You've still got me hard." He whispered low and into her ear.

Peg moaned, "Mmmmm....yes, how nice...." She liked how he was sliding slowly into her vulva and then out again, then a little farther, parting her open, then out again, tantalizing and taunting her towards more pleasure. She arched back towards him, and Gunnar took the opportunity to slide his mouth to her neck while pressing more and entering her from behind. Peg's eyes rolled back, and intense pleasure moved up and down her spine as his girth parted her thick and hard and his mouth suckled her neck sending shivering pleasure down her body. She couldn't believe he was still so aroused after his climax and was now entering her again!

Her mind started to drift back into the transcendence of her Ayahuasca ceremony and she fought between wanting the high of the plant medicine and the high of Gunnar O'Clery. His lips sucked again at her neck, biting gently and bringing her back to the room. She reached a hand up and behind to find his neck, caressing his muscles and pulling him in. The pleasure he was granting her left her speechless and sucking air into her lungs to stay conscious. She felt as if she would float away if she weren't grounded by his cradling arm and hard cock inside her from behind... thrusting...*thrusting...t h r u s t i n g*...

"Feel how you keep me hard baby? Feel me deep inside you..."

She nodded, unable to find words, never wanting him to stop, his hand slid up to her breast as he sunk his mouth down into her neck again and his cock even deeper. Peg arched back meeting him, wanting him, her hand moving to clasp his hand to her breast. A loud moan escaped her and she tried to remember to be quiet. He was making it difficult, his multiple stimulations driving her mad. His pelvic play inviting her to grip and squeeze around him. His mouth released, "You...are sooooo..."

Suddenly, he stopped, "Here, I want to feel you baby...I want to cum in you again..." He moved down the bed and up onto his knees pulling her hips towards him so she was on all fours. She couldn't believe how quickly he moved, his energy endless.

"Is it okay to, baby?" he whispered, entering her with his thick, hot penetration from behind.

Peg moaned trying to respond, "Yea...yes, of course...mmmmm..." She pushed back to him letting him fill her deeper from behind an exhaled moan escaping her at the sheer size of him inside her doggie style. Peg arched down, her tush high pushing back, meeting him, enjoying the feeling of his balls caressing her clit. He felt amazing and she wanted him deeper and deeper. Gunnar drove into her, his own exhales matching hers.

"Oh my...babyyyyy." He thrust again, and again. Over and over as she pushed back to meet him and squeeze him inside her womb. Gunnar started to move faster, his strong hands gripping her hips, one hand moving to run down along her spine. Peg's back waved and arched into it, his tender touch arousing her, she moved faster and faster, hearing him getting closer, ready to cum again so soon. Suddenly he froze, his seed pumping into her, she kept her hips moving and made circular motions surrounding him with her dripping womb, feeling him pulse and pump inside her with another seething gasp into the quiet of the room! The ecstasy like no other.

***

Peg's Journal Entry 10/22/21 (AM):
Oh...........myyyyyyyyyyyyyyy I think I've met my match! I believe I have fucking met my sexual equal. Gunnar and I ended up in my room last night...and well, I am speechless.

***

Chapter 11

AFTER

Dereck Law put his truck in drive and accelerated leaving his parking spot diagonal to Peg's house, the morning sun blaring in his eyes. He just couldn't believe she never has any visitors or male callers. Everyone wanted Peg, even when she was heavy. It pains him to see she's in shape and doing well for herself on social media. He was hoping to catch a glimpse of her now that he returned from Colorado and had time but she never seems to come in and out of the house when he's there. He was certain she would go back to the East coast when he took all the money and locked her out of the house. It always pissed him off how resilient she was. Everything he did to her, all the cheating, all the lies and betrayals, and she always bounced back! Dean even told her about the threesome with her ex-bestie Kim and he and Dean, how they banged her in a hotel room behind her back while she was in Las Ramas and he'd flown back to New Jersey. He couldn't believe she didn't care, and that it didn't destroy her! He seethed at the thought of her thriving no longer with him.

His eyes left the road and he looked down to re-holster the Glock at his leg. He wanted so badly to put a bullet in her but something kept *stopping* him. He rested against the seat, running his hand through his hair, frustration sounding in the quiet of the truck, beneath his exhale. Dean told him she had mentioned having "the best sex of her life" but not once has he been able to catch her, or anyone, coming or going into the house. He did see her roommate and kid a few times, and the skinny pot-head the roommate sleeps with. Peg, though, just seems to work and hang out with friends and a new lover per Dean. Then again, he could be lying. He's been playing both sides for awhile.

Dereck knows he should just walk up to the door and do it. Get it over with before heading up to the cabin. But Peg is smart. She'd never answer the door. And he knew, she'd be able to get a shot off on him with that damn dead aim of hers. It always unnerved him how good she was with a gun.

eg overslept, but understandably so. It had been months with no sex, no
touch, nothing but divorce stress. Enjoying the pleasures of Gunnar's sexual
prowess was not how she thought her Thursday night would go but, she
certainly did not mind and enjoyed herself immensely with him.

Stumbling to the kitchen to make dandelion coffee she smiled, wondering when
she might feel him deep inside her again. She hoped soon and based on their
conversations after their unforgettable sex, he already had another day in mind.

She chortled, the memories swirling in her head, the visuals coloring the moments
in her mind. Getting a pot of water and lighting the burner under it, she stood there
watching the flame while feeling the delightful tenderness of her pleasantly sore
vulva. It turned her on. Gunnar was very large for her, which she really liked. She
squeezed her arms across her body remembering his strong embrace just the evening
before. Never in her life had she been with a man so physically fit, so strong, and yet,
so gentle. Feeling her body begin to react, she squinted her eyes shut, thinking it
would help stop the thoughts. It didn't work. She wanted him...more.

unnar awoke to the alarm sounding on his phone. He pushed the screen
and checked the time. His dick felt extremely satisfied. He thought of her
and all they had done in two short hours on his lunch break the evening
before. The rest of his shift sucked but he was distracted by how incredibly
fulfilling sex with Peg was. She was everything he'd hoped and *more*. And it was only
the beginning. Bringing his arm up to rest on his forehead he smiled up towards the
ceiling. He wanted her again. He'd never experienced a woman like her...ever.

His mind began to replay all the kissing, her touch, her intensely tight pussy! His
cock hitched beneath the covers and he thought of more he wanted to do with her.
Reaching to the corner of the comforter he threw the blankets off so he could swing
around and stand. His hips and knees ached letting him know of all the fun he had the
night before but he didn't have time to be concerned. His body protested in pops and
cracks as he walked towards the shower wondering how he'd be able to concentrate at
the range all day with her scent and moaning billowing in his mind.

He felt Pegasus Law was everything she said she was and more and he couldn't
wait to venture further into her world. He looked down at his phone and tapped on
the icon of her pic to message her:

October 22, 2021

Hi...
Hello
Hola
In flirty voice...

Well hello there...feeling all right?

I am...you??

Very well...throbbing inside a bit...energy is still flipping out...

Mmmm...soooooooo sexxxxxxxy...

My body is like "it's been soooooooooooo long!"
Felt so incredible!

Yes...you did...yes...

I? We?? First time sex has NEVER been that good for me. Nothing like being on the same vibe huh?

Was...great...I'm still...numb...my feet and face...well done...

Numb? Oh nooooo. We can't have numb?

Face...was great...total...bliss...

Yes...blisssssssstacy....

(Later)

You...relaxed??

Finally yes...most memorable moment?

Your invite...
Laundromat...and I can't...remember who kissed who first...great memory

142

Perhaps it was mutual? We both went in...like magnets...

Was...great...like festive high school again...thank you....

Thank you. Quality time is my top human need...that was definitely quality time. You...felt soooooo...gooooooood....magic dick good...

First time I entered you...felt so right...

I'm sore...did you like that initial entry? Felt right?

Was...is...amazing...yes...

Yesssssss....

Looking up...cumming...ohhhhhh my...

Making me pulse...again...

Mine was...soooooooooooooooooooo pleasing.....

Such a pleasure to witness...so strong yet peaceful...

Was...Am I...still dripping from you?

Yes...My body is still reeling...wanting...

Well...get some rest...message soon...nite beautiful...

Night...

***

<u>**Peg's Journal Entry 10/22/21:**</u>

My body feels good, sore but good. I'm pleasantly satisfied yet there's this weird yearning...like I didn't get enough of him. So weird. Not gonna lie, I've been replaying all that we did over and over in my mind while driving around and writing this. His words, his body, the sensation of his hands on me, how big he is and how enjoyably sore my crotch is from our shared interests.

143

I don't think I've ever experienced such great first-time sex before. I mean I was nervous but something felt so natural with him. There was no awkwardness or fumbling, I wasn't offended or off-putt by any movement or position! It's as if EVERYTHING was compatible and pleasurable. Haven't had a chance to talk with him about his take but for me, I am sooooo wanting more. Can't believe how many years I went with "Mr. Abusive Manipulator Micro-Penis" in such an oppressive marriage. Look at what I was missing. Holy fuck! Damn, my loyal ways.

October 23, 2021

Helloooooo.....

Heyyyyy you...sleep at all?

I did...little...getting ready for range...you??

Little bit...didn't dream...cuz most came true...

Wow...
Best...answer...everrrr...

Oh?
Missing things...you? Range fun yet?

(Silence till evening)

Yeah...nice here...great weather...

It is a beautiful day! Body feeling okay?

Feel...great you??

Sore...
But a nice sore...the kind that only goes away with more...uh stimulation...

Mmmm....pick me...hand in the air...

Lol...please and thank you sir, may I have another...

144

Yup...
Yup...

Oh myyyyyy....

Lonnnnnnggggg day...but good...

I bet you're bushed...lostsa sun, lostsa range play...
Heading out with the gals for belated birthday shenanigans...
hard to walk in heels...can't imagine why lol....

Hehehehehe....

Mmmmm....sweet, sweet whiskey...it's an Irish thang...

Mmmm...it is this Irish kid's thing...

Yes...the shenanigans have already begun...

Having a shot? Mmmmm....
Took Benadryl...allergies killing me...falling asleep...nite...

Oh no...well sweet dreams...

Head pounding...have softball with daughter all day in El Paso tomorrow...hope allergies go...
grrrrrr...

Oh my...not fun...

Get some rest...hugs and kisses on all your pink parts...

Mmmm...you as well...dream of me...

October 23, 2021
(Silence all day)

Hi?

Just getting home from El Paso...left at 0645...longest day everrr...

Oh ok...won't bug ya, sweetie...

You aren't...was away from phone...how are you?

Feeling...uh?

Me? Wayyy tired...uh?

You all right?

Head killing me...allergies...dehydrated...tired...sun burnt...but holding up...how was your day??

So sorry about those allergies...perplexed...we good?

Good? Yes...are you good? I know you are dealing with tons of stress...

Ok...yes, stress is still a constant lol...

What's on your mind?

Hmmmm...not sure...think I'm feeling...forgettable?

**Forgettable?????? Not one bit...at all...
Meaning?**

What we did...that was...really, REALLY intense for me...and new...

**Me too...very intense...
Still numb...**

146

Numb??

My face...
I don't know how...it was all...just so rapid...but like...

Oh I see...(sad face emoji)

Why...sad?

CPTSD...processing...

I am too...
I'm sorry...wasn't ignoring...had daughter all day...

Apologies...hope softball was fun...just a simple gal...

Same...looooooong day...softball was...ok...

Oh ok...let ya go...

Going to sleep...pssst...
My cock is still throbbing...wanting more...more kisses...more hugs...hope you can relax...
falling asleep...nite...

Sweet dreams...

***

<u>Peg's Journal Entry 10/23/21:</u>

I think my body relapsed a bit...I mean my CPTSD. It's strange because the sex with Gunnar really calmed me, gave me a peace I hadn't felt in months...actually years, now that I think of it.

I ended up going out with Jan and Krystie to the Boneyard where Zena works. I was trying to have a good time but Zena just blew us off and seemed not herself. I could sense my baby girl was off. After we left, she blew up my phone about her asshole father. I think because I was the one responding to her texts, I got the brunt of her anger. Apparently, her father gave her a bag full of my mail for me but hid my Walther P22 gun case inside and she didn't know. I didn't know either!

147

She was furious in her texts and mentioned how she can't have firearms in her home and I needed to take the bag. When I told her I couldn't take possession of the firearm, or anything for that matter from him, per my lawyer, Zena flipped shit saying she'd put up with enough of our "immaturity" in our marriage and she wanted nothing to do with our divorce. I told her she wasn't wrong and apologized but now there is silence. Not my best day but totally her father's way of stirring up shit. Did I want to publicly embarrass him? Yes, it's the only way to curb his disorder. Did I? No. What I did do was go on our family chat and explain to Zena, Jaeden, and asshole the incident and why I couldn't exchange possessions (per my lawyer) until the divorce was finalized. I also asked Zena to take the entire bag of mail with the gun back to her father and leave it on the porch.

Now...I wait. She'll put me in a time-out until she doesn't and at least my son knows the deal. It's not public, but it's enough to keep that asshole from doing his sneaky shit again. My lawyer was very interested in his little power play, she's now drafting emergency motions. I want this to all go away! I don't want to deal with him...ever again.

On a good note, I still feel really good from my evening with Gunnar...kinda curious for more. And my old counselor, Dr. Adeyo called wanting to have that beer we planned so many years ago. I think I'll meet up with her. It'll be nice to finally tell her I escaped from the prison of Dereck Law... finally!

Chapter 12
WANTING

October 24, 2021

Curious...about the numb...

Face numb...bliss...satisfying...

I do remember...your face...so much peace...bliss...burned into my mind...

Wow...very much...blissful...
Ex still blowing up your phone?

Not too much...scared of me now...got my kid not talking to me tho...asshat

Things will come together? Kid not talking?

You're right, things do always come together. Yeah...He handed my daughter a bag full of mail for me and hid a gun case in the middle. She took it and found the gun so when I went to her bar with my girlfriends she asked me to take it but I couldn't take possession of it per my lawyer. I asked if she would mind taking it back to him or leaving the whole bag on his porch. He knows better and is using her which is unfair. She turned her anger towards me and told me we were immature and she shouldn't have to be in the middle of our divorce crap, she'd put up with enough the last twenty years. I agreed and apologized but I still couldn't take possession of any firearms without fucking up what my lawyer is trying to do. If I follow the rules it makes her job easier. Dereck never follows rules and he wants to make me look as bad as he. He also wants the Glock 40 I have of his because the worst thing for him is someone taking his stuff. He had demanded an exchange and used my kid after I said no. Super materialistic. So, now I have to wait until she is less mad. Wondering how you're holding up these days? Smiling, I hope?

Wow! I'm good...your daughter will be back...she will see...

True. Happy you're well! Thank you for letting me vent...How'd ya wake today?

Guess...
Hard...and wet...

Oh myyy...how my hands would travel...guiding things...to my mouth...

An amazing mouth...I was sooooo close to cumming...about 3 times the other night...

Really?

Was hot...so very...VERY hot...

I agree...hard not to think about. Honestly didn't expect it to be so good so soon...was worried our sexting would be more intense than the sex at first but...WOW!

The way you move your hips...

Mmmmm...the way you hold them...makes me want to move for you...like ocean waves...
I felt a bit...small? For your girth...

Noooo...you are soooooooooooo tight...wet...
So very wet...

You did make me...extremely wet...

Helped me...
Explode deeeeeep...

Loved that...
You did look as if you went somewhere else...then when we were on our sides, you behind me, cradling me and entering me. You sunk your mouth into my neck, and electricity flew through me...thought I would explode...from the inside out...was transcendent, like Ayahuasca...then your hands moved to my breasts... such bliss...made me want to cry out...for you...for more...

Mmmmm...soon...if you will have me...

I enjoy replaying the memories in my head...savory...
I'll have you when you decide you're no longer tied up...Lol, "tied up" (laughing emoji)

Mmmmm....doing yard work...wooohooo...

Oh fun...

Yup...weeds...trees...dump...yay...
Will holler at you in a bit...

(45 minutes later)

Wanting you...

Mmmm...ditto...scary how much...
Is this how people are?
Been dissatisfied in marriage so long...not sure what's normal. I like how you heal me...

Thank...
You...
Mmmm...you...taste amazing...

Can't concentrate...when you tease. Looking forward to "bumping" into you again...
Those hugs...yummmmm....

Right...along with kisses...

Mmmmm...kisses...on all the pink parts!
Still...gasp a lil...thinking of initial entry...mind-blowing...penetration...

Mmmm....tight...so wet...warm...

Snug...soooo tightly burrowed...stretching me....aching deep within...for moreeeeeee...your thrusting...
Deeepppp...(bites knuckle)

You made me cum so hard...mmmm...so deeeeeep....

Loved...every pumping second of it...

Your ass...tasted...felt...amazing...can't wait...

> *You sure...you want your anal virginity taken? (laughing emoji)...*
> *don't want you to feel...taken advantage of lol...*

Mmmmm...yes please...

> *As nervous as I was...everything felt so pleasurable! Want to hold you down and devour you...had to*
> *come home just now and lay down...got me all worked up...*

I wanna lick you...place tongue inside...mmmm....

> *Ohhhh savage....*

Let my fingers probe your pussy...your ass...mmmm feel you relax...whiskey sips...yes...please...

> *Yummy...*

Didn't you say something about THC...on FB?

> *THC? Trollin my FB huh? Landscaping makes you frisky...*

Would love to take you to the hot springs...

> *I LOVE the hot springs...can you imagine the heat of that water??? Get too hot...have to sit up on the edge*
> *to cool off...use my mouth to relax you...*

Mmmm...set up...half circle of candles...night time...river flowing below...

> *Oh myyy....who are you....*

Mmmm...old brass band jazz...little shots of whiskey...

> *Yes, please...*

Hugging...kissing...touching...turns to playful love making...gentle...till it gets hotter...and hotter...hickeys...fucking you like a savage...water splashing...your moans...matching my deep penetration...

> *Need some earth to grab onto here....do I moan?*
> *Hickeys?*

You are going to moan...I promise...
Hickeys? Low chest...more classy...

> *Mmmmm....*

I would lay you on your side...place candles around you...towel under you...your feet in the water...I would eat your pussy forever...

> *Don't think I'd last forever...with your mouth...on me...*

Fingers in you...make you squirt...I would lick every drop...

> *Mmmm...I'd let you do all you want...surrender never sounded so good...*

Mmmmm...and how can I surrender to you???

> *You do so nicely...I'll think of some things...I do like how you address me in whispers...but, you've not*
> *whispered my name yet...calling me "baby" is very nice...makes me moist...*
> *oh, I'll make you surrender...got an idea...*

Mmmm...you sure...I can touch your ass...if no, I understand...

> *Why would I say no?*

I never asked...
Was it ok to cum in you?

> *Of course it was okay...we melded nicely no?*
> *Did you like?*

Great...is amazing...but I never asked about birth control stuff...

Ohhh I see...there are so many places you can choose but, inside me feels right...no?

Feels amazing...greatest feeling of trust...along with initial insertion...

I do need trust...at this point in my life. Feels incredible...with you...

Mmmm...do you still have a period? Do you have sex on your period...you mentioned ovulation and hormones so...

Bleeding now actually...somehow things got kicked off early by four days! I was wondering how you feel about period sex. I can't get pregnant...

Mmmm...you ok with me having you on your period??? Does it change hormones?...Feeling?

Uh...I love sex alllllllllll the time...I know I'm weird right lol...Don't want to gross you out. "Sex on Red" helps me feel better actually (takes away cramps), just need it gentle. No oral, of course, but it feels soooooooooo soothing and healing to have penetration during. Love it in every way on every day lol! When I'm ovulating though....it's ...

Ovulation??

Yes, 3 days of a deep hunger I can't explain, indescribable ache inside, a complete hunger to procreate life...don't want to come up for air or leave the bedroom lol...love it!

Mmmmmm...you are soooooo sexxxxxy...

Seriously? I think you are as well...you play in my mind as good as you play with my body...harmony... never gotten so aroused through texting before...wet all the time. When you went silent the last two days I felt like you didn't like how we were or it was "forgettable"... felt like I had gotten our signals wrong?

**Not forgettable...ever...ever...
Just was with kiddo...try not to pay too much attention to much else...it's just me...
Your wetness was amazing...how it felt...first time...my finger slid right in...**

I may have been in my period "feels"...

Feels??

*I'm pretty resilient...independent...but still a soft and mushy woman on the inside...need connection...an
emoji...a word...even a "fuck you" is easier than silence for me lol...
silence was used as a weapon when I was a child...*

I'm with daughter today...this evening too...can I connect with you tomorrow???

I didn't know...so sorry...

**By that...I mean can I connect with you...fuck you till you moan...bite my chest...fingernails in
my back...orgasms...**

Oh...

Thinking about you on your period...taking you...hot...

It's nice to know not much grosses you out...

**Baby...
You can ask...or do anything...I am game...**

Who grew you? Is there anything you aren't up to sexually?

Not one thing...I will do all...anything to please you...nothing is off limits...what ya thinking???

*I'm a giver...thinking more of how I want to please you actually...unless I'm hurt...
Period blood is divinely sacred in some cultures...you being cool with it is amazing...*

**Hot...can't wait...
Text ya in the morning???
Daddy-daughter time...gonna go wash truck...put phone up for a bit...**

Sweet dreams you. Bye now...

(3 hours later)

One more time...hi there...

Ohhhh hi...just woke from a nap...how nice to hear from you...

Hope you are ok...thinking about you...your scent...your taste...your eyes...the usual...

Mmmm...I'm okay...thinkin' of you now...your lips...your embrace...your penetration...

Nite...baby...

Laters...

Noooo...
Soooon...
Muah!

Hope...

***

Peg smiled, happy to be able to make plans with Dr. Adeyo. She had texted that she wanted Peg to call her Josephine now. Peg knew that would take some getting used to.

They decided to meet for drinks and lunch at Ganglys. Peg said she would be there by one o'clock, Josephine said she would be there the latest by one-fifteen. Peg always liked her and thought they'd make great friends and she thought how she could use another friend who understood what she'd been through. Life was definitely looking up.

Chapter 13

ONCE MORE

Gunnar awoke in a mood. He'd never enjoyed this day, the memories of her infidelity swarmed, but mostly on *this* day. He'll play the game of course, because that's what's expected. Buy flowers, go through the motions, try to perform and fake an orgasm after pulling out, all while remembering she had a lover all that time. *All those years ago.* And here it is, another year, pretending it's all water under the bridge. That everything is normal. Preferring Peg...became his new normal.

He closed his eyes letting the hot water run down his face. He imagined feeling her soft hands on his chest, her lips around him. He can't get her out of his mind! She is a sexual goddess just as he'd thought through their early texting, only in person was more than he could have dreamed of. His dick hitched beneath the water and a desire for her emerged deep within. He wanted her.

Reaching forward outside of the curtain, he checks his phone from the back of the toilet. The green dot is next to her picture indicating she's online. Something inside him knows it's not right but he wants her again so badly. Of course it's wrong, *she* just feels so damn right. He really had no idea how compatible they would be. He takes a chance and texts her. With how his mind is racing he's not sure his body will comply and nothing pisses him off more than performance anxiety. He wants to satisfy her in every way...she's a queen and should be treated as such.

Peg moved her hands down her stomach to her lower abdomen. She hates how bloated and uncomfortable her body feels yet knowing he thinks her period is amazing somehow makes it a bit sexy. She wants his hands on her again, his cock inside her taking away every cramp and discomfort her body tries to throw at her.

Rolling to her side she cradles her arms, closing her eyes to try and bring forth the memories of the other night. He was so strong yet tender. His scent, his words...it all lingers still within her mind. Her eyes open, she follows the lines of sunlight along the wall. Exhaling, Peg realizes she's still on a high from all the emotions and pleasure and worries that her CPTSD is going to dis-regulate at any moment. She knows she needs to get a hold of herself and try to keep detached from him as it's still unclear as to how committed he is to his home situation. She'd never pretend to not understand the heightened needs of cops. She herself lived the life. She wants no one hurt...ever... ever but understands how very much sex can balance the trauma, even for just a little while. She decides that no matter what, she must contend this only be a "situationship". The difficult part, of course, is convincing her body and mind of such, and her soul may not play along as she'd hoped.

She rolls out of bed hearing both her roommate and her daughter rushing around. Peg bends forward and pulls on socks then walks out into the living room to say goodbye to them both. Her phone dings in her room and her body pulses. She heads back to where it's charging to check it. It's *him...*

Dereck was annoyed and decided to leave for his nine o'clock therapy session. Sitting and watching Jan's house since six in the morning proved uneventful. Peg had no visitors. He couldn't understand why Dean had told him she was with someone.

Pulling out onto Rerrender Boulevard he went through one light but had to stop at the next. He yawned and turned the volume up on the radio. Depeche Mode was playing.

Squinting he noticed Gunnar O'Clery, in his personal vehicle, across the street stopped at the light. He wondered where he was headed. Dereck tapped his horn and waved out of his window but Gunnar was on the phone. The light turned green and he accelerated turning left in front of Gunnar's truck staring, hoping to get his attention. Gunnar was smiling and talking on the phone not noticing Dereck at all. He thought how Gunnar looked muscular and healthy. He was so well liked by everyone too, he never heard a mean word said about the guy and remembered all the times he'd invited him to workout with him in his martial art gym. The guy never once made an effort to call or even go shooting. He wondered why that was and made a mental note to give him a call. Then again, with everything going on with Peg he didn't want to admit to the guy his marriage failed. He thought he'd call him anyway and just pretend he was better without her. No one had to know the truth that she left him. He was divorcing *her* anyway.

***

October 25, 2021 8:32 AM

Good morning...

It is...

Mmmmmm...Hi beautiful...

Hi-

What are you up to?

Saying bye to roomie, making dandelion coffee, waking s l o w...you?
Sleep ok?

Slept ok??? Roommate going to work? I am being...well lazy...

She is...her daughter to school...lazy?

Ohhhh...what are your plans for today?

Uhhh...still tryin' to see what my brain wants lol...you going to the gym?

Honestly...I want you...

Mmmmm...

Still on period??

Yeah, still vulnerably "woman" lol...

Can I...come over?
I want...want...want you...

You...want to come over?

Yes...yes I do...

I'm here...waiting then...hurtin' tho...

Hurt??

Need gentle...nessssssss

Ahhhhhh...I see...

Remember my address?

Yes...

Nice...how long can we "visit"?

Couple hours??
What ya wearing...

Lol...a tampon...so sexy...

Mmmmm...yes...it is...I want you...

Want you too...crazy, wild thang you...

(17 mins later)

I'm here...

Mmmmm...

At door...

***

Gunnar stepped sideways and slid in the door, his eyes locking on hers then down her body admiring her silk pajamas.

"Hi." He whispered reaching for her. Despite it only being the third time touching her in private, he felt very comfortable, since his dick got immediately hard walking up her driveway. There was just something about, even the slightest thought of Peg and his body responded.

"Hi!" Peg smiled then locked the door behind him. She stepped toward his outreached hand and melted into his arms as he leaned down to kiss her, her hand traveling immediately to his cock.

"Mmmmm, I love that you know exactly where to touch me."

"Uh huh..." Peg turned, pulling his hand with her. She wanted to lock them in her bedroom and explore his glorious body once again. Admittedly, she was nervous as having sex on her period is something she hadn't done in years. She was flattered he wanted her so bad, on a heavy flow day, but still a bit apprehensive since it's thought to be gross to many when women bleed.

"Ohhhhh myyyyyy..." Gunnar whispered in the hall as he watched her saunter in front of him. Her ass was amazing to him as was the small of her back that lead to it.

Feeling a bit more at ease he only half scanned the living room before turning and disappearing into her room with her. He placed his gun, phone, wallet, and ball cap on her desk and spun around to wrap her in his embrace, his mouth crashing down on hers. He loved the way Peg kissed. Her mouth was warm, moist, relaxed, but her velvet tongue sweet and searching. He slid his palms down her back, one resting on her ass, the other slightly above curve of her back. He pulled her in so she could feel the rigidity of his cock against her vulva. A moan escaped her into his mouth and he wanted her naked!

Peg again reached down and this time clasped his cock within her palm, squeezing, causing him to exhale deep into her mouth. He released from her and pulled his shirt up over his head exposing his chest which caused a smile to appear at the corners of her mouth, a sultry gaze within her bedroom eyes.

Caressing him still, she lowered her lips and began kissing and sucking down his neck to his clavicle, then down his chest to one of his nipples. He held his breath for a moment, his eyes closing for a moment. His hands roamed and he started to disrobe her, wanting to expose her nudity in the morning sunlight blaring in from the window. He reached between her legs to feel her.

"I uh...have to remove something." Peg stepped over to the tissue box and took a few. She then reached down pulling at her tampon string hoping not to offend him.

Gunnar watched while removing his shoes and workout pants, "Wow, that's hot."

She huffed a small laugh of half embarrassment and half relief. She thought about how open-minded and chill he is. For her, it's quite a turn-on that he's so eager to be with her. On the bed, she had a red blanket out and before she knew it he had her on it, on her back, her legs open and he was reaching in with his mouth. Peg tried to stop him to protect him from her blood but he insisted on inserting his fingers in while keeping his tongue up on her clit. Hearing him moan in pleasure eased her and she let him do as he pleased since he was so accepting.

"Oh my, you are so beautiful, thank you for allowing me..." Gunnar again reached in with his mouth and began teasing and taunting her clit with his warm, soft tongue.

Admittedly, Peg felt her body easing and relaxing beneath his tenderness. "Are you sure you don't mind getting...bloody? Today is well..."

She tried to finish her sentence, but the sensations he was sending through her bloated and fevered womb were taking her words from her.

"I want you so bad." Gunnar lifted up to tell her more, and Peg took the opening to swing around and sink her mouth down around his glorious erection showing him how much he's wanted. She took his breath away this time and went slowly along his shaft listening to him suck air between his teeth as he muttered to her, "Oh Peg, oh baby..."

Gunnar gently placed his palm along her ear and cheek wanting her to take more of him inside her mouth. She did so easily and swirled her tongue around the head of his penis to taste his precum and tantalize his rim. She enjoyed how healthy and silky he tasted, moaning in pleasure so he knew. She began moving up and down his shaft, lightly sucking, enjoying his sounds and reaching around to caress his muscular tush, pulling him in at the same time. Gunnar ran his fingers into her hair and lifted it away from her face so he could see her magnificent mouth taking him in and out, feeling her velvety tongue around his shaft and head, teasing his climax. He placed a palm on her shoulder to stop her.

"I want to be in you, if you keep this up, I'm going to..."

She stood with his assistance, he pushed her gently to the bed wanting her on her back. Pressing her legs open with his body he pressed into her with ease, slipping into her wetness and hearing her gasp. The heat of her felt like heaven.

"Oh myyyy baby...you are so wet..." Gunnar purred in her ear but Peg couldn't respond. She grabbed his back pulling him in deeper and deeper meeting every thrust and pulse with her own.

"I...love that you're on your period. Thank you for letting me..."

"Thank you for wanting...me..."

He smiled, pumping slow and feeling her all around him.

"You are so wanted...you feel...so...gooooood."

She smiled, "You're getting all bloody."

"I love it. Feels amazing..." He kissed her hard, cradling her body to his, melding them tighter together.

As time went on Gunnar guided them into doggie style, side-lying, her riding, doggie again, back to missionary...all passionately and slow as she needed. The hours seemed to go too quickly. She came, he came, she came two more times, he came again...their moans escaping into the little room.

They fucked like their bodies had known each other for years...and it was only...round two. Pure bliss...

***

(Later)

Can't tell you how it felt to know you locked the front door so I was safe while in the shower...

Hehehe...

(Later)

Can I just go back to bed with you?

Guy just had a seizure in my truck...had to play EMT for a bit...took him to ER...fuckin' Mondays...hope your day was better...

Wow...well...

Ugh...truck battery just died...had to get a jump...yup, going home...guess I'm not supposed to "adult" today lol...best part was you...

Started great...will be great!

From...behind...lol

Yes...deep...I came soooooo much today...

You did!

Me toooo...definitely need my own place...can't contain myself...don't want to scare roomie and her kid with my...sounds lol...

Hehehe...

(Later)

Hey...What's green and smells like bacon?

??

Kermit's finger...
Betcha smilin'...

Funny...

Told that to my director in the police academy in 1998...
He tried not to smile...made me drop and give him 50 pushups...
heard him chuckle tho...

Mmmmm...yup...

164

How are you??

I'm well...you okay tonight?

I am...
Kinda quiet...

Nice...how are things feeling?

Great...you?

Oh...so gooooood...achy...but a good achy...thank you for asking...
Most memorable morning moment?

Drive over...nervous...

Really?? Why? Do we still make each other nervous?

Just...my nature...

Oh...I didn't get that vibe from you...can I make things easier?

Performance anxiety...

Whaaat??? With me?
How can I ease things? Can I share how much I enjoy us...don't you...feel that?

I do...

Has anyone tried to destroy your "performance game" sweets? We could just lay next to each other and do nothing...and I'd cherish the time...life is short...

Never not had a girl that didn't cheat...

Ohhhhh...I see. I know how that feels then. You know cheating is always about the cheater...not the cheatee right?
Not a performance thing...

Some day...I'll get that...maybe...still jacks my head up...

> Listen...I can feel a lot of hurt and betrayal in your energy...
> especially around your chest area...
> being cheated on does mess with us...
> over beers sometime we can go over it...
> I can help you understand a woman's perspective?

I'll just re-read the Little Engine that Could...

> Well...I'm in awe of how your engine can...

Way beautiful...

> Sure is...you know, it's absolutely okay to let others have their journey...
> while you level up...just sayin'...worked for me.
> When we change the way we view things...the things we view change-
> Do you have any idea how rare you are? How beautiful?
> I've had to endure a lot...please try not too be nervous with me...

I will try...

> On a better note, had to put my hair up, it got messed up today lol...

I wanted to watch you work...

> Work?
> Ohhhhh...when you were moving it out of the way of what my lips
> and tongue were doing to you?

Yes...needed a front row...view...

> Ahhhh...yes, men are more visual...I just need to feeeeeeeel...

Hope you...felt...

> Oh myyyyy did I...needing your amazing "performance" again actually...

Mmmmm...
Guess I need to pick up my A game...

I'm going to hit the gym more...to keep up with you...
and keep things...tight...

You do...fantastic...

You...
Are...
Fire...

Gets better...little whiskey...nitro boost...

Oh shit! I'm trying to understand how you...
Balance? My...energizer bunny...keeps going...and going...and going...
I am slightly sad that your memory from today was a nervous drive over and performance anxiety...
something personal going on?

Not at all...thats just me...was a great morning...

May I ask...
Were you perhaps ever replaced by a younger guy?
Or maybe only "seen" in childhood or in your marriage
for only how you achieved or succeeded?

Not younger...I think...
I had a rough...but great childhood...not sure why...

You know...at this age, we may have to admit that no external person, force, or trophy can make us feel
successful...unless we decide...
when I began working on this my entire life shifted!
You've even crossed my path and made me see things different...

Different??

Yeah, like...just being Peg is and was always good enough. Like others who point fingers at someone else...
forget about the four fingers still pointing back at them...gotta let the haters carry their own baggage!

No...I have always been quiet...like my alone time...

Not a bad thing...

No idea...didn't want to disappoint...

Disappoint?

You...this morning...

Me???

Performance wise...

What can I say...

Wrong of me??

What can I DO to show you...I am really...enjoying our explorations...
we've only been together twice...and my world is rocked...

I have truly enjoyed every second...

But???
Perhaps I haven't shared enough yet...

Enough??

You realize how deprived I was right?
Being in a toxic marriage where I had to get my tubes tied because he wouldn't take "no" for an answer...
where marital rape was a thing...or fucking me in my sleep...

Wow...no? As in??

As in...being a good person was a punishable offense...
Telling the truth was considered "bad"...being honest was "bad" and I was to be covertly punished for being
someone he could never strive to be...

So sorry...

Don't be...you're setting me free...
Look at all the pleasure you give me...

Django unchained...

Lol...
Definitely need whiskey for more admissions like this...
Here's one...do you know I've had more orgasms with you in the last 5 days than in the last years of being
married! I'm a very sexual being lol...

You were cumming hard today...can't wait for ovulation nation...

Me either...hope you'll be here for at least one of the 3 days...amazed at how much you can cum...I enjoy your
pleasure...should allow yourself to let loose more...discipline is for work...be free with me...
I need you...we're raw...real in the bedroom...

For sure...

When so much fake shit is going on in the world...I get really tired of the game...

Game??

The adulting game...the shit no on tells you about when you're a kid. I need one area of my life where I can be
authentically me. Do you have areas where you can just be you? Not have to be or do to make someone
happy?

Ummmm....well for you...in your writing?

Well ironically yes, I mean I write fiction but it is in a way my deep truth...no one knows that...

All you...no one can capture or crush that...all you

Truth...I do hide tho...beneath the characters or plot. A lot of what happened to me in life, stuff with law
enforcement and the traumas in marriage are hidden in the pages. Cathartic yes, but still marred by the
"game". Can't offend the offend-able lol...

169

Many can be offended...by what who knows anymore...

Right? My mere breath offends some lol. Wish I could drive around with you...music playing low, your manhood in my palm...

That's a date!!!

Yezzz...please. You know my truck is pretty big in the back. Wonder if you'd christen it with me someday... Always wanted to try out the bed of it...pillows, whiskey, stars, head, tunes, laughs, fucking...Bucket list item fo sho...

Pick me...pick me...

Mmmm...chosen and picked...

Woohoo...doing the dance

You wouldn't happen to be into Guinness would you?

I could...be tempted

I hear...in Ireland Guinness tastes even better...

From Ireland?

I have some. Would love to pour ya a lil' in your...belly button...sip it out slow...

That's sexxxy...
Need Irish car bomb...

Yezzz...ohhhh Irish cream...along with your Irish cream!

Wow...frisky...yes please

I am...can't imagine why...
Now that I think of it...I have some performance stuff too. I shake inside for some reason when we're uh "connecting"?...no idea why...
Climbing into bed...

Comfy??

Yesss...I really enjoyed your lunch break...

Was nice...very nice...

Mmmm...

Mmmm....

You'll need to tell me when you want to come over...can't always tell by your texts...

Ohhh...I will...for sure...

Good. Oh, and how come you always ask if it's ok to cum inside me?

Like to hear you say it...

Ohhhhhhhh, well then...favorite way?

Whatever you like most...

You have to have a preference...

Not really...

Hmmmm...fav color?

Green...

Food?

Italian...you?

Italian...black...
Book? Drink? Hobby?

Book of 5 Rings...energy drinks...or Jameson...love LOVE kayak fishing...

Fav sexual position? Scent? Band?

You on top...your scent...Godsmack...

My, you're fun...season? Car?

Corvettes...fall...
Gonna drift to sleep...hope you can rest...

Sweet dreams...

***

Peg's Journal Entry 10/25/21:

Today turned out to be amazing in the morning. He texted he wanted me, I had my period...he still wanted to come over! Was ecstasyyyyyyyyyyy. He's super cool with gross body stuff like I am. I'm sure others would find our pleasures disgusting but it was pure bliss. I did get him extremely bloody. It's as if my body just went crazy. So narley....but cleanable!

I've got to admit, I'm having difficulties processing how good he feels. Not in a bad way, just that I'm enamored with how peaceful I feel after we're together. I know his energy and our balanced sex regulates the fuck out of my CPTSD! I mean I literally feel so calm after we're together...

Ohhhh and from behind??? He feels so damn good from behind because of some damn natural curve his dick has...and the length? It's like he's the perfect fit! Sooooooo gratifying. WTF universe??? Lol.... And he came soooo much which makes me feel really attractive and good about myself! It feels wonderful to be desired in such a way.

I distracted myself in the second part of the day with Ubering and making money, then a guy had a seizure in my truck, and I got him to ER. It brought me back to my EMT days and honestly, I missed the adrenaline and the feeling that I was part of the solution. Now, if that wasn't enough, as I left the hospital and picked up the next guy, my battery died in the truck and I had to get the guy another Uber! Now, I'm stuck home with no vehicle until I can get it fixed. Ugh! Hey life, can ya use lube? Okay, I'm through with feeling sorry for myself. Onwards and upwards Peg!

Back to Mr. Sexy, when I asked him what the most memorable moment was about today he texted it was his nervous driving over! Says it's his nature, performance anxiety, and has to do with never having a girl that didn't cheat on him! I know how that feels, really sucks, says it jacks his head all up. I could sense he's got some sort of broken heart, he mentioned his ex or wife, whatever she is, had a lover, seems he was forced to forgive as I had to once. Worst feeling...the relationship never gets good again, ya just take it in a different direction. Not sure how guys process this stuff, I know it broke me...and killed any love I had...slowly, over time. I gave it a good shot but, I was with the biggest hoe ever. Dereck cheated from day one, totally a "him" problem, so my breaking free will always be a success more than a failure. I'm now definitely a supporter of divorce. I don't feel Gunnar and my's "situationship" is balancing a score or anything...feels more like we're helping each other somehow. I know it's certainly helping me...

He seems to need reassurance regarding disappointing me. This concerns me. I'm not disappointed in the least...but the mere mention of it makes me feel I'm being pre-warned. Ouch-

I shared about the marital rape and having to get my tubes tied in 2001 because Dereck was an asshole. Wow, can't believe how much I put up with to stay in my "familiar" dysfunction. With a new baby, I didn't even know how to think to leave. Now all these years later, it feels like leaving was the most natural choice (great job Pegs). It was probably too soon to share my bullshit, especially since he has little tolerance for pity. He's witnessed too much for pity...even rehab on a relative knowing their limbs would never work again. I can understand him.

Indirectly, I think I was trying to show him he's far from a disappointment. I was married to a disappointment...an asshole! I know I shouldn't compare but, men are competitive, and I thought he might be able to understand. I am not disappointed in Gunnar at all. I think the only way I would be is if I was treated unfairly or ghosted.

He's looking forward to my ovulation which feels neat. I'm actually excited! He also mentioned how no one can capture or crush my hidden truth in my writings. So true. I appreciate the sentiment.

Lastly, he likes me on top...kinda can't wait to show him reverse cowgirl!

October 26, 2021, 9:04 AM

Good morning...
Just sayin hey before I start my day...

Why...helllllllloooo

Helloooooo...how are things?

Good...tired...not much sleep...tossing and turning...you would think it would improve my core strength...

Lol...oh no...not a good night for sleep...playing Disturbed, Down with the Sickness...

173

Love that song...

Right? Love Disturbed, The Sound of Silence...self-pleasuring type of song....

Have you???

No, saving up for...you...

Mmmm....

Massage equals 7 to 8 hours of sleep...perhaps you need a massage to induce REM sleep...

I'm not sure...we would make it through a massage...

Lol, you've got a point...

That would be awesome tho...

I can be disciplined...you would only need to lay there...and receive...

Mmmm...seeing my growing cock...would you?

I'd have you on your tummy...then we'd see what needs a massage when you roll over...I'm known to cause deep sleep...

You cause my very hard cock too...just saying...

You do get VERY hard...I really like that about you...

Are you sore??

Was...dissipating now...

Ready for more...

Really?

Josephine walked into the restaurant and noticed Peg right away. She was stunning. Tan skin, her hair back to blonde, a bright, warm smile. She stood and Josephine leaned in for a hug. She realized she'd never hugged Peg before. Rarely did she ever touch her counseling clients. Her patients at the clinic were a different story.

Peg sat pulling her chair in close and turning her body towards Josephine, "It's so nice to get together with you after so many years. You're looking hot Grandma, love the tattoos."

"Thank you, yes I've gotten quite a few more since last seeing you. How are you?"

Peg opened her hands and then laid them on her lap, "I'm well thank you, back in Ramas and ready to divorce...finally! You were so right. Thank you for caring all those years ago. It took some time but I finally broke free."

"I was very happy to hear that Peg. That's kind of why I wanted to see you."

Peg stared, "Okay."

Josephine told the waiter what she wanted to drink then continued, "Dereck came to see me outside of my office a week or two ago."

"Oh no."

"Yeah. Scared the shit out of me but you know I carry so I played it cool."

"I know you do. I think the last time I saw you was actually at a gun show."

"Yes! That's when I told you we needed to get together. I'm sorry, that was my bad. I should have made it happen."

Peg canted her head, "No worries. A lot of people stayed away from me when I was with him. Now that word is getting out that we are through, so many are getting in touch. Some just want to know what happened, but most just want to congratulate me. So weird."

"Well, it's quite an accomplishment to get away from an abuser Peg. I want you to know how strong you are."

"It was hell Dr.- err, Josephine. Sorry, it's going to take me a bit to call you Josephine." Peg touched her arm then reached for her beer.

"I know it was girl, tell me what happened after our sessions."

Peg smiled and exhaled, preparing herself to explain in a shortened, more brief interpretation of the last eight years.

"Okay well, we stayed separated for five years with him living in the spare bedroom. I watched him go out till all hours, fucking whoever, learning to drink too much, while constantly trying to talk me into reconciling. I tried and tried to somehow make enough money to leave. He always made it to where we were just getting by, it took me years to build my practice. One day he came into my room, slid down the wall to the floor and broke down so bad I thought I was going to have to call an ambulance. He was at his end. We talked for what seemed like hours and sadly I began to forgive him. It's what I do. I forgive, slowly, over time. Promises were made, boundaries were set. He closed his martial art classes down and decided to actually work a job. I opened my practice in place of his dojo and airbnb'd the rooms in our house all in hopes of raising our income. We reconciled but truth-be-told I never really regained attraction to him or forgave him totally. I just couldn't see him as a man, don't think I ever really did. The relationship was a sham for the first half and the last half was just a different fraudulence. I was trauma bonded to the abuse, not in love. I don't think I actually know what love is. Years went by, his health got worse, he couldn't hold down a job. His father died and I made the mistake of feeling sorry for him and his mother. I got involved in trying to help them and that began the end. I was unsatisfied sexually, intellectually, and in every way a woman in an abusive relationship could be. He was just as awful as his mother and I started to see the mental issues within the family. My family isn't anything great, but the narcissism I witnessed on his side, trumped anything I'd ever seen. My health started to become affected. I went to Florida to help him with his mother's house, even used my business credit cards to furnish the place and airbnb it for income to pay for his mother's care. I was a dummy. While I was there he coordinated a threesome, I found out, ended things. I returned, unexpectedly, to Ramas to divorce after completing my first Ayahuasca experience that helped me walk out of a four hour ceremony no longer having feelings for him. I had no love, no malice, nothing left for him. It's been eleven months and I'm still waiting for the courts to give us a hearing date. Recently, I heard he's been calling and telling anyone he can that I embezzled his mother's money. Only thing is the holes in that story aren't sticking since he was POA and had all credit cards and checks to the account. I never touched any of that so he can't prove his lies or that I ever had intent to hurt him or his mother. He actually set me up there, encouraged me to take care of her assets, then turned on me and lied saying I took from her. I haven't talked to him in over fourteen months and it's been the best fourteen months of my life. He is now obstructing the divorce, as narcissists are known to do by withholding financials and not paying alimony as instructed by the judge. It's at a standstill but my life is so happy now I don't really mind. Every day without him or the thought of him is a great day. That's the short version, if you can believe it."

Josephine's eyes were soft, she felt compassion.

"Oh my god Peg. I knew you were a strong woman but holy shit. The one thing that really got me though was-"

"The Ayahuasca part?"

"Well yes, that but when you said you didn't think you actually knew what love was." She canted her head.

Peg lowered her gaze then looked up again, "Oh that...well yes, I mean I know I love me kids...my family and friends but I don't think I've ever really known love from a man. Especially Dereck, he really has no concept of how to love. That came through very clear as I watched how he and his mother conducted themselves at Bill's funeral and then after...with the family. They are all such awful people. I am so happy to have gotten away."

"Yeah, I can totally understand that. You look and seem so much more balance...and happy!"

Peg smiled, her dimples showing, "I really feel so much better. Nothing feels as good as freedom is."

Josephine leaned in taking her in an embrace, "I am so proud of you and so very elated to know you got away. Great job Peggy Law, you did it!"

G unnar was inundated with shift duties and bullshit calls most of the night. He wanted to be with Peg and forget the world of crime. Feeling her body, especially the way she rode him on top, slow and deliciously torturous, was in and out of his mind all night. Any moment he was alone in his patrol car he found himself drifting off to the thoughts of how she moves, moans, breathes, and squeezes him. He shifted in his seat, adjusting his uniform pants. Checking the clock he thought of what she might be doing. He hoped thinking of him and how pleasantly sore he'd left her.

eg returned to her room turning on the light and walking to the closet to undress. She thought of her hours with Josephine and how nice it was to spark a friendship with her former marriage counselor. Hearing her praise her escape and encourage all she's been trying to do to better her life meant so much. It was exciting that they were going to get together again next week. Peg wanted to share the information with Gunnar but thought better of it. She wanted to go forward with him, not so much into her past.

She pulled into the parking lot of a pharmacy to wait for another fair and to check her phone. The green dot next to his name was lit up. She took a chance.

Hoping you're safe...thinking of you...

How you be?

Well...you ok?

Yupper...busy busy...but great...

I hear. Been out driving, counted 17 calls, all lights and sirens. Jeeeeezus

Yup...they were mines...
(Pic of Laptop Screen)

Wow, what a shift. Holy fuck...just some slight stress huh? Need dinner or drink?

I'm good...thank you...
Typical evening

Working extra to make back $200 spent on new truck battery...

Ouch...

Ah whatevs...

Yeah...could be worser...technology term...

Lol...worserrrrrr

Pretty sunset...

Very...

(2 hours later)

Meme:
My sleeping pattern ain't even a pattern anymore,
it's a freestyle that's on shuffle

Ha! Thought of you...

Yep...that's me...
How you doin?

Great. Sittin at CVS near your station...
You holding up ok?

For sure...

(Hour later)

Temp is dropping. Gettin' nipply...

Yes it is...you home??

Naw. Still out...more money at night...

After baseball game for sure...

?

World Series...

Ah, that's right. Celebratory drunks. How's my favorite body part today?

My neck is fine...

Lol, jokes...

Stab in dark...

(Hour Later)

Home safe...hope you are...

I'm good...what's next for you tonight?

Nothing much...suggestions?

Wish...me

Tonight?

Prob not...bad domestic...ladder and hammer to her...

Oh no...be safe...

October 27, 2021, 9:11 AM

Good morning!

It is...how are you?

Great...you rest?

Just got home from the gym...I try. You get any shut-eye?

Tired...rested...how was gym?

Orgasmic...

Wow...tell me how...

Core and legs today so...a real lady never tells...it's more of a show thang lol...err "feel" thang...

So hot...

Really?? I imagine guys build their kegels at the gym tooooo...

More of a show thing huh...

Feeeeel thing...

How so

Damn, I guess I need to work them harder (laughing emoji)

Absolutely not...without being crass...your pussy is amazing...you are too but...wow...

Your pillow talk warms me...lol

How warm...are you?
Self-pleasuring now??

Earlier...as I woke. Gets me going for an amazing workout and day. You?

Not yet...but I will...
What do you fantasize about...

Initial penetration with deep kissing...your chest on mine...not being...forgotten...
Thrusts...deep and s l o w...gripping you from inside...

You do...I have never been ridden like you do...

Seriously?? Aren't all women kinda the same?
You are passion x 10. I'm definitely a fan of Scorpio men!

You don't just please...
You...do...it...well...

Ah...you flatter me...
Somebody has really smooooooooooth precum...like warm...velvet...

Ohhhhhhh....really?

Reallyyyyyyy....

Mmmm...
Mmmm...good...
Still on period??

Unfortunately...
Woman shit, lol.

Not unfortunately...you were the cum queen...hormones...go good with...

I actually cum the least on red...but, I'm happy I can...

If you cum like that...can't wait for ovulation...

My fave time of the month...

What ya doin

Drinking a recovery smoothie at the table...you?

Just getting around...loving no wind

The wind was not fun...

Might have to go in office for a bit...bad case last night...follow up

Yeah, you mentioned. Those cases are not fun. Too much paperwork...

Another case...elderly abuse...grrrrr

Oh yuck...

Yeah...bad...victim can't speak...rough

How awful...Strategy for the investigation?

(6 Hours Later)

Hi

Heyyyyy

How you be

I be gooooood!! How you holding up on your hump day?

Good at office all day...got lots done...

That's gotta feel good!

Not as good as you...just saying

Stooooop. You make my inners quiver and ache...
Hope ya get overtime...extra hours is tough on the body...

We can work unlimited OT...will be doing 30 plus next week...

Oh my...

Range...

Ohhhhhh...wow...
Oof, tummy growling. Gotta find some foooooooood...

What's ya need

Forgot to eat lol

I do that all the time...

Right?
Gets kinda annoying trying to remember to eat lol...

**...my guys...just in shooting...gotta lay back for a bit
Connect tomorrow???**

Be safe!

(2 Hours Later)

All is good...guys good...Nite

Glad you're safe!

Terminator T 1000

Yeah lol. Sleep well.

<u>Peg's Journal Entry 10/27/21:</u>

Was up most of the night trying to regulate my system. I'm so tired of all these years of having to force balance and peace within my mind. I truly wish it was a natural occurrence for me.

I enjoy texting with Gunnar very much. He's interesting. Extremely busy, but when he pays attention, he's amazing. I notice I like how his mind works. He seems to process like me and if he doesn't pick up on something right away, he has the ambition to ask and learn. Impressive...

I was able to text some with Josephine and it looks like we'll be meeting again for lunch. Life has been turning in a nice direction.

***

October 28, 2021, 9:05 AM

Hi

........Hi

How you be???

Struggling. How are you??

Struggling?????

Rough night...relapsed on the CPTSD end. Trying to regulate my mind with logic and emotion. Anxiety crap lol...

I'm sorry...

I struggle from feeling soooooo damn satisfied...
Then not?

Please explain...

Not sure how...
How are you today? Sleep finally?

Not much in sleep department...and I'm...stressing you out?

No...hard when you're not close...I'm struggling with dismissal...err rejection trauma from childhood. You ever get that?

I bet several guys would want to see you...your voice...your words...makes me throb...

Ouch...

Ouch???

There are no "several guys"...I'm not like that...

185

Not you...them...I am certain...there is interest...no need for you to feel like that...at all...

Help me compartmentalize things...why did we kick things off so well 7 days ago? Why is my body taking off and my mind fucked?

What do you mean?

Nvm...

I'm sorry...don't understand...body taking off??

I need...things, having difficulties not...
Being together?

What are you needing...

I remember when you expressed your performance anxiety, I don't want you to feel uncomfortable with me...

I don't...when sexual...I want you pleasured at the highest level...

It's already there...like I'd known you already...so compatible. I want you pleasured, you want me pleasured...seems like the puzzle already fits lol

What's the new book gonna be about...

Ah...distraction. I was going to ask you permission about that...

Permission?

Would you be okay with me writing one...about...

Sure...

What do you suggest? A page turner...

Let me think on it...
What ya doing today??

Are you asking because you have time?

Yes baby...

Not up for a letdown today...

1/2 hr at your door ok?

Promise?

Yes...

This pleases me...

How...

Promises kept...anticipation of pleasure...happiness...

Mmmm...roomie there?

I'm alone.

***

Chapter 14

COMFORT HER

Peg was struggling with the extreme pleasures of the new relationship. Not in a bad way, in an endorphin-type manner. She'd spent so many years pushing away her need to express herself, the honesty within her sexual desires locked down in a place she wasn't aware could be released. Her body and mind were at odds with each other not quite sure so much fulfillment was allowed. Every time she enjoyed even the smallest bliss, victory, or pleasure in the past, she was made to regret it. Her ex did a number on her. She knew she wanted turn this around.

Gunnar understood Peg. He could sense she was mostly tough, could handle much more than a woman should but there was something soft and vulnerable on the inside. Like him. He could sense she was needing comfort. He wanted to give her what he, himself often did not get. So many times he'd needed compassion, understanding, an unexplainable freedom. He decided to move his plans for the day and make time for them.

When he arrived in her room, he grabbed her and held her tight. He'd missed the feel of her body against his. He was already erect and throbbing for her. Peg had a power over his body he couldn't quite understand yet. Just the thought of her touch, as he'd walk up her driveway, ignited him in ways he'd never felt before.

He didn't say he missed her, he couldn't allow that, but his embrace screamed it to her body. She was vulnerable and shaking slightly inside. He wondered if her asshole ex was harassing her and she was just being tough about it. His lips met hers and the feel of her warm, wet mouth made his dick hitch beneath her hand that was already caressing him.

"See how hard you get me with just your kiss?" He whispered into her mouth as she moved her soft velvet tongue to explore him. She moaned and nodded, answering. Suddenly, she was on her knees before him, freeing his cock from his clothing and engulfing him deep within her hot, moist mouth. Gunnar breathed heavily, his head leaning back. His body tingled all over as her slow, sensual sucking created ecstasy on his head, down his shaft, and in his balls. No one has ever sucked his dick like Peg, making him feel so desired. She was a master at oral pleasure and he felt honored each and every time she wanted to express her expertise. He felt as if he was going to explode.

"I want to be in you." He pulled her shirt off and unfastened her bra.

"Mmmmmm...sir, yes sir...." Peg grabbed at the bottom of his shirt and pulled it over his head moving her mouth to his erect nipple. Gunnar moaned placing his hand on her neck to pull her into him. He loved her mouth on him, her hands on his ribs.

Gunnar released her and pulled his gym pants off while removing his sneakers. Peg removed the rest of her clothes just as swiftly. Before she could even stand he grabbed her gently and backed her up to the bed laying her down and climbing in between her luscious thighs, his mouth coming down on hers, his cock sliding between her vulva to find that she was soaked with want for him. He pressed forward, her tight pussy slowly allowing him only so far. Peg released her mouth from him to breathe, as his size was something she had to allow her body to ease around. Gunnar eased up allowing her to move to him and sink around him. Both of them let out exhaled breaths of moaning pleasure at the initial penetration pleasure they so much wanted now. Their bodies melded together in perfection, she moving towards him, he sinking deeper and deeper with each slow thrust

"You...feel..." Gunnar's words hitched.

"Yes...my...I'm..." She tried to tell him she was vibrating inside, shaking from his intense energy

"Incredible...." He finished his sentence as he sunk deeper all the way to her cervix opening, his ample length and girth able to go no further in her tiny womb. Her cries of pleasure telling him so. He couldn't believe how her wetness and snug velvety canal could feel so incredible each and every time!

Peg moved her mouth near his ear, "Can you feel how much you're wanted? How desired you are baby? My body wants you like this all the time. Over...and over... and over..."

Her hot breath in his ear taunted him, her words making him feel so needed. She spoke all that he'd wanted to hear. He nodded, thrusting slow and forward, unable to answer.

Gunnar moved his hands from around her back and took each of her palms in his pinning her to the bed, holding her down forcefully but with the tenderness he always showed. She exhaled a moan in his ear and arched up farther to meet every thrust, every movement. Her body ached and yearned each time he reached her limit, taunting and teasing every inch of him inside her.

"Say it..." She whispered.

He sunk his mouth into her neck, suckling and sending shivers throughout her entire body that settled in a tingling sensation at the tip of her clit. She gasped. He moved to the other side of her neck, waiting.

She breathlessly begged, "Say....my name..."

Gunnar sunk down into her again, his mouth following, sending another electric ripple of pleasure through her that made her entire womb grip him tighter. He could feel her losing control.

"...Peg..." He did as requested and released her hands.

Peg ran her palms up his arms and to the sides of his face to hold his mouth to hers. She kissed him deep while thrusting her body up and around him, pulling him deeper into her with her legs. Gunnar kissed her back and once she had his tongue in her mouth, as deep as he was in her pussy, she moved her hands down his strong back and to his ass, pulling him deeper and deeper into her.

Gunnar could feel her desperate need for him and he felt he may begin to lose control. He slid out of her and stood up pulling her towards the edge of the bed and turning her around onto her stomach. Peg exhaled realizing that he wanted her from behind. She moved toward his cock and arched to open to his penetration. He moved his hands along her lower back and around to her ass pulling her to him.

"Oh...my...god...you have no idea how beautiful you are..." His whisper echoed in the room. "Did you self-pleasure today, baby?"

Peg shook her head, "No, I wanted you..."

Gunnar was pleased with her answer and slid in deep and fast filling her completely. Both moaned at the same time, she grabbing the comforter beneath her, he gripping her hips tighter, careful not to hurt her. He never wanted to hurt her. She was a goddess to be worshiped.

"Uh...oh, you feel so...good..."

She smiled, her face down against the soft bed that smelled of fresh laundry detergent and him.

"Oh my...uh...you are so good."

Gunnar loved when she said that and thrust a little more, feeling her move back towards him and grip him with her tight pussy.

"I...I dreamt of you...us...in the hot springs. The water reaching up to your ass, me entering you. The feel of you around me, the heat of you, the heat of the water..."

"Mmmmm...I like your dreams baby..."

Gunnar felt his orgasm getting close as the sounds of her voice swirled in his ears. He pulled out of her and gently turned her over diving into her vulva with his mouth, spreading her open sweetly with his hands. The movement was so fluid and quick, Peg had little time to adjust before her orgasm built. He moved his tongue faster, to match her breathing and was surprised at how quickly she began to cry out and quiver beneath him! He loved to hear Peg's climax, nothing in the world sounded better than pleasing her! He pulled away to let her breathe and regain her strength. He looked down at her closing in, her hands coming up around her breasts, her legs crossing to squeeze every last ounce of fluttering pleasure through her clit. She was the most gorgeous being when she came, her sexuality emanating all around them.

Peg opened her eyes, a mischievous smile beginning at the corners of her mouth, "I want you...in my mouth again."

"Oh?" Gunnar stepped back as she came towards him and stood up grabbing his lats and turning him towards the bed.

"Yes..." Peg laid him down and gripped his shaft, moving her wet mouth down onto him. Gunnar gasped at how swift and gentle she was with him.

Peg released and reached for her ice water. He watched her, his eyes widening as she placed ice in her mouth and returned to him. In one fell swoop, she slid her mouth down on him again and the ice cube traveled along his shaft, causing him to suck breath between his teeth at the shear pleasure of her oral play!

"Baby, that feels so fucking good. Oh, my ga-" He could hardly speak. Peg smiled and slurped the melting water along his shaft, the warmth mixing with the coolness of the ice.

"Have you ever had ice cube sex before?"

Gunnar could hardly answer but shook his head. Peg could tell this was a first for him and she loved pleasuring him. His moans of bliss made her swirl her tongue more, and move her hands along the base of his cock.

"Peg..."

She smiled again, feeling the ice cube disappear beneath her tongue and the warmth of her mouth heating him again. She increased her rhythm, opening her lips and mouth feeling him getting close. Gunnar moaned and gently placed his hand on her hair, moving towards her mouth, losing control.

"Oh Peg...*don't*...stop...."

Peg could feel his climax coming up through his shaft and suddenly his body postured and hot streams of cum pumped and shot against the roof of her mouth. She swallowed slowly, causing him to breathe and moan into her, his body pumping... collapsing beneath her mouth. His chest heaved up and down, she suckled until he began to relax and recover. She took her mouth off, releasing from him to let him rest.

Panting he murmured, "Holy fuck...babyyyyy..."

Peg smiled up at him, loving how his body so easily submits to her pleasure, his breathing returning, his dick still hard.

He reached down and lifted her under her arms to bring her up to his mouth to kiss her deep and taste his cum in her mouth. His tongue searched her, his passion moving through them.

Peg moved her body up on top of him pulling his hands over his head and wrapping his fingers in the rungs of the metal bed frame. A smile appeared across his lips and Peg could tell that he was very pleased with her wanting to ravish him. She liked that he looked like he'd just received the best blow job ever.

"That...was..."

Peg kissed him before he could finish his thought. She began moving her vulva up and down his shaft, teasing. "Do you give consent?"

He smiled wider and nodded, liking that she was keeping him aroused with her teasing.

"Are you sureeeee...?" She moved slower and soaked him with her slick fluids.

"Oh my...you are sooo wet, baby..."

"All for you...are you sure?"

"Like the first time...when you asked me then...I'm sure..."

Before he concluded, she slid down on him, accepting and surrounding him with her heated womb. Pushing her hands into his chest and sitting upright she began rocking deep and slow on his cock. Her hips rocking to a rhythm only the two of them created.

"Oh fuck..." Gunnar's hands released from the bed frame and gripped her hips to hold on. Peg increased her speed, gliding along the length of him over and over, his eyes beginning to roll back. Just before he lost all control she stopped. He opened his eyelids looking up at her as if she were the most magnificent creature he'd ever seen. Without a word, she climbed off and turned around.

Gunnar gasped slightly knowing that she was going to let him cum inside her reverse cowgirl. "Oh, Peg…"

She didn't say a word. She positioned herself quickly and slide down on him again, hearing him moan in pleasure. She loved how responsive he was to her. He gripped her hips once more and she began a slow, torturous rocking while running her hands through her hair letting her hips rock wildly and her pussy grip him with each gliding thrust.

"Oh…my…god…Peg…I…" Gunnar couldn't finish his sentence.

She took this as a signal that he was close and she increased her hip motions to increase their pleasure. When she did, she felt her own orgasm building quickly and picked up her speed even more! Suddenly, he gripped her hips tightly, clenching her, his orgasm taking them both over the edge. He moaned into the room, she followed, both healing each other in the ecstasy of their mutual climax…

Absolute euphoria……….

In the after glow of their reunion, Gunnar lay next to Peg caressing her skin and staring at her. She could feel his mind going and going unsure of the questions she felt coming. His breathing slowed and he inhaled, "Soooo…"

She smiled, "Yes?"

"Have you ever been with a woman?"

The smile faded and she knew she wanted to always be honest, "Women aren't an attraction for me. I was with my ex-friend Kim involuntarily after Dereck and she roughied my drink on my thirty-fifth birthday. I woke up in a hotel room with them on me. Not a favorite memory of mine. Dereck was very pissed I wouldn't eat her out. I got up and went to run myself a bath. Soaked in the water to wash them off of me and try to sober myself so I could leave. That abuse took me quite a few weeks to heal from. Got her out of my life. Unfortunately, had to forgive him…we had kids…"

"I'm so sorry Peg."

"Thanks. What else can I tell you?" She knew he had so many questions.

"So you don't prefer women…does that mean you were with two men?"

"Yes."

"Was that better?"

Peg was leery of sharing this part because she respected Gunnar and didn't want him to think less of her. She decided to continue with her truth, even if it ended their time together. "It was...life altering."

Gunnar could see her face was much more pleasant than when she spoke of the threesome with Kim. "So you liked it?"

"I felt...like a goddess."

"Really?" He smiled thinking of her with two men, how worshipped she felt. He could understand.

"It was slow, passionate, mind-blowing..."

"Seriously?"

"I ended it."

He frowned, "After just one time?"

"No, after the fifth time."

"Oh wow. Why? Caught feelings?"

"Yep, well two of us did. Dereck can't...*feel*. He wanted to pull the puppet strings on us, triangulate, he wanted power when it was about surrender...and pleasurous healing..."

Gunnar stared at her in awe, "He ruined it?"

"He did. And I ended it before they killed each other. Things got...well, intense. Was one of the hardest times of my life. It was like being broken open...set free, only to have to shut down again...but I sacrificed my desires for them both. I refused to have blood on my hands...even if indirectly. I mourned for months...but it was more of a loss of losing a freedom I'd always wanted...I went back into the prison that was my marriage. The oppression was part of why I wanted to move here. I was running from the hurt. Then here in New Mexico, he just did more, and more sneaky shit. I'll never understand why I was so loyal...never."

Gunnar caressed his fingers down her back, "I'm so sorry Peg."

"It was a long time ago..."

***

Peg's Journal Entry 10/28/21:

I allowed myself to be unexpectedly vulnerable with him...let him know I needed him. This was not easy because in the past when I would be truthful or vulnerable, I would get dismissed and ignored by Dereck. My honesty was always, ALWAYS met with punishment. Sometimes, the punishment would spill over into the night when I was asleep...and I'd wake with him fucking me! I am so proud to have gotten away from such a horrible human.

Gunnar was really decent towards me. He allowed me to express my feelings and then made time to come over and spend some quality time with me. This is new. I like it.

I am enjoying our connection, he ignites something in me I haven't felt before. I notice my body reacts to him instantly...and even just in thought. So very different.

He hugged me, but a deep hug, the kind you can feel in your soul. I liked the feel of his arms around me, his strength...the way his large chest feels up against mine. I like to run my hands along his overbuilt biceps...feeling the muscle beneath my touch.

When he reached in to kiss me deeply, my hand went right to his dick and he was already rock hard...even before I could lock the door. He even whispered, "See how hard you get me just with your kiss?" I have to admit, his body's response to me makes me feel so attractive! He's very masculine and sexy to me...

Immediately I wanted him! I sank to my knees and he was in my mouth...me pleasuring him in a way that was so pleasing to us both! I really enjoy his penis, I mean like REALLY enjoy it. He's got such a nice cock. Smooth, thick, very clean. When he sucks his breath through his teeth and moans in appreciation, it makes me want to slowly imbibe and caress him in my mouth even more. I feel I want to please him in so many ways...I think because he allows me to be me and do what I like to do.

I don't even notice my nakedness so much. He compliments me and makes sound of appreciation, caressing and whispering to me. He reciprocated orally which is blissful. What's really nice is he expresses how much he wants to be in me and I can feel I want him inside me too! It's as if our timing is so on...and we want the same things. This man is rocking my world and I am enjoying every breath, stroke, kiss, and moment. Oh, and I introduced him to reverse cowgirl today. I should let my fucking goddess out more often. Kinda feeling pretty damn savage!!

***

(5 Hours Later)

Will be away from phone...mom transported to ER...connect soon... Anaphylaxis...damn

Omgggggggggg!

October 29, 2021

Really hoping Momma O'Clery is recovering at home?
Allergic reaction?
Thinking of you...just know....

Yeah...anaphylaxis to new antibiotic...

Oh no...are you holding up ok?

Kinda tired...long night...got her back home...she is resting...

Oh good. Well try to rest yourself. Headed to gym. Dream well...

Have a great workout...

(Later)

Hi

Mmmmm...waking from such a good nap...

Much needed...how was nap

I...like sitting on your lap...

Looked amazing from where I was...

Really? You stir my milkshake soooo nicely lol...

I bet...
You working later??

I am...

I'm off...home with kiddo...

Right...trunk or treats night! Make memories and have fun!

196

We will be...I need some candy...

Mmmm...love chocolate...better than ice cubes...

That...was awesome...

Wasn't sure...

Ummmmmm...mouth full of...
My cum...

Soooo...smooth.
You're so...much fun...

(4 Hours Later)

(Pic of Peg with Uber Rider in Costume)
...and so the shenanigans begin lol
If I should die before I wake...
I thank the universe my body you did take...

Sweeeeet cos play...

Right? Was invited to a "baby shower" where he's the stripper lol...

That could be a whole chapter in your new book

Lol. You've got a point. I'll file it away in my mind. I declined the offer lol...

October 30, 2021

Hi there

Mornin'

(8 Hours Later)

Peg sent pic of Halloween Costume:
Wish me luck! Don't like people but my friends insisted. I'll make an appearance at this party but if the ex is
anywhere near...I'm out! Ya think Top Gun is ok?

Badass...

Thanx

Have great fun tonight...

Tryin'...

Make it a decision night Peg...

You said my name...

Yup...Peg

(2 Hours Later)

Yep, tried...no can do...back home. Someone sketchy showed up...can't do sketchy. Just got home, hope you
are well...

Doing good...just got home too...getting ready for back to back 18 hr days

Oh yikes...so you need me to leave you alone...

No...
Be busy...but no...going to sleep now...

198

Nite...

Night...

<u>*Peg's Journal Entry 10/30/21:*</u>

The last two days have been tough. Our connection is way more intense than I expected. Very nice...but he goes silent, and I realize I should settle into the detached state of our "situationship".

He did ask me about smoking weed and if I've been with a woman. I was honest, explained I use weed once or twice a month to regulate my CPTSD symptoms. As for threesomes, I mentioned the "roughie" thing Dereck did to me with ex-bestie Kim on my 35th birthday and then the five-time intense threesomes with Dan years prior to that. He listened so closely, I struggled with describing my "devil's threesome" dynamic with Dereck and Dan because I didn't want him to lose respect for me or pull away. My honesty tends to have that affect. I prefer honesty but end up losing people at times when being so. Now, he's distanced himself...and it hurts.

I tried to venture out to a Halloween party at my friend's house. I was able to stay about an hour and a half before the space started to enclose on me and my CPTSD took over. There was a guy who showed up that was a former student of Dereck's, so I left before he recognized me and could report back to asshole. I came home and smoked to try and rewire my brain neuro-plasticity. Helps, but I can feel the urge to do another Ayahuasca ceremony coming on. I just want to heal.

November 1, 2021, 8:34 AM

Good morning

Hi

What ya doin...I hope it involves your fingers...

That was last night...to soothe me...
Off to the hectics?

Typing...dirty girl...

Ovulation..and a bit of squirt action...damn crazy body.
Any hand action on your end?

Ovulation already??

It's a thing...

So soon after period...mmmmm....

Yeah a week...achy...horny...lol old age...
Women...are complex...

Yup...you did cum lots on period...lots

Welp, headed to the gym...today is chest and tris...and of course kegels lol...

Mmmm...wanna kiss your kegels

(Hours Later)

How's the 18hr day for you so far? Enjoying range time?

Dragging ass...

200

Oh...I bet...

How you be?

Great! Gatz family wants their massage therapist back yay!...body yearns for things....good day...you? Thank
you for asking!

Good day...long
Body yearns??

Yezzz...for sooooo many things...

Such as?

Fingers, chest, lips...tip...
penetration...thrusting...all the things..

Why were you concerned bout telling me bout threesomes?

I think/thought it changed how you view me...

I was punished for being honest in the past...especially with him. I don't want my honesty to be a negative...

Not at all...not one bit...I found your honest description...to be sexy
Your honesty is sexxxxxy...

That makes me feel good...

Well...I enjoyed you telling me...was cool...kinky...

I did enjoy telling you...thank you for creating the space for me to express it...

Was cool to hear...had sex type questions...but was just listening...

Of course...you want to know how far it went?

No...just like how it started...drinks...kissing...etc.
I assume DP happened...

201

Well...actually thats a no. Double-penetration never happened lol. Each of the five times was actually very s l o w...and sensual as I like. No pain, no kink...allllll passion. Dan said after second time...things started to get "intense" for him...Dereck started having difficulties about Dan's size...my pleasure with it...started to try and pull strings and play puppet master...triangulate us away from wanting each other

Rules were?

Dereck was changing them as we went which sucked...at first he didn't want Dan to cum inside me...

Why? Anal or vag...

Either...then he changed his mind.
Control issues I suspect. No anal ever happened in any of the 5 times...

And then he let him??
Why insecure...he wanted it all

Well...he's small...stubby (micro-penis type; turtles when flaccid)
He started to interrogate me afterwards...when we were alone...he would manipulate by love-bombing at how sexy and beautiful I looked and how sexual I was...
Then slide a question in like "but you like his size and how he felt in you right?" If I answered honestly, it was an argument. If I didn't answer it was a bigger fight. Felt awful to have something so incredible ruined so soon after Dan would go home.

Size...why such an issue...was other guy huge?
Where was he allowed to cum?

First time...he pulled out and shot on the floor per Eric's demand, cleaned it up. I didn't think much of it, thought it was a kink thing but when Dan and I had time to discuss it later he confessed Dereck told him to pleasure me but not cum in me...

Ohhhhh...did other guy get to eventually cum in you?

Yes...he did eventually, around the third time...I think. Dereck felt empowered changing rules and demanding positions, watching from across the room, then interrupting and joining when he decided. Now that I think of it, the beauty of it was diminished every time he got involved...
I much preferred Dan...as he was passionate, a gentleman, and quite compatible with my...slow ways?

How did that make you feel...

Confused...conflicted. Dereck would tell me how gorgeous I looked...how he couldn't get enough of seeing me...then on days he was loathing himself, he would begin to bring things up and slut-shame me for enjoying Dan and my sexuality. He was mentally cruel on bad days. Fucked me up...and dis-regulated my CPTSD often. Dan would make it better by explaining why Dereck was...well manipulative.

So...he turned something nice...into shit...

Yes...
He turned so many beautiful parts of our life to shit Gunnar...but I'm finally free. I think I ultimately wanted to love my "way" and my ways always intimidated Dereck...Dan began telling me what I needed to hear and that felt good.

Wow...

Dereck concluded that I was "born for sex" and that we should always have threesomes but he felt we were with the wrong person (he began to hate Dan). I never agreed to another threesome with him. Over the last 15 years, he offered me up to various men, it was extremely hurtful and embarrassing. The last guy came to me this past June (via a phone call from Afghanistan before Biden brought the soldiers stateside) and he told me what was happening behind my back. I ended my marriage while still in FL, then when I found out about the underage girl (16), I decided to file paperwork and divorce Dereck when arriving here in September...now it's November and I just want to be away from all the memories of this marriage.

Another contentious issue in our relationship was that I wouldn't swallow him...always spit in the sink...or a tissue.

Sorry...was on a call...

Sexy...

Why not swallow?

Weird...but I knew somehow, he did not deserve that honor...or me. I feel that's intimate and for a real man... I didn't see him as a man. Is that weird?

NO...not at all...Dan get swallowed?

Dereck made that some weird control issue too...at first it was no and then the fourth time...I think...he was like "you should swallow us"...was such bullshit. Dan was a gentleman of course and wanted me to be comfortable at all costs. Said he'd do anything I wanted and was just honored to be with me. Said he'd never had head so good...he was being nice...

Ummmmmmmmm...no...Dan is right...

So want you when you're being sweet...

Me too

Throbbing inside...

Are you...

I'm wrecked...heated...aching...

Mmmmmmmm.....

Wet....

Ovulation???

Must be...crazy how my body wants a baby so bad... I'm old but no one told my ovaries...lol

You touching yourself??

Watching boring TV...

**Ohhhh...
Wish I were there**

Yeah?

Yup...would be...

And...

With???

Now that we've been together...idk how to push the desire down...

You are very desired...

You are as well...
My body has become unruly...

How much???

I want you...

Mmmm...I want you...

How much should I beg...

Beg???
For?

Gonna head to bed...

Beg???

I can't...makes me feel...

Beg for?
When??

To be...
Wanted...ravished...important...needed...

How am I making you beg?

Night

Ok...nite

***

<u>Peg's Journal Entry 11/1/21:</u>

I had difficulties sleeping last night. Not sure why. Now I'm groggy, horny, and needing to drop an egg lol. I'm not really supposed to ovulate until Thursday but damn am I feeling it! I feel a yearning for Gunnar, sexually, and often. I didn't expect this...whole thing, whatever it is, especially returning to Las Ramas. I can see where I really needed it...him. This has been incredible while going through a divorce. Not so sure what he's going through though, or if I'm helping...

I've been struggling with deep subconscious "abandonment trauma" triggers...mostly from childhood flashbacks. It's more of the "rejection" crap and not being wanted by Mom...and Dereck's abuse which is eerily so close to hers. Hate that I put up with both for so damn long. Proud of myself for getting away...finally! I hope this dissipates completely someday. I often wonder if Gunnar comes from the same type of foundation of abandonment. I sense something deep within him when our bodies are touching, especially when his heart and chest is pressed against mine.

I do still wonder how our paths crossed and why. I don't regret it at all...I just know my soul crosses with other's journeys...AND for the most interesting reasons. Usually a lesson for me...but, I've been known to be a lesson for others as well.

*On one hand, I feel our connection is very much about healing. I know I needed this while going through so much rejection. Gunnar doesn't reject me in our moments of pleasure. Dereck was a constant push-pull...like a false demon energy. Gunnar is more immersive, intense, and complete somehow. I don't know if he's here to heal me, me heal him, or what this is but, I know I very much enjoy the pleasure. I am surrendering to the process and energy of our attraction...it's been incredible...and I really like his type of **incredible**.*

November 2, 2021 8:32 AM

Good morning

Hey

How are you

Well...you?

What did you mean last night...about begging?

Dereck loved me needy...triggers me to be vulnerable...I'm trying to reconcile some things in my mind...
sorry...

I don't want...or need to have you beg...
I'm sorry I get busy...many irons in many fires...

I'm sorry as well, I know you're busy...

What you doing

Laying in bed...looking at the ceiling lol

What ya thinking...

Ugh...

Ovulation???

Yes

Horny??

Is there a better word than horny?

Is there?? You are great with words

Not lately...

Rub...your pussy...

Not feelin' it...

Ohhhhh...
Sorry for assuming

No worries...

If I were there would you feel it?

Can't be in the same room with you...remember?

Right...
1/2 hour???

Today?

Yes...
On way to range...I can make a couple hour stop

You...are lovely...

How's throbbing now?

Pretty intense...
You?

Very...sensitive tip...

Yummy...

Woke up thinking bout what we talked about last night...

Which part?

All of it...

Kinda hot...honest...very hot...

It's rare a man can get me going with words...talent SGT...true talent...

I'm a linguistic Irish kid...

Ohhhh

Is it ok...
Our conversation turned me on...not turn me away

Love it...

9am...can't come fast enough...

The clock is moving...slow
Just rolled out of bed so I didn't have time to get "dolled up" for you...
But the right parts are all swollen and fevered...

I would just...un-doll you...

Please...

Peg...I'm so wanting you...

Quivering inside...

Mmmmm...answer the door naked...

Ummmm

...at door...

(Later)

So...
Gooooood...

Mmmmmmmmmm......

Such a lovely Tuesday morning...

Mmmm...how are you

Sore...pleasantly so...how's your...manhood?

Great!

(Later in Evening)

Hi

Do I have threesome written on my forehead?

Huh?

We were talking of it recently and then it came up during massage at a couple's house. I must have some weird energy or something. And holy hell its dark in Mesilla Hills!

Yup...very dark...
You get home ok??

Yes, thank you! Just now...

***

Peg's Journal Entry 11/2/21:

Gunnar decided to come by this morning before heading to the gun range. When he entered the house, I pushed him up against the wall and attacked him hungrily! I wanted him so badly, my body was heated and throbbing, I was so worked up that he was making me a priority before heading to work. He kissed me deeply and walked me backwards down the hall and into my room. Once in the room he closed and locked the door with me in his arms and mentioned how hard I get him just kissing him. My hand was already on his cock, he's always so ready!

I find him to be very, VERY sexy. I don't think my body has ever reacted so intensely to another man. I can't really recall ever being this attracted to anyone in my past. I've only been with five others, which I hear is very low for my age, but Gunnar makes me forget about all the others. I don't know what it means, I only know he feels so right to me.

He had me on the bed quickly and I clawed at his clothing which he somehow removes so quickly! He grabbed at my pajama bottoms removing them swiftly and burying his face in my yoni! He's so damn good and makes everything feel fun! He's the type that puts so much into pleasure... and is into everything I am.

I eventually ended up with him in my mouth, his cock is beautiful, and I love hearing him whimper for me as I slowly torture him. My body yearned and ached for him and before he exploded in my mouth he moved me onto my back and entered me deep causing me to cry out! I enjoy all our positions but truth be told, his missionary play is fast becoming my favorite as the weight of his heavenly body presses me down and his cock gets so deep!

Not sure when, but I ended up on top of him with him whispering "baby girl" so sweetly over... and over. During our movements, he did reaffirm how honored he was that I would share so honestly about my threesomes with Dan and Dereck. He confessed he was imagining himself watching me be pleasured and how much he enjoys seeing me happy.

This made me release from him and start to orally please him again. I purposely slowed down even more to prolong our time. This made him quiver and pulse within my mouth. He chanted how much he likes how I give him head...whispering my name over...and over. He pulled me up and asked me to kiss him. I sooooo enjoy kissing him, but I do notice he tends to break our kisses when he realizes he gets too deeply into it. I do wonder if he feels kissing is too intimate, and dejects that which he actually wants? I must remember that even as the most passionate man I've ever experienced, he's still very much a Scorpio...and as Scorpios are...well they will sting themselves to deprive themselves in certain ways.

Somehow he ended up facedown between my thighs again, then turned me over and was penetrating me from behind, making me go almost mad before turning me over again and thrusting deep in missionary again. How he holds out so long I'll never know because he insists I cum over...and over...and over.

In between kissing and thrusting deeply all the way to my cervix, he asked how I would feel about anal. I was shocked, knowing that I love it but he's the one that's an anal virgin. I asked for clarification if that was truly something he's sure he wants. He immediately apologized and I realized my question must have sounded like a "no" which it wasn't. I realized then that he's been scolded in the past for suggesting his desires. That makes me sad. I explained how I would enjoy us exploring anal. He kissed me and continued to rail me sending what felt like electric through my entire body!

We continued in pleasure, he turning me over and eating me from behind which was exquisite. He's not shy at all, and it liberates me so that I don't have to be either. From behind he feels even more "sized" for me and yet he's gentle with his movements so I'm never hurt. It feels incredible to trust in a way I was not able to all the years in my marriage. He's mentioned that he's very "vanilla" but I don't feel he is at all. He moves very confidently and with masculine skill I soooo enjoy.

Somehow he ended up on his back to rest and I, of course, did not mind at all, as I climbed on top and sunk down over his amazing cock. I love to hear him exhale with want when I do so, placing his hands on my breasts, grabbing and caressing, then gripping my hips while I slowly ride him. He relaxed and whispered to me, looking at me and telling me how beautiful I am on top of him. He says the things I've needed to hear for so, so long. Things like how sexual I am. How in control I am of my wants and needs. He makes me feel I am free and allowed to be me. He got me hotter and even more aroused, so I picked up the pace. His grip on my hips tightened and I could see he was climbing and getting close. I went faster and faster and got a bit wild. He went silent and climaxed so hard I could feel him explode inside me! His face is beautifully peaceful when he cums, and I had to softly tell him to breathe!

He did finally exhale, and a smile emerged upon his face. I enjoy every ounce of this man, and I especially enjoy seeing him crash over into his orgasm...then rest in peaceful breathing. He has to control so much in life, it's nice to see him surrender for a moment and feel the reward of doing so with me.

He dressed and talked with me. I like how expressive he is after sex and very much enjoy our banter. He was being funny at one point and mentioned how he could "talk the panties off a mannequin." I responded with "ouch". He looked at me, I looked at him, we smiled realizing how manipulative that could be. We left it alone and went on. I'm really hoping manipulation is not something that we have to suspect or even talk about within our little sexcapade. I've had enough manipulation for a lifetime...and I'm almost certain he needs no more of it in his world.

<h1 style="text-align:center">Chapter 15
BULLET</h1>

Gunner woke with her on his mind, especially the damn threesomes she did with her asshole ex and the other martial artist guy who seemed to be just as enamored with her as he is. He can't get the visuals out of his mind, seeing her being pleasured in the slow way she likes. He would love to experience what Peg explained goes on. She's so fucking hot when alone, he can only imagine what it would be like with another...but then again, he would have to share her.

Peg placed her firearm in her ankle holster, grabbed her keys, and headed towards the door. Taking the seven steps to the truck she scanned the neighborhood looking for signs of Dereck. She couldn't get the feeling out of her head that he's been following her. The private investigator was shit and knowing what she knows about Dereck, he'll "do it himself" rather than keep paying someone. She turned the key in the ignition and used the rearview mirror to get a better view of all the houses and cars parked on San Driango Court.

She drove a different way out and put sunglasses on so she could view the streets without looking as if she's looking. Dereck was never smart and she knows he's probably using his own vehicle if he is following her.

She accelerated on the main road and thought about the conversations yesterday with Cyran and Rob Gatz at their home. She enjoyed coaching them. They seemed so into each other even after sixteen years together and with the tips she gave them she knows they'll be busy for the next couple months. Peg smiled, thinking of their sexual pleasures...then *he* came to mind....*damn*. She turned onto the highway and heard the familiar ding of her phone.

D ereck watched her pull out onto the street, ducking down in his truck parked beneath a tree in the apartment complex across the way. She looked better than she ever did with him and he wanted her under him, even if he had to take her by force. He had no idea who she was with, if she even was with anyone, and he pushed it from his mind because he knew how sultry she could be. He didn't want to even think how another man could enjoy the pleasures she gave. In his mind she was still his wife...and he planned to keep it that way despite the divorce papers he filed last month.

November 3, 2021

Good morning...

Hi...

What ya doin...so guy-gal couple asked for 3some??

Driving. Well...just kinda breezed into the subject. Hubby left us for a while. Poured me wine...

Was way busy last night...couldn't really discuss...wine? Wow...

I felt you were. How are you holding up with it all?
After massage, he came back into room, we all talked for 2 hrs but they wanted more intimacy coaching...
soooo I gave my time for free...

It's good...what I'm used to...

My body hurts a bit today. She has a block in her solar plexus area...feels like childhood molestation. I
always hurt if I take on too much client energy.
You ARE used to it...like a machine...

So...3some...they just come right out and ask??

Nooooo...it's was brought up in the middle of an explanation...and then a pause...waiting on my opinion...
lol...

214

How was the energy?

Thats why I was asking "is this written on my forehead?"
How could a subject come up so many times? In the same week lol...

They swingers or just you made them wanna be more?

I'm not clear on the swinger part. I'd need more time to assess. Asked me back for massage and mentioned the rest of the fam needs me as well.

What makes you think 3some...thats awesome...

How they question...they also mentioned how pissed they were that I left for a year...it was nice to be missed... oh, and they said my ex called both of them...separately...

Called them...about???

Months back...she said he was trying to sell them his guns. She turned and asked her hubby if he did actually buy any. He admitted he never trusted Dereck and felt he devalued the guns by modifying them so much. They were happy to hear that I'd left him. Said I'm "glowing" lol...

Soooooooo...honestly...did you consider the 3some???

Nooooooo....I'm not into women and...

Sounds like...ohhhh...

I do not want any drama here...my 3some days were back in my 30's lol..

Well...I think it's awesome for you...that you were feeling desired...

How about you? You seem to be very open to trying new experiences...thank you...

I would be...never done much...just a vanilla kind of guy...

Nooooo...you are not vanilla deep down...did you enjoy reverse cowgirl at all or nah?

Yup...sure...sure do...

Nice...so period sex vs. ovulating sex...which is better?

Both...I'm greedy...

Lol...my body is...like, uh excuse me...

You were on a mission yesterday...

Mission? Oh no, did it seem I was "taking"?

A soon as I walked in...no words...knew what you wanted...needed...was very sexy...

Ohhhh yes...was hungry for you...wanted to devour...I feel you hold back in ways though...

I do? How?

You seem to have so much going on mentally...the best is when you allow...your nature to come through...
You said...come

Lol...
There's this animalistic "non-vanilla" side...it's fabulous...sexy when you start to allow it...

I would do anything to see you pleased...I wouldn't hold it to weaponize against you...would relive the points of pleasure over and over...in whatever ways that make you better...

When you free yourself in me, it makes me better...it's an energy I can't quite put into words...

Very hot indeed...
So much...that your pussy is dripping now yes...

It is...
I love riding you...never been this aroused...every damn day...it's like I'm walking around always ready...I
feel like others can tell too...

You make me cum sooooooooo much as you ride me...

You are Grade-A...I don't think you're aware of how easily your sexuality flows...

216

Flows?

> *Well...it borders on hyper-sexual...but in the best way...*

I'm sorry for wanting anal...

> *Anal? Oh...*
> *Why? Well, I'm sorry for hesitating...I don't want to be a conquest.*

Conquest?

> *You're a goals guy...open-minded...wanting to try things...which is nice...*

I wanna learn...

Were you only "seen" as a child when you made the adults around you proud? Achiever stuff...like me?

Absolutely...

Ever feel like babies feel and sense things "in vitro" or marinate in the energy of what going on around them?

Yes...and environment...

Yes...well, my mother and father were done having kids...then my mother's oldest and youngest sisters got preggers...

Hmmmm....

Suddenly, she wanted another baby...8 years after brother and sister...my father was shocked thinking they were done having kids...obliged. Energy workers always tell me they feel in me that I was "really not wanted"...created more to appease my mother's need for narcissistic attention and supply...

...is it wrong...
That I wish I were laying beside you having this chat...

> *I would love that...*
> *I enjoy learning from you...and how your mind works...*

The instant you touch me...
My dick grows...

I like how your dick responds to me...makes me feel...wanted...

Well...wanted for sure...the view of your lower back...your ass...in the sunlight...
mmmmmmmm.....

Oh...my arch? I love the way you make me want to arch...

Yes...the contour of your hips...beautiful tight ass...dripping pussy...glaze on your thighs from
cum...ohhhhhhhh my....

Sooooo...hot...

You fucked me hard...you pushed back to take me completely inside...

I did...I like your rhythm...how you thrust and move...I like to grip you so tight...

Could you feel my cum dripping all day?

Yes...a sexy reminder all day...

Oh...and the Ayahuasca? Explain?

It regulated my CPTSD and helped me not love "him" anymore. It's a plant medicine from Peru that our bodies relate to and heal from. It's saving veterans' lives. Forces the body to purge trauma. Ancient healing that is slightly illegal (DMT). Shrunk my tumors too. Very healing. Very sexual experience for me. 4-hour healing trip equaled 10 years of therapy. It's the earth medicine that helps save people from suicidal ideation. Very controversial but I know it saved me. It's a thing.

What is it?

It's a root and a leaf, boiled and prepared together and ingested from a shot glass. Feels like thick prune juice going down. Called the "death medicine" because it kills the old you. I thought I was dying but instead...well, this is the new me...lol...

You...touch yourself...today??

> *Lol...touch myself? Are you?*

Good energy today...
Figured you would...me...I will for sure...

> *Mmmm...nice energy today. So you're open to new experiences? Like a 3some? Two girls? Two guys? Anal?*

Anything that you would be pleased by...

> *I don't have a very good track record with 3somes unfortunately. I was with an idiot lol...*

Yes...I wouldn't be ego driven...I'd like to see...watch...learn...participate if time is right...
experience it in my own way...share desires...pleasures...

> *There's that methodical conquest mind.....I'd enjoy seeing you on your right side passion brain as much as you are on your left side logical brain...*

Conquest mind?

> *Achiever, pleaser...I'm the same...wow, the conversations we could have over whiskey...*

Very...
Whiskey...mmmm...it is bad...greatest turn on is honest discussion...
Need to make sure you are pleased, pleasured, fulfilled...

> *Never bad to...communicate. Big...big turn-on for me...*

Your last talk of your 3somes was hot...I enjoyed how you found ways to describe intensity...
pleasure...even with the conflict....

> *I appreciate you listening. It's not easy to share but getting it out helps me reconcile it in my brain...*

Well...it worked...made me cum 3 times...

> *Guess I should share more...lol*
> *Well, I've got to go run on the treadmill and lift. I'm on a "conquest" to get tight...goal-driven and all lol...*

Josephine checked her phone one last time before placing it down. She watched Peg walk in and greet the hostess. She looked fabulous for just coming from the gym. Josephine thought about how Dereck must be fuming at the changes Peg has made since dumping him. She hadn't said it out loud but if anyone deserved to go through the karma of losing so much it was Dereck Law. She smiled thinking how very satisfying it was to have a front row seat to see his downfall.

"Have you been waiting long?" Peg bent to hug her then slide into the booth across.

Josephine smiled, she like her energy. "No not at all, you're right on time anyway."

"Oh good. How have you been?"

"Very well. I've been thinking about all you shared last time. I'd like to help."

"You helped me more than you know...all those years back. I know it took me forever to break the trauma bond but just as you said, I did so."

Josephine nodded, happy to have helped then, wanting to help more now. She realized how grateful she was to have Aileen in her life.

"My pleasure. I'd like to hear more about your Ayahuasca ceremony actually, I think it would very much help some of my clients...oh, and what about now? How are things with Dereck, he doesn't seem to be doing so well from my perspective."

"Ayahuasca is VERY effective for CPTSD and PTSD. Did you know it's actually being praised for bringing down the suicide rate amongst veterans?" Peg looked towards the waitress and ordered.

"Really?" Josephine had not heard that. "I have a handful of veteran clients I'd like to see get relief...mental relief."

Peg nodded, "That's exactly where it heals...in the neuro-plasticity of the brain...the re-wiring of how the brain processes emotion is fire! I have hardly any anxiety anymore and no depression! I feel like I can actually think now." She smiled compassionately and Josephine could see there was a deep self-love within her.

"I am so pleased to hear this. I'm going to research it and possibly set something up for my husband and I. I'd like to experience it before proposing to others."

"I recommend that. Not an easy journey but very necessary in my opinion. How is Mark? You both seem to be loving life."

Josephine smiled realizing they appear happy and active on social media. "We travel often, life has been good to us."

"I love that. You give me hope."

"Meaning?"

"That there is a happily-ever after."

Josephine giggled, "It's not all been roses."

"I know, but still, the thought of actually working through things, having each other's backs, teamwork...and love. I am so hopeful."

"It'll happen. How are you doing with that...eh the heart department stuff. You haven't given up on men because of him right?"

Peg smiled, "I have not. He wasn't a man in my eyes so."

"Totally understandable. So is there anyone, or do you feel it's too soon?"

Peg looked down spreading her fingers along a napkin. Her eyes, dancing, looked up at Josephine, "There's someone...a new someone, well no...a new someone I'd met many years ago."

"No way!?"

"He's...well, he's fucking fire."

"*R e a l l y?*"

Peg nodded slow. The waitress served her beer and she sipped it slow then continued, "Totally unexpected but so lovely. I know people say to never rebound..."

"It happens Peg."

"I'm so grateful it does. He's making all this crap I'm dealing with so much easier. I mean the distraction is very nice."

Josephine's eyebrows raised, "Oh wow. Compatible?"

"In more ways than expected."

"Oh?"

"You ever just get it? Like how someone thinks? Ever been turned on by how someone communicates and processes?"

"Oh hell really? Yes, that's actually very important. Tell me, does he have trauma like you?"

Peg smiled, "He does...well, he functions very well in chaos, moves on quickly. Very, VERY intelligent."

"You are attracted to intelligence huh?"

"I truly am. Sapiosexual. And I enjoy our banter...the sexual chemistry is the most intense I've every experienced. I'm almost scared?"

Josephine understood what it was she'd been witnessing in Peg, "It's okay to be scared Peg, you've been through a lifetime of someone showing you what love was *not*."

"True. I'm trying to push fear away. I know now, everything I want is on the other side of fear."

November 4, 2021 9:43AM

Hi
Hello
Hola
Flirty voice...

Hi...flirty voice...

Blinks eyes...gentle hand touching...

Mmmm...able to catch up on any sleep?

I tried...on phone most this morning...you doing ok

Yep, in bed...ovulation stuff...contractions lol...you doing ok?

Way tired...almost exhausted

Same...new moon...zapping everyone's energy...tough stuff...

Yeah...long hours suck...

November 5, 2021

Goooooooood morning

Heyyyyy

Feeling better??

Tryin...How ya handling the temp drop...bet your knee is stiff?

Yep...hobbling around...but it's ok...

Oh good...keep it movin...

What you doing today??

Gatz hooked me up downtown to open my practice in a new spa. Negotiating lease 3pm...you?

Sweeeeeet...gotta run range all day...

Ohhhh another long one...

Very long...days...

Yeah
So sorry about that...life...

Right...very exciting bout downtown mall...

Thnx...wishing you the best birthday weekend...make memories!!
Finishing up getting fondled by hydro-massage at gym...then headed home for shower...

Mmmmm...shower...

Mmmm...

Wish I had time...to join you...

224

Be nice...time is the problem, unfortunately...

Yeah...my curse...

Lol...yeah...

You upset?

Nah...readjusting expectation...it's what I do...new life Peg...lol

With me? Life? New prospects?

New prospects?
Life? This is a new life for me...no longer married to someone who discards and secretly hates me...free...
wahoo!

Prospects with new massage job...not guys...

Ah lol...I'll be opening my practice downtown (LLC). Bodywork, relationship coaching, reiki, and be able to
publish next book. All I need in one spot...sorry was driving...

Sounds like you...have a great big smile...

Taking life as it comes...trying to be balanced lol. How are you handling the "tough shifts"?

With smiles...

Headed to my storage unit today to get massage practice stuff, moving in new space wahooo! Now...how does
one notify 1300 former clients that one is back in town?

Social media...social mafia...

(Hours Later)

How was meeting??

Moving? Hopefully be up and running by Monday. Excited...How are YOU Doing?

225

Kinda lazy...

Really??

Long day...just getting home...day off my ass!

Burning that candle at both ends...

For years...

Gotta take care of you so your babies have you...

(3 Days Later)

Hello...
Beginning of another mammoth week...4 straight 16 hour days...well...let's go!

Hi...how are you?

Doing very well...how's new massage shop??

Up and running! Thank you for asking...

(Later)

Hi...long day...but full heart...full smile...

Good to hear!
Hoping your birthday is memorable tomorrow and all your wishes come true...

Beat up...tired...thanks

(2 Days Later)

Good morning

It is!

How was your yesterday...any plans to make today better

Always looking to make a day better lol...yesterday was narley...coached another couple. How was your "Life Day" for you? Happy Birthday!!

Loooooooooong...long hard day at range...but was good...what you doing

Lying in bed...

Ohhhh really...

You? Why up so early?

**Wish I was there...would have slipped hand in front of your pjs
Getting ready for another long day...**

Mmmm...

Would massage your clit...but make you focus on conversation...

You do speak in distracting whispers...

Yup...take you to the brink...

Oh?

Yup...then back off intensity...rub nipples...stomach...then back to clit again...and again...make you so wet...clit throbbing...sensitive...

Mmmm...such lovely hump day banter Sgt. O'Clery...

Wish I could fill you now...

That would be...

Would want lips connected...as we came for each other....

Kissing...yummmmm....

Feeling my passion...my desire...throbbing release...all inside you

Mmmm...passionate today...

Keep thrusting...keep dripping...draining every ounce of cum in you...for you...when done slowwwwwwwwly pull out...sit at edge of bed...you open legs...show me our cum...rubbing slowly...

Mmmm...touching yourself this morning?

I am...
Will you?

Hmmmm...not sure just yet...

I think you will...great big orgasm...for you

Maybe...over did it at the gym...feeling vulnerable...weak...

Soooo...if I were there???

Yes?

Would I be able to kiss my way down???

Don't think...I'd resist...do you?

Certainly hope not...would love to lick you...rub g-spot...as you begin cumming...look up...beg you to cum...
Saying...Peg...cum for me baby...

I know I would...hearing you whisper my name...

Leaving my fingers inside...feeling your spasms...

Would you? I spasm huh?

Yes you do...as you cum...

Ohhhh...yes...

Slide your hand down the front of your PJs yet??

Unfortunately, no...roomie is hangin around the house. I like to focus...no distraction...

I know...wish I was there...would lay you on your side...quiet...gentle...slide in you from behind...gentle strokes...whole length buried in you...

I did enjoy that our first night...ruined me when you sunk in...and then your mouth on my neck! Gets me wet...makes me pulse inside still...
How's my favorite sensitive tip?

Wet with precum...would love to run it along your pussy lips...tease you...till you push up... release..as I slide in you...

I do enjoy your...slide in...

Mmmm...babe...you are soooooo tight...get sooo hot...sooo wet...

It is...
Sooooo hot...

Yes...was amazing last time...sunlight was perfect...looking down...from behind...

You remember? I did hear you mention the sunlight from the window twice...

Was an amazing view...buried as deep as I could...slow pace...could see your glaze all over my shaft...

Oh myyyyyy....

Could see that...when you were on top...facing away too...

Ahhhh yes, reverse cowgirl...

Had me on the verge of cumming the entire time

Oh? Well...we could have allowed that...I do like you pleased and satiated...5-star cummer...

You do...you do...do you like my multiple orgasms?

*I do yes...like me. I haven't been with many men but...you are not like others...
Most...are once a day or worse...once a month!*

Month??

*You know how you mentioned you had a "rough" marriage? Mine was r o u g h...especially when it came to
intimacy...used to have to finish myself off in the bathroom after sex...if even had it once to twice a month...
he would put me down for us not having sex but as you can tell...it wasn't me! Dereck was not the kind of guy
one could be attracted to for long...*

Thats...wow...
Even threesome guy????
You seemed...very pleased by him...I enjoyed the stories...

*That was in 2005...and no, he seemed to not be able to get enough of me. I had to end that and I did go
through "mourning" that connection...Dereck ruins good things...ruined many pleasures in life.
I want all pleasure now...you know, being 48 and all lol. I'm actively designing a blissful life daily...
How's your head feeling this morning?*

Yes...you do know how to pleasure...
Feeling great...wished...not to be crude...I was in your mouth

*Don't think you're crude, I enjoy you...gliding in my mouth...you have a very nice lingam sir...don't let
anyone ever tell you otherwise.*

A what?

Lingam...it's the name of the male member in Tantra...yoni is the female part.

Mmmm...welll...then thank you...

Welp, heading to the shower...happy hump day!

You toooo

Going to the shake shop next door to brighten my day again.

What shop

Senta Nutrition a few doors down from my office.

Sweeeeet...go network

Always!
Same guy that robbed the salon next door lives in the apts behind. Emmanuel Garcia. They say he hasn't
been picked up just yet because the PD is down 60 officers...like you said.

65

Oh myyyyyy....

Yup

(Later)

How you be

I be fabulous! You?
Headed to the gym...to work things tighter...hoping you're safe...

I'm good...p.s. tight already

Glad you're safe...ooooh you speak such nice words to me...

Mmmmm....

November 11, 2021

How are you

Well...you? Dream?

Too tired to dream...but just today left to go...

Left?

Training class...today last day...been loooooooooong week...

Yes. How are you feeling about the class?

Great...good peeps...

That's the best! I miss teaching...fills the heart...

**How's your budding awesome business...
I wanna fill something alright...**

*Lol...still budding, any suggestions?
Mmmmm....wish you would...*

Just let it...social media...promo...

Yeah...

If my math is right...close to period??

*In 3 days lol...
Wow, didn't realize you were paying such close attention...*

**Can we???
Again?
Now no nerves...just well...hormone filled amazing...**

*Odd for a guy to like hormones...most run from hormonal women lol. I think we're past nerves...
comfortable...and compatible...*

**Nope...not this guy...
Gotta head to class...so wish I was looking down at you...**

Your lips...that mouth...you let me cum...in your mouth...you climb up...slide my hard cock in you...you kiss me deep...we taste each other...

Gunnar saw Rod pull into his usual parking spot and get out. He moved slower then in years previous, he was getting up there in age and the death of his wife seemed dim his spark.

When he made it to their table Gunnar had his coffee already served. He kicked the table as he slumped down and spilled some of their drinks. Gunnar laughed and used napkins to clean up.

"You okay sir?"

Rod exhaled long, slightly eye-rolling, "Yeah, just having some lower body issues."

"Lower?"

"Yeah. Do me a favor, don't stop using your dick and balls."

"What the fuck..."

Rod smirked, "Serious. Keep things flowing...so things...you now...continue to flow."

Gunnar searched his face, he could see fear behind the his friend's eyes. "What's going on?"

"Doc says prostate shit. I don't know, that's his expertise, I'll let him worry about it. My expertise is more upper body." He fist bumped his heart then lifted his hand to his head.

"Anything I-"

Rod cut him off lifting his coffee to his mouth and taking a sip, "Nah, should be fine. Just waiting on some test results. Let's get my mine off my dick. Speaking of, how are things going with...you know..."

Gunnar didn't want to talk about how amazing sex with Peg was while Rod was trying to learn how to live life without sex with his wife. "Uh-"

"Now listen, we've been friends for too far long for you to be hesitant about such matters. Besides, I'm old, not dead. Let me live vicariously through your youth yes?"

"I'm no spring chicken...but damn."

"She certainly makes you feel so huh?"

"Like I'm in high school...but with a slower stride...and I can hold out now."

Rod smiled, happy to see him happy.

"Nice isn't it? Listen, don't slow it. I want you to feel as much as you can for as long as you can. I made the mistake of burying feelings to be tough, not showing vulnerability with my wife, not touching, communicating enough. The worst thing we ever did was stop having sex. Now my shit is...*well* gone to shit."

"I'm sorry."

"Don't be. It's a "use it or lose it situation" so take my advice, don't stop. Don't make her feel unwanted, don't neglect her. Some women don't want it, they're all wrapped up in their heads, but some...those that need it, want it, often, and all the time...those are the women that will keep you alive."

"I'd have to agree. I don't think I can stop now."

"Good. Stay alive. Let her breathe life into you..into every facet of your being Gunnar, because the worst part of this life is trying to live it half-dead. Stay...alive."

November 13, 2021

Hi

Wondering...if you're wearing as little as I?

Mmmm...what ya wearing...

Zero...well, maybe fingers...I love the way your fingers feel along my...

Yes????

Feel...along my...swollen lips...

Mmmm...someone is super horny...

Headed to the office to distract myself with healing others...thinking of my lips kissing along your...

***

<u>Peg's Journal Entry 11/13/21:</u>

Life has been interesting as of late. I haven't had much time to jot things down...err rather, I haven't made it a priority lol.

I have a client that I've been coaching on the whole twin flame stage of her life journey. The twin flame union is quite fascinating. First of all, it's said a twin flame is different from a soulmate because the twin flame is like the "other half" of one's soul, whereas the soulmate can be anyone or a few someones who come to teach lessons or be lessons. A twin flame is referred to as our "mirror image" and interestingly enough has stages. Many don't know or believe in this energetic soul stuff but the information I've studied is at least worth a listen. Kind of fascinating...

As my client and I enjoyed coffee at a local shop, I taught her about how twin flame union forces our awakening and definitely an awareness and working on our "soul wounds". It can happen at any age and can come in stages like the following:

-Yearning for "the one"

-Meeting/glimpsing them

-Falling for them

-Dream relationship

235

-Turmoil stage
-Runner/chaser stage
-Surrender stage
-Union/reunion!!

My client feels that she is at the runner/chaser phase so we talked a lot about that and easing into the patience needed as the surrender stage is coming. I felt great helping her and sent her home with the following information:

<u>Twin Flame</u> - *A twin flame is an intense and unforgettable soul connection with another soul, thought to be a person's **other half**, sometimes called a **"mirror soul"**.*

Twin flames are based on the idea that sometimes one soul gets split into two bodies. It's not common, in fact thought to be very rare.

Characteristics of a twin flame relationship is that it will be both *challenging and healing*. The mirroring nature of a twin flame shows the deepest insecurities, fears, and shadows. ***BUT...***they also help one overcome those shadows, fears, and insecurities - the other twin flame will be equally affected.

When twin flames come together, they are **physically drawn to each other**. Not only is the *sexual connection* strong, but the partners also feel ecstasy and harmonious when physically near each other. This must be prepared for. Life changes will occur, sentences are completed by the other, incredible synchronicities present, and a bond that is unbreakable will ensue. Many end up together but if not, they're never able to ***forget each other***

Common Traits of Twin Flame:
1. Both don't always embrace the reunion
2. One or both unusually experience a triggered spiritual kundalini awakening (often intense unexplainable sexual opening)
3. The masculine energy will not understand the same as the feminine energy
4. Obsessive or telepathic thinking of the other is VERY common
5. There is often separation and reunification of twin flames but they aren't guaranteed to come back together after lessons
6. The purpose of twin flames is for soul growth and healing
7. There are some who experience a "happily ever after"
8. You CANNOT cut a cord on a twin flame connection no matter how hard you try

My client and I had a lot of fun exploring and talking about her possible twin flame encounter. I'm excited to see how her life unfolds in the next year as she's been pining after him for the last three.

As of Gunnar, he's been super busy lately. Not gonna lie, I want him in my bed again...and again...and...againnnnnn. I don't want to make his life more stressful so I don' bug him too much but I would soooo tackle him if I could. He's scrumptious.

My new office is working out so far. Coming out of retirement to start all over again has been challenging for me but I'm not complaining. I am super grateful I still have my skills and licensing. I can' take back all my clients I gave away to my students, that wouldn't be fair to mess with their money like that. Building new clientele will be slow but the ones I've already accepted have returned so that's a plus! Onwards and upwards...still lol.

***

November 14, 2021

Wow...wake up with wet pussy???

How did you know? Dream much?

Yes...

Oh, and the goatee...so hot, great job...

You like

I likey...a lot...

How are you

I'm well, thank you. How are you handling life?

Busy...but good...can I visit you tomorrow???

Still want to? Looks like I'll be alone...

Yes...and yessss...

Mmmmm....

Are you okay with it...

I am...very...

Goooooood....cuz I want you....

Yummm...how?

Want your naked skin touching mine...kisses...caressing...arousing...deep

You mind being...gentle? Want your nakedness on me...that body yummmm...

I would truly enjoy that...

Looking forward to your enjoyment...and thus mine...

Chapter 16
PLEASED

November 15, 2021

Thought you might find this humorous. Client is on the table face down and says, "Peg, I took a gummy from this girl I was seeing and holy shit, I was able to have sex for 3 hours! What was that all about?" I laughed so hard because she must have only given him 2mg, if she gave him 5mg he would have gone for 4 to 8 hours!!!

Lol..

I educated him on the effects of THC and gummies affecting the liver...love my work!

Liver?

Yeah, edibles fuck with the liver so a 4 hr high can last days sometimes...I don't mess with edibles much... unless tucked away safe at the hot springs for a weekend.

Ohhhh...
Has the throbbing...begun?

All...night. You?

Yup...
Did you self-pleasure?

No...

Well...I will take care of you...

Mmmm...promise?

Just say when...

Good...lay back...I will gently kiss...lick...do all you need...
Will you smoke before I get there...be relaxed...

Mmmm...maybe...those hands, that mouth....your engorged...cock...

Rubbing tip along those lips...slowly...deliberate...deep inside...
When is roomie gone?

8:55 AM

Sooooo long....

It is...
You sure you want to be a part of my crime scene (day 2 of period) then again...there is healing in your
magic...

Yes...I do...won't bother me one bit...kinda a turn on...that you allow me...
Are you ok with it...

It's a turn on that you want it! And me...I'm ok with many, MANY things...

***

Gunnar woke rock hard and thinking only of Peg. He's wanted her for days and days. His excitement was now like a deep fluttering within his loins and he could not wait to bury himself deep into her wet, wanting body. He loved what it did to him. He thought how it bordered on obsession.

Since she liked his goatee, he decided to leave it and shave it off later before getting into uniform. He showered quickly, then pulled on his workout pants, a shirt, and sneakers. Grabbing his keys, off-duty weapon, wallet, and sunglasses he bounded out the door and to his truck. Oddly, the sounds of a vehicle accelerated quickly away from his street and didn't resemble the sounds of any of his neighbors' cars. It was more of a peeling-wheels-against-the-sand-on-the-road type sound. He put his keys in the ignition and pulled off hoping to catch up to whoever was driving like an asshole in his neighborhood.

Dereck drove off the road and hid down into a steep ditch near a pecan farm. He looked in his rearview mirror and hoped the mist of dirt would dissipate quickly! Not sure if Gunnar O'Clery would go right instead of left out of his street, he waited almost holding his breath.

Dean was wrong about Gunnar. It wasn't his truck he saw. His truck was clearly dark red and not beige as Dean swore. He waited a few more minutes, making a mental note to never listen to Dean Pelgus again. He used to be loyal, but lately, all he'd done was give him incorrect information and piss him off! He knew Dean always wanted Peg, and try as he did, he couldn't get her to commit to a threesome with them both, so it never happened. However, Dean had been wrong about her and her whereabouts and who she was with more often than not lately. He'd gotten sloppy and Dereck wasn't trusting his intel anymore. There was no way Peg would have ever given herself to O'Clery anyway. He refused to believe anything Dean told him and decided it was all to throw him off her trail and protect her. Damn her ways, everyone protected Peg eventually. It was like she was some magnet or something. He hated that about her.

He put his truck in drive and slowly crept out onto the road heading in the opposite direction O'Clery's went. He was most likely, one of Peg's massage clients since she worked with a lot of law enforcement and firemen. It unnerved him how many people loved her practice. He remembered when he used to enjoy her skills... and her others talents for that matter. But now that he could no longer have her, he'd find out who had been dicking her so well and make sure they no longer have her either...

Peg finished rubbing her Egyptian oils into her skin. Her freshly shaven legs were like silk to the touch, and she ran her fingers along them thinking of all he would do to her in the next few hours. She adored when he had time for their pleasures. He was an extremely busy man but when he focused on her, she felt like she was the only woman in the world. Her phone chimed again and a smile reached the corners of her mouth. He was on his way. Her heart thumped against her chest, her crotch moistened, she walked toward her bed and lay down as he'd requested.

(texting continued)

I'm heading your way-

Good. Roomie left for work...

Oh....
Bout 5 out....door unlocked...you naked on the bed...please...

Uh...ok...however sir likes it...I get to watch you undress...my favorite new hobby...

Mmmmm....

***

Gunnar opened her door and slid in moaning at the sight of her spread on her stomach, legs open, naked on her bed. Peg placed her phone on the side table, her eyes finding him across the room. She loved his facial hair grown after a week of teaching at the gun range. She smiled and flipped her hair away from her eyes. She watched him looking at her, whispering how lucky he was and throwing his items and hat on her desk. She enjoyed watching him kick off his sneakers, pull off his pants and shirt, then walk to her, fully hard and sexy as fuck!

He reached her and caressed her tush with his hands. Peg's eyes blinked slow at the warmth and passion in his touch. She loved how he touched her. Rolling over onto her back she felt his mouth come down onto hers, his tongue warm and sweet from whatever gum he'd been chewing. She brought her hands up and around his face holding him to her and joining her tongue with his. She exhaled a long moan realizing how much she'd missed his scent. Her skin, cold from the ceiling fan, shivered beneath his heated touch. He felt familiar again.

Peg moved a hand from his cheek down to his dick, loving the feel of his rigidity through his underwear. It made her feel amazing that she did that to him. She released him from his clothing and eased him lovingly into her mouth, slow and easy. Hearing him gasp and try to maintain composure made her smile. Peg loved the sounds of his pleasure. She moved her body so that her head was hanging off the side of the bed, him leaning over her, his cock in her throat.

"Oh Peg...oh my god...you are..." Gunnar's words hitched in his throat, his mind unable to formulate more words. He missed her slow, torturous, velvety mouth sucking gently along his shaft, moving to swirl her tongue around his head capturing his precum along her lips. Sucking him into submission.

Peg moved her hand around his base and balls, her mouth further down his shaft. Suddenly he bent down and his mouth was on her as hers was around his! He felt so good, his slow sucking and kissing making her quiver all the way inside. She felt he was so good at how he followed her pace and touch. He may not realize it but Gunnar was incredibly energetic and could easily be the most intense, tantric lover she'd ever felt.

Gunnar gently moved them from their sixty-nine position and had her sufficiently aroused before switching around. He could hardly wait to feel her and pressed between her legs, parting them sensually to find her slick entry. Peg sucked on his nipple but ended up gasping with her head back as he thrust into her body, burrowing and stretching her tight, wanting pussy. He exhaled, the pleasure of penetrating her making him almost lose his mind.

Peg grabbed at his body, caressing and pulling him in deeper, meeting his every thrust, loving how his pelvic motion eased and relieved her cramps while his mouth taunted and tantalized her senses.

After some time, he wanted her on top, Peg complied delightfully then turned around for reverse cowgirl, where he spread her tush open so he could see the glistening of her slickness all along his shaft.

He laid her down on her side and spooned her close to enter her from behind, feeling their pleasures while they rested and continued to build their climax. Gunnar leaned in, kissing and suckling at her neck, sending electric pulses up and down her body that made her quiver and almost cry out. He slid his hands around cupping her breasts and whispering in her ear "I want you again, riding me..."

Peg, loving how much ecstasy he was giving, happily agreed and swiftly maneuvered him on his back as she slowly and meticulously sank down on top of his glazed, rigid cock, beginning her hip rocking that pleased them both...

(Hours Later)

Thank you for locking my door on the way out my king...
Hope your day is amazing!

Mmmmmmmm....amazing morning...

So...true...

***

<u>Peg's Journal Entry 11/15/21:</u>

So he made time for "us" this morning and walked into my room a little after nine, breezing across the floor to my naked body on the bed and touching and running his hands along my tush and arch of my back. He looked hot, his chest broad, waist trim...newly grown goatee which felt good trailing along my skin as he kissed my shoulders and back! He removed his clothing to the floor as I caressed my tummy, my breasts, my neck, wanting him to touch me more. I like his touch. He's very gentle but intense. He was already hard for me which is an incredible turn-on, his mouth whispering then moaning for me. I was soaked before he even made it across the room. He pressed into me and kissed me deep, my hand wrapping around his hard, warm cock. His body felt so good on mine, especially since the overhead fan had chilled me while laying naked. His connection overtook me, and I slipped my tongue in his mouth tasting his sweetness. I slid my hand in his underwear to feel him more, and he stood up to take them off. I turned myself and pulled him into my mouth, I love the sounds he makes when I do so.

He started chanting my name and turned me vertically somehow so that his mouth was between my legs sending bursts of pleasure throughout my body. I moved so I could take more of him in my mouth, my head hanging a bit off the bed. We were in a glorious sixty-nine position and I'd realized it was our first time! It was so gentle and comfortable, we were devouring each other staying in our slow rhythm and feeling the exquisite pleasures. He stayed focused on my clit as I had a tampon in still. It feels so validating that this man love, LOVES that I have my period and doesn't want to stay away but rather do more!

We moved to standing so I could get tissues and remove my uh, feminine product into the trash can. He was impressed and eager taking me in his arms to lay me back down, pressing in between my legs to penetrate me with his supreme penis. Initial entry is such a fucking turn-on, especially since we both have to ease into it. As much as my body soaks for him and is ready, I'm too small for his size, and this makes it all the more blissful! He goes quiet when burying inside me...I gasp no matter how much I try to stifle it. My body wants him and grips and squeezes him. I push towards him and feel him all the way to my cervix where he can't go any further! Aching pleasure shoots through my womb and up through my body vibrating my energy center chakras. I can't explain it but I've never enjoyed a man's body or energy as much as Gunnar's. There's just something about him, about how he moves in the world...moves within my body.

He guided us into an amazing rhythm and then started whispering as he does. He asked, "Do you like being made love too?" I could hardly speak so I nodded. He commented, "Wonder how this would feel for an entire weekend, at the hot springs." I smiled, still unable to think straight as my eyes wanted to roll back from how damn good he felt thrusting and thrusting deeper. Every so many humps, he'd arch harder on the end to make me gasp loudly. I laughed because he's fun and sneaky, playing in my body but never hurting me.

My uterus had no choice but to relent and ease, letting go of tension and cramps. He so open-minded about the yucky stuff it makes it enjoyable to be beautifully woman. He suddenly admitted, "I can't believe how tight your pussy is, I can't get enough." I felt flattered. I was already on top and he said, "I have never had anyone ride me on top like you...like this." I looked down smiling and put a little more rocking and slow squeezing into my movements. I remembered how he told me he was "a simple guy" and "very vanilla" which actually surprises me because I've experienced him EXTREMELY ADVENTUROUS and so very good at sex. He looked up at me and asked again, "Are you sure you were okay...with me cumming inside you last time?" He's very good at clarifying in normal dialogue and it's interesting that he does so in the throws of sex too. This leads me to believe he's been manipulated and lied to by someone. Someone who made him feel he was okay in one way and then took that security away later or guilted him for cumming inside them. I feel bad that at a man's weakest, most pleasurable moment they might be made to feel shame. Women who do that piss me off. I looked at him and asked, "Baby, who's scolded you?" He just stared up at me and knew he wasn't going to explain it while deep inside me. I smiled and said, "Of course I'm okay with it. I love your cum inside me." He smiled and gripped my hips more encouraging me to grind deeper and slower. It pains me that he may have felt rejected or learned toxic shame in the past surrounding sex. I want him to know I don't reject him at all. I'm honored to share such pleasure with him. It's the kind of sex I've dreamt about for years. I don't know how to even begin explaining that to him so I just show him.

We moved into reverse cowgirl upon his request, and after a while, he took me from behind and also on our sides when it was time to rest for awhile. I enjoy that nothing is rushed and each position feels as if it builds into the next. He has amazing control to hold out and I can tell he really enjoys spending time in each position, getting as much pleasure as we can from each other!

I did feel him get close when I was in reverse cowgirl and encircled my hips for him to add a little "extra". He spread my tush open and mentioned our slickness and how beautiful I am. It made me want to please him more and he let go, cumming and cumming as I moved on him. I timed it with how his hands grasped at me and then slightly started to relax. He was quiet, and as he crashed over and then relaxed, I eased. I slid off and turned around, he motioned for me to ride him, wanting to see me. I eased down on him and rocked keeping him hard!

He looked up at me watching me slowly coax his dick into building and staying hard. He asked, "Was it odd to have me cum in your mouth last time after so many years of never swallowing him?" He was referring to Dereck and how I would spit his cum in a tissue or go to the bathroom and spit it in the running sink water. I was surprised he remembered but I told him the truth and mentioned how something in me knew Dereck didn't deserve it...but with him, "I want to" which is the truth. I really enjoy pleasing him, I want him to know I feel he is worthy...good enough, even if he has a hard time believing in himself.

After we were spent he laid with me for some time. I enjoyed resting with him at my side. His body feels good next to me, on me, in me, there's some sort of neat comfort I have with him. He looked at me and said, "I've got to get going or I'm going to fall asleep." I smiled knowing full well what thats like. He kissed me while climbing out of my bed and said, "I've got to head to the gym to workout and think of you." It made me chuckle because I do the same damn thing when I'm at the gym. Our VERY memorable moments help my workouts go so much smoother.

While dressing he asked me about my daughter and how she was doing with the pregnancy. I told him well with expected nausea. He turned and said me becoming "A grandmother at 48 is hot!" That felt good and I was happy he remembered details about what's important in my life.

He asked me about work and wants me to try to be safer since the town is going to shit. He said he had driven downtown to try to find my office but didn't see my truck. I smiled saying, "My office is super private when Karen is gone. No windows, no cameras." He looked at me seeming to pick up on my hint and said, "Wow, would you do me in your office?" His smile was cute, like a little Irish boy waiting for any answer I would give. I nodded saying, "I just might Lt., I do have a couch that folds out into a bed." He smiled and sat to put on his sneakers while talking to me for another fifteen minutes or so before leaving. I made my way to the shower thinking how I could go back to bed and sleep all day from all his splendid loving. Was...soooooooo good.

November 16, 2021

Hi

Mornin...

Sore?

Heheheheee...my legs...how are...things?

Great...doing well...

I like hearing that...shift go smooth?

It was...very smooth...

Gooooood. Slept well?

Not really...up at 0630...home bout 0200...

Ugh, no bueno...
Kinda excited this morning thinking of you losing your...anal virginity...with meeee...

Yeah...what you thinking??

When you're close...we'll move on our sides...so things are relaxed. I may smoke before...after yesterday, I'm ready to do so much more. What were you thinking?

Don't wanna hurt you...if you can't enjoy it...I don't want...

I do feel that and thank you...but it's mind over matter lol. I'm deriving so much pleasure from you...I think it will be amazing...

What will we need???

Just you and me lol...I'll take care of the rest. You deserve pleasure...as do I...

When???

You're the one with the curse of time...

Time...
Are you pleasing yourself...

Headed out...saving me for you...
Are you touching your sensitive tip?

No...just laying around...holding cum for you...

Mmmmm...yes, please build it up...
I know you're busy...I'm with my last client but then heading home...
just wanted you to know someone on the other side of town really likes your cock...
And the brilliant mind attached to it!!!
Nite-

Made me giggle...out loud...
Nite

November 17, 2021

Helloooooooooo

Hiiiiiiii

How are you

Missing you...how are ya holding up?

I'm great...what ya missing

Hmmmm...where shall I start?

The tip...I mean the beginning...

Bahawahaaaaa...somebody's got jokes!
I do like your sensitive tip...my mouth especially...

Your tongue...does amazing...

You have a very nice...uh manhood...for my tongue to enjoy!
We should spend more time exploring that...

We shall...
Loved that you swallowed...every drop...

Was nice...

Will be again...

I always hope...are we resting today???

Had to call in sick...my mom sick...but trying...you relaxing?

Oh no, is she still having antibiotic issues?
Takin the day for me yes. Too much giving out so I've got to replenish.
Took my baby girl to Indulgence Cafe...can't believe my baby is having a baby...

Wow...great day!

Really hope your Mom gets ahead of this...

She will...

Hump day!

Yes...it is...

Trying to nap...but all I can feel is your lips on me...damn...

(Later)

Bored at the laundromat so I'm gonna bore you...

Mmmmmm...laundromat...memories...

Mmmmm...great, GREAT memories.
So...my kid (has dark humor like her mom) was explaining to me how her man got up from the couch to get her a drink and she said since his ass was eye level she did what came natural and reached out to poke him, but his jeans were a bit "snug," so when she did her fake nail snapped and he yelped out "Oh my Perineum!"

Wow

So she says, "That's what you called it when you were an EMT right ma?" (Thought of our first message) and I nodded and said yes while laughing. So I told her, "That's kinda crazy, baby, ya know they say if your man rally loves you he'll helicopter for ya..." and without missing a beat she says, "Oh hell mom, I can hear him all the way down the hallway coming towards me...and if I don't lose my breath laughing he'll take his towel and stuff it in his crack while walking away!"
She had me rollin'. Damn, it's scary when they turn out like us huh?
Then...she told me she was moving!

Moving...where?

Alamogordo...my grandson will be a bit far to see daily...

You can find a way...you are resources abound...

You're sweet...Ok, gonna go back to daydreaming about necking in your truck in the parking lot lol...

Was awesome...

Really was. That first kiss...

Very sexy...your hands wandered...immediately...

How could they not? Your dick felt so good in my palm...warm and sooooo hard!

Very hard...tip...dripping...

*That's right...so slickkkkk...with precum...
I remember trying to work out afterwards,
but it only made me want you more...then you showed up in my room that night...
I was done! Years of oppressed sexual energy just came to the surface...
Ugh, now I'm...pulsing lol...*

You do cum often...and hard...

*I've always been like this, very responsive...just wasted it on someone who didn't deserve me...but very uh...
sexual...*

Yes...you are. Tongue swirls around clit and few times...you start to moan...

You do make me "vocal"...I've never been this...vocal...

Was great to look up at your face the other day...you straddling me...deep...pulsing cum in you...

I do like to look at you...that peaceful look...as you cum...I likey...

Visit tomorrow??

You've got time? I'd like a visit...

I will...

Yes...

Yes...for sure...

Mmmm...exciting...

Leave the door unlocked...be in room...naked...wanna walk in...see you fingering yourself...

Oh?

Yes...I will take over...after I watch you for a bit...as you rub your pussy...see my cock grow for you...

It grows so nicely for me...usually already hard...

True...remember as you walked me to your room...first time...in hall...first kiss...solid saluting cock...

Is that why you hesitate sometimes...to kiss me...

Not at all...you are a great kisser...

You are...don't want you to hold back...makes me throb inside...
When your mouth comes down on mine...your arms slide around me...
that chest...pressing up against me...

Feeling my...

Mmmmm...then when you hold my hands to the bed...forcing my surrender to your pelvic bliss...filling me...
stretching me...holyyyyyy fuck...
All these years I've been teaching everyone else...all the tantra classes, students, couples...
I was always helping others. I'm actually scared...

Scared??

Perhaps I'm a bit...hyper-sexual?

No...
Just know how you want to be pleased...

Hmmmm, I hear that...
I'm gonna stop bugging you now...headed to the gym to tighten these kegels and cellulite! Namaste hottie!!

Mmmm...I'm gonna kiss those kegels tomorrow...

Promise???

Yes...

Chapter 17
PROMISE

Gunnar rubbed his hands over his face and around his head. He was tired but really wanted her. He shook his head a bit, trying to wake up, hoping the energy drink would kick in soon. He needed his best game since today was the day with Peg. She'd promised anal, and Peg has yet to break a promise. After texting with her he picked up his keys and gun then headed out the door using his other hand to fix his cap. His dick was already responding to the excitement of seeing her. There was just something about Peg Law and her seductiveness. *He couldn't get enough.*

Dereck slammed the backdoor to the house and stomped across the bedroom to the hall. He was furious, his round, chubby body jiggling with each over-pronounced step through the living room to his office. He slammed down into his office chair regretting the movement as soon as the pain shot up through his low back, reminding him of the injuries that often made him have to sit down to pee. He ignored it and dialed aggressively, unable to believe his mother was taken from the facility he'd put her in. His cousins were the bane of his existence, and he was appalled that they'd actually gotten the judge to believe them. He called and the phone rang four times then went to voicemail. He slammed it down on the desk and leaned back against leather chair. All he wanted was to wake up and go watch Peg to see where she goes and what she's up to. Dealing with his family kidnapping his mother was going to take up time. Too much time!

P eg finished shaving the last part of her leg and rinsed off still texting with him. She ran her hands up and down her body in the hot water thinking of his sexy body. It'd taken only a few times together for her to realize how passionate and gentle he was. He made her feel alive and desired more and more. It'd been years since she's had anal sex and admittedly, she missed it. The thought of being Gunnar's first was exciting to her. He was a natural at everything else they'd explored and brought her so much pleasure, she was certain giving herself to him in this way would be just as worth it.

November 18, 2021

Helloooooo

Heyyyy

What ya doin

Jumping in the shower...you?

Running daughter to school...get in shower...drive to your place...lick you till you cum...

Sounds like a fantastic morning!

Bout 9...door unlocked...you naked...facing door legs open...fingers inside yourself...shot of JD...please...

My...myyyyyy

I woke up hard...wondering...how you taste...after a full night of sex...

Hmmm...I wonder too..haven't had that yet, have we...

Still sensitive...little sore...absolutely willing...taste our mixed cum...mmmmm

I'm ready...

Readyyyyyyy...

255

How?

Throbbing inside...yearning for your touch...your kiss...that chest...and all the pleasure below it. I think I'm developing my first addiction at...48 yrs old. Your penetration...slick sloooow thrusts...your whispers...I think I've been a very deprived woman thus far in life lol...

Mmmm...can I buy you a drink...first shot...please...

Lol, yes...

Describe...the sensation...for a lady...as a cock first touches your pussy...

Hmmm...warm tip, slick...feels good with slight pressure then hard, thick glide into opening...stretching fully...sliding all the way in deep...you make my body convulse...gasps as the energy pushes up into my throat. The retraction is another beautiful sensation...makes my pussy want to squeeze you so you don't leave...another thrust and it's even more intense...more energy...dopamine high. Difficult to describe the ecstasy. Makes me wetter and wetter...makes me want to open too then squeeze so you won't retract...a mind-fuck for sure...

Mmmm....soon...

Laying on my bed...

As my cock pushes in...tip glides in...you slightly push up and open legs more...inviting... submission...pushing up...to get exactly what you need...

Mmmm...I think you like my submission...simple needs...simple guy yes?

Mmmm...think of that first kiss...my hand sliding down panties...finding your wet...wet...wet pussy...2 fingers pushing in...circles on clit...
Yes...I'm simple...really am...

You had a very good sense of direction that first time...
I like your simple-nesssss...

Your hand stroking my hard cock...kissing me deep...

Felt...natural...

I am simply...going to fuck you till you scream today...
Are you naked?

I'm not a screamer...am I? Lol
Yes to naked...

On top...yes...doggie for sure...when cock buried...yup...
Anticipation is building...

Anticipation is what gets me...

We have...great sex...

We do! I've never been more satisfied Gunnar...only thing I'd change
is to take you when I want...you'd tire of me always touching and sucking...

You would be...very...very sore...I'm very spontaneous...

I would be then yes...but I enjoy your "sore"...it's a lovey reminder all day...just like your cum...makes me feel
like a goddess inside!

You make me cum so much...
I wanna walk in...middle of you pleasing yourself...glistening...
How's the drink?

Smoooooth. So weird having honey whiskey for breakfast...

Mmmmm...that's sexy...truly...

Fucks me up for the day tho...

Between that and the orgasms...cummm....

I like this part of adulting tho...lol

You are good at it...

Mmmm...you are as well...second shot going down...
as requested...

Mmmmm....

Mmmm...soaked...need...your...cock...

Need??

Soooo neeeeeed.....

Roomie gone?

Gone...

Mmmmm....gonna cum all over...and in you...

Promise...my fingers are too small...need youuuuuu...so much bigger...

You like?

Soooooo much yes! My favorite...stretches meeee...
I'm cold naked....need your warmth!

(13 minutes later)

Here...

***

Gunnar and Peg explored their favorite oral, missionary, and other preferred positions but ended in the slow, sultry completion of mind-blowing anal to which both found a unified climax and a new favorite orgasm. Their trust increasing...their bond undeniable. A new level...of trust...*for each*.

(Hours Later)

Uhhh...just so we're clear...that...was amazing...and you are very, VERY good at anal...ohhhh wow...

Mmmmm...rookie...but thank you...
How you feeling?

Really good! You? I mean I do feel a nap coming on lol...

Tired...
Mom still sick...had to call in...

Aw...well rest while keeping her company no? Naps are life!

(Later)

Partner at the spa just said I have a red mark on the back of my neck...
I was like, "Oh I do? Thank you." Lol...

Mmmm...taste test...

Was nice...

Was...
Backside ok?

Very...you were so gentle...I want more...
You feelin' okay? Seemed tense in your hips and low back...shoulders...burdens?
Maybe mom burden stuff?

Yeah...but gotta deal...day to day...

Good deal...
My mother called me last night drunker then drunk to tell me my ex tried to fuck her and she's so proud of
me for finally dumping him. Ironically, she said she hopes I start dating and get with a cop because Dereck

would hate that. I told her I no longer care about him or what he would hate. Life is too awesome to be looking in the rearview. Doesn't matter, she won't remember anything today. It took her 6 mos to remember she has a daughter named Peg lol... Hope you're resting that fine bod...

Yup...trying...
Today...was amazing.........

Was...yummyyyyy...

Mmmm...hottyyyyyy....

Yes...yes you are...so hot!
I've never been much into heels...always preferred swat boots and Uggs...
but after today...I may get a few more pairs in fun colors for us...

That was...bonerlicious...

Omg...I may have just pee'd a lil'...you crack me up!

Hahahahaha...first you squirt...now this...

You've got me cumming undone!

(Later)

Random thought...

Yes...

Would you ever do...

Yup...
Yup...
Yuuppp....

Lol...
A threesome with me and another female?

If you wanted...for pleasure...yup...not for ego...

Nice...

You?

Me? I'm not into women...they hit on me but the only one
I'd ever even been slightly attracted to was...

Was????

(Sent clip of Selma Hayek in Dusk til Dawn dancing bar scene with snake)
Selma...but it was the dancing...acting...the song..the snake...

Best bar scene ever...

Right? You...are so much fun...and coooool

I am...I am...like baby Yoda...

I'd be afraid to get drunk with you...

Why...

I tend to...laugh too much
when partaking in adult beverages...and your humor...
would get me going waaaaayyyyyy to much...

I'm a funny guy...
Like rodeo clown meets porn star...wink...wink...

I have a feeling...lol

See...jokey jokes...

So nice...taking time off looks good on you...

Why...thank you...

(Later)

(Sends pic of hickey on right trap) Ohhhh myyyyy…my first O'Clery hickey…
been 20 years since I had one…yummmmmmmmmm…

Ummmmm…was…occupied…not totally my fault…

Occupied as well…when did this actually happen…

5th amendment…

Mmmmm…

It's…a thing…

Had no idea it was so pronounced…just got out of the bath and saw it in the mirror…

Nibbles…

I enjoy your…nibbles…

Was…a great day…I came lots…smiled more…

Love hearing that…I came lots too…even lost count…smiles upon smiles…

We were like high school kids…

Yes…so fucking hot though…

So…
You wanna go to prom with me…

Lol, prom! Love it…
I've written a lot of erotica in my books but this…holy hellllll…

Real screen play….
There would be whiskey…and anal…

I did finally relax...and you felt...gooooood...

You took...a kinda big dick...

I did...the pressure...the gliding...you're a natural...

And...you squirted...all over...was sooooooo hot....

You made me...from my giney...
OMGGGGG I took your anal virginity!

Uhhh...you fucked me into oblivion...

Felt soooo good...so much more I want to do to you...in so many places...

Did you enjoy the anal...or just do it for me...

I actually enjoy anal...so much more now...been years...I don't lie to you...

No pain??? Never wanna hurt you...

At first there was some pressure...a lil pinching...well, because you are a very well endowed Irishman lol...but there is an A-spot in the anus...very pleasurable once relaxed...
Dereck had ruined anal for me years back so I never allowed him again...but since I've been able to trust you and relax...and you slid in slow with lube...not gonna lie, turned me on in new ways...

Mmmm...soooo...you likes....

I likes... I think we should try it in your new favorite position...reverse cowgirl!

Ohhhhh my...
S
O
L
D

And...definitely when I'm droppin' an egg and my body wants...your baby...

Gonna smack that egg around...
Like a ping pong ball in China...booooooom....

Ya killin' me...lol

Mmmm......

The kissing was magical too...when you held me down with your hands and covered my mouth with yours...

And then...slid right inside you...

You did! So good, I like how you devoured me...
there seemed a hunger deep within you...sexy AF...

Tasted...mmmmmmmmmmm...

I still have your scent here on my pillow...our scent on the bed...

P.S. loved...loved...loved...loved...loved...the heels....

I'm so happy you did...the way they felt on as you bent me over the bed felt soooo...
empowering...the way you held my hips, commented...touched the arch of my back...let me slide back on you
and squeeeeeeze you tight....

Yes...the black heels...one leg up...the other leg down...
me deeeeeeeeeep in you...mmmmmm.....

You are amazing...from behind...

Why???

The way...you thrust...your timing with mine...how you fill me...and let me sink back on you...perfection...
But...then again, I don't think there's any position that doesn't feel incredible for us...

Ohhhhhh...
My cock is blushing...

Blushing? Bahawahahaaaa....

I just want to squeeeeeze...and suckle...and swirl my tongue...and....

...and...and...and...you look at me and say...breatheeeeeeee....

Yezzzzzz.....

I go cross-eyed...then straight to puppy...

Awwww...love that. I go a bit cross-eyed as well...especially with anal...

You...really like it?

I don't lie to you. I really, REALLY enjoyed you. You are a very desirable and respectful lover...I want it...
again...
Did it meet your expectations? How does it feel for a guy?

Sure did...you gave yourself to me completely...
was...great...
If you didn't hurt...more anal!!

I believe in pleasure and to be able to feel it and give it freely feels so natural and good right now in my life.
Feels empowering as woman to...me? Thank you for being patient with me with the decision. You've helped
me work through some oppressed CPTSD issues.
I feel like I can enjoy pleasure...and it's not wrong...

You...know pleasure...for sure...

Best...stuff...ever...invented...

Adrenaline is pretty awesome too...

Like that huh? What's the best adrenaline boost? Fire? Hunting a douchebag? Gun fight?

The initial call out...
Knowing I can contribute to a solution...

That's a fuckin' rush for sure...love it!

New thing in shootings...EMS runs BP...shows elevated stress levels...last couple they said...
serious...you just got into shooting...yet your BP is great...

No shit? You actually balance in heightened situations???

Thrive...
It's the little things that stress me...

That's some talent my man...lil' things? Oh, like brushing hair into a ponytail yes? Lol...

Yup...damn ponytails...pigtails...curls...sheeeeeeesh.....

You're amazing...lol...

Gonna try to sleep...on range all day...believe this...I shoot better than...
I do hair...

I think you do better with the lil' stuff more than you give yourself credit for...
G'night sexy...great talk...even better day...peace out...

Mmmmm....hugs and kisses on all your pink parts...

***

<u>**Peg's Journal Entry 11/18/21:**</u>

Today...was incredible! He requested the door unlocked and me naked on the bed while he walked in. I improvised and added heels with a scarf since I was cold. OMG was I rewarded!!!! He loves heels apparently....mmmmm...soooo nice.

He walked to me whispering how much he admired my gifts. He kissed me...hard and pressed into me. He climbed on top of me and took me, making me feel wanted and desired, burying himself in me so deep I gasped. I love his body and how he uses it so gently to climb into my womb... and mind. He took my hands in his and held me down to the bed while covering my mouth with his. He felt amazing and I felt safe as he devoured me.

He went on to taste me until I came, stood me up and bent me over the bed driving me into ecstasy as he complimented me on the arch of my back. He made sure to thank me over and over for adding the heels as it was turning him on in every position. He went on to slowly eat my ass, lick, suck, fuck, flipped me over and did oral again...and again. He climbed into me again and hiked one leg up to make sure he got even deeper, thrusting, whispering about how my threesomes turned him on as I explained them. I climbed on him and rode him till he almost lost control then I turned around in reverse cowgirl and rode him until he spilled into me. He then got up to get a drink and I noticed he was still hard. I laid him down and pleased him orally for quite a while, which admittedly was so nice, not just because he is an amazing length and girth, but more so for how he whispers my name and how he's never been blown so well. He's very expressive and kind, he makes me feel happy to give and give...and please him fully.

After an hour of doing all our newly favorite things I mentioned to him gently that I'd like to go forward and try anal with him. I said that I had promised and was honored to be his first experience. He asked if I was sure and I could tell he wanted it so bad as his face was like a curious little boy. I taught him about lube and he was so respectful and gentle with it. It was a warming lube so it felt amazing for both of us. I told him since he was "sized" it may take me a bit to relax and allow my body to accept him. He listened and only pressed into me when I was ready and instructed him to. We were on our sides and I explained it was better since things weren't as "pulled apart" but rather more relaxed, ready to accept. To my surprise my body wanted him so much and he was in easily by three or four slooooooow presses. He felt fucking phenomenal after my body eased around him. He used small, slow movements and I was able to press back deeper and deeper. His arms around me, his body pleasuring mine, his breath in my hair...his voice murmuring my name..."Oh, Peg...oh my...." It was super slow and felt magical. I enjoyed him more than anyone before and honestly moved to a new level of trust with him. I could tell his mind was blown and when he came with me...he came loooong and then quieted with satiation. It felt wonderful to find yet another level of pleasure with him. I don't think there is anything I can't enjoy with this man!!

November 19, 2021, 10:55 AM

Hi...

Heyyyyyy...how's the range today?

How are you...

Missing that "O" face lol...

November 20, 2021, 12:16 PM

Hellooooooooooo

Heyyyyyy

How you be…

I be great! How you beeee?

Like Winnie the Pooh found honey…
Was at range…gonna take daughter to trampoline park with her little bestie…
Woke up…thinking bout you…anal…

Ahhhhh…still remember? Sooooo nice….

Very much…can't wait till your ovulation…wowewey….

Makes me happy you're such a fan…

Very…you working today???

Nah, lawyer crap. Next week could be…fear based for me…ugh…

Fear??

Lawyer put in an emergency motion stating military spousal abuse. Asking judge to transition me as the owner of the marital home as he broke the divorce decree locking me out on Oct 5th. Second motion is for him to pay all her fees as he broke the decree by moving all monies out of joint accounts. Third motion is for (not transitional as she told me) but for permanent alimony as he manipulated me into retirement, let me go take care of the FL home for his mother running up my LLC credit then left me with no home to return to, no money, no way of running my massage practice (which is lic in my home) and trying to sell the home for $378,000 when it's appraising for $420,000. She's pissed. You were right, she's savage. Anyway, next week when he gets the paperwork…he'll either leave town or come looking for me. I know him, he'll come lookin'. I hate this fear shit. Guess it's just part of my journey. Hoping he heads to CO soon. Apologies, that was super long.

Heading to my office. Got a lil' fridge and microwave to set up…
Heyyyy…no trampoline jumpin' on those knees and hips…gotta save some for me ok?

268

Will do...text in a bit...

Have fun! You're a cool dad...makes me miss my cool dad lol...
(Later)

Finally getting back...these kids have energy...

Hmmmm...someone else I know has energy as well!
Does Winnie-the-Pooh still wear a red half-shirt and no pants?

Yes...naked little devious bastard...

Mmmmm...little lol...

What ya doing....

Driving drunks around...

Be careful...plans for you this week...mmmmmmmmmmmmmm

Mmmm...can you elaborate?

Yes...
I plan on cumming...lots...and lots...all three ways...for sure...

Really??????

Yup...yup...yup...

3 ways? So ambitious...

Very...very...

I think I need to really get serious and get IN SHAPE...

Why...
I think ya beautiful...

***

<u>Peg's Journal Entry 11/21/21:</u>

My certainty and security were rocked today. I shouldn't have but I signed into the iPad that links to Dereck's texting and read texts he was sending to more people fabricating that I embezzled money! It's amazing the lengths a narcissist will go to, to distract others from his own behavior. He even put a number on it of $15,000. Where he gets this shit from is beyond me. He told his friends I took it directly from his mother's account. This is what I get for trying to help them both. I'm sorry I even ever believed in them as family. There is no love in that family and the two of them have the same delusional brain issues. I think back to 2018 when Bill died and how everything went to shit. I should never have felt sorry for her losing her husband and not being able to run her life. I'm pretty sure it was past trauma for me, remembering how my mother was when Dad drowned. Fuck it, no good deed goes unpunished...just like with Mom, helping always results in pain. I lost time, clients, my home, my business, money, and my credit helping her and her pedophile son. I went to Florida with his urging and need for help, racked up tons of debt while he's buying expensive items (ATV, hot tub, sauna, tile flooring, etc.) and now I'm the thief? Such fucking bullshit. I am so happy with my decision to divorce him. That motherfucker and his fucking douchebag family are the shittiest humans I've ever been around. Covert narcissists definitely breed more covert narcissists. They use your good intentions and character against you...because they have none and want you to suffer for yours! Ugh, I'm just so over this.

The worst feeling though is the feeling that he's been following me or worse, watching me. He's a creeper now from what I've been told by neighbors and read in his texts. I can see that he talks to women at the local golf course restaurant or from around town and tries to entice them with rides in his ATV or flatters them about their children. Same patterns. He's desperate and although I like that he's distracted at times, I can see once he's ghosted or dumped he tends to focus on what I'm doing. I know he'll never find someone better, especially in the bedroom. How I put up with his mini-member all these years is a mystery. What the fuck was I doing all this time trying to make a marriage like that work? I can't believe how peptide-addicted I was to the lies and keeping the waters calm. Fuck that. Dereck Law is by far the worst human I have ever known. I will forever be grateful I chose freedom...and actual passionate sex! I have never been happier with my decisions than recently...even though they fuck up my stomach. This is all temporary!

Now, if I can keep him away, especially away from my bedroom window. I don't want him heaving his fat-ass through the glass and spraying me with bullets. I know that sounds a bit rash but many don't know what a fucked up brain he has. I remember him telling me if his cousins ever won in court or even attempted to kidnap his mother from the assisted living Alzheimer's unit in New Jersey, he would get in his truck, drive to Arizona, and blow them all away with his sniper rifle. They wouldn't even know which direction the bullets came from. I just stared at him thinking he would say he was kidding but, the look in his eyes told me otherwise. He is a coward and hates to be exposed, but that doesn't mean he wouldn't take this all out on me since I'm now back in Las Ramas.

I deeply regret ever trying to love someone who had no capability for compassion or love. All I learned from this whole marriage was I should have never given out my love so freely. I am truly on a journey to love myself right, in order to love those who deserve me. Fuck him and thank bejeezus I never have to again.

Chapter 18
TO THE TABLE

Dereck tried continuing the strokes. His eyes lifted up focusing back to the television, even porn with a blonde that looked like Peg getting railed by two young guys couldn't help. He knew he was wasting his time and took his hand out of his shorts and threw the remote across the room. It landed on the bed. He stared. Their marital bed. He could not fathom never having her again. Her slow, velvety tongue exploring his mouth then down his body to his dick. No one ever blew him like Peg. No one ever took the time to explore pleasure the way she did. He stared over at her side, seeing her empty pillow.

Depression seeped in again. He knew it was going to be another day in the recliner...his father's recliner that she hated and said brought bad luck into their bedroom. He should have listened to her.

He rubbed his eyebrow trying to will away another headache. Jacking off didn't work, stalking her didn't work, lying about her character didn't work, hiding all the money didn't work, locking her out of the house didn't work. Nothing was working! He exhaled long wondering what else he could do to smoke her out. Peg had never *not* cared before. He had always known her to show up, be the one to work things out, forgive! He wondered if he could take much more of her silence. It was ruining him. Even thoughts of her with another guy was waking him up over and over. He knew too much of what she was like and that no woman could match her. He hated this, all of it. He looked at his phone wanting to text her but the courts said to stay away. How could he stay away? She was his wife!

Gunnar slammed the door to his truck and looked over at all the students lined up ready to begin another day of shooting instruction. He was dead tired. Truthfully, he wanted to slide into Peg's bedroom for the morning and slide himself into her gorgeous, tight pussy. He couldn't deny that there was some deep connection between them, but his love for his career came first. It always came first and he wondered how many more years he could do it.

He maneuvered in his 511's and walked, trying to will his cock to go down. As much as he wanted to think about all she does and makes him feel, he can't allow the distraction while sharing his expertise at the range. Peg would have to wait but he certainly would make it up to her.

P eg said goodbye to her roommate and started the shower water. She was excited for the day and hoped it would just be about helping clients and making money instead of being forced to feel emotions over all the drama with Dereck. She hated days where he was even a thought.

The hot water ran over her body and ignited her senses. Gunnar came to mind. His hands, his overly built chest and back that felt so nice against her body. Peg tried to wet her hair and run her fingers through it but her body quivered with want for him. She smiled reaching for the shampoo bottle. She squeezed a generous amount in the palm of her hand and lathered it in her hair and over her body. Feeling her skin heated and wet, her breasts and stomach, then thighs, reminded her of how he touches her so tenderly but with want. She liked it. A lot. Gunnar had a way of making her feel desired, even with the slightest of strokes.

Leaning back to rinse the suds from her hair and body, Peg smiled, thinking of how she'd actually prayed years prior for passion and sex, like it is with Gunnar. She giggled remembering how she had even put it on her vision board, which Dereck hated. He would interrogate her constantly about her dreams and wishes trying to make her feel guilty for her desires. Removing him from her life was the best decision she'd made...and allowing Gunnar to fill her mind and body was proving to be the most fulfilling decision she's ever allowed.

***

November 22, 2021 12:59 PM

Thinking of...
That mind...the humor...that
B
O

Mmmmm....

Hoping you're safe...and smiling...

What ya doin...

At my practice...thinking of things...you?

Getting ready...work...

Mondays...

(Later)

Sooooo....

How are you...

Missing you...how are you?
Soooo...the guy that gave my roomie the STI?
Just came out of her bedroom (shocked emoji)

Ummmmm...
Awkward

Sooooooo awkward...lol

Guess it was that good...

She did say it was the best she's ever had...

Well...there is that...

Yeah...there is that huh?
You holding up alright?

I'm ok...how's your stress week?

Can we start with a less complicated question? Lol, we both deflect well, don't we?

Well...
Ok...how's your gorgeous tight wet vagina...

Damn...that made me smile...
How's your thick, juicilicious cock?
I think I should leave, they just went back in the room lol...

Well...I can come over...have a version of dueling orgasms...

We would win! Not sure if they do anal...

They might...give her a shot of that whiskey...mmmmmm...

Was that what did me in? Mmmmm....

Was it really ok?????? Did not want to hurt you at all...made me cum so hard...

Was better than ok...you treated me like a queen...we eased into it...
it had been so many years I thought I might hurt but remembered it's a patience thing...

Was great...so amazing...you let me cum...in both...super sexxxxxxyyyyyy....

Pleasure is my first love language lol...

You speak it fluently...

You speak it with meeeee...
Any dreams lately? I like when you dream...

Yes...
Went into your room...you had a swing for sex...you said no words...just dropped robe...
climbed into swing...invited me to join in you...

Oh wow, sex swing dreams!!!

Saw it on an HBO special years ago...

Yezzzzz...Real Sex! Great show...nice dream. Was I sitting upright...or on my stomach?

Upright...legs open facing me...

Ever tried a tantra chair?
Open huh? Yummmmm....

No...not yet...
You tell roomy...how well...you have been???

No. Should I?

Girl talk...so brutal...honest...

I'm way too honest...especially with you...

Ohhhhhh...I likes that...

I've told you threesome stuff I've never told anyone...let you climb inside my body...
and truth?...kinda make sex sooooooo yummy....

Very...
I'm sorry he ruined your threesomes...
I would savor watching you pleased...and pleasing...a man or a woman...all eyes on you...

Oh myyyy...why? Dan and Dereck both mentioned watching me being "pleased" too...
is it my face? Maybe my...gasps? Dereck's insecurities ruined everything pleasurable in our life together...so
happy I got out-

Connection...exploring seeing your pleasure from the outside...
I wouldn't have the issues...of insecurities...

Do I ever make you feel...insecure O'Clery?

Dereck was...doubting himself...
No...you can't make me feel...I either have it or not...
If I don't bring to the table then...
I've never had a threesome before...wouldn't unless you were 100% comfortable...

I feel you bring it...especially to my table lol...and our "first time" sex...still blown away by that first night...

Great every...time...

Still processing how it all feels so...pleasurable...every position...every movement...

Very...very pleasurable...

Ugh...so wet...

Wanna slide...tongue inside you...you smoke your weed...

Mmmmm...that would actually be another first for me...never nookied on weed lol...

Did you get some???

Yes...
Horny...

Way horny now?

Worked out, hydro-massage, tanned...now...horny! Ugh...

Wow...how wet??

Dripping...from vulva lips wet...
Throw you up against wall type wet...lol

Just...well...soft kissing type...

I like your soft kissing...makes me want to reverse-cowgirl...and glaze you up...

Yes...

Thats amazing...the way you ride...that...that...that is sexxxxxxxy...

Your face...amazing when you're high on pleasure...I ride to please you...

And...you have made me cum numerous times from that...thank you...

Love it...

Are you rubbing...your clit??

Saving...for deep penetration...

Mmmmm...what happens with deep penetration???

Sends ecstasy and blissful shockwaves up and through my whole body...

You are soooo tight....suck me so well too...
What does naughty Peg do?

Hmmm naughty? Do I have a naughty Peg side???
I see everything as pleasure...more than naughty...

Do you??

I've used feathers...food...massage...ice...flogger...blindfold...cuffs...and...

Well...you were playing with my ass..thats hot...naughty

Ohhhh...pleasure...not naughty lol. We'll do more of that...
now that I know you're not...squeamish...

I'm not...
Anything to please you...

Oh...you please me...

Tell me...

Never pain...toys, oils, ties...clamps...
When you kiss me intensely...it gives me deep tingling way down deep in my secret...garden. When you press
your chest to mine I feel a warmth inside...when I feel your lips and tongue...

Mmmmmm...yes?

...on my nipples...my neck...my....yoni lips and clit...I get tantalizing bursts of pleasure searing through me
that makes me moan...almost speaking some weird language or in tongues lol...hard to describe...

I'm so happy you are pleased...
the squirting the other day was...way...way...hot...

The squirting always happens with intense build-up...

We build...well...

So...welllll....

So...you kinda like how I touch you...

Touch me? I yearn for your touch...as soon as you come through the door, I want your touch...hands all over
me...skin pressing against skin...

Me too...

Your body long on top of mine...your cock in my hand with my lips searching...until I find and reach your...
sensitive precum tip...

So amazing the way you swallow me...

I enjoy you...it seems...to make you happy...
I like when you're pleased...

Your pleasure...makes me happy...

Really? Guess we're...two givers...

It seems...

Still wet??

Very much...so...

Like...cock slides right in...no foreplay needed wet?

Bingo...

Roomie still occupied?

They're not coming up for air till morning I bet...

I bet...
You should smoke...then rub...

Mmmm...maybe...

Do you cum harder when you do on weed?
Shot of whiskey does wonders for you...

Not sure...never tried on weed...whiskey makes it smooth...

You fucked me into oblivion the other day after a shot...

Whatever do you mean??...lol

You were so...relaxed...no tension...thats when...you gushed...

I do gush when I'm chillaxed lol...

You did...very much...nice.......

...your girth...the length is...just perfect...the curve so natural...feels so fucking gooooooood inside...yep...
makes me a gusher lol...

Imagine...
If we weren't baby safe...big trouble...wouldn't stop us though...

280

Ohhhhh my...I'd be so knocked up right now...probably from the very first night lol...

Be like...wait...get a condom...wait...hurry...wait...just fuck me...wait...pull out...noooooo

Is it fun...being baby-safe for you...or kind of a bummer that I...

It's goooood...but....we wouldn't have been "safe"...nope...

Oh?

We would have taken off condom halfway through...guaranteed...

No way I would have wanted to try to feel you through a rubber...
hard to go back from bareback O'Clery...you feel tooooo good...

Sooooo...true...

With all our positions...we'd break'em...

Wish I was looking down upon you...now...

I'd really like that...

Rub my tip along your pussy lips...along clit...

Mmmm...love that...

Tease you...till you push up...beg me to insert...

You know I would...wanting you long, deep...hard...
wrap my legs around you...my tongue exploring your mouth...

Mmmm...yes...
Will you be alone tomorrow?

Not sure...roomie doesn't work tomorrow...

Was she there when I came by?

When?

Last week...

No...

She works mostly Monday through Thursday...this week is weird due to the holiday...

Ahhhhhh...I see...

Touch yourself...pretend its me...

Mmmm...cock throbbing...

O...m...g...I'd so straddle you...

I'd...be in all of you tonight...allll of you...

Allllll?

And every...

Every???

Yes...every...

Mmmm...I'd give you everyyyyy...

Soooo....hot...

You are indeed...

My cock...is growing more...

Mmmm...love that...sexy in your uniform. I remember...you pressing it up against me...so hot...love that you get so hard for me...

You...make me so damn hard...

282

Mmmm...you make me soooo...
Wet...

As wet as the laundromat?

More now...

Wow...how???
Why???

Well...it was pretty intense after not seeing you for years...when you wrapped your arms around me and our pheromones mixed...gush...instant wet...haven't been the same since...

Little sex machine...

Not sure...what it is about our chemistry...

Great...GREAT...chemistry...

Right???
Like how? Feels like liquid electricity...

Just is...don't know the math of gravity...know it when I see it...

Feels like your mind thinks...as sexually as mine...things just click...

Very much...
Like a lego...

Snap, snap baby...lol
How's it feel knowing the mere thought of you makes me wet for you?

So...amazing...
Truly
How does it feel...as I walk in...few seconds...kissing...my cock is rock hard for you...

Flattering actually...

Red Bull...with boner...

283

Lol…

How's work?

Trying to keep busy…not run into Dereck…rough week. You holding up ok?

I'm great…he calling again?

He might once he gets motions from my lawyer.
Happy you're feeling great…
Roomie just apologized, said her bed was noisy…segway into sexy-time TMI. Peeps just tell me things lol.
Apparently, nothing can be heard from my room!

Told you…

I was mid-bite into my salad at the table and…she just unloaded…

Bout???

She admitted she went downtown to find him! I was parked in the driveway when they both came pulling in. I was shocked to see it was her ex! They went running through the garage and into the house…it's been 9 months since they…broke up.

She know bout us??

Never hears a peep…

Well…

I mean she knows about us…when she mentioned her bed I said, "Mine is noisy too." She was like, "No it isn't, half the time I forget you're even in the room." Lol…

If that bed could talk…

Oh hell yes…I've never been a fan of twin beds, but I'm kinda taking a liking to mine now…

We make it work…

284

She mentioned he finally started to kiss her with his tongue...
and that she's sending her kid to the Dad's house more often lol...

Ahhh...
The big O can do that...

9 months is pretty torturous...they have the same HPV...
she laughed about that and felt not having time to shave her legs was fine since he was high...

Good night I guess...

Are you doing alright out there?

Kinda busy tonight...what ya doing...

Hibernating now under the covers...I'm cold...

That sounds great...

Feels...ok...

Feel better...if???

If??? Do you have warm fingers...

Yup...

Love that...and that warm, wet tongue. Dream at all today?

Yup...
I did...

Swing still?

Hot springs...

Mmmm...bet anal was involved...

You riding me...squirting...you thinking anal??

Thinking...all of it. Hey, you think lube works underwater?

Think so...kinda new so...

We can experiment and see...ever been blindfolded?

No...not yet...

I know you enjoy visuals...but there is something that happens when one of our senses are taken away, heightens the others...I think you'd find it...stimulating...

Oh really...

You'd have to trust me...

**I would...
I do...**

*My mouth...would feel even more intense for you...
I trust you as well...new for me...*

**Hard to do...
Your mouth...feeeeeeeeels great....
Roomie home tomorrow?**

You've...got time?

Trying...have a couple meetings...

Morning?

Yes...you free?

Mornings are always my free time...

She says she's going to work at 9.

(Later)

What ya doing...

Layin' in bed...roomie wanted to tell me more...and more...and more...
I have one of those faces where people want to share their deepest confessions...lol

Ahhhh...yup...
Wanna sneak in...

Come again?

That too...
Wanna sneak in your room

Tonight?

I do...

You can...

How are you still awake?

Life...need my upset tummy kissed...

Mmmmm...what's wrong with tummy?

Are you...on your way?

Wish...on a robbery call...grrrr...
Morning?

Nite...be safe...

Mad?

Chapter 19
EDGY

November 24, 2021 7:31 AM

Nah...
You dream?

I did...heels...

Ohhhhhh....

Very hot...very...

Mmmm...headed to shower...let me now if something...comes up?

Well...let's do this...0900...eat you till you scream...meeting with DA at 10...when done...come back...your turn again...

Sounds...interesting....

Yes...quickie to start...you ok with that...I know it's not your style...

Lol...roomie just left...

May I???

See you soon...

Mmmm...vrooooooooom

Drive careful!

I'll try...

Door open?

Yes

***

Gunnar opened her door immediately seeing her black panties and tank top that matched perfectly with her heels. A moan escaped him and he went to her placing his hands on her tush and softly murmuring.

"Ohhhhh my gosh, you look so....."

"Hiiiii. You like?" Peg whispered into the bed as he caressed her body with his strong, warm hands.

He nodded, "Mmmmm...oh I likes, here...."

Gunnar rolled her gently over and pressed down onto her body kissing her mouth, exploring it with his warm, eager tongue. He hugged her and melded their bodies together to press his engorged cock in between her legs. He couldn't wait and slid down her body to pull her panties off and dive into her vulva with his mouth. Peg folded, her head coming off the bed as he sent sheer bliss through her. She was so wet already, he couldn't wait to enter her. He stood up disrobing and gazing down at her. He crouched in and opened her legs with his hips. In one fell swoop, he buried himself deep into her, forcing her to cry out into the room in ecstasy.

"Oh, Peg...baby...you are so..." Gunnar groaned into her neck and ear beginning his deep, slow thrusts she loved so much.

"I am...all..........for.....you......." She breathlessly whispered.

Gunnar dressed telling her about his meeting with the DA. He noticed Peg was quietly listening and somewhat exhausted. He felt it was more than just their amazing sex. He sat on the bed and asked her what was going on. She sat up not wanting to darken their moment. She downplayed it but explained that Dereck was accusing her of stealing his mother's money. Peg searched Gunnar's face. She was fearful that being honest about her intentions to go to Florida and help with Dereck's mother's house and it all failing and going to shit, would annoy Gunnar. She knows he deals with enough drama, hearing hers could cause him to stay away. Instead, he reminded her of how far she'd come and that Dereck is scrambling for some sort of control over her. He told her she need not entertain it.

He kissed her and was gone.

(After)

You ok? Seemed...edgy after...

I'm sorry...hope you're feeling relaxed...wanted to do more to you...

Want you to relax...
Listen he has no case...two reasons...you didn't steal...and by the way...you didn't steal...his control is your reactions...all he has left is that...

You're right...just need to get my head straight...it's hard to be accused of his embezzling.
Working on relaxing now...wanna touch myself...but you do it so much better...

Ohhhh I likes...

(Later)

Hi

Hey

You ok

Yes...you ok?

Gooooooood

290

You...are a beautiful man...

Mmmm...thank you...
you sure you ok...

You told me not to worry...

I know...
You shouldn't...you are doing awesome in freedom...enjoy the journey

Thank you. I really do enjoy my new life. I fought on intense personal levels to break free from his covert narcissistic imprisonment.
I just need to remember that...on the tough days. Thnx for the ear...

Anytime...p.s. you squirted...lots

p.s. I really did...somehow that happens when you come around...
Oh, p.s.s. you did too...that "O" face is ooooo so lovely...your cum is like heaven...

Lots...of cum...was it ok...to cum on your tits...in pussy...

Was A LOT! Loved it...seeing you pleasured and happy makes me elated...
see it's not so bad to choose where you want to cum right?

Was...great...

November 25, 2021

Happy Thanksgiving

Happy Thanksgiving!

How are you today...better?

Yes, thank you...feeling all right?

I am...little tired...but good...what are your plans today?

Probably gonna head to my office...give roomie her family privacy...you?

Working...woohoo...

Oh noooo...picked up the Turkey Day shift huh?

I did...easy $$

Yezzz! Usually a slow shift from what I remember. Lots of fire calls tho lol...

Yup...later on...domestics...

Always...can't have dysfunctional family and alcohol mix...ugh, and the paperwork blows...

True...
Honestly...wish my cock was pushing inside you...

Mmmm...that initial entry...that "May I?"...

And deeeeeeeeeeep thrusts...stretch you...fill you...

So gooooood...ahhh, did someone dream?

Always...

Mmmm...great minds...hope I was in it just a smidge...

You were...as I pulled out...cumming on your pussy...saw you rub it in...fingering my cum inside...

Oh...myyyyy what a sight...so fired up...

Once pussy glistening with my cum...you guide me back in with your hand...

Soooo nice...where, which uh...

You tell me...

Lol...was your dream...

I think you wanted me to...push my cock in your ass yesterday...to cum for you...

Thought of it, yes... I also wanted to swallow you but the time rush kinda messed with me...

Yeah...as I fingered you...you relaxed...pushing back...were enjoying...wanting...

I do want...you...

Mmmm...

You...like to taunt and tease? I was wanting to ride you...wanted to slow grind...

Me too...when you taking off?
Slow grind deep...your hips move so well...feel your clit gliding on me...

Aligns me...connects me...taking off?

To your shop...

Oh...noonish...you?

Taking Mom to breakfast bout 1030...work after...

Oh cool! Hope she's getting around better with those lungs...

I'm manifesting to be able to cook Thanksgiving in my own kitchen by next year...this year he won but I'm not one to stay down!

Enjoy your mommy time!

He certainly has not won...I have seen your smile...

Well...you do create that...

Mmmmm...

(Later)

Holy fuck it's nippily out! If my headlights are on I know yours are lol...

Yes...yes they are...

Mmmm...need to be warmed?

Totally...

Mmmmmmm....

How's shop???

Warm...heated bed, yummmmm....You know I like to be warm...and moist...

Have you??

Last night...first "O" on weed...ommmmgggg...

Tell me...

It was as if you were there...full body orgasm!

Mmmmm....

Prolonged it tooooo...

Wow...really...fingers only??

Only fingers...my favorite filler was asleep lol...

Wow...imagine...when I'm buried in you...

I am...makes me throb...already getting wet...

Sooooooo hot...

I keep thinking having an orgasm is going to satiate me...then you text me,
and I get all horny again! Hot? Yessss...you are...

When can we...

When can we?

You...tell me

I'm always ready for you Gunnar...

Wow...best answer...

Truth no?

Mmmm...soooo wanna do hot springs...whiskey...weed for you...wow...

I'd love that...truly...
would be a memory I'd cherish...

Yes...we would...

Bucket list!

Good "O" huh?

So good...I felt really icky yesterday but a lil' puff puff and easy to bed...
started thinking of you...touching and caressing...was explosive...and loooong...

Wow...so real cock might be???

Is the best...
Even started dropping an egg....

Ohhhhhh myyyyyy....

Just a day off from calculations...

Well...what shall we do bout that?

Any suggestions?

Yes...heels...weed...seed...

Lol...your mind...
So much like mine...

Roomie home tomorrow?

Nope

9?

Mmmmm...sounds lovely...

Can you...smoke before...bout 1/2 hr before...
pour me a drink...be ready to be ravaged...

I would but I have to drive so...
Pour you a drink?

Yes plz...anal?

I'm fine with that as a chaser...
Feeling stressed?

Always...

Are my crazy body demands too much stress?

Not at all...

Want you so bad...body aching...what do you do to me...

Feed you what you want...slide right inside...

Mmmm...loveeeeee

Lick you...slide fingers in...

Did I tell you my office couch turns into an office bed?
I hope to christen it someday with someone...any suggestions?

Pick me...pick me...

Sold!

You rubbing your pussy??

No...just moving ever so seductively in my jeans...jean-gams are amazingggggg....

I'd rather the tip of my cock be pushing on your cervix...

I'd prefer that yes...double sensation...

Mmmmm....

Your inner play...and your outer play...yummmmmm...

(Later)

Hi

Hiiii...How are you holding up tonight?

Easy peasy...you?

Great money day. Easy. I like easy days...

Lots of DWI

I believe that! I was driving most of them to their cars this morning, then home from family this evening...

Still out???

298

Yeah...

Uber??

Yeah but a lil dead right now...

Figured be busy

Here and there...
Great tips, people are generous when they drink lol...

Holiday cheer

Right! I'm fine with it...missing your arms...

My "hold you down" arms

Mmmm...loooove that! Now ya got me going again...

Yes...you do

This thong...
These jeans today...ugh, sooo done lol, just done...
Aching inside for you...

Soon...all of me...in...all of you

Mmmm...yearning. Love the feel of you...can't get enough.

Chapter 20

BROUGHT IT

Dereck blew air out of his lungs and murmured curse words under his breath. He pulled out onto the main road away from Peg's place. Her roommate was home all evening but Peg never showed which means she's out having Thanksgiving with others or worse getting laid. Dereck looked down at her little Walther P22. It annoyed the fuck out of him that she had his Glock and all she has to do is hand it to him and he'll give her hers. He had planned to maybe fuck her in the exchange, pointing her own gun at her temple, making her blow him the magnificent way she does, then violating her body in every way he could until escaping out the window again. He knew Peg to be strong but would she go along with a bullet near her head. He smiled thinking of the power he'll feel once he does get a hold of her.

The roads were empty, everyone but him out enjoying the holiday with family. He called a few friends and old students but it seems Peg was able to get to all of them. He thought how his dick in her mouth would keep her from telling people too much. How she found out about him forcing Candice to blow him in the parking lot of his mall dojo is still a mystery. He can't believe she knows. He went twenty-two years without her knowing and the second she finds out, bam she commits to divorce. *Bitch.*

The sound of his blinker annoys him so he hits it off. The light turns green and he accelerates turning left onto Golf Club Court. He sees a patrol car approaching and his headlights flash into the front windshield. He beeps once he recognizes it's Gunnar O'Clery and slows but the car pulls off at high speed. Dereck thinks how he should call O'Clery and convince him to go shooting or better yet, get him to buy some of his guns. He won't mention Peg at all because he doesn't want any of the cops to know they're divorcing...or that she's single. He'd hate if she dated any of them and told them why they're no longer married. He doesn't want her to have a legal advantage either. She could get a restraining order against him and he'd end up losing all his guns.

Dereck watched in his rearview mirror as Gunnar disappeared and remembered when he tried to convince Peg to do another threesome. He was going to bring up Gunnar to her but never got far. She just flat-out said no. Dereck hated when she said no. It unnerved him that she grew boundaries. He tried to break them all but she held steadfast to the "no threesome" one, even found out about him and Kim and Dean. He only hopes she doesn't know about all the other ones.

He pulled into the driveway thinking of seeing her with Gunnar behind her and he in her mouth. His dick hitched in his jeans and he looked down smiling. It might be a good Thanksgiving after all. He turned the truck off, half elated that he might actually cum tonight and half annoyed that it's always Peg, or thoughts of her, that gets his dick to work again. *Biiiitch.*

Gunnar looked in his rearview mirror happy to see his taillights disappear. He frowned, wondering why Dereck Law was coming from the street Peg lived on. He knew she wasn't home, but it alarmed him that Dereck might know that now, too. He really wished Dereck had moved to Colorado as Peg hoped. He was certainly the type of shitbag who's absence would be felt fondly.

He wondered if he should check on her once more while she was out working. A call blared across the radio for a domestic two neighborhoods over. He made a u-turn and keyed up on the radio to let dispatch know he was enroute. He hit lights and sirens pressing his foot to the pedal a bit since the call involved firearms. He decided he was not going to let Peg know he saw Dereck. She had enough going on already. Their sex was incredible, no reason to diminish it with memories of her ex. Poor bastard really fucked up in Gunnar's mind. How he let Peg go was beyond comprehension.

Peg walked down the hallway and opened the door to her room. It was dark, quiet, smelled of essential oils, and made her sad. She spent the entire day, her first Thanksgiving, alone. She looked around, threw her keys and phone on the desk, and slumped down on the bed. The glow of her salt lamp illuminated the ceiling. She wanted to cry but no tears would come. He didn't deserve her tears ever again. He may have taken her life, the kitchen she used to cook Thanksgiving in for everyone, her home, and all the money she worked half for...but she vowed it would be the last Thanksgiving she ever spent alone and working to pay for his actions and disgusting body. Dereck Law may have taken her life but, it was the old one, and as far as she was concerned, a sucky one at that. He could have it.

She turned over and fell into a deep sleep...one where Gunnar O'Clery's arms lulled her into a beautiful slumber.

***

November 26, 2021 8:31 AM

Ohhhh myyyy, I overslept!! Please tell me you're ok?????

I'm great...getting ready...to...

Need to know...
If you can surrender to me a bit today...

Absolutely

Let me take over...

For...sure...

Need to devour you...

Ohhhhh...how's that egg

Savage...making me silly lol. How's my fav bodyyyy...

Getting ready to be against your body

Mmmm...love that answer...roomie is leaving...

Door open...please

Door is...just getting my wits about me...

***

Gunnar opened her door and before he could get fully in she grabbed at his shirt, pulled him in, closed the door, and pushed him against it kissing him hard while her hand found the lock and turned it. She then slid her palm around to his hard cock and gently squeezed his shaft as her tongue moved slowly in and around his mouth. He moaned into her, tasting her and feeling all she was doing. Peg aroused him beyond expectation and he found her assertiveness so sexy.

Placing his gun and wallet to the side on the desk he cradled her low back with one hand and used the other up the front of her shirt to unclasp her bra. She let it fall to the floor and grabbed at his workout shirts, lifting them up and over his head. His chest and neck were exposed and Peg went in to nibble all around his ear and then down his neck and stomach. He lifted her face to his and kissed her again backing her up against the bed so he could remove her jeans. He took his shoes off and pulled his pants down, stepping on them to get them off quickly. Peg reached for his rigid dick, loving how engorged he was.

"You...are so wanted, baby..." She whispered into the quiet of the room seeing him smile. She heaved forward and took him full into her mouth, leaving him gasping for breath. Peg moved slowly, up and down his shaft, feeling him pulse from the pleasure.

"Oh my...baby...ohhhhhh...Peg...." He brought his hand down cradling her face. He absolutely loved the way she gave head. He's never had it the way Peg did it. She was so gentle but purposeful, like she really cared about his pleasure and the build-up. Feeling her tongue and lips swirling and caressing him, all of him. He lowered and took each ball into her mouth giving one just as much attention as the other. She stopped a minute and pointed to the area of the bed she was on. She got up.

"Lay here?"

"Okay." He watched her as she made sure he was comfortable and then she put a drop of lube on her finger. Next, she opened his legs and climbed on the bed in between. Gunnar moaned not knowing what she was planning but knowing everything she does is his favorite. She slid her mouth over him again and he gasped watching her slide her lips and mouth further, down to his base. He relaxed, leaning his head back against the pillow, and she reached, inserting her lubed finger into his anal opening. Gunnar gasped louder loving the feeling of her gentle finger sliding warm and slow into him. The feel of her sucking his head and shaft along with her rhythmic slow fingering was mind-blowing. He felt he was getting too close and going to explode. He reached and gently grabbed her under her arms.

"Kiss me?"

Peg followed his request and straddled him, kissing him deep.

"Oh wow...you are so wet baby...you're dripping...."

"I'm sorry."

"Please don't apologize..."

"Do you?"

"Do I?"

She smiled, "Do you give consent?"

"Please?"

Peg pushed into him sliding his hard dick in and up inside her in one thrust. Gunnar gasped again in her mouth and Peg exhaled her pleasure into his. He filled and stretched her in a way that made her want to give him all of her. She thrust...and thrust and caressed...and thrust so slow, taking him into her, squeezing and then releasing him for another deep thrust.

Gunnar grabbed at her ass, holding on, letting her take him, surrendering as she had requested. Peg rode him for what seemed like hours. She felt he so big and fierce inside her and yet he felt she was so tight and snug around him. He especially liked how she sunk so deep on him he could feel her cervix suckling his head and her clit rubbing on his pubic bone. Peg knew how to fuck, she was all about slow pleasure, not only his but matching his with her own, and he felt that was beyond hot. She knew what she wanted and he thought she was the sexiest woman he'd ever met.

She lifted up and before he knew what was happening she was crouching down between his legs again to take him into her mouth! He was only able to take the extreme pleasure for a few seconds and stopped her then got up.

"I'm going to cum if you keep this up." He reached for the honey whiskey on the desk and uncapped it taking a huge swig.

Peg stood up to stretch her legs and watched him. He'd never drank before and she realized it being Friday meant he was not on shift. She smiled and walked towards him caressing his tight muscular ass. He put the bottle down and turned to push her to the bed. He bent her over and sunk deep into her from behind. Peg moaned and braced herself taking in all his desire and realizing he wanted to take over. He drove into her whispering about how he can't believe how she takes him into her mouth and pleases him until he almost explodes, then rides him like no other woman ever has. Gunnar grabbed on either side of her hips supporting them both and drove in deeper causing her to cry out and push against the wall to meet him.

"Oh my god, the way you push back makes me feel so wanted Peg. You are amazing..."

Peg smiled, pushing again, "I like what you do to my body..."

"I'm going to cum baby..."

Peg pushed more and more, picking up the pace to make him feel all of her as he came. With a few more deep thrusts Gunnar gripped her hips and went silent while Peg pushed back on him over and over and over until she heard him inhale and felt him pump and release and pump and r e l e a s e. His cum spilling inside her while his hands loosened and his legs began to relax. He caught his breath and she waited.

With that, Gunnar pulled out and flipped her over onto her back. He pressed his mouth into her and began flicking his tongue along her clit until she curled up into him. Her arms flew back and she pushed against the wall feeling his glorious mouth on her. His tongue felt amazing, and suddenly Peg felt her eruption come crashing towards her and over. She screamed his name into the room and it echoed. He smiled and moaned, loving how pleased she was. It aroused him and he was happy to feel himself hard again. He lifted away and Peg's arms came in to cradle her breasts, her legs closing to squeeze every ounce of throbbing orgasm through her yoni. She turned to her side to recover and he took the opportunity to lay behind her and put his arms around her while sliding his cock between her tush. She arched back opening to receive him and he slid slick into her womb, filling her as he grew again and making her gasp in her post-orgasmic sensitivity. Peg's head flew back he cradled it with his chest and took both her breasts in his palms as he drove deeper and deeper into her. She moaned with pleasure and he sunk his mouth deep into her neck causing her to cry out in ecstasy! Goosebumps and shivers rang through her and she clenched around his dick harder.

Gunnar bit her again then asked, "Would you ride me again?"

Peg nodded and he got up helping her to her feet. He laid down on the bed and instead of straddling him she turned around and sunk down on him in reverse cowgirl.

Gunnar was very pleased, "Oh wow baby...I love when you do this..."

Peg began swaying and swirling her hips slowly and built up to a faster pace. Gunnar loved to see her move and reached forward to open her tush and watch her come up and down his shaft. He murmured how beautiful they were together and how she was so hot. It aroused Peg to hear his gratification and she picked up the pace, moving and humping him rapidly. Gunnar sucked air in through his teeth and began to clench at her hips, Peg could feel him start to cum again and she went wild making sure he surrendered. He did and so did she, they both yelled into the tiny room, crashing over into pure bliss...together.

While dressing, Gunnar talked softly to her filling her in on calls he'd gone on the days he'd been busy and away from her. He mentioned how weird it was to go to an overdose and see the guy's mother put frozen pork chops from the freezer on her son's crotch to wake him up. That reminded him of a drug addict they had to restrain as a paramedic pulled out a syringe from her hair and shot the guy up with Ketamine, totally freaking him out because the guy could die...days later. Peg could see the stress in Gunnar and how the holiday shifts brought on some unwanted emotions. He even explained how there was a two-vehicle DUI crash and upon review, he could not understand how there wasn't a fatality. Peg watched his eyes and recognized his trauma words as very *familiar* to what she spoke when she was debriefing about CPTSD trauma as well. She admired Gunnar for trying to get it out and could see why he took a small shot of whiskey. She just hoped she wasn't a part of his stress and instead a way for him to relax enough to process.

"If you weren't fixed you'd definitely be pregnant already!"

She smiled at how his mind shifted back to her, "Oh really?"

He laughed, "Yep, I'm super fertile and....Irish!"

"Ah...I see."

"Thank you for sharing and giving yourself to me." He touched her face, then sat down to put on his shoes.

"Thank you back..."

(Later)

Ohhh...you brought it...

You like???

My legs are still shaky...I think I likey tooooo much. You?

Feel great...whatcha doin???

*Baby girl asked me to get her chicken noodle soup
and snuggle watching a movie.
I may fall asleep now that someone rocked my world...
feel an ovulation nap coming on ...*

Great plan...I love chicken noodle soup

Do you? I'm learning so many new things...about you...

I do

My kid looked at me and said, "Ma, you okayyyy?"

...and???

*She squints, "You sleeping okay?"
I was like "Yeah, just overslept."
Then she smiled wide...(oops)*

That's funny

307

So I was like, "Well...I'm droppin' an egg so...
" She says, "Ohhhhh, well I'm not anymore!" (Laughing emoji)

Well...thats the truth...she feeling ok

Queasy...but momma brought her food so she's smilin'.
Thank you for asking.
That...was sooooo good today. I'm addicted...Feeling better after your pull-ups?

Very...
Very relaxed

Mmmm...I like knowing you're relaxed...
I heard you when you explained how your night went.
It's really difficult to be the supervisor on a call...that can go to shit so quickly.
You handled yourself well...like that you're watching your six...
I'm happy to help you relax when you have rough shifts like that-

You did...believe me

Hoping you're warm and safe...

Hey...gonna back off phone...daughter was scrolling through...will call next week...

Yeah

Peg couldn't help but feel confused and slightly abandoned. She knew it was because they had such closeness, she opened more herself to him and then he ghosts mentioning he'll call next week. Her body started to react in ways she wasn't wanting. Thoughts came rushing in one after another, after another, and another. Dereck came to mind as he loved to keep her in a constant tailspin so she couldn't feel good.

Peg got up putting her boots on and grabbing her keys. There was no way she was going to sit ruminating and feeling like a K9 dog he was "handling". As she made her way down the hall to the door she scrolled through her messages to Tommy's last text and opened it. He had invited her to the grand opening of the bar he worked at but she never made it. She texted her old student and asked if he was working. He answered right away and invited her to join him as he had three hours left on his shift. Peg started the truck and told him she'd be there in seven.

Tommy Michens watched her as she made her way into the dimly lit bar. Peg Law was the type of woman that looked stunning in dim light but he also felt she'd look good in any light. Tommy was seventeen years her junior and a former student. He liked being a massage therapist but bartending was more his tempo. He also liked their easy friendship but would happily explore more now that she'd returned. There were many nights he pleasured himself to the thoughts of his cougar instructor. Her touch was like no other.

She made her way to the bar and before she sat down he embraced her, inhaling her scent deep within.

"Oh myyyyy, I've missed you!"

Peg let go a small smile offered, "How the hell are you Tom Tom? I'm so happy to see you, you look amazing as usual."

He smiled, releasing her, and making his way back around the bar as she sat on one to the bar stools toward the end away from all the other patrons. He prepared her

Tito's and cranberry with lime and thanked her, "You are very kind. Speaking of, how much weight have you lost? You are one hot momma!"

"That's sweet...actually, it's grandma."

"No fucking way! Who? Jaeden or Zena?"

"Zena, she's due in late July." Pegs shoulders relaxed and she sipped her drink nodding.

Tommy raised his hands open, "I haven't seen anything on Insta or Facebook."

"She's not announced it yet."

"Doesn't want the douchebag to know?"

Peg chortled, "That and well...it's very early."

"Oh right. Well, congrats to all. You are way too young to be a grandma woman."

Peg shrugged, she really wasn't.

"Well, you look too young." He touched her arm then retracted to wipe down the counter.

"Thanks Tom, that feels good."

He winked, "So what's this?" He waved his hands in front of her.

Peg's eyes looked sad but she smiled, "What are you talking about?"

"This...*mood*. You're usually more, I don't know, peppy."

"I'm just coming down off the holiday. Tough one this year, but next year will be better."

He knew there was more but it would take way more than one drink to get Peg to open up. "Oh for sure."

"Just glad it's over."

Tommy knew to change the subject, "So, when can I throw you an "Unhitched" party? My boss is really cool with that sort of thing you know."

Peg raised her hand up, "Oh well, it's gonna be awhile. That would be fun though."

"I'll get you a stripper...all your old students and friends would..."

"Please bud...*noooooo*."

Tommy loved seeing her smile, "Aw come on teach, you deserve a hot, tempting, uh..." He saw her evert her eyes down. "Wait, do you?"

She looked up, blushing mildly.

"Ohhhhh, I see, you want me to do it. I'll be your huckleberry Instructor Law. I can shake my ass...assets for your..."

Peg laughed trying not to. She sipped her drink through the tiny straw, "I don't know why I torture myself by coming to see you. I knew I should have failed you...you know your anatomy and physiology test scores were not as good as they..."

"Hey, hey, hey now." He laughed, leaning in. "It's so good to see you. I'm happy you're here."

"I am too. Thank you. Can we talk about something else perhaps? I don't want to think about my ex, or parties, or any of that stuff right now. Tell me, how are things?"

Tommy refilled a beer at the tap and slid it to a guy down the bar with a MAGA hat on. He came back and leaned on the bar to make eye contact with her.

"Things are...okay. Hey, I actually wanted to pick your brain a bit about-" He paused and looked at Peg, furrowing his eyebrows.

"About?"

"Well, remember when you explained energetic sex versus genital sex?"

"Oh gosh, that must have been in 2018 right before your graduation."

"Yes, actually I think it was one of our last classes and a few of us had asked you about spiritual sex...or Tantra, that's right it was Tantra!" He pointed at her, recalling the memory excitedly.

Peg smiled, "I remember. So what's the question?"

"Well, I have this girlfriend now. We've been going strong for about a year and we're exploring more uh, sensual play."

"I love hearing that, great job."

"But-"

"Uh oh, there's a but?"

"Yeah." His eyes everted down then up again to hers.

Peg knew what was coming, "Have you cheated yet?"

He inhaled and exhaled loudly, "I'm feeling the need to."

"Oh wow, that's heavy Tom. Can you tell me what you're feeling?

"I feel...well, have you ever heard the term "throwing a hot dog down a hallway"?

"Wide-set vagina."

"What?"

"Let me guess. She has a wide-set vagina and you feel uh...small?"

He raised his eyebrows, "How do you just know shit!?"

"I just know things. Do you love her?"

"What?"

"Okay, that answers it. You don't bud, might be time to let her go. How long have you gone without being able to climax inside her?"

His eyes widened. He couldn't believe she knew, "Since the beginning."

"But you can cum from oral and anal yes?"

"Uh, yes? So weird that you know that."

Peg gave him a small smile, "I have a lot of stuff I know, and tons I don't yet. Tell me, are you insecure about your size?"

He smiled, "I wasn't."

"Listen, all bodies are different. It's okay to say that she may be shaped a bit different and shaped for *another man*. You may be just right for a different woman. Better to know now."

"So true but-"

Peg softly cut him off, "You don't love her bud. You may be very fond of her, but you don't love her and sex is very important. If you are feeling insecure it's going to affect your dick. Men are ninety percent mental, ten percent genital. It's just how it is. Let me ask you this..."

"Okay?"

"Did you have this problem with other girlfriends?"

"Not a one."

"Wide-set vagina."

He squinted, "I had no idea."

"It's a phrase from a movie, Mean Girls I think, but it is a thing and can be an issue for some men who need to feel more when inside in order to release. Again, no one's fault just different bodies."

"Fuck..."

"They say there's a perfect person out there for everyone." Peg sipped her drink and winked at him.

He laughed, "I feel so much relief right now...I mean it's not the best news for she and I but-" He paused.

"No one is to blame, it is what it is."

"Yeah, I mean I was really conflicted."

Peg nodded. She understood the confusion, the anger, blaming, denial, then the wanting to cheat to get answers or to have release. She had coached quite a few clients over the years who just didn't "fit" well together. She herself didn't even fit well with Dereck but she made it work when she should have set herself free. Now, she feels there is no better fit for her than Gunnar.

"Well, enough about me. How are you doing in other areas of your new life? Work, friends, family...love?" He was super curious.

"Hmmm...work is awesome, somehow I'm making it and have more money than I ever did married, I have a whole new set of friends, my family is healthy and my kids are still awesome, law-abiding humans, so I think I did okay in that area."

Tommy stopped cleaning classes and waited. He wanted to know if she was free. "And..."

Peg smiled, pondering what she should elaborate on. "And...I'm open to love...should it come along." It wasn't a lie.

"Aw, come on. This whole fucking town breathed sigh of relief when you returned no longer married. What was it your profile said...oh yeah, a big fat "Divorced"."

Peg rolled her eyes, "Wow, I didn't realize so many were paying attention."

"We were ALL paying attention."

"Wow." Peg felt a slight pang of hurt.

"You know he didn't deserve you *Teach*. You were so happy in ever aspect of life except when it came to him. The light in you would go out when he was around or even texted your phone. So many of us hurt when you left but we also knew you had to. Just so glad your back."

Peg smiled, "Thank you. That feels good. I almost didn't come back. It was hard. I returned and had to start all over again but I don't pity my situation. It's actually been very freeing. I mean I'd prefer to live in my home, have my practice again, friends over, my garden, amazing sex, bonfires in the courtyard. Ugh, I dream of laying in my hammock again..."

"We all loved your bonfire nights...amazing sex?"

She laughed, "Such a guy..."

"Well yeah, I mean with who?"

"With whoever I want. I love being free."

"I bet. Been a long time-"

"You know Tom, I will never understand why I was so faithful to a man that never deserved my loyalty."

He huffed, "Yeah, he was quite the hoe."

"That is truth. I'm so much happier. Never again."

"Never?"

She winked, "I will never put myself in a cage like that again."

Peg drove home feeling a little better. She knew she was confused but convinced herself that it was normal to be confused in whatever it was she had with Gunnar. She turned down the street she lived on thinking of how if she didn't care for Gunnar, she wouldn't be feeling the way she was. Exhaling she recognized she'd need to really sit and think about how much she felt for him.

Parking in the driveway, she cut off the engine and placed her head on the steering wheel trying to ease the thoughts. "Peg, you need to dig deep girl...figure this shit out. It's okay to help everyone else but you gotta help you too." The words lingered in the quiet of the truck. She knew it was time to consider her true feelings just a bit more.

Hopping out of the truck she walked quickly to the door and locked herself in the house. It still wasn't safe to be out after dark or lingering outside the house since Dereck could be around. She always felt like he was watching.

I'm sorry bout other day...daughter had phone...scrolling...I panicked...

Sounds like you have a lot going on...perhaps

Just..my life

As you're out there working and trying to navigate the stress...
Just remember you're worth
and that there is someone out here that thinks you're doing a hell of a job. I know what it's like to be pulled in
ten different directions, not be seen, not be heard, and worst...
to work and live a thankless job.
I wish you some ease...and most of all peace
I see you....

Gnite

...gnite...thanx

December 2, 2021 12:18 PM

Helloooooooooo

HIiiiiii
Dreams lately?

Yup...yup...

Me too

Really???

Really

How's shop? Busy??

Gettin' there! How are you holding up??

Tired...been working at NASA all week...loooooong...

Oh myyyy. Yeah, thought you went undercover or somthin' lol...
Did you get to teach peeps how to aim and squeeze?

Trying...they're good guys...just poorly trained...can't have much phone use at facility...

Ugh...hard to break poorly trained gunplay...but...if anyone can lol...

Yeah...it's a process
How's things on the divorce side?

Uhhhh, I try not to think of it too much. He canceled my truck insurance, but I was able to catch it in time
(yay Peg) and then he canceled the wifi at the FL house so my two tenants are thinking of moving...
Lil' wins is what he loves. I'm patient. I like peace...and big wins lol.
The paramedic with the needle in her hair incident go away?

Gosh...juvenile...he is...
Yeah, he didn't die...no harm no foul...yet...

316

Glad he didn't...you don't need more stress.
I'm in Alamogordo meeting the other grandmother of my kiddo's baby. This baby will have lotsa strong
feminine energy around him!

Strong energy??

Yes...she's retired military...
Then there is me...my daughter...is fire!!

(Later)

Hi

Hey, you ok?

Yup...wishing...

Wishing??

That I was...pushing inside you...

Ohhhh...now I'm wishing...

Yup...your feet...flat on my chest...

Mmmm...no heels tho?

Yes heels...for sure

Mmm...fire!!

Sorry...I have missed your...
Well you know...

Missed yours as well...

How so???

I've missing your thrusting...kissing...connection...heat, words, whispers, chest....

Ohhhh...is it ok? I have been dreaming about....

Yes

Honest??? I really like you fingering my...

Yes...of course. I like how you dream...

Was...very hot...

Thought so too...you chanted my name...

Two fingers next time...help me...relax

Yes...whenever you want...

Chapter 21
FOLLOW

Peg pulled out of the parking spot and onto the main road. She could hear the sirens in the distance and felt bad that Gunnar was so crazy busy on shift. The town was going to shit and with so much crime, there was no time for "them".

She went around the circle and then straight. She thought she'd stop off and see Tommy again. Admittedly, she was curious about how he handled things with his girlfriend. He also texted he wanted company while closing up but she knew he wanted to ask her more questions.

In her rearview, she caught sight of headlights off in the distance. Not many cars were out so she checked all her mirrors and made note of each car approaching from every direction. She turned left to head home and alarmingly the headlights in the distance ran the light and turned in the same direction. Peg frowned. It was past midnight. For shits and giggles, she decided to make a quick right and then a left down a side street. She got all the way to the end and in her rearview, she saw the vehicle creep up, look down the street after her, then speed straight trying not to be recognized...but she did. Only Dereck had an obnoxiously decked out baby-truck. She was familiar with the running boards, the stupid oversized KC lightbar on top. She exhaled, shaking her head, and pulled in the opposite direction to head to a different part of town away from him. Why he was following her or even remotely interested in what she was up to was beyond her. She just wanted him to forget about her and go to Colorado.

Dereck drove home pissed that she might have seen him. He hit his hand on the steering wheel, annoyed that he let her spot him. *Impatient Idiot!* He'd watched her for a few hours. Sat watching her truck even after she was in it in the parking spot for another twenty minutes. He cursed his anxiousness. He knew if he waited enough hours she'd at least have had a client or whoever she's been fucking show up. Dean said she'd been happier than ever with... someone.

He pulled in the driveway of the home they used to share. He looked at all the twinkling lights she'd hung in the courtyard garden. She made it a beautiful home. He still had difficulty believing she'd left him. All the years together and she actually left him! He knows if he gets enough time, enough time to explain and twist it all... convince her of his love, she'd relent. He just needed enough time with her...days maybe...days away and alone.

He turned the truck off looking again at their beautiful home. How could she leave all this? How could she leave him? He stepped out thinking how he'd rather have her dead than let another man have her.

Gunnar felt like shit. If he hadn't been in this line of work for the last twenty-eight years, his body would surely break down. He bent down and grabbed his gear to walk to his truck. It was still dark out, and a bit cold. He thought about Peg and how he was unable to get with her. She didn't deserve to be pushed aside. She was too much woman to be put aside.

He wondered if she was awake at such an early hour. He opened the app and saw the little green light next to her pic was lit up.

December 3, 2021 6:39 AM

Hi...sorry bout last night...got home little early...crashed out...

Yeah

How are you?

Well....you?

Getting to NASU...text in a bit...

Have a good one!

(Later)

How's...you?

Better suddenly...you?

Good...you working?

At shake shop. Heading back to my office, done for the day...yay! You?

Finally done at NASU

Great job! Bet it was an awesome week for you...

Looooong...long...week...

Exhausted?

Not too bad...how was your session this morning?

Meh...he had fragile masculinity...but the $140 made it bearable...

Ohhhh...like me!

Stop...not you at allllll...

So...a tour of shop???

Really? Kinda got a visit from Aunt Flo...

Sweeeeeet!

I'm vulnerable...lol

You at office yet?

Yes

Ok...I'm here

Secret door in front of my truck...see it?

Ohhhhh...

Do I come in??

Ok...

***

Gunnar slid into the side door of the building and looked down into her eyes. He then scanned the room and whispered, "Hi."

"Hi there." Peg shut the door and locked it, waving him to follow her around the corner and down the hall to her office. She was nervous, not that he was there, but that her partner had come in and had a client in her office. The music was loud so that would help. As soon as she let him into her office and turned to lock the door, he pushed her up against the wall and kissed her long. Although her shoulders and heels hit the wall, she relaxed immediately beneath his touch. He put his hands on her hip and breast, she reached for his manhood. He was as ready for her as she was for him.

"Please take this off," he whispered to her and pointed to her shirt. He backed up and took off his shoes, pants, and shirt watching her do the same. He missed her body and groaned as she took each layer off. She loves how he looked naked and hoped she could someday be as in shape. His body was thick with muscle but trim in all the right areas. His two-hundred and twenty-pounds looked phenomenal on his short five-foot-seven frame and Peg felt herself get even wetter for him. She loved the way he held himself, the way he walked, the way he looked like a football player ready to tackle criminals at any moment.

Fully erect and naked he stepped towards her wanting to place her down on the bed but she sat and took him inter her mouth completely forcing his surrender. He couldn't believe how gentle and caring her mouth was wrapped around him. His breath hitched and he stood taking every stroke of pleasure Peg offered. He felt he was going to explode, it had been a week since feeling her wanting him...and she was soooooo good!

Gunnar reached down and helped her to her feet. He reached down remembering she had her period which he admittedly loved so much. With confidence, he pulled at her little string and removed her tampon. He placed it in the tissue she offered and threw it in the trash turning to replace where it was in her womb with his erect cock.

Peg backed up and he laid her down on the futon, parting her legs with his body and penetrating her the way she loved. He heard her gasp near his ear and pushed in all the way to her cervix wanting to caress and stimulate her, helping ease her cramping womb. His mouth met hers and his eyes closed, rolling back at the familiar bliss she gives accepting him into her tight body.

"Ohhhhh my Peg...you feel incredible..." He moaned it into her ear and Peg almost came squeezing him tight inside, never wanting him to stop his slow, torturous ecstasy inside her deepest parts.

Gunnar brought his hands up on either side of her face and looked into Peg's eyes, "Look at me." She focused on his eyes as he thrust deeper and deeper into her. "Where's my cock baby?"

"...I feel you...up...in my throat..."

He smiled and kissed her mouth arching and humping her harder and harder.

Peg broke from his kiss, "You are so fucking hot baby. Feel how much my body wants you?"

He groaned trying to answer her, wanting to do so much to her body...then again, wanting to stay safe and buried inside her...

***

Unexpectedly he got a hold of me today after getting off of work at a NASU teaching gig early. He mentioned wanting a "tour" of my office, which I was super excited about until I showed up and

Karen was in her room with a facial client. It was a bit nerve-wracking, as I'd thought we'd be alone. I was able to sneak him into my office and we had a mind-blowing reunion after a week. I can't believe how pleasurable and balancing our encounters are. It's as if all my CPTSD symptoms fade off for days and his as well from what he says.

He was forceful but gentle. I could feel his hunger within, like he was hyped after a successful week and excited we were rewarding each other. I locked the door, he pushed me again the wall and started going after me. I hope my partner didn't hear much, if she did it was merely my shoulders and heels hitting the wall. She had her music on so she really shouldn't have heard much.

We were groping and touching everywhere, clearly having missed each other. He was so engorged and frisky! It turns me on like crazy that he wants me so much. I pleased him orally, but a few minutes in, he stopped me, not wanting to cum too quickly. I love hearing his breath hitch as he tries to prolong things.

He was very eager and climbed into my body possessing me and making me want him deeper and d e e p e r in my fevered, swollen womb. I played orally with him and made him lay back and take my gentle, caressing mouth. He was very vocal, trying to finish sentences, but his breath kept hitching, and his cock pulsing as he was trying not to explode. So much fun. He was extremely hard, I could tell he really needed our connection as did I.

*We did most all our favorite positions but ended up back in missionary again and again due to how deep it feels and he likes to talk to me during...while looking down into my eyes. He admitted he'd had naughty dreams about me wanting him and asking to have another guy! This seems to be reoccurring for him since I told him the intricate details about my positive experience with Dan... not so much positive with Dereck. Sadly, instead of my mind wandering to how pleasurable Gunnar would be in it, I thought about how Dereck always offered me up to other men (asshole) and how he'd not waste a moment to offer me up to Gunnar if they spoke long enough over drinks. Dereck idolizes Gunnar still, all these years later. And he'd want to fuck him too which I'm sure Gunnar is not into. Then again, if Dereck knew we were together, he'd probably knock on my door and just shoot me point blank in my heart. His ego would never allow him to accept how amazing Gunnar and I are together. He'd imagine us in his crazy mind and it would send him over the edge. And...I think he's been following me to see what I've been up to, if he knew I had a lover already, and Gunnar O'Clery at that...he'd surely ruin it all. I have to make sure Dereck stays away, he would hurt us both if he could. He did tell me once that it "he ever goes down" he's "taking everyone with him." Dereck is such a coward. Can't believe I actually **believed** in him once.*

(Later)

Nice to see you as well...nite-

Peg answered the text from her friend Trent. He was asking if she wanted to meet for a beer at the newest brewery. She knew he needed to vent. Trent was a safe friend. She never had to worry about him trying to hit on her as he was an old friend who knew her and he was madly in love with a women he couldn't seem to reach. He'd want to catch up, bitch about how she ghosts him, and then after he had his tantrum he'd soften and finally relent to Peg's advice.

She welcomed the distraction. Her body was happily satisfied but she wanted to talk with Gunnar...and couldn't.

Aileen opened the door to Josephine and smiled lovingly. She'd missed her oldest friend as it had been months since they had a wine night.

"Bitch, bring it in. Damn, it's been forever." Aileen took her tiny body in her embrace. They talked often but getting together had been tough due to such busy schedules.

"It has. How you be woman?"

Aileen released her and backed up to let her in. She hobbled a bit then closed the door.

"I'm alive. These damn legs keep me from doing much though. Thanks for coming here as going out exhausts the shit out of me."

Josephine worried about her as she had obvious edema, a weak heart, and took every medication the doctor's threw at her which obviously weren't working.

"For sure. You really should come in to my office for a full workup. I know I could help you feel better."

"I know, I know. I just would never want to scare you with seeing this body naked." She chuckled.

"You know that shit never bothers me."

"Well, it bothers me. I don't even recognize myself in the mirror anymore."

"Aw Ai, I want to help you. You worked all those years, now you're retired, you should be able to enjoy the second half of your life."

Aileen smiled, "I am. I kind get to do the fun stuff now. Speaking of, we should discuss Peg Law. I've been able to gather some intel on the idiot up the road."

"You are not going to believe she shit she shared about him. Wow, he is worse than I remember."

"Ha! You don't think narcissists get better do you?"

"Oh I know they don't, I just think he progressed to a more dangerous level"

Aileen agreed, "Oh my yes, he's infested. Total sociopathic narc, the TBI from the military and obviously martial arts does not help at all."

"You know why she left him?"

"I've been catching on to some of his conversation over the phone. He touches on subjects but turns everything around to how its her fault. He really has no one else to blame but her...and now she's gone."

Josephine nodded, "Well, he'll never take accountability so he'll blame her until he finds a new victim."

"That might be harder than he thinks. That motherfucker can't get a date to save his life."

"Well, he's known to try to pick up single moms, with young daughters by the way, and trash Peg's name to bait and hook them but then when they look her up and realize who she is, they end up ghosting him. He get's livid and bitches like a sissy to his friend Kelly and some guy named Dean that was living with him but moved out."

"Yeah, that is the two-faced friend who plays both Dereck and Peg from what she's mentioned."

"Oh so you've been able to talk with her?"

Josephine smiled, "We meet for lunch or dinner, she's quite the looker, but also a real decent person. I've been enjoying our growing friendship. Kind of wish I'd nourished it over the years."

Aileen liked how her friend explained things, "Well, we can help her now. Come, let's drink too much wine and talk about young girls stepping forward."

"Yes, lets. You know it only takes one, then they all begin to reveal truths."

"True."

December 4, 2021 4:50 PM

Super wasted...ask me anything lol...

Wow...what ya drink?

Guinness...

At home...or office?

Home now...went out with guy bestie, he says...I'm

Oh wow...great time?

Says...I'm oozing sexual prowessssss lol

Yup...I would agree...

Don't even know if I spelled that right...
Says I could turn a gay man straight...I disagreed, reminded him who I was married tooooo bahawahaaaaaa

Wow...went there huh...

Ppft...

Mmmm...bet you will rub your clit...

Last night...thinking of all you'd done to me...

We...had...
A great time...

Did you like the tour of my office?

So much...

Is this how people are?

How???

> *So much...pleasure...my marriage sucked...*

You liked???

> *Dudeeeee...seriously?*

You tell your friend...how well you were fucked...

> *He didn't ask for details lol...just knew...he was concerned tho...*

Concerned??? About???

> *Worried...I'm getting wild...lol*

Well...you tell him you rode a big cock...with multiple cum shots...

> *(Laughing emoji) Ya killin' me...just drooled M&Ms down my boobs lol*

I bet...he asked bout...details?

> *Not too much...I won't reveal anyway...he's worried about my ex...*

Worried bout?

> *He knows how unstable he is...*

Well...thats true...
Where you guys go drinking?

> *Icebox*

Ahhhh...

> *So my friend told me that in high school someone said cum made your teeth whiter...*

Well...that or crest...

Lol...so girlfriend was like, "Peg, no shit, I was swishing that shit around in my mouth everytime...for like a year!" I almost peed myself!! Crest...lol!!!!

Wow...
How's your ass today...you had me deep!

Feelin' good! You likey?

Ohhhh my...you had me cumming everywhere

Some of us ladies enjoy that a-spot orgasm...I believe everything can be pleasurable with the right person... love to see/hear you cum...

You make me cum everywhere...every time...

I had no idea sucking your nipple like that would do so much! Uhhh, I've only experienced you cumming a lot....

Lots...you get me hard...turned on quickly...
Want to fuck you in the morning...BJ at lunch...eat you till you scream at dinner...

There's nothing I don't like about that lol...you holding up ok lately?

I'm good...long hours...tired...but good...
How are you...you tell your friend today...that you...have been getting fucked like a queen lately?

I might have mentioned...that I'm really enjoying being single and not married...yes...

Ohhhhh...tell me...what you told him...

And...I am now aware of how good great cock feels...

Ohhhh...my...I'm blushing...

Mmmmm...the thrust play of your hips... He's worried cuz...

Cuz??????

It's so soon after my ex...I told him about my Ayahuasca trip...and
How I was told of you...

Told of me??

Well not you specifically...no names...Ohhhhh, I didn't tell you about that?

Not yet...

Haven't been able to share much lately...

What...are we talking about...

I like the way you kissed me as I locked us in my office...instant wet!

You were...moaning...biting...squirting...cumming....

That...I was...

Very much...

My brain...fails me in your presence...

Fails? Thats a victory...

Lol...

You make it home ok??

It's sexy when you care...

I do...I do...

Friend thinks...I'm just a booty call...

Not...what I do...

330

Mmmmm...throbbing over here...damn hormones...

You do that soooooooo well...great period sex!

It's sooooo good, feel great to be a woman around you.
Roomie asked why I look like shit last night lol...

You tell her...you were ravaged in every way...

Even fucked my makeup off! Lol, not too much.
We did discuss anal...per her topic. Seems to be a "thing" this month lol...

Wow...she learning too?? Just like me...

You are my favorite student! Naw, she just wishes HPV guy wasn't playing hard-to-get...

I am...I am favorite student...

Thank you for being so...and so gentle and open-minded! You've restored my pleasure centers after so many years in a shitty marriage lol...

Very open minded...anything... ANYTHING to pleasure you...no questions asked...

How'd...you get to be so cool?

Well...a long time ago..in a galaxy far, far away...

(Laughing emoji)

You get home ok??

Sir...yes sir! I don't drink and drive. Home safe, under a blanket freezing' my tits off...

Sounds fun...really does...

Lol...no it doesn't ...you're just being sweet...

I'm sweet...like valentines candy...

Better watch how sweet you are...could result in tongue lashings...

Promise...

Sooo...I'm curious...

I bet...

Do you often get that hard throughout a day?

Yup...very...

Really???

Irish kid...

Your whole life?

Kinda...

December 5, 2021 5:41 PM

Sooooooo many drunks out...

Yes...very...NFL Games

Lordy...

How's that vagina...which I wanna...kiss

Want those kisses...so much...
One just told me to call my boyfriend and tell him I"m bringing someone home...

I bet...

Told him that was slightly disrespectful...he apologized and said he'd probably get himself shot in this town...
Are you well?? Happy today?

Yes...
Yard work..wooohooo...

Mmmm...Gunnar O'Clery earthing...sexy...

Burning shit like Godzilla
(Gif of Godzilla breathing fire)

(Laughing emojis) Don't make me laugh...gotta peeeeeeeee...

(Second gif of Godzilla sent)

(Laughing Avatar sent)
Testing your inner pyro huh?

That was me...went full pyro...

Nice...smell good? Always wanted to make love by a fire...on a beach...

Smelled kinda like...well weeds...but we can pretend...

Was long day...how are you?

It was a long day! I'm great. Oh, and apologies about my drunk texting...went to the gym to get rid of it lol..an old lady scolded me at the laundromat!

Laundromat?

Yep

For??

Told me my undies were too "skimpy" lol...and that I had too many sheets. Old people need to complain to meet their need for significance...

Should have told her...you had a huge cock cumming in you...in pussy...in ass...in mouth...

Lol...might have given her a stroke...she was concerned about what my profession is and was less judgy when I mentioned "therapeutic massage".

Wow...

Lol, roomie just asked me if guys like being told they deserve to be "sucked and fucked"...

...well...if she likes to be licked...and pricked...

Ahhh...good one!

Got jokey jokes...

You do...

Roomie working tomorrow??

Uhhhh....

Yes?

Working it into convo...life coaching at present...

Oh...

Tell her you need pleasure...
(Hi, my name is pleasure)

I do....I need to be pleasured for balance lol..what are you needing??

Have it
With you

Wow...that felt good! She said she works Mon - Wed, off Thurs/Fri...

December 6, 2021 7:51 AM

Hi

Mmmmm...

Mmmmmmmmmm??? Did...I...interrupt?

No, not at all...nice way to wake...

Ahhhh...better way is by licking you...as you wake...
Dream well?

Yezzzz...you?

Very...how was coaching sessions with roomie?

Looooooong but it makes her happy so...how are you feeling today?

I feel great...

Nice...

What ya sleeping in?
I would...push into you...

Was putting on jeans and high heel boots...but if you wanna play...

335

Roomie will hear you moaning, sucking, and being praised for sucking me so well...

She left...works next 3 days...

Ohhhh...I see...we're you leaving?

Yes. Didn't know if you wanted to...pleasure today...

Mmmm...did you touch yourself last night???

Noooo...saved me for you...but you ghosted so wasn't sure...

Ghosted???
Fell asleep...thought your roomie was home today...

Ah...Thought so...yard work wins that war lol...

It did...

Nope. She works next 3 days then off 2...

Ahhh...you work today??

Later...you?

Can you smoke this morning...I wanna see you mega cum...
I do work yes...

I mega cum regardless lol...

Can I come by?

You asking??

Mmmm...bout 1/2 hour...door open...heels...on bed...2 fingers inside...

Mmmm...va-giney is occupied momentarily...might need to be all about you today...

Huh?? giney?

Va...giney lol

Occupied??

Still bleeding...sorry, messiest day!

Ummm...it's ok...you will be licked...touched...pleasured...

Mmmm...so good...

Mmmm...hormones...can't wait...speeeeeeeeding....zooooooooom

Nooooooo speeding...want you safe...I'll keep things warm for you...

Nothing from your ex???

Haven't checked...

Ahhhh...

Makes me have to puff puff...I just want to be happy...was hoping he was in CO by now...

(Later)

Think I want to get into hunting...

Sweeeeeet

Can I catch you and mount you??

Good one...

I can be witty...
Does my face ever remind you of a wrench?

Wrench?

Do your nuts tighten when you see me? Lol...

That's funny...

Can we play strip poker? I'll stripe and you can poke me?

Frisky...

Ok...I'm done lol

(Later)

Lawyer sent some paperwork, went home, got high, finally opened it, he's not contesting or responding to divorce. Appears as if things are going in my favor...so now I'm super high and can't stop smiling. Is it wrong that I'm aching for you again already?

Wooohoooo...not wrong...how you feeling?

Soooo...fuckin' horny for you...want that hard...dripping...precum cock inside me...
How are you feeling?

Feeling good...seems you are frisky

Right??! What the hell is wrong with meeeeee...

Wanted to mention how enjoyable you were to be around today. I could hear how much you care about people you'd rather be a team with and trust to do their job well. It's difficult to feel your loyalty has to shift instead of grow. I've always admired the empathy and care I see in you. Great job. Hoping things turn out as you prefer...

Still working on it...but thank you

***

<u>**Peg's Journal Entry 12/6/21:**</u>

Unexpectedly Gunnar asked to come by this morning. When he arrived he said he was coming over whether my roomie was home or not. One of the symptoms of CPTSD is spontaneity, lol. It's understandable. When it comes to the fight-flight-freeze-fawn dynamic he's definitely more on the fight side whereas I, will fawn more. Somehow it works though…

I do enjoy it when he visits on Mondays because he seems to have had rest over the weekend and he tends to be VERY focused on our pleasures. This guy puts 100% in when he focuses!

He wanted to disrobe me immediately and then wanted to be in my mouth while doing the same to me. It was so hot…him chanting my name…as I sweetly pleasured him, missing him over the weekend. He was quick to move us so he could slide in. I commented, "Wow, want in already huh?" And he eagerly responded, smiling with "Yup!" His slow entry felt so phenomenal, I gasped. He took my breath away further with slow, deep kissing and I wondered what had gotten into him. He felt so good, I wanted to devour him as I felt his body sink so deeply into mine, his strong arms engulfing me and his broad chest pressed up against me. The pleasure he gives is almost indescribable. He whispered into my ear how much he loves the feel of my pussy around him and continued with deeper and slower thrusts that shot ecstasy up and through my chakras like electric.

He started to get close again and slid down to orally pleasure me. He pulls me to the edge of the bed to position himself just so and have his way with me. He enjoys looking down and seeing how he's entering me and then watching my reaction. I come undone with him. I looked up and said, "I want to ride you now, it's your turn to rest." I didn't have to say another word, he helped me up and took my spot so I could sink down onto him and set our slow torturous pace. He looked up and mentioned again that if I weren't "fixed" I'd be so pregnant with his child already. I smiled and nodded. I can tell he secretly likes the thought but it would have us both coming undone if he were right. It's sweet that he loves his children so much he'd think of more. I love kids but…I'm "seasoned" lol.

He enjoys talking during our "connections" and looked up caressing my breasts and asked, "Do you like all your orgasms?" This made me smile. I replied, "Of course, and I've had so many with you so early on in this." This pleased him and when he smiled I locked my lips to his wanting every inch of his happiness. I love to see him smiling and pleasured.

I continued to bury him inside myself and he broke the kiss to remind me of how the first time he ever came inside me was the first night and in the position I had him in. I nodded again remembering how amazing that was. It's nice he reminisces about the details. He's very good with details, I like that our moments are imprinted in his mind. I mentioned how he looked in the candlelight of my room and how we both peeled his uniform off revealing his nakedness. He smiled when I told him of how I was in disbelief at the size of his cock! I knew he had a nice body from his gait and how he carries himself, but nothing was like seeing him naked! I had no idea what all was hidden under his clothes.

I reminded him that it was the BEST "first-time" sex I'd ever had. He continued to hold my hips, letting me rock us closer to climax and nodding. I looked down and told him, "I can feel all of you... every amazing inch." He moved with me and praised me for using him against my clit. I kissed his ear, his face, his mouth and said, "I like how this mind works, the humor, this...b o d y...." I sat up to ride him long and sultry hearing him chant, "yeeeeesssss". I looked at him and said, "Say my name." He purred it as I swayed and rocked to our slow rhythm. I told him, "You're soooo good." He countered with, "I can feel your cum running down me..." I apologized instinctively but he said not to, that he loves my body and he's honored I let him cum in me, my mouth, and ass. I wondered again who, in his life, has rejected him doing so. He asked me then to look at him, I did and he said, "Thank you for giving all of me...you." It felt amazing and I simply replied, "You make it easy for me to want to."

I sat up and really began grinding deep down onto him, squeezing him deep within my womb. I saw it pleased him and so I went a little faster...then a bit faster. He grabbed onto my hips and I knew he was losing control. I continued more until he began speaking my name....then went silent into a blissful release! He pumped and pumped his seed into me and I kept going until after a while, his grasp on my hips began to ease. I smiled, loving making him cum so peacefully. He is divine beneath me.

We laid together for a bit and he described his struggle at work with possibly having to end an officer's fifteen-year career because the guy neglected to conduct a sobriety test on a "friend" who had too many drinks at a local bar and ended up killing an old man, hitting him head-on. I could see in his eyes he hates this part of his work, where decisions and supervisory duties include altering the careers of those you work with. I get why he compartmentalizes the way he must and how the CPTSD processing can be daunting. He let me know he won't be too available and he'll be traveling later in the week. I was grateful we could get together and bring "ease" to each other for a bit.

Somehow we got on the subject of our kids as we were dressing. He said he named each of his children as soon as he found out about them. I found this endearing and remember doing the same with my own as I felt them in my womb. He went on to ask me if I was born in Florida then quickly shifted remembering I'm actually from New Jersey. He then asked oddly, "What were you known for in school?" Like what would people say about me. I tried to clarify by saying, "Like cheerleader or choir chic?" Which I was both. He said no, would people say I was a party girl. I was truthful and said no, I wasn't, didn't do drugs or drink much. Told him the only thing I ever heard, which I thought was amusing, was people would say I was a "rich girl". He said, "Rich girl? Really?" I told him It was comical because we weren't rich, only comfortable, but because my father built us a huge Spanish Hacienda home, people assumed we were wealthy. I told him my father was big into family and enjoyed it when everyone could come over or swim or play football on the front lawn. My heart hurt for a moment thinking of Dad and the unconditional love he had for me. I looked up at him, I know he could see my pain so I brushed it off. It was at that moment I realized he again, reminded me of my father and that I will never regret our tiny connection, for however long we have it. I'm beginning to think no one is as special as an Irishman.

December 7, 2021 6:21 PM

Hi

Hey, hot stuff...you holding up ok?

Loooooooong...day...

Oh...I'm sorry...things looking better?

Just...cop stuff...how are you?

My pink parts...are missing...
yours...

Ohhhh myyyy...
Did you touch yourself last night???

Uh...nope..sleep...
You able to rest tonight or still dealing with shift stuff...

Ohhhh yeah...and more crap...

Oh noooo...it got worse?

Yupper...
Been here since 0800...

Oh shit...I was rooting for it all to go the way you hoped...

Just is...what is...

Headed to the gym to tighten the jiggle...here if you need me.
Anytime for us in a.m. or super busy?

Busy...
9 meeting...
10 training...

342

12 range...
2000 shift start...

Got it...

Wanna be in ya...
On ya...

All..in time...office nookie was badass...

Yes...it...was...

Chapter 22

STALKER STATUS

Dereck looked down at the little Walther P22 handgun he bought her. He smirked, feeling clever and slightly poetic at his decision to use her own gun on her. He walked to the bed and picked up the black hoodie pulling it over his head then placing the tiny gun in the front pouch. He wasn't entirely sure tonight would be the night since he hadn't been able to catch her at home, but he decided if he could somehow get into her bedroom window, he was going to at least fuck her one last time and then do her in. He knew he'd have to because she hated him now enough to rat him out. She was different. Not like all the years before where she'd keep her mouth shut if he shamed her or when she wanted to keep the family together so she went along with whatever he did to her. Now that everything had disintegrated, and she had learned of so many of his indiscretions, he knew he'd have to kill her...then disappear.

He huffed a small chortle as he left his bedroom and turned off the light. He might just leave her alive a while longer in case Dean was right about her being with someone new. He'd like to know who she chose after so many years. The best scenario would be to catch her fucking. He always loved the way she moved and seeing if she was like that with another might satiate him for awhile. Smiling he thought he might just watch through the window and let her live, then again he might hate it. He wasn't sure if he could handle seeing her with someone better. Perhaps she was with some Mexican dude. Peg was always the best he'd ever had, and he wondered if someone new now thought the same.

As he backed out of the driveway, he smiled eerily, feeling mischievous. Minutes later, he parked a street over and diagonal to her place, turning off his engine and lights. Dereck leaned his seat back, exhaling in annoyance because her truck was not in the driveway! He wondered where the fuck she could be and how long he might have to wait. This was not how he'd planned his evening, and it was already the middle of the night. He considered using the time to break into her room and look around. He opened his middle console and took out a tiny LED flashlight, wondering how *quiet* he'd have to be in case the roommate and kid were light sleepers.

He opened the door quietly and stepped out onto the curb. When he tried to bring his right leg out it caught on the inside panel causing him to stumble and catch himself. A fire felt like it ignited inside his sacrum as the nerves in his back spasmed. He grabbed onto the top of the door to catch himself, cursing under his breath at the weakness of his spinal injury. The pain was so bad he had to hold his breath and almost dropped the flash light. He could feel he was losing control of his bowels and tried to get back into the truck without falling. The pain was brutal but he managed to slam the door before screaming. He felt the hot wetness leaking from him and soon smelled his own shit. The numbness came on quick as he began losing his control. Turning the key in the ignition he started the engine and pulled away to head back toward home. Peg had always told him his evil was going to come back at him and haunt him. She called it karma. He thought about how he wanted her dead. It would have to wait.

Chapter 23

THIN WALLS

December 8, 2021 8:48 AM

Hi...I want you...so you know

(Later)

Heyyyy...I want you more...just so you know...my inner cowgirl wants...a ride...

Me tooooo

Mmmm...that makes me happy...my kitty is purring...
Might have to lock myself in my office for a bit of O'Clery self-pleasure time...

Mmmm...tell me more

It's like...our first kiss...
Then your warm hand reaching down to find if I was...aroused sitting next to you in your truck at the laundromat...
Your fingers...my slickness...just from conversation...then our kissing...
Hmmm...couch in my office is comfy...one leg up, the other hanging off...fingers...hood skin swollen...warm...slow circles to match my breathing...

Wowwww...

Clit...very happy...but yoni pulsing and aching for you...your penetration...filling...stretching...your perfect thrusting...
Whispers in my ear...your hips...driving forward...into me...love when you grab my hands and hold them to the bed as you move deeper and let me meet you...then thrust at the end making me gasp!
When you cover my mouth with yours...my breathing muffles...your chest on mine...your tongue exploring...want to grab your back...pull you deeper...pull your ass...into me...soooo missing youuuuu...

(Later)

What ya doin

Thinkin bout...things...you?

Things??? Tired...head bobbing

Oh noooo...you driving? You could come lay it on my chest for a while...

So wish I could

Mmmm...Burnin' that candle at both ends

Been my pace for many years

How's that workin' out for ya? (Sad face emoji)

Yeah...

Survival...

I'm good at that

Can't fault ya...I do it too.

How was your...session earlier...cum??

Mmm...yep, loooong. Dreams lately?

Of course...I dream often...

Can you share or is it secret?

You...
Anal...lots of cum...

Oh myyy...it's nice to enjoy anal again after so many years...to enjoy allll of my favorites...

Favorites??

All our various positions feel soooo good. Wasn't like that for me...before...

You...are very sexual...so sexy

That feels good to hear, thank you. I feel honored to be able to be free and accepted with you...you're fucking hot...
I feel like you're as sexual as me!

Anything...to please you...

Awww...why? It's to please US no?

Cuz...yes...you first...always...

Mmmmmm...such a gentleman. Favorites?

I'm ok with anything

Gotta have favorites...I'm a patient gal...I'll figure them out...definitely want some lube for my office!

Lube...ohhhhhh my

So gooood...

You really enjoy???

I really do...I'd always been sexual...but not like this! I want it allll the time since doing Ayahuasca in September and then experiencing youuuuu...

You are like a badger

(Laughing emoji)
WTF?

Intense little creature

That savage? Temperamental? A lil' too much huh?

Not at all..not one bit...

Hmmm...

Hmmmm??

Well...
I guess I'm your intense little creature then...
So...how's your sensitive tip the days?

Very...

Mmmmm...

December 9, 2021 9:29 AM

Good morning

Hi!
Holding up ok?

I am...you? Working already?

At the gym, then massage at 2:30pm with a dude I'm not particularly fond of. How's work today?

I'm off finally...

Oh great...catch up on sleep?

Roomie home?

Unfortunately yes...think she's depressed...she's in bed. You have time?

Yes...I...do...

Mmmm...love your...yes...

You???

I'll try...my room or office?

Office ok?

That might be more fun. Gotta shower, meet me there at 11?

Yup...please bring lube...

Lol...your wish...
Is my...
Pleasure...

Yes baby...I want your tight ass...

350

Yes...
Sir yes sir...

Ovulation?

Feels like it but not just yet

Wow...super horny???

It's my curse...

Wear those yoga pants...no panties...

K...they won't be on long

Mmmm...

(45 minutes)

HOLD UP !!!!!!!

Huh?

DONTTTTTTT

Ummmm...ok

Partner just...
Said walls are too thin...busted...
Fuckkkkkkkkkk

Heard the other day?

Her...and her client...ugh...

Heard...us?

Yep

Ummm...in trouble??

Being interrogated...rain check or go to my room?

Room...

Meet ya there...need...hug...

Are you gonna get in trouble???

Hope not. Leaving now...

Hope not???? You need this gig...

All good...leaving now...

Sure???

Yep...you?

Sure you still have job?

Lol...yes. Have to clear up miscommunication...roomie leaving...

You sure it's ok?

Yes...tough day...need you...

I'm here...ok to come in?

Please...

(Later)

Hoping you'e safe?

All good...you ok at work?

Karen won't look at me but said hello...walked right to her room.

Will you be...in trouble?

Don't think so...tough day. Had a client who jizzed all over my table...had to deep clean. Ugh...

Jizz?

I could sense he has sexual trauma...trapped in his body...

Ummmm...that sounds complicated...
Just say he has a kink in his slinky...got it...

(Laughing emoji) cop humor...

Soooo...you kinda had a jizzy day!

It was quite...a day..
You had a jizzy day too!

Hands down...best BJ ever...everrrrr...bestest...you are Jedi...

Really?

Yup....

Blushing...

I was...VERY happy...

Jedi? Mmmm...I like that so much better than badger lol...
I get to play with your lightsaber...

Yup...good one...

December 10, 2021 8:17 AM

How are you?

Struggling...how are you holding up?

Why struggle...

Communications with Karen are tough. She derives her significance needs by judging others and holding onto her ideals but at the same time wants to be coached into open-mindedness to free herself. Tough...but this is what I do lol. I think she wants me to feel remorse for being with you in my office...but that's not me. How are the doggos?

I'm sorry...
What do you do now?

Best case...clarity, communication, ease...lol. Worst case? Move out and move on...

Don't want you to lose place there...great place...

Of course not...but I've learned this year to move onwards and upwards in all things. I've taken accountability but that's not what she wants so what's really going on is deeper within her. I have heard from the shake shop that she can be super "stuck up" and is having trouble keeping the place...but that's just in listening to others. Not sure what's true or not. Would rather be shootin shit up today than dealing with these issues. You're ok?

I'm doing ok...kinda stressed bout your situation...

Oooo...I'm sorry...didn't mean to elaborate so much...

No...it's good...just think. You are doing well there...don't want it to stop your progress...

It's all progress...even the tough stuff...

I know...you are correct...

Want you still...dreams?

No...didn't sleep well...

Oh no...unable to nap on the plane...or just strange surroundings in general? Thought my magic would have helped...

Was magic...be assured...

Mmmmm....

Back on plane...zzzzzzzz time...

Niceeeeee...Sweet dreams...

***

<u>*Peg's Journal Entry 12/9/21 - 12/10/21:*</u>

So life took a bit of a turn on me! I kinda always wanted an office booty call experience. It'd been on my bucket list and came true last week when he met me in my office and we had crazy-amazing sex. I will admit, I didn't expect Karen to be in, she showed up while he was on his way, we snuck in...making dope memories.

Unfortunately, allllll weekend, Karen stewed over apparently "hearing" us (my feet and shoulders against the wall when he kissed me then the refrigerator door slamming) and was a bit shady about confronting me, which led me to learn some things about her character as she was trying to put mine down for enjoying sex. She became very interrogative and judgy, not willing to work through things. She seemed infuriated and used a tactic (shaming) Dereck used to use about how "others" were uncomfortable when I know she only had one client and they didn't hear us all that much as she was trying to put forth. I could see her manipulative ways, and as a relationship coach, I know that what she was judging in me were actually unhealed parts within herself. I left before she escalated and told her I would be back to discuss things. I ended up meeting him in my room instead so we could discuss it. He was concerned and supportive as he is...and we eased each other with our sexual pleasures. I did want to bounce it off him for his advice and let him know I was concerned with how she wanted to know who he was. The saddest part was, she was trying to insinuate that I do inappropriate "intimacy coaching," like sleeping with clients, which showed her distrust and her personal issues. I've never once in all the years of working with students and clients crossed a line. Gunnar is not a paying client, nor would I ever allow that. He had to leave for the airport, and I headed back to talk with Karen.

When she arrived she stormed passed me and straight to her room. I believe at that point I knew I'd need to move my office elsewhere as she was overblowing things and quite upset with herself more than my lunch-time quickie. Things did not go well with our texting as she wanted to judge and interrogate more...and my vague answers were more antagonizing her. I understand and take accountability for my actions, quite honestly it's the first time I've done something so fun but "naughty," but my apology was not what she wanted. She wanted to shame me over and over and over and it was best for me to end the situation. I called a friend and negotiated a shared office space around the corner and moved out within an hour...

R o u g h times...

December 11, 2021 2:22 PM

How's it going?

Hi...tough weekend...you ok?

What happened...
I'm good...so far doing ok...
Work???

I start at my new office tomorrow...

New office??? What happened!!

I wouldn't reveal you...she wasn't happy...I left...

Reveal me?

Yeah, not sure why she wanted your identity...I don't need drama...moved out...

She wanted to know who I am?
Where new office??

Yeah...I moved around the corner at Ruby Sans...called in a favor..half the rent, twice the space...my gut said to take it so I moved...

She sounds...kinda creepy...glad you are out...

It got weird...

Yeah...
Reveal me by name...
Hmmm....

I have not...not to anyone...She thinks you're from out of town...I didn't correct her...just let her believe what she wants. Awful few days for me but hoping she lets it go now that I left...

I'm sorry...

Thnx...me too...

What you doing?

High...laying on my bed...you?

Just picked up buddy...for dinner...

Oh ok...enjoy...

How's high?

Just enough...to balance the CPTSD symptoms...why?

Just wondering...if you will...rub clit...

I could...

Should...

You should...

December 13, 2021 1:04 PM

How's new place?

Good! AZ?

Yeah...airport...

Oh noooo...blows...

How are you??

Lonely...how you holding up?

Tired...things ok??

Can't complain...livin'...new book this time on plane?

Same one...almost done...new office ok? Better?

It's good...functional-

Ovulation?? Needing my...swimmers...

Lol...teasing???

Nope...thought of you swallowing last time..
Allllllll weekend...

That was the main thought? Ovulation is tomorrow...

Mmmm...

How are your...sensitive parts?

Very needing your pink parts...

Mmmm...same here...

359

Sooooo wanna spend time with you...wanna cum in mouth...cum in pussy...cum in ass...just stare down as you are exhausted from sex...pleasure...

Wow...

Just saying...a gentle thought...

I like...

Mmmmm...goals...

I enjoy your...gentle side...and you are goal-oriented for sure. How was dinner with buddy? Fun?

Very...good guy...known him since college...

Very cool! Love those types of timeless relationships...

Yeah...he's my oldest best pal...we went to academy together...

Love that...

You play today???

Not yet...gym, tan, shake shop...I'll play if I feel stressed...or lonely...

Ohhh...so when my tongue darts across your clit you will???? Explode?

I doooo...so compatible...you dream any?

Mmmmm...soooo yummy your cum is...Yoda voice and all...
Yes...3somes...

Lol...Yoda...
Ohhh...I must have some sort of 3some vibe...

Was thinking bout your story...very hot...

You like? I do have stories...but I think yours are better...humor and all...

I do...I do...

Making new stories...

More offers lately??

Offers?

Clients...wanting you?

No...
Assholes on Messenger and Instagram, so I just block them...

**Ohhhh...know how the difference will be if you ever decide to have one with me...no rules...
trust you...love to watch...participate...explore...but you and your boundaries...are yours...**

Didn't realize you were so into it...it's been a VERY long time for me...

Been...never for me...but whatever you desire...pleases you...

I enjoy your pleasure...
But 3somes change dynamic forever...you have to be sure...

Would you?
I liked your stories...how the intensity built...and built the more you guys...ya know...

Depends on the connection for me...I may seem like I'm ok with disconnection...but it fucks with me. I knew
Dan for years before letting him kiss me...and things got...well out of hand emotionally...

Ahhh...I see...

Do you have anyone you trust?

**No...just dreaming...great to look down and see you pleased...be great to watch too...you are so
sensual...**

It's not easy for me to feel comfortable with just anyone...the more we're together the more I want to open up...sensual is yummmmmm....

Mmmmm....and that's yummy...

Very...scares me a bit...

Why?

Just new...well, I mean I told you for years I had to hold back, imagine a different face, try to be me but guarded...I heard how amazing I was but from a liar, how no one's ever been so sexual...but again from a liar. It was hard to feel there was truth in it, hard to be free...don't know, was like I was always jiggling the lock of the cage.

...and you jiggle well...so you know...

Thank you...you've got great skill yourself...your missionary play Thursday was amazing...felt like my body was being taken over...

Oh...it was...

Deep kissing...deeper cock...

Very deep...I can feel your cervix...

Good...I was trying to meet you...so good...making me ache now...

How hard did I cum for you?

For me?

In your mouth...I felt I exploded...

You did...in an intense and pleasurable way...you went silent and pumped...and pumped...was amazing. Still learning your...rhythm...and wants...

Was...amazing...

I enjoy learning...studying us...

I wants...you to cum...over and over

Same...your body is magnificent to me...I feel it hasn't been celebrated well...liberated enough...

You certainly do that...

...or touched in all the right ways...places...tied up enough...blindfolded...

Mmmmm...yes please...

Flogged enough...massaged enough...kissed...sucked...caressed...enough...

And you??

Me?

Your needs...desires...

Desires?

Yes???

I want to do it in the bed of my truck...under the stars...whiskey...blankets...music...definitely want to feel you deep in me as we relax in the hot springs...want to do it high...blindfolded...

Me too...love to come by right after you smoke...see the changes...never seen it...never done it...

Lol...probably not that exciting...sleepy eyes, giggling, loooong slow climax...

Yup...thats what I want...

Want to be your first for "high" sex...but not sure how that would happen...

We will figure it out...

Like you...I waited...was a saint until I turned 45...

Wow...

Yup...never did drugs...ever...

First time...what it feel like? Only weed?

Only weed...first time was...safely with my sister. Felt amazing...until we ate a whole bag of chips and laughed at Gigolos on Showtime until she drooled chip dip down her shirt. Was awesome...then we went into her hot tub and I felt like my legs floated away lol...

Perfect story...

Lol, now she tells me I need to come home (NJ) so she can have "puff puff" time lol. She has an amazing husband so I tell her to get baked and smoke with him. She says I'm more fun lol...can't imagine that...

You are...

They think I'm a saint...if they only knew the sexual side...or if I told sis how I now have toxic shame to heal from a prude who couldn't handle my office "lunch break" and how I have a new office...she'd break my balls for weeks!

That chic seems to have psychological issues...like cra cra

I think 3 orgasms a day would keep the cra cra away...lol..

Right...at least...

At least!
What's your opinion on...butt plugs?

You tell me...I'm rookie...

For a rookie...you adapt well...

You tell me...Butt plugs??

I have a feeling you've been a natural at quite a few things in life...they add...more intenseness...to final climax...

Have you used?
Would they be for you...or me??

Both...

You asking for me...or for you to use? Do you have?

Was asking to ascertain your comfort level...

I'm good with whatever you want...Anything...

How's the layover...are you stuck in AZ?

It's ok now...almost boarding...

Oh good!

Untucked shirt...wet precum dripping tip...thnx

Save me some?

Mmmmm....

Now I'm moist again...thnx lol...

I bet...home?? Work??

Driving...picking up rider. Might need to stop home after...for pleasuring lol...

You should...lots

December 14, 2021 12:33 PM

Uhhh...please tell me you're safe? You boarded a plane then vanished (sad face emoji)

I'm good! Got home...crashed out...running around on errands...how are you?

Whew...k...

How's today?

Today was good. Coached a realtor that walked in on a tenant in a casita spread eagle with porn playing and a dildo inside her...facing the door. Took all my strength not to laugh...love my work. Realtor will be fine, has to deal with her own deep-seated issues at catching parents fucking. It's all good. Now, just sitting on my bed playing "author".
How's the stress?

Wow.
Stress free me...zoom meeting...

Oh funzies...

Right
How's next chapter of book?

Cumming along...

Ahhhh...got jokes...

Me??? Noooooo....

Mmmmm....

So, do you remember what sentence or at what moment you knew you wanted to be with me?

First time text...then when in truck...100% knew when walk in your room...was scared... nervous...wasn't sure you were 100% there...at house...yup...we knew before that...yes with sex talks...

I was trying to fight it...but when you showed up in my room that night...the low lighting...taking uniform off...the kissing...that BODY...mmmmmm...yup
We knew!

Mmmmm....cuuuuuuumunication...

366

Foreplay for me...
Heading out to dinner...kisses to your sensitive tip...lol

You too....

(Later)

You okay?

I am...are you?

I ammmmm....

Cuz????

Just like knowing you're safe...the weirdo in me...

I am...I am...how was dinner?

Was fine...I was the happy life coach as usual. Meet people's needs and they'll love you right? lol. Have the night off or surviving another shift?

Night off...back to the grind tomorrow...

Ahhh...back to the grind...

Grind on you...

Lol...

How are you?

Me?

Yup...honestly?

Feeling...too much going out, not enough in...

On???

Oh...with energy. How are you these days?

Tired...getting worn down...energy with??

Just giving to others...need a reboot...

How you get that?

Hot springs...hiking...probably just need to smoke and regulate my brain lol...

You upset with me?

Not at all. Why do you think that?

Just seem off...not sure...can I ask kinda serious question...

Yes...

Will you push back?

Push back?

As I enter you...
In the morning...

Do I ever...not?

Anal?

You wants?

I certainly do...

I enjoy...

Can I come by...cum in??

Can you?

Yes...you???

I might...

Ok...............
Things ok with roomie?

Yes...she's bending my ear as you're
Making me wet...

Ohhh...well tell her to listen in tomorrow...tutoring for orgasms in your room...ovulation nation baby!

I ammmmmm...still ovulating now that you mention it.
She'll be at work but she'd probably like listening in...

Well...9 ish?
I'll be PhD of cum...

Not really wanting a quickie...messes up my chi...

No quickie...I will cum for you...all three...

You sure?
You seem...very distracted?

Not at all...want you to do what you do...

Mmmmkayyyy...

Yes?

Yes...
She just asked the mother of all questions...

What question?

369

Ummm...she asked me if she should say the L word first...
but this guy isn't worth it yet. I advised allowing time and actions before words???
Idk. Not on my best game tonight. Had one of those egg-dropping naps where I had no clue who I was....one
shoe fell off...and she was asking me if I was all right lol.
Anyway, I'll let ya go. Thinking of you...nite-

Wow...thinking of you...nite...

Chapter 24

NOT HOME

Dereck sighed, pissed her truck had not returned to the house. It had been a week or so since he had time to watch her and it'd been hours, she still hadn't returned. He decided to take a chance, since it was pitch black out, and go peek in her window, maybe gain access as he had planned before but lost his nerve.

He stepped quietly through the houses, relieved there were no dogs out in their yards ready to reveal him. His heart pounded in his neck and he thought about turning back towards his truck as the coward within him tugged at his insides. Part of him liked the adrenaline of it all but more of him was concerned about what others would think if he were caught, dressed all in black, breaking into his ex's room with her own gun. After losing her and his entire life though, he just wanted to fuck her one last time, make sure she could never tell, and be in the mountains by the time they came looking for him, elude them, and maybe take a few out before they get him.

Running alongside her roommate's house he made his way, crouched low, to her front bedroom window. There was a low light on which didn't seem right since Peg wasn't home. He lifted his head and peered in between the blinds. Shocked he lowered quickly. The kid was on the floor inside talking to someone on her Ipad! The room was a fucking mess with no items that looked like Peg's belongings.

Dereck cursed under his breath and continued on along the side of the house to the next window. He had told the PI he hired, she was in the front room but obviously that was wrong. There's no way Peg would be in a room that messy, nor would she share a bunk bed with that brat. He could never stand the kid, or her mother, even though he tried to fuck her to hurt Peg.

Just before the next window, Dereck stumbled and hit his big toe. He pursed his lips, muffling the pain annoyed. He was wearing flip flops–they were all that fit his fat, swollen feet. Recovering, he crept up to the window and recognized the low light of her salt lamp. Peg loved all that energy shit so he knew he was at the right window. He lifted his eyebrows and peered through the blinds. Her room was clean, beautiful, and serene just as she was. He exhaled, trying to hate it, but it was her style. Peg always had such style.

His eyes went to the door, it was shut. She had a desk, her chaise, a small twin bed, and art on the walls he recognized from the office she had designed in the Florida house. He wished she'd stayed there. He really thought he could manipulate her for at least another year. Why she didn't want the house, all the belongings, the hot, humid air was beyond him. Convincing everyone she embezzled and wanted his mother's house was gonna be tough now that she left it all and came back.

Her bed was made, her room clean, it made him miss her for a moment but he squinted pushing the emotion away and deciding he was still going to kill her. His eyes searched but he couldn't stop returning to the sight of her bed and pillow. He wondered if that was where she was getting dicked so well, per Dean. He fumed thinking about how she's "having the best sex of her life" and he can't even get a call back from bitches in town. His mind wandered, he could see her riding on top of whoever she was giving herself to. He seethed, thinking about her tight pussy wrapped around him, squeezing and caressing him into oblivion, the way she does. Anger shot through his chest. He could see in his mind how she blows him in her slow, sensual way that renders a man willingly vulnerable. He hates that she probably swallows him and gives him anal too. Peg gives so much when she's receiving pleasure. He shifted his weight on his crouched, aching legs, wanting to punch right through the window!

Suddenly, her door opened and light from the hallway shot in. He lowered, keeping his eyes on the figure in case it was her man. He wouldn't mind taking her new love interest away from her, let her feel that pain before he puts her out of her misery. He recognized her roommate, and her kid who was talking non-stop to her mother who placed a few small amazon packages on the desk, looked around, then left closing the door behind. Dereck exhaled long, realizing how irresponsible he was with his visit. He decided to make his way back to the truck and get a better plan in place. He didn't like that the roommate and her kid were in the house and could identify him if they found him in her room. He much preferred to come back and catch her fucking her guy, maybe put a bullet in them both. The same bullet, through both of them would be a grand story. A smile curled the corners of his mouth as he turned to go.

eg pulled into the driveway feeling a bit exhausted and deciding an Epsom salt bath would do nicely before bed. She had to admit to herself, she was excited at the thought of seeing him in the morning. She really enjoyed their moments...and the lasting memories she regaled in her mind for days and days after.

unnar tossed and turned in his bed. He wished sleep wasn't so elusive on nights off. He was looking forward to seeing Peg in the morning. He turned onto his back, looking at the ceiling and seeing her in his mind, above him, riding his cock so slow and sensually the way she does. He's never felt a woman so tight and pleasing. He had to admit he did want her soul and often felt she was handing it over as he was inside her, but Peg was beautifully complicated...and not so easy to tie down.

His eyes started to feel heavy and as he saw her in his mind, doing so many pleasurable things to him, him driving her into ecstasy and hearing her gasps. Drifting off, he heard her whisper "save me some" the way she would and he smiled, liking when she would ask for anything. Visions of her intimate toys flashed through his mind, then her sleepy bedroom eyes...then her...smile.

December 15, 2021 7:24 AM

Hi

Hi

What ya doin?

Waking...
You?

Wow...wish I was waking you up...

That would be a memory to cherish...but I think I'd prefer to wake you...

How would you?

Tongue...to sensitive tip...swirling around...areas

Wow...well done...precum dripping now...

Mmmm...

So roomy was flipping out??

Not flipping...just suffering rejection...breaks my heart...

She ok...you ok?

Yes...thank you. You feeling alright? Dream?

I am...
I did...blindfolds...butt plugs...lots of oral...

Oh myyyyyyyy...

You moaning...begging...for pleasure...and anal...

374

Mmmm...I'm working on moaning softer...others don't seem to be able to handle our pleasure...

You dooo...you handle it well
Can I come over? You suck me...I cum inside you...slide my cock in your...
Just a thought

Wow...lots of thoughts there...

Analysis is my thing

So true...

Roomy there??

She's getting ready to leave for work...

Would you like me to cum by?

Lol...Yes...

Wooohooo
How's your ovulation today?

Dripping...needing your...healing?

Dripping...ohhhhhhhhhhhh myyyyyyyy...

You drip...I drip...we drip! (Laughing emoji)

Funny! Can you puff puff before I get there????

Uhhhh...let me see if she leaves early enough...I can go out on patio.
Want to analyze me high huh?

Yes...
I do...very much
What ya thinking?

Today...in general?

Yupper...

Hehehehehheeeeeee

The tip of my cock...is throbbing...

I can help with that...

Yeah?
Roomy???

Rushing out...has to be at work by 9...

Ok

Left...

Door open?

Heading to the door...

Walking up...mmmmm...

(Later)

Mmmm...I've decided...

Yes?

Age 48...
Best Sex Of My Life...

That...was very...VERY intense....

Hands down
Is there a stronger word...for intense?

376

Not yet...

(Later)

Del told me today at shake shop that my multiple orgasms are some sort of magic dick leprechaun shit...I was laughing hysterically.

You are giddy...

Sorry...

It's awesome...

My goofy side is not pretty...I usually tuck it away. Hope your shift has started easy...

Will be a great day...

Still...dripping. Damn...that was phenomenal...You're good!!

Wow....yeah!!!!!!!

Wanted to mention...
It meant so much to me that while you were entering and tantalizing my cervix...you took the time to whisper in my ear and let me know how remorseful you felt about my having to move offices because of our "lunchtime tryst" at the old place. You've been supportive and kind to me in a difficult time. To hear your apology made me feel less alone in it. Thank you for caring. Gratitude to you for being a man in my eyes... while ravaging my body as no man ever has. I appreciate you...

Wow...uh...

No words needed. Just...thank you.

***

<u>*Peg's Journal Entry 12/15/21:*</u>

He was apologetic for his part in our lunch-time tryst and showed remorse deeply...while in me DEEPLY! He went on to apologize if he came off as "vulgar" regarding threesomes and our texts about them. I enjoy his passion and his ability to think things through...even in our intimate moments. I enjoy pleasuring this man more than any other and he reciprocates in kind! I can't remember a more compatible lover and told him I feel I am having, at age 48, the best sex of my life. I believe it's almost perfect...if I could have him on the daily, or wake up with him in my bed...then I'd say with confidence it was perfect. Very grateful to have his pleasure at this juncture of my life. He is lovely...

After so many fun, slow and sexy positions we ended with anal and he cried out my name as we climaxed. It was amazing to hear him calling me as he crashed over. Looooove it!

Afterwards, he regaled me with tiny shares about himself. I learned he has a brother he doesn't care for very much, he's been a Lieutenant for years and cares not to go any father. Of course, I asked why he isn't a chief, and he shook his head and said he'd never want that job. I agreed and felt the same when I was in for a short time. Too political, not enough hands on problem-solving. He is definitely great "hands-on" (lol).

He spoke of kayak fishing and how he was a boat owner. I didn't share how much I love paddle-boarding and kayaks because watching his eyes light up and a small smile grow upon his lips entertained me immensely. He mentioned a lot of travel coming up and I noticed he isn't as much money-driven as he is about the growth and contribution parts with a little "recognition" spice thrown in there. I totally get him as I am very much like that but he doesn't need to hear that.

His mind is beautifully twisted like mine and he's much better at hiding his CPTSD symptoms. He showed great empathy when explaining about a pastor whose wife passed from cancer and asked him "What am I going to do without her?" He shared that his first thought was sadness but his immediate second thought was the old, "The best way to get over a woman is to get under another one." Of course, I cracked up laughing because I'd think the same damn thing in a weird trauma-minded cop thought but like him...would never say it to the intended. He canted his head and we both laughed again. He thinks I'm the one who's complex...but it's really the "survival warped mind" that causes the complex part. I'm not quite sure why or how we crossed paths this way but I can say I kinda get the guy. Best dick in Las Ramas too...

December 16, 2021 8:56 AM

Hi
You holding up?

Hiiiiiii...
Just waking up...my kitty...is still purring...mmmmm

How you doing? Sore?

378

Yezzzzz...pleasantly so. Magic-dick type sore lol...slept in like some lazy gal...

Wow...

Wow?

Yeah...your pussy felt amazing yesterday...you made me explode with cum...just...wow...

It was...a lot...

Yes...3 times...

Yezzzz!! I think my most intense, although I loved each, was in reverse cowgirl...with the anal a close second... you?

You came so hard riding reverse...squeezing me....creaming...

Yes, you made me cry with a full-body explosion. I've been able to relax...more and more...

Yes...you have...you just laying in bed??

Yeah...supposed to be in the shower...you get any sleep?

I tried...rested...slide a finger in your pussy...

Already done babe...couldn't resist remembering your breath on my neck and your cock deep in me...

Wow...soooo hot...you have appt?

Yes. Later, after 2pm. How are my favorite pink parts today?

Tip wet...

Mmmmm...love that...

We're you quiet this morning? Wake up roomie?

I'm quiet unless you make me...not. She was gone already. I have a hard time keeping my breath when you thrust...

Yes...you moan...lots...especially with anal...

Oooooh my yes...analgasms are a whole different world lol...I enjoy your moans too...

Was my cum dripping out all day?

Yep...

How's pussy feeling now...throbbing?

Achy...pulsing yes...

You're sooooo...hot...

My body reacts to our...communications...

Yes...yes it does...

Never really got this worked up before...I guess because we started out just sexting...

Well...you cum so much...your pleasure is amazing to watch...

Feel the same...I enjoy bringing you to pleasure...

You gonna shower?

I'm trying but...

But??? Round 2...I'm thinking your should rub your clit...

I could...

Dick is growing...your glaze on my cock in the sunlight of your room...mmmmm

Loooove that...your cock grows so well for me...

Yes...you make me soooooo hard...

Mmmmm...

Are you rubbing??

Done...when you mentioned glaze...I could imagine you entering in long and deep...warm...
thrustinggggggggg....

Yes....
Deep yesterday...you pushed...up and back...

Your perfect curve gliding my g-spot up to my cervix for a perfect womb...kiss...

You naked???

I like to push back and try to grip before you retract...not naked...only you get me naked...

Peg...

Mmmm....yes?

Wanna fuck babe?

I...do...

20 minutes...naked...legs up...rub your clit...I'll walk in...just slide deep inside you...kiss you deep...

Mmmm...sir, yes sir...

Driving...how's clit feeling?

Swollen...
Tip?

Can I walk in...
Just thrust in you?

381

Yes...

Mmmm...how many orgasms already today?

Only 2...

Only...wow...

Sex I dreamt of...for years...

You like...bigger cock now??

Yes...you've corrupted me...

Mmmm...

Ok...ready for you...

We shall see...

Mmmm...

(Later)

Mmmmm....

Was...great...

So...was...

Wanted to mention how much I enjoyed our talk. I heard you when you were sharing about the tough retirement decision stuff. I recognize you have to make tough decisions all through every shift and it's got to get so tiring. I commend you for thinking ahead on whats best for you though and I feel it's incredibly logical to perhaps get out while things are good. You have to admit having the reputation of "O'Clery was a damn good cop" is desirable because that can never be taken from you. I like how your mind works...keep that shit up. Gotta watch your six because nowadays it seems no one else will. Great job... Damn sexy.

Thank youuuu....

Gonna head to bed...kisses to all your big parts...

Mmmmm....make me...

Would love to...still wet for you after all these hours...

Damn girl...

Been a great week...

Yup...yup...

Still taste you...damn boy...

Damn...girl...

Gift that keeps on giving...

Yup...yup...

Nite baby...sleep warm and safe...kisses to your sensitive tip...

***

<u>Peg's Journal Entry 12/16/21:</u>

So...to my pleasant surprise, he visited again. Two days in a row is amazing and despite being sore, we made it so much fun! He mentioned drinks and how he'd like to watch us begin to relax, dance close. I asked, "You dance?" And he replied, "I can tear it up a bit." I was impressed and thought about how I enjoy his open-mindedness and zest for adventure.

He was super slow and everything felt even more intense. I asked at one point if he knew how he'd "like to cum today" and he whispered in my ear, "I'm waiting for you to tell me. I will, anywhere you say it's okay." I replied, "Thats not how this works, you give pleasure, you get pleasure." He looked down and smiled at me, driving deeper and deeper into me causing me to lose my words.

We went on and on to do many things. At one point he got up and walked to the window to open the blinds a bit more stating, "I love the sunlight on your pussy." It was endearing and made me smile but there was a part of me that felt Dereck could be lurking right outside my window. I wouldn't be surprised if he sits with binoculars, watching our passion, and jerking off his thumb-sized pecker to the sight of Gunnar's gorgeous ass. I smiled opening my arms to him and inviting him back to me on the bed.

I pleasured him orally again...and again, then climbed on him sinking down in cowgirl position as I know it's a new favorite. I tortured him slow and rocked my hips in a way that he could catch glimpses of his huge cock entering and opening me. The visuals blow his mind and after a long while of building up his climax, I picked up the pace and took him until he could hold on no longer. Once he grabbed onto my hips and went silent I knew I lulled him into ecstasy and I rocked and rocked and rocked until his grasp and breathing regulated.

When I lay down along his body he mentioned my heart was beating "so fast" and I smiled not mentioning how he gets me so hot I just want to cum all day. I love our sex!

We started talking and he admitted he's been considering retirement very seriously before something happens or he gets "jammed up". I shared with him that in martial arts I had always thought it was best to depart when one was "on top" or won their championship, that way they go out a winner, nobody challenging the title, and for the rest of life everyone gets to "wonder" if they could have ever taken that title. He stared at me and nodded. I then mentioned if he leaves now as a "top cop", he'll always be remembered as that. I feel for him though. I don't know if he'll ever be able to really leave. The mindset anyway. Tough stuff.

He shared information about a foster kid situation where he really couldn't see a solution unless the court got involved. I listened, then mention I was a foster parent. He was surprised. I told him it was truly a different world and that I had, had eleven foster kids but Dereck ruined it and the money I was bringing in. I shared with him about Geraldo and the plastic hanger slip-in-fall anal surgery. He found my story very amusing and I realized again we'd have a great time over drinks with all the shit we've seen and been through.

As he got up to dress he mentioned Dereck's father and how he felt he was a "good man" but that he never spoke of Dereck much at the shake shop they all used to frequent. He sat down on the bed beside me to put on his shoes and mentioned how my ex always wanted something from him in the way of coordinating trainings but he just couldn't bring himself to do it, there was something he couldn't trust about Dereck. I told him I was happy he went with his gut!

I enjoyed today very much and feel wondrous sleep coming on. I continue to enjoy our "quality time" so much...and two days in a row. I'm sore, but a damn good sore.

December 17, 2021 12:42 PM

Hey you...

Dropped my phone...screen totally fucked...grrrr

Oh nooooo...are you able to fix?

Sending one...grrrrrr....

I'm sorry...

Daughter has softball all weekend...

Try to destress watching her...

That's my plan...
Will be away from broke phone tonight...muah...muah...

December 20, 2021 11:42 AM

Hello...
Phone soooooo jacked...can only use 1/2 screen

Hey...

Stupid phone...

I understand the frustration...

(Later)

Holding up ok?

I am...how are you...hate broke phone...

Gym time...

Good workout day?

Tough how much phones have become a part of us...

Ivhatesss...
I hates it...

Lol...Well...I'll let you go...
Ease your frustration...

Not frustrated...how was your weekend?

I'm alive...happy to know you're safe...

I'm great...

Love hearing...

(Later)

What you doing tonight?

Nothing...you? Just got home...

Just working...woohoo...

Fun times...
Roomie is all showered...waiting on ex to come over...for sexy time...

Oh wow...she need tips??

Lol...got jokes tonight...

What ya doing...

Being a couch potato...wondering if you've forgotten about my...gifts?

Ohhhh no way! Your gifts are many...roomy get stood up??

Yep...she went to bed...very sad, breaks my heart...

Ohhh shoot. Sorry, was on homicide...couldn't answer

386

Oh myyyyyyyy....

Don't rob stores...won't get shot...

Right!
One less criminal...

For sure...tried to rob the smoke shop...dude walking in plugged his ass...

Wow...one bullet do it?
Thoracic or headshot?

The one to the chest did it...

Love it...
Well, on that note I'll bid you farewell-

Farewell??

Meant goodnight. Hoping you're warm and safe...

Will be bout 0200...kinda cold out...but...better than bad guy with bullet in chest...

Oh, hells yes. Hate that you're in the cold...keep all my favorite parts warm and protected. You did well with half-cracked phone screen...

Sucks

Yep, you're resilient for sure lol
Roomie set me up with her psychic tomorrow...should be interesting!

December 21, 2021 12:34 PM

How's psychic?

Hi!

Uhhhhh...interesting to say the least. Didn't expect you to come through...apparently, our connection is...

Is??

More intense than I'd thought. How are you today?

I'm lazzzzzy...gotta work...

Awwww...gotta rest up in order to deal with all that shift crap huh?

**Yupper
What ya doing today?**

At the shake shop. Krista just shouted from the back that her kid gave her a golden shower (she was changing his diaper)

Wow...

Wow???

Golden shower...

Yeah, joke was about my last name and...well, ever had?

No...you?

No. I have many talents but I can't say that's one of them...

Soooo many talents...

Psychic asked me to ask you if you feel there is a "corruptive" female energy in your home. Someone "lacking in mind and body that you wish would...evolve? Told her I did not know...

Don't think so...

She's never met me...but asked me who drowned!! Was like, "that would be my father...in 92'...scuba diving accident with my brother and 20 other divers. They couldn't save him."

388

Shit...

That was just the beginning...I'll spare you the details. How's your shift? Full of homicide paperwork I bet...

Tons...called in early...bolo...violent robbery...
She ask about sex???

These robberies are fucked up...She asked me if I shake during or after sexual connection with my...

Your?

Twin Flame lover?

Flame?

Yes? I shake huh?

Yup...yup....

She mentioned your humor...

I'm a funny guy....
What else?

Then she blew my mind with..."yeah, that's why he sent him, they have that humor" so I asked "who?" She says "you know who Peg, that's why they have the same hands..." I about pissed myself. When I met you at the laundromat and held your hand I noticed you have the thick Irish hands...

Dad...

Yes...
She asked first time I met you...I couldn't remember the exact year...I said 2012? She asked if my ex talked about me to you sexually...says my "evil" (ex) crossed paths with you...

I understand...he never spoke to me bout that
What else?

Head spinning...going through my notes here....

Wow...I bet

Mentioned I was too confined? Imprisoned energetically. With ex, which I was already very aware of...

Sooo...you like being set free...stretched?

Yes, O'Clery...I do lol...
I should stop boring you with all this...

Hehehehe...not boring...what else?

Uhhh...she mentioned endings must take hold for beginnings coming. Uhhhhhh...stagnation can kill growth...speed bumps are necessary. She didn't clarify that because the next sentence was weird...she said it was about the October secret...

Oct secret?

Right...I asked same...she mumbled, "The baby will have his humor."

Huh?

She looked at me funny...so of course, to clear things up I said, "I can't get pregnant." She said, "You can't?" I said, "I'm almost fifty." She laughed. Then she said, "What baby is a secret then?" I told her my grandson is due in July and is currently being kept a secret from my ex because my daughter asked that he not be told until he moves away. She doesn't want him staying and using the baby as an anchor to stay close to her in Las Ramas.
She then nodded and said again, "Yes, the son will have the same disposition and humor as your father."

Ohhhh...so she didn't ask about great sex?

Lol...not too much. She told me this is an extremely important time in my life...could last next 9 cycle years.

Wow...

Says there is a female energy around me who's "condescending" not always "for" me, more so jealous and competitive. She told me to be careful of those who appear supportive but are not...and to watch closely who I live with...shit...

Old business partner?

> *Roomie I think. Do you know she just told me tonight she*
> *fucked her ex-hubby today while I was out...*

Good thing?

> *Noooooooooo...She was with STI guy 5 days ago...ex-hubby is her baby daddy!*

Ohhhhh....

> *Yeah, limp noodle diabetic ex-husband...who now will have STI...*

Ohhh nooo....limp?

> *She mentioned he was able to get semi-hard but not finish...yikes. None of my business really....*

Well...if she shared...

> *Right.*

What you think...
About psychic...

> *Still processing...*

Bout?

> *Body...*
> *Mind....*
> *Hell, all of it...was a good day but lots of info in...*
> *Trying to process out...Hope you're well?*

I'm good...been busy...busy...get phone tomorrow...woohoo...

> *I bet that makes you happy!*

Yes...how are you...needing at all???

Are you offering? Are you at all...needing?

Yes...yes I need!

What do you need?

Big...hug...

Ohhhhhh I likey your big hugs...

Mmmmm...I'm a hugger...

Master hugger...make me...gush...

Yes...you do...
When's roomy gone?

Works Thursday...but she owes me now..twice lol...

Fuck it...she can listen in...take notes...

Stop...lol

Been...needing you...

Really?

Yup

Blushing...

(Later)

OMgggg...roomie's STI ex is on his way over to fuck! She asked, "Should I shower?"
I'm dyin'! That's both guys in same day!!!
I told her yes to shower!

Wow...

...and yes...on shower power

Lol...right? Two guys in one day?
I was like, "Yes! A shower is a must!
He was concerned with my whereabouts...in the house. I'm staying in my room. Music on so they think I can't
hear. Godsmack...Metallica...writing book...so wet for you....

(Later)

So...he stayed...to watch a movie out in the living room...I think he was trying to listen in thinking we were in
my room...
Gnite...you're wanted...just so you know...

Muah

Muah

Peg's Journal Entry 12/21/21:

As an early Xmas gift to myself, I booked a psychic session with my roomie's psychic she speaks highly of. I've had luck in the past with readings, at least in the area of helping me manifest life forward. I take what I like and leave the rest. This one was interesting, to say the least. The following came through for her:

My energy came through and showed things work out for me quickly especially when I remove fear, guilt, and harboring. Harboring was explained as my "secret thoughts"

Says there's an evil energy after me. Arbitration is needed and will work out so no need for fear

Mentioned the word "widow". Says she got chills that the word widow keeps coming through. (Weird to hear)

Congratulated me on "coming home" to Las Ramas. I must retreat, reflect, and trust my inner instincts. There will be mystery and passivity

She stated I am in Tempress Energy, sexually attractive, alluring and seductive in a way that can bring about balance and patience (thought that was interesting)

Says I need to master my raw emotion to overcome challenges

I am to let go of harbored guilt with my children and years of trying with a fraud (ex)

Mentioned an older woman, sharp-witted, candid, stepping into my life that protect and assist me to overcome problems

Says I MUST rest as my manifestations are coming

393

Asked why I wanted a reading when I'm already clairvoyant and aware. Do I need validation? Said I'm already a "badass" and must believe in me

Again said I must rest before all that's coming so as not to hinder the ripple effect

Says to pay attention to the ringing in my left ear, it'll be higher pitched at times I must pay more attention

Must attune with frequency music for "healing"

Asked about dots...like a first connection to "him" (Ellipses!!)???

Went into "the new people in your life will be your soul tribe you need" and that I shouldn't be standoffish, I should allow them to fall into place and come into my vibration

I need to manifest more often for smooth sailing (income, quantum leaping, indigenous resilience, etc.)

Says I need to tread on eggshells with "him", very alluring, tempting. He's having a hard time "letting go" of something, wants to "become single"

Manifest and send love towards him

He's a "feeler" and "lacks in unhealthy ways"

Says to protect my energy, ask guides to "show"

Mentioned "he" has someone in his life with a corrupt female mind who cannot evolve, someone lacking in body/mind balance

"He" must clear his conscious by letting go of what no longer serves him. Endings will foster new beginnings, he must stop hindering growth with stagnation and suffrage

Says my soul tribe does not want me to be confined or imprisoned, they want you to enjoy yourself

Mentioned I must continue to draw in kundalini awakening, use my body (oh myyyyyyyy)

Said to be patient with Karma and allow it to be captivating! Your father is finger-wagging "I sent him but not right now, you must be patient." (WTF???)

Asked "who drowned"? Says he watches over (whoa)

Mentioned a twin flame lover (holy shiiiiiit)

There was a lot more she "sensed" but didn't make sense just yet. I am thoroughly exhausted and have much to study. Overall, my life is gripping...I just hope to get a grip lol. Wow!

December 22, 2021 11:50 AM

Gotta lay back on phone today...getting new one...will hit you up tonight

(2 hours later)

...I'm baaaaaaaack...woohoooooo...

Hey

HI there...

Hi

What ya wearing???

Hoodie, leggings...etc.
And you?

Superman underwear...only

Nice! With a cape?

No cape...can get caught in gun when I draw

Oh wow...yeah, can't have that...

What ya doing...phone all good now...

Chillin after Xmas Party at work today...too "peoply" out. Hiding out at home. You?
Feel good when the phone works well huh?

Daydreaming

Mmmm...share?

Bout your...pussy

Really?

Very...yes

Elaborate Mr. Details...

...mmmmmm...swollen lips when stimulated...erect clit...taste of your cum

Mmmmmmm...

When full of cum...how it dribbles out...

Does it? I don't get to see that angle...

Yup...beautiful view

You're sweet...good for my self-esteem

You're great for mine

That makes me happy...

You touch yourself???

Not so much lately. You?

Having any whiskey?

*Naw, been a rough few days energy-wise. Processing.
Have you partaken in any fun holiday cocktails?*

I wish...energy?
Need a monster drink

I bet you're exhausted...

What's wrong with your energy?

Ya ever just feel off? And...the psychic stuff has got me researching and such...I love to learn. The place I'm at is requesting a Tantra class...was approached twice today by two different gals. Gotta get my energy in check lol. How are things with all this Xmas extra? Not my fav time of year lol...

I am ultimate grinch...

Ahhhhh...more we have in common. Roomie took me out last night to a store and I think I'd rather put a bullet in my big toe than be around shopping idiots. I wanted to escape to Ruidoso and stare at freagin' deer drinking from a stream. Bah humbug lol...

Great deer...bad-ass stream...

Beautiful there...

With you there for sure...

That...was nice to say...
Wow...what I would do to you tucked away in a lil' cabin...

Such as...

Starting out...would really like to caress your sensitive tip...shaft....balls...backdoor with my tongue...while naked on a rug in front of a fire...then christen every surface in the place as the weekend unfolded...and...

Wowwwwzy...What have you wanted sexually...but never had...

Haven't done it in the snow yet...

What else?

Done pretty much everything my body wants...haven't done it on a beach...or the back of my truck...you?

Whatever you desire...
Beach

You told me you've been all over the world...

Never had sex on a beach...

Mmmmmmm...best place to have sex? Should make the bucket list? Country...state?

Ruidoso snow storm...

I think the hot springs. Under the Aurora Borialis in...Alaska maybe...
Snowstorms are soooooo...yummmmmm
Always wanted to on a private jet...

What you and roomie doing...watching Die Hard?

Lol...I'm banging away at the laptop keys...more chapters in my book here on the couch...she's hibernating in her bedroom...says she's meditating. She's got a lot going on...
Are you watching Die Hard...The truest Xmas movie lol...

**Best Xmas movie
E V E R**

Lol...makes this shit holiday easier to get through for sure...

What's this chapter on?

Anal...anal virgin chapter...

Wow...soooo...a documentary....

People who read it will definitely make sticky pages lol...

Like Scooby doo???

Meme: When you take 3 Tylenol PM and try to crank one out before falling asleep (Scooby doo passed out with pink toy in hand)
Scoooooooooooooooooobyyyyyyy lolololol...

Ohhhh my...
That's soooo funny...I took 3 Benadryl last night...totally in fog...

Be careful...

Right
Slept well

That's good! Probably like a rock with 3 benes...

Been tired lately

Just promise me...

Yes...

You'll switch to weed and kayaks when you're done being a top cop overachiever. The uppers of 5hr energy/ monsters then benes will fuck up your BP and then your penu will quit working by age 51. So many of my clients are...
Dealing with it.

Penu???

Big...cock...

Ohhhhhh...that...

Must protect your assets...

You touching your assets???

Last night. Orgasms soooo long and strong this week. Not sure why. Hormonal I guess. You?

No...running around...last minute Xmas crap...was clit throbbing?

Yep. Swollen. Sensitive

Wow...hormonal???

Always...One-rolling into next...

December 23, 2021 10:44 AM

I would love to watch you masturbate...start to finish

I don't think it's a pretty sight lol...but I love that mind of yours...

It is...you pleasing yourself...mmmmmmmmm...study guide for me-

I haven't felt you need to study me much...not one thing I don't like...

I could watch....as you begin orgasms...I would stroke myself....as you continue to cum...I would be kneeling over you...my sticky hot cum...all over clit...lips...pubic hair...you keep rubbing with my cum...

Mmmm...such a beautiful visual...

Yup...your fingers...sticky...both our cum...

Mixes well...
Welp...now that I'm sufficiently wet in my outfit. I'll be off playing Santa w/the girls at the shop. I found gold-colored travel-size vibrators for them!! Gonna be so cool

Very cooooool. Wanna kiss your wet places...

I would like that, O'Clery...holidays suck.

Why???

I plan to be high through this one...the next ones will be memory makers!
Was asked to teach Tantra in their yoga classroom...seems no one in Ramas is doing so. Could be interesting to get back to it.. Thinkin' on it.
*I'm thinking I could end each class with "Namaste M*thaf*ckers" lol...just kidding...*

Now who gots jokey jokes

Lol...sometimes. I tuck that away most days.

Nahhhh...let that dragon loose

400

Hmmmm...with this dark mind...most don't get me...

(Later)

How's was gift giving??

Uhhhh...gifts are in my truck. Have to wait until their kids aren't around...will be a hoot!

Yes it will...
That's hot they get those little fuck trophies

I can figure out people's needs pretty quickly most days lol...Fuck trophies? Bahawahahahaaaa
Was a big hit! Lol. Induced blushing and excitement.
They gave me earrings lol...

I bet...

(Later)

Video Sent: Metallica: Nothing Else Matters
Those moments...when nothing else matters are my favorite...

...I just listened to that on Spotify...listening to for whom the bell tolls

Nice!! Love! Traffic sucks but at least the music is good...

Very good...

How it all started...
Meme: Just so you know, nothing accidental goes in your butt.
Sincerely, The ER Staff

Now we are allllll about the ass play

Bahawahahahaaaaaa...

What ya doing...wish it was me...

That would be sooooo nice. On my way to the gym. You?

Out fighting crime...

Mmmmm...sexy. That uniform...I remember seeing what was under it that first night...

Ohhhhhhh girl...I'm blushing

Well, I'm gushing...gotta work out so I finally sleep...

I have seen you...gush

I've never...seen you blush

Seen my eyes roll into back of my head

Soooo wanna see that....or

Or???
You did with last BJ...

Last one? Or anal play one?
Or...I like seeing your toes point when I reverse ride you...

Anal one...omg

Hehehheeeee
I have got a few Santa surprises for you, I think you'll like them...

Ummmm...hints????

Sorry, no hints...it must all be felt

Ohhhhh. My...how's workout

*Ran 12 mins...now I just wanna f*ck...*

Rolling orgasms

Lol. Just abs, ass, kegel combo. Oblique kegel combo is causing some heat...

Very warm...lots of heat

So...

Yes???

No words...if you can believe that...
Had to take a cold shower...how's the shift treating you?

Good...wish I was...in you

Wish too...kinda bummed. One of my gifts for you.
It's too big...lost my DDDs so things are falling out...
My nip...won't stay in the slit...
(Pic of black lingerie front)

Ohhhhhhhhh...snap

Snap huh...lol

Like the button on my pants

Yummmmmm...wanna see the back?

Yes...I...do...

You sure...

Yup...pleeeeeaaaase...

I like when you say please...and my name...

When deeeeeep in you...

Oh yes...

You rubbing your????

Lol...no trying to distract myself watching TV...

Meme: **Horniest**-*Taurus, Virgo, Aries, Sagittarius, Scorpio*
Naughtiest-*Pisces, Cancer, Libra*
Kinkiest-*Leo, Capricorn, Scorpio, Gemini*
Wow...

Twice on list!!!

Right???? Only sign that's listed twice. I likeyyyyyy

Wanna bend you over bad...

Mmmmmmm...I do like your doggie...style...

Deeeeeeeep...thick...stretched

Sooooo deeeeeep...
Your perfect curve...hits my g-spot...perfectly...

You cum hard doggy...and reverse

I do...I do...but, if I remember correctly...you do as well...

Yes...very...great view

It'll get better...6 more months at the gym...

Looks amazing everyday

Yes...you do...every damn time...

Wet?

Torturously so...

Mmmmm...slide two fingers in...

I really need you baby...

How????

Any way you choose...

You choose

Any way you want...

You select

(Sent pic of black lingerie back with side-boob)

I would kiss every part in that pic

Mmmmmm...yes please...

I like your legs up too...clit glides on shaft

YES please...

You cum so much...you get sensitive and stop me

I'm sorry...

I like that...

Like which part?

That you cum soooooooo much...know what and when you need

I've never cum this much...you and me together is...

Wow...you are electric...

That felt great. Thank you!

Wish I were there...would wake up your roomie with your moans

Lol...maybe. I'm learning to...be quieter...

Ummmmmm...no....

Besides...when I'm quiet I can hear all the flattering things you whisper into my ears...which get me hot for more climax...

You are so beautiful...keep me hard for long time

I hear that's your natural magic dick leprechaun way lol...

Irish energy

My favorite...

Touching yourself yet???

(Sad face emoji)

Ohhhh no...you ok???

Yes...you?

Very...tip of dick wet...

Mmmmm...what my mouth would do...to your tip...

How hard did I cum in your mouth...when you were fingering my ass?

It hit the roof of my mouth...hot...slightly faster...

Lots??

Yes...had to swallow..and then again...so I wouldn't...
drool lol...

Can keep in mouth...straddle me...fuck me...kiss me...share our cum

I could...yes...I guess I shouldn't be so...greedy?

Up to you...almost period time?

No...sorry

Ohhhh...unless I sent seed and it worked

You better hope not...

Why

Seriously?

Just saying...

Saying?

Preggo you...be hottttt

You think I'm horny now...that would be intense!

Right...amazing

And my luck and your fertility...we'd have triplets!

Mmmmm...Ex bugging you anymore???

Feel bad each month...it's like your soldiers are all searching doing their best...and my egg is floating out
there somewhere like duuuuuuh...lol
Not since I threatened him-

It's ok…I enjoy…your ovulation…your menstrual cycle…hormones are awesome…

Seems like the "in between" week we're not together though. No interest?

Ohhhh hell no…very interested
V E R Y

I miss…

What you miss?

Your eyes, your lips on me, your twisted mind like mine, your chest, those arms holding me down…your thrusts deep…when you make me feel important…and alive…

You are alive…and beautiful…and wanted…needed…desired

You…are a beautiful soul…
Welp, I know it's your Friday so TGIF lol…be safe. I wish you the best Xmas my grinch (lol) with lots of hugs. I'll be thinking of all your kissable pink parts…muah…muah…gonna "pullback" as you say, to process better…

Meaning?? I understand…ok

Chapter 25

TIS THE SEASON

Dereck looked down into the glass of crown royal he'd almost polished off sitting in his father's recliner seething. His eyes everted to his crotch. He hadn't had a full erection in weeks. His eyes scanned the room they'd once shared, all scent of her now gone except for the few pieces of clothing in her laundry basket. He'd kept them unwashed to hold onto her pheromones, but even they were fading after a year.

A commercial blared on the flat screen. Christmas Eve sales at Walmart. He thought about how everyone is out doing their festive holiday bullshit. He thought about getting up and driving over to her, having his way with her tight holes, but with the state he was in, she'd surely overpower him. Peg was scary strong for a woman. He'd always regretted training her. She was a much better black belt than he ever let her believe. She would have to be taken by surprise when he did get her. He couldn't have anyone know, and he **couldn't** ever have a record. With so many of his former martial art students being in law enforcement, it would be much more embarrassment than he could stand, and he knew if Peg was left alive, she'd turn his ass in without batting an eye.

He took the last sip, tilting his head back, the recliner inching farther and squeaking a bit. He let his arm fall, and the glass rolled out of his hand and across the tiled floor he had done for her and she never got to see. His eyes moved and he tried to focus on the textured paint of the ceiling. *Chocolate milk.* He even remembered the name of the paint they picked out when building the house he'd locked her out of three months ago. There was even a time he thought he could shoot his load as far up to the ceiling...thinking of Peg, not anymore. He couldn't even get hard now. He watched the ceiling fan blades go around and around, still in disbelief that she was not coming back. Out of everything he got away with, it was the sixteen-year-old student who blew him in the parking lot in 2002 that did it. Her boundary was an underage girl. No doubt because of her own issues from childhood.

Dereck rubbed his forehead still baffled at how she found out. Every day, he waited for the others to come forward and wondered why Peg hadn't pressed it all further. She always fought for justice, he could always get her distracted with some tasks, but this time, *this time*, she really left. She didn't care anymore.

He slammed his hand down, unable to believe she was really gone...and that she could turn him in at any moment.

Gunnar sat watching the movie but couldn't quite shake Peg's texted brush-off. It pained him that she was feeling things he couldn't understand. He hated Christmas, such a bullshit consumer holiday that only proved to increase his workload times ten and make people act worse than normal.

He stood up and walked across the room to the kitchen to pour himself some Jameson. He thought about the honey whiskey she kept in her room, how her lips tasted after she'd downed a shot. His dick hitched in his underwear, and he thought of her lips around his shaft. The woman unhinged him in ways he'd never known. Part of him wanted to grab the bottle and head over to her room, spending the holiday celebrating with her in his arms, hearing her breathless moans in his ear. She made him feel so good, the way she appreciated him and always wanted more, making him feel desired in ways he'd never expected. Something about it scared the fuck out of him, and although he wanted more, his body said yes, but his mind said no.

He picked up the bottle and his glass and walked down the hall to the spare bedroom, sighing and promising himself a better holiday next year.

Peg woke up feeling better than she deserved. She was well aware that her CPTSD processing would always be a challenge, one she had committed to working on, but still a challenge.

A twinge of guilt bit at her for turning to weed the night before. She needed it in order to sleep and not spend the night tossing and turning in an overthinking cloud of abandonment or rejection trauma. She hates that her mind resorts to both as a knee-jerk response.

Walking towards the kitchen she ran her hands through her hair, thinking she might need to explain things to Gunnar. He didn't really need more to analyze and think about since he already did that daily but, he also didn't need to be confused about how she responded when she was dealing with her trauma triggers. She sighed, annoyed that holidays bring it all on.

Peg bent down to grab a pot and fill it with water. She placed it on the burner and set the fire. Staring at the blue flame wavering beneath the pot, she realized how much she struggled even all these years later. She shifted her hips and huffed a small laugh. Realizing that although difficult to work on herself, her life was tremendously better than it was years ago with the demon she was married to. He never allowed for a moment of self-awareness or self-growth as he was afraid she would leave him if she ever got strong enough. She blinked slow and felt gratitude to be able to stand in her roommate's tiny kitchen and actually be able to think. She vowed to step forward and continue to work on herself however long it could take. Being free of the mental torture of Dereck Law felt like a gift...every day.

She poured the hot water in the cup filled with dandelion herb, mixed in cinnamon and creamer, and stirred it while looking out the window. The sun was shining despite it being a cold Christmas Eve. She decided a little more weed and some coffee on the porch was in order to further process. She walked towards the door remembering this was not the first holiday she'd spent alone, the worst were when she was married, in the same room, and still felt completely *alone*.

December 24, 2021 10:19 AM

I'm beginning to hurt...

Another weekend...another holiday...so many years of just being an option...it's been kicking up again and I

don't know how to process it...

Got super high...apologies for anything said offhand yesterday...

It's ok...how was...high?

Meh...high now...lol

Now...how high?

Heheheeeee...what do you mean?

You are totally high now???

I'm fucked...

Wow...with roomie???

411

Naw, she went out

You fingering?

Lol...can't really...feel

You ok?

my fingers lol

Wow...great day

Yeah

I'm sorry about last night

CPTSD relapses are less but still happening when I'm not ready. What do you mean?

You seemed quite upset

I'm sorry...

I'm sorry you were upset

You're sweet. I appreciate you caring...thats new for me. Are you feeling well today?

Kinda tired...lazy...gonna bring daughter to movie...

That's a great idea. Can rest in the recliners there. Taking mine on Sunday.

Spiderman too???

Lol...Matrix

Wish I could go over...make love...laugh...have shot

I really wish too. Need you...

Will msg soon....going to movie

Bye babe

(Later)

Hi

Hiiii Are you holding up ok?

Tired...but good...you??

Are you sleeping? I'm doing well thanks. Got my period (ugh) I'm really sorry for my emotional night. I get one here and there...

Ohhhh period...mmmmmmmmmmmmmmmm

Lol

What ya doin

Thinking about heading to bed...you?

Rub your clit? Watching Die Hard

I may...have to...

You should...for sure

*I watched that yesterday lol.
I should rub huh?*

For sure...

I do every day...sometimes I just need...to be filled...

Filled with???

Filled with your amazing engorged cock preferably.
Touch yourself lately?

I did...today...shot my cum to my chest...lots

Holy fuck...that's hot!

Long thick streams...
Thinking about...anal

What thought helps that happen
Ohhhhhhh

How you push your ass to me...

Mmmmm...how big, yet gentle you are...makes me want to push towards...

As long as it never hurts you

Nothing we've done has hurt...that's why it's so good. I like your style...respectful, pleasurable...only problem is...

Is??

It's so good...leaves me always wanting more...and more...and

Me to...best part...
Walking in...you naked...high heels...absolutely beautiful

Hope so...
As soon as you open the door...your energy reaches me and my insides start yearning and aching...then I see your eyes, your huge chest, and arms, and I want them around me...

No hope so...know so...please...know so

Feels like "home"...safe...

When you enter me...I lose my mind...along with my breath...please know you are sooooo desired...so wanted...

Thank you...
Rub my cock along your wet pussy lips...tip pushes in...full hard cock in you

Slides in...mind-blowing. Soooooo hard...stretching me...
Perfect curve...like made just for me...

Slow pumping...till you open...accept fully

Those first thrust makes my eyes almost cross with ecstasy...
My hands on your broad back...I always want to pull you in deeper...deeper..

Tip...touches cervix...you moan

Yesssss...that causes moaning from deep within...

When I cum...I drive entire length in you...

Yes...you do...love when you cum...

You have let me cum in pussy...ass...and swallowed...wow

Let you? Isn't that how things should be? Pleasure is healthy no?

Your pleasure

Since coming back and being with you...I have way less relapsing.
Pleasure and bliss is super healthy for our CPTSD...

Yup...you cum so hard...creamy...squirting

I do...yes...and wildly so. Very often...

When you were reverse the other day...you squirted lots

Oh no...made a mess on ya?

Nope...was glorious

Oh good. Reverse is...

Amazing view...tight lower back...great views of side boob...tight...gorgeous ass

So...fulfilling and slick...and stretching...electric in so many ways. Going slow...is mind-blowing...then your sounds...how you hold my hips...rock with me. Would love to do it on a yacht...with the waves rocking us...you know?

Yup........

Josephine sat and stared at her Christmas tree. The glow of the lights illuminated the room and she felt completely immersed in the beauty of the season. She sipped at her wine rolling the tart flavor around her tongue then swallowing. She was excited to see all her family tomorrow but something was gnawing at her. She couldn't shake some of the conversations she and Peg had been sharing. Her heart ached knowing that Peg was home in a stranger's house, no kids, no presents, no holiday cheer, because of one degenerate who loved the power of taking away the life she worked, the last twenty years, trying to create.

Exhaling disgust, she thought about how she would get rid of Dereck Law from the face of the earth if she could get away with it and not suffer the guilt of ending him. She took an oath to preserve life but, she began to feel she would be more so preserving lives by eliminating him, rather then sitting by watching his destruction.

She knew Peg didn't spend much time in pity, she actually voiced so much and then would come around to healthy and proper processing. It almost unnerved her how Peg was tremendously *disappointed* in Dereck but not so much angry at him. On one hand, she was proud of her, but on the other she would love to see Peg receive justice. She certainly deserved the scales to balance.

Josephine squinted looking toward the white lights inside the tree. She thought about Aileen and what the two of them might be able to do once more intel was collected on Dereck. She was hopeful with her vindictiveness and Aileen's skills for extracting information, a quiet resolution might present in the next few weeks.

od picked up his cell and decided to reach out. The loneliness of the first holiday without his wife was almost too much to bear. He dialed hoping Gunnar would pick up. He knew Gunnar slept as little, if not less, then he.

"Merry Christmas sir." Gunnar answered, his voice low, a television played in the background.

"Hey there, thought I would have heard more of a bah-humbug from you?" Rod chuckled.

"Yep, would have for sure but my kid is here sleeping on the couch next to me. Got me up at the ass-crack of dawn."

"Ah, to be young."

"Right. How are you? Holding up okay?"

"Not so much."

"Yeah, rough day."

"Roughest so far. My Joyce loved this damn day."

"I admire those who can find the joy. My youngest here still sparks up the day... well, until all the presents are open and she's back to snoozing."

Rod smiled, "That's funny."

"Yeah."

"Are you doing well Gunnar? Got some time off?"

Gunnar huffed, "Yes, but truth-be-told I'd rather be on the street in uniform. Just trying to be the family man today."

"I know, you've always been more comfortable on calls."

"It's just a thing."

"I hear ya. I've been wondering about you and our last conversations. Have you made any decisions about...well, about your unexpected *connection*?"

Gunnar felt slightly uncomfortable, "No."

"Oh."

"This is why I'd rather be at work."

"It's not wrong to feel conflicted son. Emotions are there to be felt."

Gunnar was annoyed, "Rod, you know I'm a solutions guy...but greedy."

"Tell me about that."

"Well, I don't really have any answers yet to be able to give you answers."

"No, about the greed."

Gunnar sighed, "I have a wife that doesn't want or appreciate me...and I have... well, Peg who wants to give me the world. I'm the problem in it all because I'm greedy. I don't know how to leave what feels wrong without everyone getting hurt or judging...and I don't fucking know how to let go and hurt Peg...who doesn't deserve more pain. And...then there's my greed. I want what I want."

"Okay, now we're getting somewhere. Acknowledgement is a very good first step."

"Doesn't feel that way Rod."

"Well being greedy never feels good."

"For some it does. Greed is easy, it's the fucking guilt I hate."

"Ah, yes."

Gunnar exhaled, "Now I really want to go to work."

"Overworking is a good distraction tactic."

"Well...I am a tactics guy..."

Rod laughed, "True, but this heart stuff? You can try to logic through it, use all sorts of tactical solution...at the end of the day though, the heart wants what it wants."

"Right. Well, lucky I don't have a heart then."

"Okay O'Clery." Rod felt a pain in his gut. He knew to drop the subject as Gunnar was one who often spent time alone figuring things out. He'd stirred up enough dust and trusted Gunnar would come to him in the coming weeks and share more. For now, he just prayed he'd use his supposed missing heart instead of his head for once.

December 25 10:53 AM

Hi

Merry merry sexy...

(Later)

Hi...

Hi

How are you

I'm well...you?

Tried to sleep...kid woke me up at 0400...

Oh shit...
Well...Xmas is for the kiddos lol...

Yeah...what you doing

Writing...you?

Watching tv...wanting to lick you...

My kitty...just...purrred...aching...

Mmmmm...wanna fill you deep with cum....lots of cum

Stooooooop...making me looney over here...
roomie is like "why ya smiling at your screen" lol

Tell her...

Tell her what?

That a man...at this moment is fantasizing about my touch...my taste...my gaze

Are you???

Yup...sure am

Mmmmm...I like knowing you think of me...

Tell her...you rubbed your clit today...thinking about me stretching you in every way...

Lol, she's eating unhealthy Wendy's...not sure how well she'd receive the information lol...

Why not...it's true

When I've shared tiny tidbits here and there...about our "truths," she's said she's jealous so I don't elaborate too much. Any friend thats ever joked saying "jealous" has not been the friend I thought they were lol

Ohhhhh...well you do fuck me into bliss...she could learn...from you
And how to be a friend too...

Blisssssssss...

Very content...never had a woman do things you do...how you move...touch...give...receive...

We're just beginning...

Ohhhhhhh my....

I am ready to...push back some...when you're ready...

Push back??? I'm ready

Mmmmm...my kitty just meowed again...

Push back???

You say you like when I push back...take you all in, yes?

Yes...tell me more

Relax...let you thrust...push back...grip tight...give you my vagina hugs...
Kegel squeeeeezes...So goood...
Want to wrap my legs around you...never let you go...

Such a beautiful tight warm wet pussy...so beautiful of a lady...beautiful breasts...perfect nipples. Make me cum multiple times!

Never been perfect...but I will use and enjoy what I've been given for as long as we can...I do enjoy your pleasure and multiple orgasms...Never had a lover quite like you...

What ya mean

Everything feels good...everything is fun and so pleasurable. Each movement, thrust, caress, kiss, penetration, phrase, breath...It's like energetic bliss for me. You seem so...
In tune with me?

Each time has been like first...

I've NEVER had "first time" sex that good...

It gets better every time

I'd have to agree...

Your wetness turns me on so much

You've mentioned...
All for you...Was that surprising to you the first night? Even after our kissing/necking at the laundromat?

No...I knew you would...well...fuck me into oblivion...

How does a man know that?

Way you kissed me...how your hand went straight to my cock in the truck

Ohhhh....The kissing...

Yup

I was quite impressed with your manhood...beneath my grasp...and your kissing...tongue...

I knew...You were impressed?

Yes...you hadn't really mentioned...such size...

Have you...had bigger?

No...you?

Me???

Are perfect...a bit girthy for my smaller size...but it feels perfect!

Don't hurt you??? I don't want to hurt you

I think I'm handling you well yes?

Very...you ride cock...like no other...

You haven't hurt me...just takes me a bit to acclimate after so many days of missing you...and I really enjoy riding you...

You make my balls tingle...like the beginning of cumming...for entire time you ride me...

Really? I like that...knowing that...

Yes...on edge of orgasm constantly

You have excellent control...I do enjoy slightly overtaking that though...lol

You do...with ass play...and in your mouth...

Edging is a very sought after skill in tantra...I love to explore your body with my mouth...can't wait to massage you...and explore moreeee...you have a body that is a massage therapist's dream...

Edged?

"Edging" is what powerful men do...

Which is???

Holding their seed! They understand how powerful they are...sexually, and use that power to excel in life. It's getting to the edge of orgasm and holding back...letting things settle then bringing it forward again...and again...and again. Not easy. Men who control their ejaculation tend to have more power.

Ohhhh...not easy with you for sure...your sexual energy is (bomb emoji)

I feel the same about yours. Rocks my world. I do think we deal with our CPTSD outlets similarly. Tantra taught me how to circulate my overly sexual energy...I'd be dead or on drugs if I hadn't learned how to use my sexual energy to heal...

Mmmm....wanna take 3-4 shots...watch you smoke....relax....then just fuck you till you can't walk...over and over...orgasms for both of us....I wanna cum in your mouth.....in and on your pussy....then in your ass....shower...clean up....in shower you stroke me hard again...

Wow...sounds like you've got plans...been dreaming lately?
I'm happy you feel so comfortable cumming with me...

I do...I do...love how you squirt too...soooooo warm...wet...tastes amazing...

Mmmmmm...
There was a moment...that first night when you placed me on my side and entered me from behind while sinking your lips into my neck and wrapping an arm around me...it sent an awakening through me that I have no words for...feeling your cock so deep it felt almost in my throat...then your kiss on my throat...I felt I'd almost lost consciousness...ecstasy....

First time you let me in your ass...I came so quick...kept going...to please you...

Aw...I'm sorry...that's not easy

Was amazing...soooooooo amazing...didn't know if I could cum inside...

You do please me sooooo much...

How wet is your pussy now...

You can always cum with and inside me..I'm only with you...

My...parts are quivering and aching mostly...giny is occupied currently...but I'm sure I'm sufficiently trying to lubricate. Just our sexting gets me going for freagin' hours...

Occupied??

Tampon...
Would much prefer you occupying...lol...

Mmmmm...yes....
Hormone fueled fuck-fest...

Lol, most men run from hormonal women...

Run from your pleasure...not at all...you let me cum in you...your mouth...do ass play...not one thing I won't do...

Why wouldn't I "let" you? It's all so enjoyable...don't you know how good you are? Has no one ever told you how much pleasure you invoke? Everything you do to me is electric. You need to know how good you are in bed...

Just try to please you....

No need to try...I'm VERY pleased..we can relax more now...
I think we please each other well lol...

Yes...what's on your sexy bucket list?

Hmmmm...definitely different outfits, more heels, feather-lite massage, flogging, blindfolding, food sex, more surfaces, shower, in nature, on a yacht, hot springs, other countries, beach...I have so much more but...

But???

Not always sure of your wants and desires...

Want...anything...you desire. I'm in awe

Blushing...

Wanna put your legs...over my shoulders

Mmmmm...you soooo spicy...twisted...like me...

Tip to cervix

Mmmmm...yes please?

Cream hitting as deep as you have ever had

*So true. Honestly...never had it this way...or deep (drooling and dripping again)
you torture meeee....Roomie has the Jeff Dunham Xmas special on and I'm giggling because Ahkmed is
making fun of Irish dicks that are magically delicious (in leprechaun voice) heheheheeeee...Mmmmm...soooo
delicious...*

Ahkmed knows...like encyclopedia Britannia of dick...

My favorite now...

Good dick??? You high??

*Best!
Noooo but you seem like you've had a cocktail or two?*

Three...or four

*Mmmmmm...you're so sweet...and sexy...what I would do to you...
Whiskey?
Are your walls down enough to where I can ask anything? Lol*

ANYTHING

Hmmmm...I wouldn't take advantage. I know you'll always admit what you want...

K...so I'm high now...how ya feeling?

Amazing

So happy you're relaxed

You???

Mmmmmmm...very...

My gsl

?

December 26, 2021 10:33 AM

Good morning

Heyyyyy

How you be

I'm well!! You okayyyy?

I'm okie dokie...woke up...wanting...

Oh??? What specifically?

To fuck you till your body shivers...and you say you need a break

Ohhhhh wow...that...you do...

Then on your side...you guide me...

Mmmmmm...yesssss...you are sooo...gentle and sweet...

You tell me harder...harder...

...and

And I do...I push deep...you push back...

I curve and arch into you to get that extra electric tingling you give...right at my cervix...

You turn me over...take me in your mouth...taste our cum

Mmmmm...you and me together...swirl my tongue...suck...s l o w...to prolong and build. Maybe two fingers...

Please...two fingers...

However you need it, baby...

427

Whatever you desire...pretty sure 2 fingers...wow...explode cum for you

2...maybe 3 swallows after...this week...

Lots...did you rub pussy today?

Not yet...on the way to the gym to run away my cramps and the torture you put me through being so damn "snack" like lol...

Bad cramps???

Nothing I can't handle...I prefer how you take them away...

Orgasms help...

Sooooo much. Remember, 3 a day keeps a woman balanced...

And analgams...

Those are lovely with you...full body orgasms. Hard to function through the day after...soooooo nice...

You sure...no pain???

Well...you are large lol...but when we go slow and use lube...it's...just...sooooooo intense...trusting is nice after allll the years of...not?

Never hurt you...but...I think about anal with you...lots...

You do??? I think I've turned you on to new things...

You saying you would like my cock in you...turns me on...

Yes to cock in me...

When is roomie back to work...

Not so sure...

Baby...I want to lay you down...

Love when you do...part my legs...find how wet you get me...

Lick...suck...finger...fuck you...leave cum in...on you...watch you quiver as you cum...

Yes please...

You so horny now...just the touch of the fabric or panties rubbing clit turns you on yes?... throbbing...

Yes...and it doesn't help with tampon in making me squeeze...too small...want your big dick penetration...

Would you let me have your ass?

Have I ever denied you??

Would you ask for me to be in your ass...

I would probably beg at some point yes...maybe even twice...

Roomie gone tomorrow?

Yep. Save me some...

Can we????? Plenty of cum...

Neeeeeeed you...

Still on period tomorrow?

Yes...3 more days...

Its ok...I really enjoy that...really enjoy.......realllllllly...reallllllllllyy...

So nice...that you do...

Hormones make you cum more...and more...

I always cum lol...last week was the loooooong, intense ones.

Why orgasms different?

Between ovulation and period week...just preparing I guess. Phenomenal...so missed you...

Wow...wanna brush your hair away...watch you suck me...precum on your lips...

My lips like your beautiful skin and precum tip...tastes yummmmmm...

Wanna fuck you in every position...reverse riding...wanna have you gush...great view...

We can do all that you desire...I likey it all...with you...

How's your pussy feeling....

Better. Tightening with leg squats on last ten of reps. Camps halted...

When you get home...will you??

If I think of you...or see that pic of you...

Mmmmmm...really wanna just watch you touch yourself sometime...not tomorrow...tomorrow I'm gonna animal fuck you

Hmmmm? I may do you!

When you are riding...I watch you...so beautiful...watch you...how you move...first time I came inside you...you were riding me...

I'll never forget that...
Psychic said that's when my body began to...awaken. I mean I felt something during my Ayahuasca ceremony but when I said yes to you and let you in...ohhhhhhmyyyygoshhhhhhh

You kept going...grinding...every drop of cum was yours

I know I'll never go back to being oppressed and stifled...I wanted all of you...your seed...

We did a lot of amazing positions that first time...what made you decide you wanted to cum while I was on top?

You were cumming...how you were moving...
Was kinda nervous...to cum in you...

Well...we've established you can rest at ease with that. You can cum in me every way...

I think...we have. You never had a guy...cum multiple times???

I was nervous until we got your uniform off lol...I told the psychic I can't understand why I shake in my core. Why I want more and more. I'm not usually nervous with sex as it's my dominant energy. She says it's my kundalini awakening since I left "him" who I had entrapped so much of myself inside with (hence the illness/ tumors) so coming back to LC and "opening up" was a very good choice as I'm healing. But...my body will have a hard time with all the energy until I learn how to harness it.
Multiple? Not even in the 3some. Once they were exhausted and came...it was talk, awe, and beer. You...are very special. Have you had multi-orgasmic women? Its a thing-

One...in college...nothing...like you...we were kids. She always wanted to be fingered...that was her thing...

Lol...darn. You should see the look on my students' faces in Tantra classes when I teach them multiple orgasms are a good thing.
Fingered huh?

Home now?

Hydro-massage then tanning next, then home.

Would love to walk in tanning bed while you are in there...tan nude???

Yes, tan nude...that would be wild if you did. I'd have you on every surface!

My kid is asking me to go out. Wants me to meet up later...but I'm kinda having a hard time being around her beau...

Why??

Gunnar...I think she went out...and found her father
just in a 30 yr old version...my gut tells me...he requires way too much attention...ugh

Grrrrrrrrrrr...

Well...anyway its not my journey. I'll love her anyway. But, it's his addictions, how he touches her, how he
needs attention more than anything...something bothers me deep down.

Addictions? Does she still see other guy?

She was so angry with me for suffering for so many years but...he smokes/drinks to deal with his childhood
shit. Other guy is here in weed fog too much. She couldn't get any attention from him...shunned from
Jehovahs Witness family so...terrible rejection trauma (sad). Real mess while I was gone in FL. Just want her
to be loved...hope she feels so...

Damn...

Anyway...they want to take me out. Matrix movie I guess...Keanu is great but...I'll be riding you in my mind
the whole time....

Sweeeeeeeeeeeeeeeeet...have fun with your girl....

Hope your day is amazing
Want your...

Yes...

Glorious cock...

Mmmmmm....me wants you...

432

Chapter 26

CAN I

December 27, 2021 10:34 AM

Hi...hello...hola...

Hey

What ya up to

Nothing much. You? Get some sleep?

Not much...roomie home?

No
I'm alone today...

Babe
Can
I
Come
Fuck youuu

Don't
know
can you?

Open door...find out in 10...

Mmmmmmm...maybe...

Dereck loaded up the back of his truck and slammed the tailgate shut. He walked around to the driver's side door, looked over to see Juan wave while watering his trees. Dereck stopped and shouted to his neighbor and new closest friend. Juan couldn't hear him, he shut the nozzle to the hose off and put his hand to his ear.

"You got time to go to the range? I'm bored. Headed over to blow through some ammo and destress!" Dereck forced a smile. It had been a week since he talked to anyone or even heard his own voice. The loneliness was beginning to get to him. He hated the holidays and was tired of hibernating in the house.

Jaun laughed, "Bored? What about all those repairs you talk about in the house?"

"Are you busting my balls?" Dereck opened the door.

"Yeah. Hey, when you gonna go out with the ATV again?" Juan sprayed a bush and turned the hose off again.

Dereck's face fell, "The damn thing won't start again. I don't know what's going on with the battery."

Jaun shook his head, "Dude, I have never known anyone to have so many problems with a new side-by-side. I think they sold you a lemon man. You ever think about turning it back in?"

"I thought about it but then she'd be right...can't let her be right, man." Dereck nodded his head towards Peg's old truck to indicate he was talking about his ex.

"Oh...right." Jaun faked a smile. He knew Dereck would have nothing if he didn't have his ex to blame for something in every conversation...or bring her up. He tired of it years back. The guy did nothing but bitch...and his ex was just the next in line to be at fault so he didn't have to recognized the issue was actually him.

Dereck asked again, "So, you game?"

"What? Oh, shooting? Nah, I'll pass man." A smile showed on his face.

Dereck shook his head, "Pussy. She's got you locked down dude. You don't know what you're missing."

"Uh, yes...yes I do. I'm missing the divorce I don't need." Jaun sassed him, chuckling.

"Whatever. Later."

"Bye."

Jaun turned the hose on again and waved watching Dereck climb in his truck and leave. He thought about how he never wanted to go shooting with his half-nuts neighbor ever again. The guy was a loose cannon, in his opinion. Since the day he and his wife moved next door, he'd had to keep an eye on him. He pretended to be close, listened to all his complaining, even kept his secrets regarding his infidelities and all the wrongs he did to his wife. But, he knew he wasn't a man of honor...a man he'd even trust around his own daughters.

Everyone in the neighborhood agreed, she left him so much later than she should have. Peg was too ambitious to keep putting up with Dereck. He was a horrible husband and a worse human. She seemed to be the only person who believed in him...until she *didn't*.

Jaun thought about how he and his wife didn't really care for them as neighbors, but as things went, Peg was way easier to get along with than Dereck. The things he'd done to her, and was continuing to do, were shocking. He really never deserved her and despite how he tried to take her down or lie and blame her for embezzling...everyone knew he was the real culprit and blaming his wife to distract others from his dishonesty.

Juan raised his eyebrows and strode along, spraying the shrubs. Dereck Law would always be an enemy he had to pretend was a friend. He didn't want to think about what the guy would do to him or his family if they ever got on his bad side.

Dereck pulled off the highway and headed toward the shooting range. He sighed, annoyed. He hated being alone. He wondered if Gunnar O'Clery would be there. He should have called him and invited him to meet up. It annoyed him that the guy was still the best shooter he'd ever known, but something in him made him want to hang out with him anyway. He could show off his AR's and some of the modifications he'd done. O'Clery was always good at banter and competitive conversation.

He pulled the truck in and drove slow, passed each of the bays looking at each shooter and their gear wondering who he should park near so he could feel something other than depression. He smiled at how he could think of Peg, and whoever she was fucking, while pointing downrange. He was getting more and more comfortable with thoughts of taking her out...he just needed to decide if he wanted to fuck her first, after, or take her and her man out at the same time and stage it as their murder-suicide, sending everyone sniffing on the wrong trail.

eg's stomach swirled as her mind readied to see and feel him again. She remembered months ago when her stomach was a mess. She much preferred how it was more excited now because of him. She bent down to fasten the strap of her heel...he loved when she wore heels.

unnar entered the house and looked around. He could hear the low sound of an 80s rock ballad coming from her room. His dick was already rigid with want for her and he shifted himself in his sweatpants as he walked to her door. He opened it, and his eyes were immediately on her, his arousal heightened. Heels, legs, tan skin, bare ass, tight lower back, blond hair, bedroom eyes on him, and that smile...

He couldn't help but groan low in his chest, throwing his items on the desk then locking the door. He swiftly headed towards her, eager to be inside her, remembering how she felt perfectly formed just for him. He reached for her...and she for him.

(Later)

Mmmmm....so much fun you are...(Yoda voice)

Awwww...love Yoda. That...was incredible...

Mmmmmm...yes...how are you

(Later)

Hi

Hey, sexy. Everything ok?

Yeah...need more paperwork...grrrrrr

For Mom's POA stuff?

Yeah...insurance crap...

Ugh...

Just make sure she's of sound mind and body and not in distress. That's how the Puerto Rican side of my ex's family got him on elderly abuse. (said he forced her to sign at the bank) You have a brother you don't really like yes? Don't want him coming back at ya later...if he's a part of her life. Family loves to put opinion in but never step up. Wish you ease with this...not a fun part of adulting.

For sure...he completely ignores her...but will show up with outstretched hands...for sure

Ohhhhh fuck. Yeah, good thing you're doing the responsible thing then. Great job!

Sux...I'm having adult beverages

Yummy...yeah, I'm considering having an adult puff after these cookies my son baked and sent in the mail for me lol...cuz, today was...(bomb emoji)

Yuppppp...bomb.com

That actually directed me to a site...you crack me up bahawahahahaaa

437

Wow...I'm a dork...

Nah...adult beverages...and lots of cumming...

Lots

Ditto

Not sure what we did today...but every time I pee I have an aftershock orgasm lol...sorry if TMI....yummmmmm

Mmmmmmmmmmm...deeeeeeeeep...

(Later)

Still have your scent...like a wolf...hungry...

Me toooo...you just got me going again...

Metallica...of wolf and man...

Yezzzzzz

...out from the new days mist I come...
Best Metallica song everrrrrr

Okay...I'm putting it on while I write...fuckin' love Metallica...didn't know you did!

...so everyone in my work loves...loves sheep dog stuff...fuck that...I have worked with the toughest dogs noooooo one could work...
Each one would be destroyed by any beta wolf...only thing that can stop a wolf...is a better wolf...Metallica song nails that...along with anything from Van Halen!

Mmmmm...liking how your mind is this evening...not seeing the sheep dog thang why do they prefer? My better wolf lol

Easy scapegoat...not a wolf to fight wolf...sheep dog...same genetics but empathy for group...or sheep...or citizens...

Ah, I see

Well...panda has same genes as grizzly...but well...

Hmmmmm....

Or...band stuff...Dio...Ronnie James was 5 foot 2...but has lungs of angels

Yezzzzzz sir!

Watching vids on shootings...tired of badged up pussies

Love that shit...I try to stay away tho...

Need to find way...we are losing...

Yes
Losing is not your style...

True
If not for the Ewoks...the evil empire would have won out...

Bahawahahaaaaaa

(Sent Ewok Dancing gif)
God...you wants me now
My Ewok swerve...
S T R O N G

Fuck yeah...

You...got giggles

I got giggles...

You...also had...cock in mouth...cock in pussy...cock in ass...mmmmm

Yes...I'm fun...like you

We be like a Mc D's play land...woohooooooo

We be...lol

Yup...yup...you were on fire today

Was...really good after 11 days...I was starving for O'Clery cock...got so distracted...forgot to give you Xmas gifts we could have played with...but probably best...was a freagin crime scene...had to use baby wipes to clean up, bed rails, wall...ya slayed my kitty babe lolololo...

Way great day of baby girl pleasure

Mmmmmm...sooooo pleasurable...

In...soooooooo...many....ways...

I enjoy every way...need more time with your sensitive tip tho...precum was amazing...slick and warm...

Velvet cum...throughout...insane anal today..

It was intense...feels so good with you...a bit big...but...just had to relax..

Ummmmmmm...ok though??

I thought so! You?

3 orgasms...in a row. Yupppppp

You did cum a lot! Love it...

I did...I did...I did...x3...wooohoooooo

Mmmmm...I like when you do...each and every time...makes me feel happy...

Would you let me...take you tonight???

Don't tease...but yes-

Would roll over...ravage you...wake up...ravage again

Only when I wasn't ravaging you...no way I could lay next to you and not touch and caress...that body...

Mmmmm...so cum...every morning...night...

You'd get tired of my insatiable-nessss....

I think...you would

Lol...doubt it...hmmm what a fun challenge...

You would beg for mercy...again

Lol...okay, you've got me there...that's new for me...begging...never had to before...

You have...me likey...

I think you do yes...lol. Which was your favorite orgasm?

All...since day 1

Awww...yeah, come to think of it...they've been pretty damn phenomenal for me too since Oct 21...wow, but I did like how you were touching my low back, caressing me, and really into my boobs today...

Ummmm....yeah...you be hotttty

You be...can't keep my hands to myself...

Tag...no tag backs

You're fun...I'll always let you win...It's a Libra trait...

Scorpio. Can't lose...scorpion and frog story

I'm familiar...
It's okay...Scorpios are my favorite now...sultry in bed...yummmmmmm

Found out did ya...

Done found out...so glad I did...

Mmmm...good night baby girl

Nite sweetie...hoping I'll be in your dreams...laters

***

<u>Peg's Journal Entry 12/27/21:</u>

We reunited today after eleven days apart with Xmas in between. A particularly rough holiday for me this year, but not the first I've spent alone. Our time together was amazing! I was shocked at how in tune things felt after two weeks. We both seemed affection-starved, as we disrobed each right away! He was in a VERY good mood, even fiery. Already rock hard for me as soon as he opened the door to my room and walked in. He placed my hand on him and said, "See what you do to me?"

We started out orally for him, of course, and went at it from there. Soooooo much pleasure. When he entered me, it took some coaxing and stretching despite my substantial wetness for him. After so many days, my yoni just tightens, and my, my, my how he loves to slowly, torture me then fill me fully...to my cervix! He teased, thrusting over and over, then hooked his arm under one leg, hiking it high so he could get even deeper making me gasp at his offered pleasure. I cried out, and he loved it, so much energy shooting up through my chakras, driving me almost mad.

We took our time with me riding on top, then reverse cowgirl, and ended with anal, which he near about lost his mind with. Everything feels so damn good...with just the two of us going slowly through all we enjoy and it is exquisite!

As we dressed, he shared how he wanted to take his ten-year-old to see her older brother and sister in Phoenix for the holidays but doesn't know if it will happen since so many flights are grounded or unavailable due to the covid omicron crap. He regaled me with all the ridiculous robberies over Christmas and how carjackings are on the rise. He brought his phone out and showed me a gangrenous untreated bullet wound on some dude. Says his officers were puking due to the smell, which was indescribable.

I smiled, enjoying all that he wanted to share. I miss the calls and understand much of what he talks about, we tend to have the same type of CPTSD warped mind, and I'm grateful we can find comfort in each other. Today was awesome.

Sadly, he had to leave and take care of some POA and LLC legal paperwork. I've been there. Not such fun stuff.

December 28, 2021 12:12 PM

Mmmmmm...best tanning sesh thinking of you interrupting it...ty

Ohhhhhhhh my...sore?

You know it. You? Lol

Little bit...

Awwwww

Gooood sore...was awesome...session...

I like a good sore. Hope your day is stress-freeeeeeee

Very...gotta meet guy doing LLC paperwork

So proud of you...that's awesome!!!

(Later)

Hi!

Helllllooooooooooo

Hi baby...how was your LLC day?

Good...kinda overwhelmed...but good...new chapter stuff...anxiety a little...ok lots

Thats all part of it. It's gonna be amazing...you wouldn't step forward towards it unless your gut told you to do so, yes? Overwhelm...anxiety...all very normal human response but everything we want is on the other side of fear. Your doing great! Even more for your babies to be proud of...

You are so correct...how are you today

I'm well! Did good for others...helped a marriage, healed some bodies...avoided a narcissist. Can't complain...

443

Narcissist???

My drunky mother...no biggie. POA stuff go smooth?

It was...but its...end of cop stuff...it's time...but all I have ever...really known...kinda struggling...

Absolutely! But it can be a great ending. You are NOT losing just adjusting. You'll always have it in you... always be great at it. Not losing the "known" just adding more to your expertise. You'll mourn the certainty of the routine until you get to build a new one. No one can take away all the good you've done...and there was more good than not. That's success, baby!

You are right...gonna try to close eyes...sleep...nite

Me tooooo. Nite

December 29, 2021 2:44 PM

How you be

Missin...us...you?

Loading up...taking kids to PHX tomorrow...

Oh great! Finally got flights?

No...son flying...daughter driving...meet them all there

That's awesome...so happy for you!!! Need that connection and love now..life changes warrant it...

Sooooo true

Great way to ring in the New Year! I wish you nothing but snuggles, hugs, and smiles...

Thank you...daughter will have my phone most trip...for tv...games...will need to be careful

I won't bother you babe...hope you make great memories...

January 1, 2022 12:01 AM

Happy New Year!

Happy New Year

January 3, 2022 8:34 AM

Wake up!!!!!!

On treadmill...already awake...

Whattttt....

Lol...how are youuuuu?

I'm great...how is you doing

Livin! What's making ya smile these days?

Why at gym so early...had great weekend...my 3 kiddo all together just being goofballs

Love that!
Can't sleep...gym helps

Why not...need some Benadryl???

Lol...nooooooo

Why not sleeping?

Who knows...so 2022 looking good?

Well...nervous bout business stuff...lot of uncertainty, unknown...you???

Same. Trying to ignore the anxiety lol. Your kiddos supportive of LLC stuff?

**Yeah...more supportive of retirement...
Your ex bugging you??**

Thats fantastic!! So Happy for you.
Him...nope. Other than missing my...
Uhhhh...abilities...

Missing your?? Ohhhh he texting...calling...well he should...your abilities are...well...can't be measured...

Lol...telling friends he really loves me. But...narcissists do not have the capacity to love. Thanks. You catch up on rest...I hope...relax at all?

I tried...I tried...you ok? Seem...like weird energy...

Meaning?

Don't know...just feeling...you ok?

You feeling?? I am!

Just me...how's your day looking...I'm back at work...one of my guys got with me...he's having rough time...need to have chat...

All good. Good luck at work...tough to get back after all the fun. Hope he's ok-

He was shot...couple years ago...residual coming on strong...he's not in a good place...

Ooooh nooooo. Well, you're the guy who can get him thru the tough PTSD...just needs to be reminded of his worth no?

Yeah...was awkward initial chat...

Oh really? Like suicidal ideation stuff?

Very...he was not kidding at all...his eyes...were...already dead...

Oh shit...

Yeah...You gonna tan?

He needs vagus nerve reset bad...and Ayahuasca like...yesterday... Headed home...

Ohhhh...how was workout???

Did the trick...mind is clear...
How is yours...able to work out while in AZ?

No...just hung with kids...good...I can connect well to workouts...

Yes...nice!
Bet they loved "Dad" time. That's awesome.

Yeah...you rubbing yourself today???

Lol...idk am I? How are...things?

Things...miss you...yes...rub yourself...ovulation???

Aw...ummm...

Ummmm???

Had to check my app...next 3 days...

Feeling build up???

Are you kidding??? I'm dying.

??

That was...super dramatic...lol...
I'm ok...you?

You finger yourself last night??

Yep

Smoke??

No...too many beers with Gina at Game II. Don't like to mix.
Talking about micro-penis issue lol.

I'm sorry mine is little

(Laughing emoji) We know THATs not true...

Will you smoke today? Off? No roomie...

She's working today then off all week...

Ohhhh...well???

I'll smoke when needed. Just use it to balance...

Ohhhhhh...my bucket list...wanna see you high...then...

I promise...

I know...you in shower??

Just got out. You?

Wish I was in shower with you...waiting for mom to pick up my daughter...she is off all week...

Oh yes...yummy...
Yep, the lil' ones don't go back till 10th/11th.
How is mom?

Still rough on health...but always smiling

Ahhhhh...now thats how to do it. Bet she missed you...

Any naughty dreams lately??

Pretty much all the time lol. Did you feel my telepathy last night lol? I can't believe how strong my orgasms
can be...getting older is NOT that bad at all...lol

Strong...what was on your mind...and yes...yes...yes...after couple beers???

Those were during football earlier but may have relaxed things. I'd been writing and damn... I think what took me over the edge was the missionary and deep penetration as you whisper to me...visits me in my dreams. What are your naughty dreams about these days?

You...riding...swallowing...some scenarios...

Mmmmm...new scenarios?

Yes...you have clients...couple working with...you ask if they can...watch us...hot springs...

Wow...you think they'd like to watch...

Yup...watch you and I...watch how you move...you caress...suck...accept...we ravage each other...they are on chairs watching...after I cum...in your mouth. Pussy...and ass...you put on robe...talk them through intimate and performance issues...they begin...we sit on chairs...watching them...they are so in tune...you are so proud...
They have couple long orgasms...you begin to suck me hard again...we move over to water of the springs...we begin to fuck again...they also keep fucking...no swap...just sharing hot springs...

Oh...your mind is...my favorite...

At end...you begin to massage them as a couple...your sensual touch sends them over the edge...you see his cock growing...her nipples are erect...you see the cum dripping from her...your touch is magic to them...no words...you grab my hand...we walk out...as we walk out you hear her moaning again...

You tell me to drive...as we drive...you give me the greatest blow job ever...I cum in your mouth...

Quite a scenario! I...likey...
I do like when everyone is pleased...mmmmm road head!!!

You kiss me deep...sharing...our cum...lean head on my chest...saying thank you for assisting you...

Best assistant ever...lol. What fun!

Yes...then...they send you a $1000 tip...and the pic of a positive pregnancy test

Awwww I love happily ever afters...

See...like Bambi...but no fires and shit...

Lololol...you're awesome...

How's your about-to-be-fertile-little-pussy doing?

Purring...how's my favorite...
pink parts???

WTS
Wet
Tip
Syndrome
It's a thing

Mmmmm...precum

Waiting on mom...sooooo I can...

Take care...
Of your WTS?

Take care???? Yes

Mmmmm....

There will be lots...of cum

Save some...

Yes???

Well...you know...

Yes

Yes???
Yes?????????

Yes...for me...

Say when...

When, when, when...

Can I???

Can you???

Mom just left...want me to come by?

Is that a trick question? Lol...

Are you fingering?

Saving...but getting...very...

Mmmm...door open...heels on...legs spread...fingers in...

Damn...gotta undress now...but...you're soooooo worth it...

Yup...facing door...pussy glistening as I walk in...
Mmmmmm.....

Waiting...

Wanting??

Always...you???

Throbbing...

Soooo much. Been soooo long since I've felt...your penetration...

Where??

Can I?

Have I ever refused???

What are your wants today?

To connect again...feel you...be important for a while...

Always important...never just awhile...

Have hope 2022...mmmm...wanting you...your hands...your mouth...your cock...

Yes...

In my mouth...my wet...womb

Mmmmm
And??

All...the warm places...

(Later)

Mmmmmmmm...sooooooo satisfied

Awwww...that makes me so happy. Is it wrong to want...
You again?

Nope...I do too

Oh...(gushhhhh)

(Later)

Hiiiiii

Heyyyyyy

How you be....

453

I be sooooo…balanced??? Thank you. I like our therapy lol.
You feeling ok? Hoping your guy is doing well on your swing shift?

Busy…busy

Forgot to tell you…I think you're phenomenal in bed…

Ohhhhhhhhhh my……

***

<u>Peg's Journal Entry 1/3/22:</u>

So, after seven days, we found time to ravage each other. I had bought him a black lace lingerie bodysuit for me to wear with black heels. He was VERY responsive and made me feel so wanted, even thanking me a few times. It was glorious to connect again!

We teased and taunted each other with oral until we couldn't wait anymore. He slid into me deeeeeep in missionary to we could be so close. I really enjoy him, his voice, his body, his tenderness… Somehow, we ended up at the edge of the bed, me rocking on his lap but moved into more oral (sooooo yummy). Most of our time was spent with him beneath me, as I rode him he reiterated a fantasy dream he had of me teaching a client couple of mine about how to be more intimate. He liked that they were watching us (at the hot springs) so they could learn and that I had them practice what they saw us demonstrate.

At one point, he asked me, "How did you learn all this?"

"Isn't this how everyone is?" I responded. He just stared up at me and I laughed.

I switched up to using a toy on him while pleasuring him again orally. He had an intense and immersive orgasm, which I was hoping was full-body! He was in such a great mood and ended up staying a while instead of rushing out.

He shared how worried he was about one of his officers who had been shot in the throat and how he's trying so hard to help him move away from depression and drinking. I can feel his heart come through his words and feel for him and the stress of caring about others. Law enforcement is a constant struggle because if one isn't dealing with the "worst" that people go through, they're dealing with making decisions CONSTANTLY in an environment where their hands are tied by politics and human judgment. I always found it a thankless job…unless, of course, one gets injured on duty, then a medal is granted (ugh). He mentioned his officer is receiving a hero's award but is not feeling the heroics because he drove up and got shot, he didn't have a chance to do his job.

I always found it odd getting shot in a war on the streets could warrant a medal. I feel for the guy, he is infested with ego regret since he was unable to return fire. His wife divorced him, replacing him as a husband and father with a new man...ugh, pain. Sadly, alcohol has become a coping mechanism and we all know alcohol is a depressant. Gunnar is conflicted in how to help him when he has to follow protocol. He is challenged at possibly having to betray his officer's trust by getting him help. Really sucks.

After sharing some information about Dereck's VA disability, Gunnar opened up about a piece-of-shit brother-in-law criminal in the family that has been mooching off the VA and walking around in a "stolen valor" bubble for years. The shame of being married to someone like that still hits me every now and then.

Speaking of shame, Gunnar mentioned he ran into Dereck at the movie theater! He said it was startling because Dereck called out his full name...and no one calls him by his full name. He said Dereck's appearance was alarming, he'd really aged with a lot of gray in his overgrown hair and beard. Annoyed because his hands were full and he was trying to get his daughter to their seats, he had to shift items in order to shake Dereck's outreached hand. He found it odd that Dereck mentioned how he'd seen Spiderman the day before, yet he was back again to see another movie. I told him Dereck is all about sitting in recliners, watching movies, and jacking off with a dick that only works a few times a year. After I said it, I realized I don't much respect Dereck as a man anymore...and how much I value my freedom after so many years in his narcissistic prison.

After he left, I gave gratitude over for my new life and for finally finding the strength to leave a liar. Dereck was by far the worst decision of my life, but what I take from the experience is the desire and want to NEVER be like him. We have to thank our haters...for showing us who not to be...

January 4, 2022 11:00 AM

Hi...wanting u

Hey big guy...always wanting you...

Wishing...I was...in you...

Mmmmm...makin' me wet....
Thank you for sharing your hot springs dream with me
and how "we" helped another couple. I enjoyed your descriptions and love how your mind works. Namaste
lol!!!

Right...

(Later)

Hey you. Someone out there knows you're going through it and having to make tough decisions...and they
think you're great.
Proud of you...

Thank you...still...a shitty process. Thank you.

(Later)

WTS...just saying

?

Wet...Tip...Syndrome

Ohhh yezzzz. Oh yummy. Why?? Whatcha thinking bout?

Lips...swallow...

Ohhh you remember that huh?

Ummmmmmmmmmm...yup

Mmmm...I'm putting the batteries in your other...present. I have plans for you...

Share any??

Nope, these are for you. I prefer your warm toy...for me...

Mmmmm...

Your mouth...was amazing btw...just sayin'

January 5, 2022 9:31 AM

Mmmm...woke up on my side...dreaming of your warm chest against my back...your arm around me...hand cupping my breast. I arch back into you...feel you growing for me between my slickness...already dripping for you...your hand slides down my tummy and to my swollen clit...I arch more...taking you deep...within... my breath...hitching...your lips on my neck...ecstasy begins...

Wow...you are throbbing this morning?

I...am

You touch yourself??

Last night...you?

Not yet...but I might...helping kiddo on 3D printer...

Lol fun...ok have a good one...

What you doing today?

Just Peg stuff...

That sounds...delicious

That was....sweet...

(Later)

How are you

Home...pit stop for food...pleasure...how are you holding up??

Wow...super horny???

It's my curse...

Wow...sweeeeeeeet

Tryna keep my energy balanced so it doesn't spill over into client session (reiki)
Wow, that sounds so weird...

Feeling...little horny????

Naw...lotta. It's my new life...

Ovulation not helping...I wants you...just saying...

Want youuuuu....

When is (egg emoji) ready?

Lol, cute emoji!
No egg yet...but damn the aching is crazy...always wants you...

Wish I was there...would knock it loose...

I do believe that...ping pong fun! Lol
Hope your week has gotten easier on you...

It has...long...but good...how's...your...welllll...beautiful pussy...

You're so kind to me...I'm truly struggling...

How struggling

Sexually...well, physically. I guess emotionally. Idk whatever this woman shit is...

How can I help

Connection maybe?

Explain???

Tell me something good?

Everything about you is good...like Rudy plays football inspired

OMG...haven't seen that one in years! Lol...thanx

Right...how was work today?

Great, thank you. I feel like a tiny hero. Healing someone's pain...freeing another to go for what she wants instead of settling with a micro-penis...yay!

Micro? Day off...been here at work since 1400

Oh nooooo...I'm sorry I didn't know...

Micro junk?

Micro-penis. It's a term women are using now to describe when their man is "declining" due to all the hormones in food and diabetes diminishing things. Hypogonadism per se. Penis shrinks and inverts; stops working. How's your...well, beautiful manhood?

Hope that shit never happens to me...want my shit to work like Harry Potters magic wand... always!

I think you're definitely on the best path with your Potter lightning bolt. If you've been the tripod you are since college you're fine. I hear men who work out tend to produce testosterone at higher levels for much longer. I don't mind helping if needed...

Yezzzz
Are they married??

Unfortunately yes...a minor technicality at present...

Fixable? Ohhhhhh...

I can't advise that no...She's never had an orgasm with him in 14 years and no sex for the last 6! Truly unhealthy...she deserves happiness now...in Peg's world anyway lol...we have our work cutout for us...

Wow.......

So what's been making your happy these days? I'm glad the week is better for you.

You...you make me smile...

You make me smile...a lot...thank you for saying that...missing your...

Miss that lingerie

Like that huh? You made me feel so admired...

3 step boner...yup

I think I want more...love your 3 steps...

Within 3 steps across room...full boner

So...hot...best my hand...and tongue...have ever caressed...

Damn...

Love your pearl...of precum...WTS

It's...a thing

Mmmm...would do anything for it to be...mine tonight...

Roomie work tomorrow???

No (sad face emoji)

Want...your...ass...

Yeah?

Yup...I do...

I likey...O'Clery style...my fav...

O'Clery style??

> Slow...slick...thick...feels sooooo good...

Feels sooooo good...really does

> I didn't expect it to be this good...all of it...
> And..each time...like it's getting better...and better...and...

Very much gooderrr...you rub pussy tonight??

> Not yet...

Mmmmmmmm...you should use new blue toy...then rub clit...

> Mmmm...but that's your toy...

I would love to hear you use...rub clit...ass pleased...mind-scorching orgasms...

> You'll be the one crying out...blue toy...reverse cowgirl...oh myyyyyy...

Yes...I...will...with other toy...in me...please try...

> Nervous?

Not at all...wanna hear about your pleasure

> Oh...so...that first time...we were together...

Yes

> You weren't worried I would get knocked up?

Caught in moments...but was...lot of cum

> You said your first time cumming with me was when I was riding you...

Yes...deep...hips grinding...rhythm

It was amazing to know I could...please you that way...makes me feel really good...

Was instant...cream pie...

I wasn't as frisky Monday...I didn't tell you, but I had a rib out on my right side. I popped it back in a few hours after...I was relaxed enough...
Gym injury...

Huh...what happened...ohhhhh....

Yeah...sorry. Happens when I give too much during massage...

Couldn't tell...at all...you sucked...me clean

Lol

Very...u slide toy in your ass yet???

Nah...prefer...warmth of you...

Can't wait

(Later)

Hey my hero, thank you for brightening my night...

You tooooo...hope you rest...

Took your encouragement...your blue toy is...divine...
You have great ideas!!

Reallllly????? Tell me

OMG...I squirted!!! Literally passed my fingers...thinking of you penetrating...thrusting in while whispering in ear all the sweet things...how deep you are...how wet I am for you...how good it feels...

Toy was???

Inside you??

Yes...created two types...of climax...one rolled over the other. Combined...it was mind-blowing...like when you're inside me...plus clitoral...omg...want youuuuu

Wow...imagine...that...while my cock stretches you...

Oh...so imagining...

Toy in ass...me buried in pussy...nipples stimulated...biting your neck

Mmmm...yesssss. The way you move...and fill me...burrowing...stretching...up inside me...your hands and mouth all over me...you're so...fucking hot...

So glad you tried toy...

Mmmm...you're so convincing lol. You have great ideas... Kisses to your tip...nite.

Nite

January 6, 20 22 10:40 AM

Wish I was woken up...in your mouth...

That is a wish I'm capable of...

Very...cumming in your mouth...made my face numb...toes crack...

Mmmmmm...

What ya doin

Isn't pleasure the best...love to see you happy...
I'm struggling today...but got workout in...shower...trying to figure out if I need weed to balance...or more
chapters written lol...both can help. No clients on Thursdays. You? Finally got a day off?

Weed...blue toy...clit rubbing...Gunnar prescription for pleasure...

How's the "shot-in-neck" officer situation for you..able to strategize it?
Thank you...like that prescription...

Tell me about last night

You first...still no egg...

What did you do to pleasure yourself so amazingly

Well...when we...connect my body reacts in a heated...dripping sort of aching??? Things swell over time...but
if I'm patient...the throbbing begins...then I start long breaths...

Yes...please continue

Clitorally it's always easy for me but the clit extends down into the insides...sooooo
I turned your blue toy on...running it slow...from the hood, sides...circling...

Wow

Then longer...slow...strides...

465

Ohhhhhh my

> *Thinking of you...inside...deep...inserted...vibrations...tantalizing all my senses...radiating out...*

Sooooo wish roomie not there...inserted...ass...vagina...

> *Thought of you tantalizing...*
> *Roomie owes me. Said to just tell her when...*

Reallllllllyyy

> *Says she envies me...both guys dumped her. Been on coaching time with her all week...*

Ohhhhhhhh.....

> *I think karma came calling...*
> *Not good to infect others with STIs or trap into pregnancy...no bueno.*
> *Just my gut but...think karma came*

Ohhhhh...she was trying to get preggo?

> *Says no, but my stomach swirls each time I look in her eyes...*

Ohhhhhhhh.....

> *Could be preggers...behavior kinda erratic...moods...*

Her kiddo there?

> *Yes, got her covid shot at 7 yrs. Sounds like they are getting ready to go out.*

Ohhhh...out??

> *Shall I inquire? Like I said she owes me...*

Yes...please

Anything for you...

Mmmm...please...smoke...naked...door open...toy inside you...unlocked??

No, I have to come answer

She home???

Yes. Says she just woke up...

With kiddo there???

They're hibernating in their room...

Should I come by??

Yes, she says as long as she knows she won't disturb or have kiddo around...can't make me noisy tho lol...

Ok...smoke???

No time...

Ohhhh...shot? Today is Peg day...

Its not a fast thing...I'm sorry. Shot I can do...

All pleasure...for you...

Pleasuring you pleasures me...

Your turn...

Thank you for making time for me...you have no idea how much it means to me...

Woohoooo...hard to keep quiet

I must...

I'm here

Mmmmmm...

(Later)

Best quickie yetttttt...

Was...amaaaaaaaazingggggggg

OMGgggggggggggg
BP ok? You scared the fuck out of me for a sec there today...

Was awesome sauce

That wasn't for me. I need to work on relaxing you more...

Wasn't??

The moment where you looked as if you might pass out was not awesome. My gut went wonky...worried me. And...did you bite me?

Nibbled

So...hot. Friend took me out for beer...he says I'm so hyped! You...are amaaaaaaazinggggggg...

Hyped??

Says I'm emanating some crazy vibe lol. He's like are you preggo? Bahawahahaaaa...

Wow...vibes...what you thinking??

Me? I'm thinking you're just a fucking god when it come to my pussy...you?

Mmmm...we can't get preggo...can we???
Sexy preggo you...

Babyyyy...I'm gonna be 50 in two years..let's just pretend to try...like bunnies lol...

I want to shoot wild boar from a helicopter in TX, kayak rivers, jump out of a perfectly good plane, and fuck on every beach I can...granted I would love your baby as you are an amazing father in my opinion...but my baby-maker is "aged"...how fair is that?

That's fair...
Meme: There is no hunting like the hunting of man, and those who have hunted armed men long enough and liked it, never care for anything else thereafter. -Ernest Hemingway

Wow...Hemingway.
I am pretty hot preggo tho...but horny..can't imagine more of it at this point

Freedom horny

Ohhhhh myyyy...yes. Love how you liberate meeeee...

(Later)

Do you know how happy you make me?
Thank you again for our "lunch time quickie"

Was greeeeeeeat

Was...already self-pleasuring to the memories...dream of me...

Ohhhhh yeah

Mmmm...

***

<u>**Peg's Journal Entry 1/6/22:**</u>

Today has turned out quite well. Zena texted that she had her first ultrasound, and she announced her pregnancy on social media. It's wonderful to celebrate a grandson at this juncture of my life.

Gunnar made time to visit for a lunchtime quickie. It felt amazing! He warmed me up with his mouth, although I was already pretty warm for him when he arrived in my room. Not gonna lie, I

469

became completely swept up in him as he took me in his grasp and fucked me deep. He kept whispering he wanted to please me over and over. I don't think he realizes he pleases me 110%!

At one point, he turned me over on my tummy and lubed up his blue butt plug then inserted it gently into my ass while entering me vaginally from behind. It was incredible to feel him so deep while having anal play as well. I could hear him whispering how amazing the view was. After a while, I was on top, and he was whispering how hot he knew I was during my threesomes. I can tell he would love to experience a threesome. At one point, he said he'd love to see me pleasured even if he was across the room just watching. I can tell his brilliant mind has many fantasies as his imagination can take over sometimes. I really enjoy pleasing him, but the way life is at this time, I just don't know of anyone we can trust to not destroy his or my life if things go south. There aren't many who can handle the threesome dynamic.

When he did finally cum, it was after he asked me if he could. Of course I said yes and helped him to where he was cumming long and deep inside me while I was lying on my back, accepting it all. He held his breath, and I had to remind him to breathe.

Somehow, he ended up getting up too quickly, and as he checked his phone, I watched him start to talk to me telling me his "guys were already starting to call out". His eyes glazed a bit, and the next thing I knew, he was leaning against the wall with his hands on his knees looking pale as fuck ready to pass out! It scared the fuck out of me to see him gassed like that. He tried to play it off, a slight smile forming at the corners of his mouth. It was at that moment I realized he puts himself last. I started to sit up in bed in case I needed to get across the room to him. He played it off well and dressed as I watched him closely. I realized at that moment I cared very much for him and his well-being...much more than I thought. (I'm scared)

He changed the subject and brought up how sexual I am. He asked a few questions about Dan and when in our threesomes was he allowed to cum inside me since Dereck was such a controlling prick. He sometimes apologizes for his curiosity and did so as he heard the question come out of his own mouth. I have no reason to lie to him or about my past, and I feel someone has shamed him deeply for how his mind works. I don't want to do that. I told him the third time and that seemed to please him.

I explained how uncomfortable Dereck could make things when he would try to be overbearing or a control freak. He shook his head, and I mentioned that surviving my marriage was a lot about pretending. I resented Dereck because as a liar, it was as if I had to be one too just to make it through one trauma to the next. I even shared how having sex with him left me needing to fantasize about someone else in order to get to climax. Oddly, I always envisioned someone like Gunnar, his body, his touch, even his face, in order to cum. I may have been sensing him all those years since he seems now so familiar and I am wildly comfortable naked with him...like I've known him for a long, long time.

I did notice that while he was on top of me and everything felt so good, I whispered how much he's wanted, if he knew how much I desired him...but he stared down at me and got quiet. As magnificent as he is, I feel deep down he's a lot like me, always wanting to be wanted...but rarely believing he is.

January 7, 2022 11:11 AM

Hi...want you...thats all...

Hiiiii...always wanting you...
Out with my friend's kid, he needed help choosing a healing crystal. Love kids!! Missing you...

This morning's shower thought:

He...will hunt man, caring for nothing else thereafter
He will take life, to protect and honor

He will hold her with the gentlest of hands, rapturing her soul, filling her womb
He will love his babies more than his own life, bringing them forth in legacy, requiring the world to cherish them...

or be the hunted

He is man
A simple, beautiful man

-Peg Law

So very true

Real quick...most defining moment yesterday?

Your smile

Thank you...
Your energy and the things you did to me...
Ohhhh myyyyy gawwwwd.
Put that phone down! Just saw you drivin!!!!!

Ooooohhhh...hi...

Heyyyyy

472

Trying to staff instructors for range next week...

Ah...yes. Busy, busy...

Can't get reliable help

I hear that...the worlds going to shit

Such...16 hours days all next week...grrrr

Wow...blows

15 instructors...only 1 said he'd help

Seriously?! WTH?

Bunch of goobers

I agree. Is it money?

Just...burnt out

Miss...your...

Yes...hugs...that's what you were gonna say

Lol...yeah...or deeeeep, hard, penetration, thrusting type hugs!

Name the 80s movie...”your hot beef injection”

Can't remember

Clue: “Don't You” (forget about me) by Simple Minds

Adam Sandler?

Breakfast Club. Good guess tho!!

Not one I have seen...

Seriously??? Ohhh my bad.

Ask me anything from...Blackhawk Down...on

Love that one!!

American Sniper kills me...fuckin' Clint Eastwood. He always said he was better behind a camera than in front of one. He knows how to pick a script. My son worked with him here on the set of The Mule. Says he's quite the "ladies man".

He is badass...through and through

Dropping an egg...Ouchers

Hmmmm...that is hot

Sooooo...yearning...

What's it feel like??

It's a deep aching inside...like a milking? Only an orgasm can ease. When you...

Tip meets cervix...motion

Right...when you hike my leg up and thrust hard there's an ache that surges through everything...hard not to scream out...

Me too...so deep...

Thank you for asking. It makes me happy to share with you. Right ovary this month...ouch...
You want to scream too???

I do...moan...scream...cream...

Mmmm...love to hear you in my ear.

As I enter...as I cum

474

Omg...soooooo good. How is it so good???

Irish loving

Is that right?

Irish

My favorite.

Mmmmm...

Needing Irish loving againnnnnnn...

And...again...and again...and...

I'm sorry...

Sorry??

I'm your support badger!

Meme: Do you suffer from anxiety attacks? Are they often caused by stupid people? Get an emotional support honey badger. Unlike other companion animals, the honey badger physically attacks and severs the nuts off the idiot bothering you, removing the source of anxiety. Much more efficient. Ask your doctor if a honey badger is right for you.

Badass little creature

Want to...give you a hug...with my...

I wants that

Looooove it so much...your...giftednesssssss

That a technical term??

Just made it up...Irish loving word
So how was it using your xmas gift on me?

475

Ammmmmmazing...you...well...loved it

I'm like that...
It was hot...but you?? So prefer you there...amazinggggg...

Have you played alone...since. With it???

Ummmm...no. Just disinfected and put it back for when we have more time. I have played with our memories...so I can sleep. How are you these days?

I'm good...looooong week ahead...just relaxing

Good. Gotta rest. Ever find any loyal instructors to help?

Not a single one...bitches

OMGooooosh. Wow. Welp, guess you're the go-to-guy again. Sorry, shouldn't bring up work while you're relaxing.
Instead here's a Meme: When she rides it, hops off and sucks it, then climbs back on Lol...

Yes you do

Meeeeeee?? Not me....

Yup...you...I look down...you lick, suck, engulf

Who wouldn't...have you seen how amazing your cock is?

Seen. Your glaze all over it...

Meme: Be with a man who opens the blinds just enough to appreciate how the sun glistens off your skin... Or glaze...

Yes...I...do

Mmmmmm...

Chapter 27

BIRTHDAY GIFT

Dereck opened one eye, the sun shone through the curtains waking him before he wanted. He reached for his phone to see the time. There in big bright letters was proof he was exactly fifty-two years old:

January 8, 2022

He clicked the button to turn the screen off and threw the phone back on the end table. Sadness washed over him as not one text was waiting to be opened. He thought of Peg. She always did something for his birthday to make his existence feel known. Every birthday was memorable if Peg was around. The silence that now filled the room was deafening. *She was still gone.*

Dereck rolled over aggressively to face the other way. Her spot in their bed was empty. He thought about how January was the sixteenth month she'd been gone. Her side of the bed had been untouched for over a year and four months. He let out a long sigh, hoping to start hating her again as he'd done so well the day before. He decided that even though not one family member, not one student, not one friend or neighbor, not even his mother...called to wish him a happy birthday, that didn't mean it couldn't be a memorable one.

Throwing the covers off his body, he slowly slid out of bed, trying to ignore the back pain of lying down too long. He huffed out air and brought himself to sit at the edge of the bed. Looking down at his swollen, stubby hands, he nodded and whispered into the room, "Happy Birthday, Dereck, today is the day you give yourself the gift of her death. If you can't have her, no one should." He then stood and limped to the bathroom and through to the master closet to get her gun and visit her room one more time.

eg made a left out onto Telshen Road as she did every day when leaving the gym. She put the blinker on to turn right onto Spree Boulevard but then turned it off and continued straight. Something inside told her to keep going in that direction and stop at the gun shop for a holster. For so many years, she'd gone against her instincts, especially living with Dereck, but now she knew better than to ignore her gut. Even Gunnar was a gut decision, and she was more than happy with the way their relationship naturally unfolded.

She made a left and parked to the side of the building. The store was relatively new compared to her favorite gun shop out on Valley Street. She thought about going there but the risk was too great that she'd run into her ex, or Gunnar...or her ex and Gunnar at the same time! She huffed a laugh at her droll thought, then again, with the way life had unfolded, stranger things could happen. She just needed a concealed carry holster for under her scrubs in case Dereck decided to pull his shit. Her gut was telling her he wasn't well...in a way it was more screaming at her.

unnar sighed while texting back to his higher ranks. The department was getting hit hard with Covid cases, and the pressure of forced vaccination was causing unneeded stress as well as surprise early retirements and a ridiculous amount of resignations. He could feel his body resistant to all the changes.

Wishing there was a stronger word than fuck, he pursed his lips and continued to be politically correct in his text messaging as he agreed to attend yet another morning meeting. Honestly, he wanted to text with Peg and forget all the bullshit that had become his life. Less time was not what he'd been wishing for. Peg was the type of woman that needed more time...took her time...deserved time.

Hopping into his truck, he started the ignition and turned the music up until he could feel the drums in his chest. The one thing he could always trust in was his ability to compartmentalize for focus, and distraction, to ward off pain. He pulled out of his driveway trying to decide which one he would need more of to detach from Peg Law...if that was something men could even do from a woman like her. He touched his phone screen to check to see if she was on.

January 9, 2022 10:47 AM

Did you...rub...your...

Was soooo...incredible. Kept seeing you looking down at me...sliding deep...whispering...You?

Cum shot all over chest...use your toy? Our toy...

Mmmmm...cum...I didn't have to lol. Soooo sensitive. WPS lol...

I was reliving...your ass and pussy filled

Ohhhh myyyy...yes please!

That was hot...great view

It feeeeeeels so good...gonna have to go to the ladies room if you keep making me relive the pleasures you give meeeeee....

Wow...really...wow. Would follow you in...

That...would please me very, very much. Just that feeling...your hand down my spine...grabbing both my hips and driving in me slow...then a lil' harder...deeper. I can't help but lose myself...surrendering...squeezing you...

Buried...balls touching...

Mmmmm...love your balls...touching my...

As I cum in you...from behind

Loooooove that, now...I'm pulsing. My right ovary is punching the shit out of me like "got cock"? Lol. My egg is desperate today...my vag wants to hug you soooooo...tight lol...

Wow...you are in the mood...

Yes...our...connection...calms me, regulates the CPTSD! I was trained for years to be dismissed...he'd always said I was so incredibly sexual but...played games to control it...ignored me...as punishment.

I know he's regretting much now...

Mmmmmmmmmmm....so very (fire emoji)

Yes...you are. Scorpio...Irish loving...my new all-time favorite...

Made me smile all over

I like to make you smile. And...the way you were nibbling me the other day...your mouth makes me want to
gush just thinking about it...

You are...quite the squirting gal.

Sorry. Off to the laundromat.

Ohhhh my gush...I mean gosh.
Still trying to staff 40 hours of range.

Oh no...40 hours is hella long...

Be more like 80...still work after range...covid is kicking PD ass...

Oh shitttttt..too much baby. Can you postpone range courses due to covid crap?

Neg...gotta go...

Oooof. Well, it is kinda fun for you yes? It's the shifts after such a long day that's dangerous right?
Drowsy copping no bueno.

Dereck parked and stared at the house for a while. He didn't give a fuck that it was the middle of the day with full sunlight and birds chirping. He'd tried so many times before after the sun went down or in the middle of the night and just couldn't seem to go through with anything he'd planned for her.

He fumed at the sight of her truck missing yet again. He had a thought that maybe she'd been parking in the garage. He decided he was going to go right up to the door and ring the fucking doorbell to see. It was, after all, his birthday, and blowing her away, then driving up to the mountains where he'd never be found, sounded like the most memorable birthday he could ask for.

His heart pounded in his ears, but he didn't care, he reached for his truck door. Suddenly, his hand ceased and a sharp twinge of pain ran down his arm and to his fingertips. He retracted, grabbing it with the other palm. *Fuuuuuuuck!*

He slammed his head back and against the neck rest. He couldn't understand why he got like this when it came time to execute plans. He closed his eyes and tried to breathe. It was all happening again...like so many times before...just like in the military. He slammed his head again to erase the flashbacks. His whole life, he'd been a coward...just like she knew but never said. He hated her most for that...for being Peg. She kept the secrets, even when she didn't have to. That's why he had to kill her... because her existence reminded him of who he'd never be. He had to do away with that, with her...but maybe tomorrow.

Chapter 28

WIMP

Dereck was silent. He couldn't believe what he was hearing.

"Mr. Law? Are you there?"

His voice was barely audible, "Yeah...I'm fucking here. Are you serious?"

The nurse tried not to laugh at his half-whispers. She remembers how dramatic he was when it came to the long q-tip. She'd seen a lot of patients, and Mr. Dereck Law was definitely one she put on her "wimp list".

"Yes sir, you are positive for Covid."

"I haven't even been around other humans!" He slammed his hand down on his desk, his heart beginning to race again.

"I'm sorry, I know this is tough news for you. As we discussed yesterday, you'll need to quarantine in your home and continue to stay away from the public." She wanted to get off the phone with him before he got belligerent.

His nostrils flared, "Oh you know what? Fuck the fucking public, this is bullshit, lady!"

He looked at his screen and touched to red x button to end the call. His new powerlessness in life reserved him to only be able to hang up on people to feel significant.

Throwing his cell down on the desk, he leaned back in his chair and ran his hands through his overgrown hair that was beginning to resemble more of a Brillo pad. If he didn't feel like a truck ran him over, he'd head out the door and go cough all over Peg and her overly healthy immune system, which always pissed him off. She could die slowly, but then he thought how that wouldn't be as exciting as violently.

He stood up, his head pounding, and shuffled his feet towards the office door and out into the living room towards the master bedroom to return to bed. He mumbled about being stuck in the house for another fourteen days but not even the pets cared.

unnar slumped down into the patrol car seat and slammed the door shut. He hated January in the desert, even all these years later, it was cold as fuck. The wind didn't make it any easier, at times it felt like his bones would snap. He put on his seatbelt, but before putting the SUV in drive, he picked up his phone to text her. Peg always responded. It was one of the things he liked about her. She always had a nice thing to say and never rejected him. That was rare...and he liked rare.

***

January 10, 2022 12:13 AM

So cold...

OMG...I've been thinking of you working out there...please tell me you're ok?

Doing great...just cold...

I'd keep things warm...

Sooooo wish you could

Someday...

(Later)

Thinking of you...just so you know...

Just home...long day...good day...how you be?

I'm well thanx. Happy to hear your home safe...

Loooong day...but good

I understand. Just checking in...writing chapters. Wet lol...rest up...nite...

483

Nite...

January 11, 2022 1:20 PM

Heyyyyyy...just checkin on ya. Hope you are well...

Loooong days...how you?

Well...stay safe you...

(Later)

Sooooo...sleepy...back to range...

Hiiii...Metallica/Godsmack therapy at the gym.
Sleepy is the vibe this week. Hope you're feeling like you make a difference out there...cold mornings...

I am dragging ass...looooooong week..days on range...nonstop last couple nights...sooooo tired...almost done tho

Proud of youuuuuuu...

Just is...my job...28 years...had many...many...shifts...weeks like this...

How ya doing with it? After 28 loooooong years?

Just is...but...tired...doesn't have the flavor it used to...how you be?

And thats how you know life is throwing a curve ball lol...you can duck, catch it, or swing right? Lol...I'm
holding up, thanx-

Irish kid...only know how to swing

I hear ya...

***

<u>Peg's Journal Entry 1/11/22:</u>

I'm beginning to get downloads while driving and signs in my dreams about how and why this crazy thing with Gunnar came into my life at this juncture. I woke this morning to the words TRAUMA BOND, and as I opened my eyes to look up at the ceiling I stare at all too often, I sensed and felt the ayahuasca medicine still in my body telling me I am exactly where I'm supposed to be with this thing with him. I don't know why I need it...but the lesson is there...and so is the yearning for his pleasure...still...

Fuck-

January 13, 2022 8:57 AM

Hi...miss...your....

My?

Kisses...how are you?

Awwww...I do miss kisses...

I am...thinking you are touching yourself...

Did last night...putting on workout pants now...they feel like your hands...

Wish I was pulling off those pants

That would feel even better. Have you? Touched and thought of me?

Yes...I have...

Mmmmm...makes me happy...

Hot streams of cum...

That...is hot...

Was dreaming I was in your mouth...

Really...

Yes...feels soooooo good as you swallow...

Reeeeaaaaallllllyyyyyy.....

Amazing...seeing you suck your glaze and cum off me...mmmmm....

Wow...someone is on this morning....

Wish I was on you...

Mmmmmm....

In you

I do remember how good that feels...

Dripping...from you

Do I...drip?

Yes...you...do...

WTS = WPS muah...

Want my lips on it...use vibrator last night?

I do like your lips...

And my tip...slowly pushing in...

Just my imagination...tantric breath...and skilled hand.
I do like your s...l...o...w teasing tip...

Wish it was teasing your ass...

Mmmmm...

Slowly passes in...

I like your gentle pleasure...

Orgasms from anal...ohhhhh my...

So...good...

How's gym?

487

Lol...trying to get there...a bit wet...

Mmmm...slide those pants off...vibrator...right on clit...

Lol, might never get there if...gotta increase weights...build chest and boobies lol...

Boobies looks great...rub your beautiful clit...

My yoga pants rub it with each step...rep...breath...and no one even knows. Peg secret...

Mmmmmmmmm...I know

You do huh?

Yup...yup...

Needing help with my two characters in my latest chapter...it's their first "encounter". Perhaps you have suggestions?

Mmmmm...dress rehearsal...mmmm...

Lol...that may be a very good title for the chapter...

Seeeee...already getting my brain in gear

Mmmmm...that brain of yours...sexy-

(Later)

Wow. Today just tanked...

How?

Roomie's mother stopped by...

...and??

Told me she needs to move in and doesn't think there's enough room for me...then told me I look hot and my makeup is great. What a manipulative wanker.

488

Ohhhhh....

Already knew she was a covert narcissist...not sure if roomie knows, is uncomfortable with me staying, or if mother is testing to see if she can triangulate. Yay, fun times.

What's plan??

Processing...

Not NJ...is it???

Not my preferred state...

Nor mine...

January 14, 2022 10:08 AM

Off to PHX...again...

Oh wow...excited?

Meh...shooting match...sponsors...back Sat night...then Albq for teaching on Monday...grrrr

Well...that can be fun...

Tired...

I bet. Burnin' that candle at more than both ends...
Curious.. what's your process with winning at the shooting/competition stuff over the years... Do you visualize, or feel yourself doing it? Is there a dreaming or meditative part for you?

<u>***Peg's Journal Entry 1/14/22:***</u>
    Today was a day I could have done without along this new single-life journey. With all the changes and how up-in-the-air my life is, I needed my "certainty" needs met in the ways of shelter, food, comfort, etc. Sadly, with one conversation, my world went a little wonky, and now I'm needing a new place to live.

I've always known my roommate's mom, who lives next door, was an awful person. Angry, dishonest, incredibly manipulative...and that's just what I picked up from the first few years I knew Jan and the "idea" of her mom. She, herself, has always had some intense characteristics, and in my experience, they come from a tough parent who has identity issues. My gut tells me to get away from these people, they are the types that pretend to want to help but really only want a front-row seat to watch someone in pain go through more pain then they actually feel. I had moments during recent meditations where I asked for evil and conditional types to be removed from my life. I guess I shouldn't complain if the universe is looking out for me lol. Just sucks I have to move again.

I'm going to take the weekend to try to find a place to live. Worst case scenario is sleeping in my truck, second worst is throwing in the towel and calling my sister to ask if I can move back east with her, both feel too much like giving up. I don't want that. I'm going to call in some favors and see what I can come up with. I'm sure with proper funds, I could do whatever I want, like get an apartment, but money has to begin to flow for that. I'm going to try to be positive. Who knows, maybe something better is about to unfold.

I think the saddest part is in remembering all the years I was friends with Jan, never her mom, but I truly tried to be a friend to her even though I could never trust her after she sexted with my ex. It felt awful to know how she was underneath it all, and yet I still ended up apologizing to her for his disrespect. Even after I learned about all the gossip she told her co-workers and why her jealousy wouldn't allow her to invite me along to events with them, I still let it go. I'd thought we were tight, she even helped me move from my massage office and let me store my belongings in her garage...but then again, nothing was without payment. That's Jan.

For years I supported her emotionally, giving countless hours of free coaching via text and in our woman's group. I'd wanted to see her flourish. Living with a person definitely shows more truth. There seemed to be a falseness and I didn't want to admit that...a deep depression or apathy of some kind lingers in the house along with a feeling of disdain towards me. I'll probably never know why. That shit always has to do with the deep wounding of the person, not who they project it on.

I'd overheard her and Crystal on the phone recently. It saddened me to listen to so much judgment and criticism with no real accountability for why. My daughter had warned me years back about them and how small minds stay stuck. I didn't want to believe that but well...no growth means things die...and I have to let it. This is an opportunity to break trauma bonds, so I must let it happen. Who knows, maybe Jan will come around and stand up to her mother not allowing her to bully me out of living in the room I pay for. Then again, my gut tells me that Jan may have wanted her mother to get rid of me so she didn't have to have the confrontation with me. Time will tell. In the meantime, I've got to keep going. Onwards and upwards, Peg!

January 15, 2022 8:02 AM

Very much visualization is part of it...not really meditation but more of sequence of complex skills...how are you?

Love that! Thought so.
Moving some things to storage. Hope you are well?

January 17, 2022 9:00 AM

So tired...couple more days of grind...how was roomie situation?

Hi

3 guesses...

She lives in her truck and showers at the gym...

Ummmmmm...who????????

She's with her bestie (sister) in NJ...

Wait...you?

She called in a favor and a friend let her rent a room in her house out by Field of Dreams...

Ummm...better be field of dreams. What's going on?

(Later)

Apologies...had to FaceTime client. Talking her off the ledge.

Please tell me something happy. AZ trip go as needed? You smilin'...I hope...

Was good...you staying with friend???

Yes. I'm ok. Was rough week. Sister tried to send me a flight. Can't give up yet.

No giving up...not you.

Tired...long couple weeks too...weather has been great...where you staying now?

Legends Way across from FOD. Not a fav neighborhood, houses icky on outside, roomies very clean inside.

Last roomie was a piggy. Drove me a bit batty lol.

I know you've got to be burnt out...

Roomie allow visitors?

Lol...of course...

Ahhh...gooooood...how's...that vibrator...

492

Lol...idk...tell me how you really are...

I'm good...great

Toys are packed in the closet. Had to move in one day.
I'm happy you're feeling great.

How are you?

I'm hangin' in...grateful for resilience lol...

That...you...are...

Lol

You at shop?

It's a holiday...

Ohhhh...you home?

Yes. Rough weekend. Trying to regulate lol...my brain...

Ahhhh...I wanna regulate...your clit...

Really?

You seem needing...seed?

Are you needing?

Love to suck you...lick...taste you as you cum...

Someone's back...

On period?

493

Was late...stressy week. Started today. Got things in your calendar?

My mind...just a feeling...need to give you some hormone orgasms

I think mine are all hormone orgasms lol. Thank you for caring...

Mmmmmmmmm....

Smilin' through the cramps

Would you be able to sex me up with cramps??

Sex you up? Lol

Do that thing...when you ride

How's that? What thinggggggg?

That hip thing...

Mmmm...I think I remember...

I know I do

I kinda can't stop seeing my hands holding you down...
rocking my pelvis to your...engorged...sorcery...lol

Wowwwwwww

Wet...

Well...

Gonna be...super tight...after sooooo long...have to acclimate again to your...girth?

You like? To be stretched...

No...I loooooove it...

494

still...takes my breath away...

Mmmmm...and your ass??

On the menu...if you're still...into that sort of...

Are you...if you are...I is...

Intense connection...I'm always into...pleasure. You know that's my jam...

Mmmm...any toy play recently?

Sadly no, they're packed but I'll find them. Did pick up some...

Some???

*Skimpy lingerie...can't seem to find green.
I believe someone told me green was a favorite color?*

Very sexxxxxxy...how are you doing?

I'm well today, thank you. How are you holding up? I'm curious...

I'm beat...but...get to Thursday night...I can relax

Wow...you've got to be exhausted...are you enjoying any of it?

Love it...wish more days...more hours...do more

Really?? Is it more you stuff, less work?

Both...of'em

Lol...that's great...gotta feel good!

What's you doin

Sitting on the couch writing...you?

Just work...wake up at 0400...woohoooooo

Tomorrow?

Yes...work till 0100...couple hour sleepy time...then off to races

Ohhhh myyyy...well...as long as it makes you happy your energy should hold up!

Pre workout!!!

Lol...looking forward to the gym tomorrow. Gotta get rid of all the aches and pains from moving lol. Still got that chest I enjoy nibbling?

I hope so...not much working out this week

Yeah, tough schedule for self-care...

Yeah...how's your gym stuff

Great actually! Increased weights this week, skin is getting tighter, tanning to detox and shrink skin, so hoping the next 6 months will show big decrease in chubbies and more defined muscle. Missing my grasp on your lats and...ass...
And...your whispers...

Ohhh and I forget...who kissed who...first?

Easy...you

Are you sure?

Not at all...but sounded good...

Sure did! Lol...you make me laugh...
So...real quick. When one is driving away from a laundromat parking lot after touching and necking with someone he's been sexting with for weeks but met years ago...what is one thinking?

Ummm...was thinking...wow...what a great kisser...

Right, got that part and the hours in between?

Ummm...don't remember that part...I know...I was amazed how fast you started stroking me...

Mmmm...so good...I remember thinking "how will I even handle his size" lol...

Was great first kiss...great first entry...great first orgasms

OMG...I'll never forget

Damn...I mean...damn...

Great memories...

It's amazing-

January 19, 2022 10:35 AM

Hey? Everything all right?

All is great...in Albq...teaching...loooooong days

497

Finally back in groove...how are you?

Heyyyyyy...I'm kinda missing things. How are you holding up after so much fun?!

I'm...beat...but solid as woodpecker lips

WTF?? Lol...

Solid

When can we...well...

Yes...well???

Mmmm...just need a lil...I mean if you have anything left?

Left? Plenty

Really?

Always

REaaaaaaalllyyyy?

Yup...yup...what you doin

In my room...writin'...you?

Was gonna go to gym...is your roomie home??

No, she works till 5...

Ahhhh...can you?

Can you?

Be fucked till you moan...and are cross-eyed

Really?

If you will have me

Should I? I might...have a difficult time stretching...after soooo long being apart...

Wanna try??

Do you remember...how my body needs...you?

Tell me

Well...you know the slower...the better...
We women feel more inside when it's slow...and torturous like. Fevered, wet, filling...

Wow...how wet???

Well now that you're arousing me...kinda dripppyyy...but messy...it is my day off...
I could do a lil' puff puff

Yes...please

On second...puffffff...

Whats address

2378 Carrots Ct...

(Later)

Mmmm...how was nappy time...

No nappy time yet.
You...felt incredible...know you are VERY desired and wanted sexyyyyyy...How are you?

I'm...beat...but holding up

I'm sorry if I ..."took" too much energy...
Your penetrations are sooooo...yummy

No take...was amazing...

OMG...your body...what you do to me...

The weed is nice physically but...it tends to "distract" the mental part...and I feel I wasn't doing all the things I wanted to do lol...the connection seemed off?

I thought you were funny...giggling

Noooooo...was I?

Cute

Oh nooooo...that from behind action was hot and then my feet on your chest!!!!

Was sooooo hot...deeeeeep

OMG feeling you in my...throat...feeling your broad back under my hands...you tasted amazing tooooo...

(Later)

My kitty...is sore...

I'm sorry

I'm not. Just...needs you...

Hehehehe

And...I wanted to mention, but I had to get my thoughts clear...

When you wanted me on my stomach...when you entered me from behind...filling, stretching me so completely...thrusting deep...making me succumb and want to arch back...taking my breath away...then I felt you...Lean down, when you bit my neck...there was this electricity that shot through me...and ecstasy...

Sooooo...hot

***

<u>**Peg's Journal Entry 1/20/22:**</u>

It'd been 14 days since he and I were last together. Wow...so needed it!

I even live in a whole different room, in a house way across town, and none of that mattered once he stepped in and we locked the door. I was high on a few puffs of weed. Never had sex high before. I'd definitely had too much because everything was intense but kind of chill...almost humorous. I mean I tried to think of it as humorous but the passion gets me to my core.

It was a day off for me and he'd wanted me to be high. Not sure I like it as I kind of felt forgetful...or mentally distracted. He seemed to have way more energy than I did and usually I match his efforts. Weed slows me down in ways I wasn't expecting.

We started out with oral, then ended up on my back, me pulling his ass and back into me to feel him as deep as possible. I love sucking on his nipples and neck, I can feel how it affects him and makes him gasp. He did all the best things that feel so good to both of us. We're so in tune it still freaks me out how enjoyable our sex life is. My legs were up, out, open, on his chest...then I was on my stomach, he entering me from behind, me pushing my hands against the wall to push back and meet his every thrust. He felt full...incredibly so and then suddenly reach down and sunk his mouth into my neck and trap! My eyes rolled back and I thought I'd go mad. I'd blame the weed but every damn time he sinks his mouth into my neck I feel an indescribable electricity or surge of some sort of energy. There was so much more intense missionary and edge of the bed play. He has such good rhythm and timing...so strong too but has never hurt me! Love that so much. He genuinely has no malice inside him when it comes to women. I can feel it...he's masculine and even animalistic at times but never has he wanted to invoke pain. He even treats his mother with respect. I am convinced that a man who treats his mother well, despite their history, is a man who'll treat all women he encounters well. Dereck hated his mother and when it came to me, there was always a blackness inside him. I was never sure totally if sex was going to be pleasurable. There was some weird unspoken demon energy...like a block between us. I was always able to cum, but after I felt... lonely or as if I'd pleasured myself with no connection. There was never a connection with Dereck... just sex...and loneliness after. With Gunnar, the connection is so effortless, it scares me. Even across town or when he's gone for days and days, I still feel and want him. I don't understand and I know nothing lasts forever...but the moments, the memories of what we do creates something inside me. Some sort of lasting...limerence? I try to shake it off because I know my CPTSD plays a huge part. I don't fully understand it...but I know I like it.

After we'd finished he talked about his fears of retirement and about what he'll do if he doesn't do what he's been so accustomed to for over twenty-eight years. His eyes were heavy and

501

exhaustion wore on his face. He mentioned his kids and I could see how he just puts out fires, and fixes, and steps forward...all for them. I can see he wants so badly to "hero" forward for them...it's truly his "why". Admirable.

At one point he let me know he was happy to see I'd moved to a better place and not back to New Jersey with my sister. He also let me know that I would never be sleeping in my truck and that felt really good to hear.

I'm aware of his need for progress, and I fear there will come a time when he'll fade away because we are no longer "achieving". I'll never not admire his drive...I've often done this myself. Progress equals happiness for types like him and me...

January 21, 2022 11:03AM

Hello...

Soooo...about yesterday...

Yes?

(Later)

Ugh...clients.
Anyway, I see you.

I saw in your eyes yesterday the exhaustion, like deep fatigue...but I heard what you said about your kids...
Please know...I do see you. Your drive and purpose are admirable...All you're doing and striving for...it's the
stuff a real man is made of...in my eyes anyway.
All that you're doing is for your babies it's soooo...

That is one of the kindest things someone has said to me...

(Later)

Sorry...couples massage. Lunch w/the girls.

No seriously, please know there's so much that comes through...and your intentions are correct. Your
reasoning behind your uh..."disease to please"? Is seen. What you're creating for them is going to heal...and
"hero" forward. On your low days, please remember your "why" because there should be more men like you...

Thank you...that truly made my day

Oh and I wanted to mention how much it meant that you said I wouldn't be sleeping in my truck. I had the
worst weekend but knowing you'd heard me and would say that made it all disappear. Thank you for that.
Truly...

You will never sleep in a truck...

Thank you...lawyer put out another emergency motion for Monday.

That good??

503

Yes, she's pleading to have him understand the urgency of my situation and how his "military spousal abuse" should be stopped immediately. I'd live in a box as long as I don't have to be imprisoned by him anymore. Life is good!

Very good

Please tell me you've been able to rest some?

I have...have to work in morning

(Later)

Hello...

Hiiiii

How you

Great! You holding up ok sexy?

I am...worked today...relaxing at home...having drink

Mmmmm....

Yes...Jamison has new orange whiskey...

Your opinion of it?

...

Chapter 29

DREAM

P eg spun the fidget spinner between her middle finger and thumb, making it go faster and faster. Her kids had bought it for her years ago, and somehow, it ended up in her massage supplies. She looked at it and huffed a small laugh at how her two favorite humans think she needs a fidget spinner to balance her CPTSD...or the side-effects of it.

Her daughter recently tried to have an entire texting conversation about how Peg has undiagnosed ADHD, which is super common in women who suffer from CPTSD. Peg spun the spinner again, not giving much of a shit about all that now. She smiled wide, looking around the tiny room she rented and enjoying how great it felt to be free of Dereck Law and his mental torture. She thought about Zena's last text and how she slid in there that her father has covid. Peg almost felt sorry for him. She wouldn't wish the crap on anyone and knows Dereck was probably throwing a tantrum at the news he was just like others. He was always convinced he was god, as most narcissists do, and that nothing would happen to him. She raised an eyebrow thinking how he always thought she would stay too.

Placing the little spinner to the side, she rolled her body off the bed and up to a standing position. She'd recently gotten some lettering for her truck and decided it was time to apply them to the back window so she could drive around advertising her business. She was a bit nervous to have her name on her truck windows but knew it would deter Dereck from taking the truck away from her should he find it. He has a key and if pissed off enough, he would come steal it just to see her struggle. She knew it was only a matter of time before he started feeling better and started to come looking for her.

The thought of him hurting her never left her mind from the moment she drove back into town in September. He was not well and she knew that, not in a Covid way, in a mental-type way. She squinted her eyes to try to erase the visual of him pushing the head of a sixteen-year-old down onto his thumb-sized cock. She shook her head, opened her eyes, and grabbed the lettering to go distract herself from the fact that she

505

was married to a monster all those years and didn't even know the extent of it. Her stomach swirled and she tried to will the queasy away.

Stepping out of the door and feeling the sun on her skin took it all away. She smiled again remembering that she was in fact free...she was even dreaming more, a true sign that she was feeling more liberated and able to express herself...especially with Gunnar.

***

January 23, 2022 8:58 AM

(Gunnar posted a photo on social media of his daughter)
Some of the best memories I have are of painting my Dad's nails and also hammering nails with him in the garage! Love when dads "Dad" well. Psst...you're doing it right...great job!!

Muah!

Mmmmm...thank you. So needed that today!

How are you?

Leaving gym. Good! You?

Need to go to gym...gotta find motivation

Hmmm...well, you're a hottie underneath all that clothing. Maybe that helps?
But on another note...it fuckin' gets the mind straight...so just...goooo.
Even if for just the sauna and resetting the adrenals. You'll thank yourself later!

I needs to

Did I ever mention it's dangerous when I get bored?
(3 pics of lettering applied to truck by hand)

Well hell...looks great

Ya think?

506

Best part...clearing bubbles...with CCW card....fuck yeah

I knew you'd pick up on that lil' detail...
That mind...

I get paid for details...

Mmmm...you've mentioned...I likey details...

Yup

January 24, 2022 8:27 AM

Hi

Hey!

Alright?

Sorry...was dreamin'...

What about?

Making you smile

How

Mouth...vagina hugs...anal...

Wow...anal...

Mmmm...our lil...secret...

Whats that

Our pleasures...

Mmmmm...you like anal...sooooo hot

You've said...feels gooooood...

Sooooo good...you rubbing clit?

Getting out of shower...that was last night...thinking of your hands all over me. Helped me sleep. How are you these days?

Normal work week...kinda nice...

Yay

You?

> *Normal as well...*

Shake shop?

> *Later perhaps. If I don't go they all text me and worry. Nice.*
> *Feeling like you might "gym" today?*

I needs to...

> *Mmmm...feels good...*

So do you...

> *That was...nice to hear...missing your...affection...*

I want to stretch your

> *I likeyyyy...how you fill and burrow deep...makes me crazy*

As my tip rubs g-spot...goes deep...so deep

> *Soooo deep. How you do that?*

Easy when you push up...push back...grind deep...

> *Feels soooooo good...*

So thinking about...
Pushing my cock in your ass...

> *Mmmmmm...I like how slow and gentle you are...*

You sure it pleases you?

> *I'm very sure...tough at first...cuz you're uh...well endowed?*
> *But when I relax...it's alllllllll pleasure...*

Mmmmmm....

                    Mmmmm...

What was your fantasy last night...as you were cumming

                    Promise not to laugh?

Yuppppp

          You were saying goodbye to the last of your students in a classroom.
          They left and you were cleaning up...

Ohhhhhh....

    I took papers out of your hands and pulled you by your belt to a side closet...

Yes please

          You moaned like you do when you're interested in me...
          Kicked the door shut with your foot...

And???

          My hands went to my favorite place...

Yes...

          Was impressed...

With

          You still wanting me...so I

Fuck yes...I wants you

          Pulled your shirt off, unfastened belt and pants, you kicked off boots...

Kissed your neck...chest...mmmmm nipples...tummy...found my favorite places...warm oozing tip, hard shaft...

Instant hard cock when you need

Always seem to need... you get me going...even just texting...I used my wet, fevered mouth to help you relax... my hand gliding on your shaft to the base, my tongue swirling and sucking every drip of precum...

Mmmmm...throbbing as I cum in your mouth...

Pumping...so much...

Spray the top of your mouth...throbbing...squirting...moaning...

Mmmmm...I love to hear your pleasure...

You give amazing blow jobs...amazing...

You make me want to...

Amazing...
Your pussy tastes amazing...

Really? My kitty really, REALLY likes you...

After you cum...sooooo sweeeeeeet...beautiful tight...pink...perfect

Blushing...

After I cum in you...it drips out...slowly...

Like that huh? You have very nice, healthy, cum...white...warm...

Fuck...very sexy

Mmmmmm...

Keep me hard...rub along pussy...push in again...

Looooove that penetration you give me...sore all day...cum dripping here and there...
subtle reminders of intense connection...

Lots of cum...

Agreed...You are special in that way...

Which way

You produce a lot...

Ohhhhh....

It's impressive...

Taste...feel ok??

Very much. Didn't like so much in past. Haven't been with many.
Yours is...idk...like mine somehow. Feels and tastes...

Wow...

Comforting? Not sure how to explain...

You make me cum so hard...
You explain things well

What does that mean?

Like explosion...meets electricity

I love to see that...makes me feel...like...
I'm finally doing something right...like healing you...

Yes...please

Mmmm...I look forward to our "healings"...

So dreaming of healings...

> *Mmmm...me too. I enjoy dreaming these last 4 months...makes me smile...*

I had dream the other night...you were gently kissing a girl...
her fingers in you...yours in her...

> *Oh myyyyy...*

You were talking her through techniques and showing her...she was rolling in multiple orgasms...

> *Well...multiple would be YOUR doing lol...*

When done...she left...you undressed me...
took me in your mouth...instant cumming...

> *You were dressed?*

Kept stroking me...told me...you wanted me to see that...you with her

> *Just watching??*

I would...I want to see you as you are pleased

> *You would be participating...I wouldn't be pleased unless I had you during....3somes are VERY overstimulating...I would need you...because women don't stimulate me...*

I would stimulate you...yes, I would...

> *Mmmm...just seeing you look at me gets me going...*

I have dreamt...of sharing you with a man too...

> *That...can be...intense...*

Buried...in you...deeeeeeep

Would share...watch...study you...

I'd probably want your "deep" more

Yes...not for narcissistic control but to please you...see you pleased

I get you...

Yeah?
See you lose yourself in pleasure...

Watching tho...it works the studying mind...different from pleasure side...

I was so intrigued when you talked about your 3some

I know...what else do you need to know?

You seemed so pleasured when talking about it...almost...re-living
When you discussed it...you allowed me in...was tough...but you did...to see you...open up

I don't mind letting you in. You're very intense like me. I think you call it "complex"? It was pleasurable but it essentially ruined my marriage. Sooo...its tough for me because something so liberating, where I could be "open" was then used against me later.

Yeah...sounds like...
I'm sorry to bring it up...

Why?

Not cool to re-live the bad...

It's the only way I can heal...

I know...but...feel bad

If I don't work through it, it'll stay stacked in my body...
Feel bad? I don't want you to feel bad...

Not bad...but it turns me on greatly...to think about it...but one ruined your marriage the other...well

Well...I do know that you wanting me, connecting, it's liberated me more than I expected. It's been very validating. I feel more myself. So it returned me to the good parts of the threesome. Like when Dan said...

Said???

He never knew I was like that, never been blown so good before, was like it was just us and Dereck wasn't in the room, my breathing, my touch, how my pussy made him feel, he said it was like I only wanted him...

And you felt it with him...instant orgasm for you...the first time he came in you?

No...he wasn't "allowed" at first. They had to go out for beers and discuss things. Not sure how that went down between men. Found out later from Dan. Said he had a hard time with how Dereck was "pulling puppet strings". The third time, when he was allowed...things changed. Got more "bonded"?

For both him and you

Yes...that's when I started to sense danger...

Ohhhh....sorry to bring it up...

No need to apologize. Maybe you have some sort of guy view...that can help me...

Such as?

Not sure...I only know my experience...from my eyes outward lol...It was a very profound time in my life...So much pleasure. Yet so much mental abuse after Dan would leave... Dereck had a very hard time with loving it and the visuals of me pleasured... but then hating me too? He also had issues with Dan's size...

Well.....I think....you were at point in marriage that you knew...in love wasn't option...stalemate...but have passion to be....once passion was actually allowed....your pleasure was amazing...

Not sure now if it was all about his wanting Dan...I believe he has a preference for men.
Yes, thank you for articulating that...

So when allowed to feel you for real...you and Dan both took time...enjoyed every kiss, touch, moan....were lost..then filled you with cum you wanted...needed....pleasured for...as cloud of passion feigned away....Dereck's jealous aspirations became shame to you...they shouldn't have

True...which ultimately swayed my loyalty towards Dan who was treating me like a woman, worshipping me, understanding me.
Dereck has a deep hate for women (his mother, 7 female cousins suing him, not being born female, etc) which I wasn't fully aware of...I think Dan and I "understood the assignment" lol...

Well...I so desire your pleasure

Same here...

Assignment?

It's a TikTok phrase, lol...
I believe Dan and I had a deep maturity, passion for the pleasure of what a threesome is supposed to be...It did go more toward intense emotion than expected, but I stopped it after 5th time. His life was worth more than my pleasure...and Dereck is not a safe person. He would get a glazed, black look in his eyes when speaking of Dan.

I see...what you doing?

Laying on my bed thinking of you...

Rubbing???

Should I?

Yes...yes...yes...

Are youuuuu?

Getting ready to go to gym...sooooo lazy...work after

Adrenal fatigue will do that...almost killed me.
But, I'm on the mend. Hope you think of me at the gym.

Whoa...of course

(Later)

Energy holding up ok?

Ummmmm....sure

Oh good. Seems like a quiet night out...

Lots of ODs...junkies...

Oh fuuuuuck...I hear fentanyl and meth...

Yupppppper...boff of 'em

Damn

It's everywhere

Yes...well you did mention a lil war between gangs...err cartel?
Sad times in Ramas'...

Nonstop

Fuckkkkkkk

January 25, 2022 10:33 AM

Gooooooooooood morning

I hope it is! Sleep ok?

Little bit...how you be

I be great! You holding up alright?

I am...gotta go in early...assist academy...finish paperwork from homicide last night...

Oh myyyy...busy day. Ugh, homicide huh? Drug dealers killing drug dealers?

Yupppppper

(Later)

Hoping your day has been good...missing things...

How you be

I be goooood! Stress minimal?

Always

Lol

January 26, 2022 11:22 AM

Hello beautiful

Hello you

How's you doing...I hope at peace...with some parts aching

I am...aching as you know.
How're you holding up with all the crazy?

**Good...trying to go to gym...
but lazy druids have attacked me...star wars style...**

Lol, better than badgers...err I mean Wookiees...

Wish I had pet Wookiee...

Right? Lil' fuckers are savage...and cute...

Best of both worlds...like me...

Mmmmm...got a point there...

Baby Yoda ohhhhh so cute...till he force choked fuckers...

Yesss

(Later)

What ya doin?

Mmmmm...Uhhh, just chillin'...what are you doin?

Done at gym...gotta work...did you...touch...

I didn't have help...

I'm sorrrrrryyyy....

Thinkin' you've lost your mojo for me...

Ohhhhhh...hell nope...you?

Uh...don't think that will happen...nopers

Baby Yoda dancing...woohooooo

Awwww...

(Later)

This couple behind me just said I look familiar lol...
(Pic of couple groping each other in the background while standing in line)
Guess what they asked me to join in on...really?

Wow...really???

W...t...f...

You is hotttty

For the record I have never done anything in this town to look...familiar...lol
Thank you-

Way hottty...

Muah...

They just asked?

I was standing in line for a beer and they waited until I was near enough...
I thought it was weird they kept staring...Segway in was "Do we know you? You look familiar." Lol...

Then bam...we wanna...

They're pretty drunk. Hope they call an Uber lol...

Right...an uber...

Lol...I'm off tonight...

Uber...your beer

Just one...gets me through this shit with my girlfriends. Rather be in bed lol...

Shit??

Half naked men...hoping your night is quiet? And you're safe...

Naked men?

Have I not told you about my life coaching clients who dance?
My girlfriends love the free tickets...

Ohhhhh

You do know this goes on in your town yes? Lol
200 screaming women is not my idea of a fun Wednesday but whatevs lol.
I stand in the back...no one touches me...just you...

Did not know dudes dance here

It's a show that comes in once a month. Ramada, whiskey dicks, grapevine. Not very covid conscious. One
dancer just deep throated bridal party bride with a lime from her drink. Ewwwww...

Sounds...great

Nope

I go told once...you look familiar...Told'em I was a stunt double for Brad Pitt...fight club...

Yezzzz!! That's awesome lololo...love your quick wit!
Can't complain, they're playing Metallica sooooo...

521

But if one of thee new fuckers tries to pick me up one more time...I'm a big girl, but ironically, one of the smaller in the room...

Hotttty...

(Later)

Hi...hello...hola...

Heyyyy

How u be?

I be good! You safe?

Affirm

January 27, 2022 7:33 PM

How ya holding up?

Good...you holding up???

Of course, lol...being lazy tonight...jacked my hip a lil on the treadmill so it's a "non-gym day". Happy it's your Friday?

Not...gotta work tomorrow...and Saturday

Ohhh yikes. Jeeeeezus. Well...you did say you were married to the job lol... As long as it meets 3 or more of your human needs...you'll commit!

It does not...how are your needs?

Meh... You feeling ok physically...emotionally? Able to do anything fun lately?

I'm holding up

Hope so...

...almost had to shoot a guy...

Fuckin' serious?

Yeah...domestic...he had gun...mine was nicer

Sexxxxyyyy...glad you didn't have to...had to use your big boy voice? Scared'em?

Easy day

Lol...proud of you. How's it feel to still be great at your job?

523

He knew his love light was about to stop shining

Ahhh, he did? How long it take him to decide?

As soon as I took safety off mine...

Badass...

Gave his wife a brain bleed...previous conviction of murder...

You have to draw...or just use your hands? Murder? Fucker needs to go bye bye for life-

AR15...pointed at his head...

Nice!

I don't get paid to lose

I hear that...gotta be feelin' good.
Great work...

Feel bad for the lady...

Of course...no one deserves a brain bleed
because of someone else's unhealed childhood...

He accused her of hiding whiskey...

Oh christ...alcohol his vice? I mean I know it contributes to 73% of domestics but was he sauced or showing
signs more so of psychosis?

(Later)

He's just a dick...met a bigger dick today...Me...I can be...very not nice

Hmmm...kinda necessary...I like your bigger dick btw...

January 28, 2022 7:38 AM

Hi

Awake?

Back at work...got home at 0230

Holy shit...

Easy day...

Lol...how's that? Easy dayyyy...
(Sent pic of legs in tub water)

I would drown

Mmmm...I wouldn't allow that...we take turns well no?

(Later)

Hi...I want to fill you

Killin me...I'm soaked...

Wanna take you from behind...
Long
Deep
Filling
Throbbing...cumming

I would thoroughly enjoy that...

You ok...seemed mad that I went by...

Mad? Not at all. Felt nice actually...seeing you gets me going...So sorry my roomies are covid quarantined.
Just sitting here manifesting my house back
(Sent pic of home locked out of)

Huh? House??

Just waiting on the judge...no fun renting rooms to live in...

Ohhhhhhh.....

Oh, and I never get mad with your surprises...you are welcome any time...

I was daydreaming...

Mmmm...details?

Wanting you...bad...bad...

Wanted to climb in your truck and make you moan...

Ovulation?? I was daydreaming bout...anal...

Tomorrow?
Anal is needed...

Mmmmm...love your analgasms..

Thank you...Love alllll the gasps and gasms you give lol...

(Later)

What ya doin?

Bored...you?

Just hanging with daughter...getting stuff ready for range tomorrow

Ahhh, more fun tomorrow!

Yup...then one full day off...can I please drive somewhere with you...seed you?

I would like that baby...

You ok with that...kinda cheesy...but...I need your...youuuu

Not my fave or first choice...but you are so...

I know...crude...want your pussy all over me...

No place we could meet?

Hmmmm...room?

?

Room...hotel...I have $$

Mmmm...would I get you for more than just 45 mins?!!

Yup...yup...yup...

Well..thats a yes then...

January 29, 2022 4:18 PM

Hi...hi...hi...

Hiiiii

How you be*e
In sauna...damn buttons

That's hysterical lol
Oh yummmmm...

How's...egg day...

Tough...but so am I. Quals better today?

Yeah...didn't...nice out...great to see so many old pals

Aw, I bet! Good day...

Yeah...another homicide...at park tho...grrrrr

Jeeeeezus...drive by?

Dope deal...at park...

Wow...well, they're still weeding each other out...lol.
Curious...what do you wear in the sauna?

My cock...jk
Just workout gear...

Ah...lol...

You???

Me?

Sauna?

On the cruise ships...bathing suit.
The one in my house I haven't had the chance to use yet...locked out of the house lol...

Ohhhhh my...

Let ya go...you seem busy...

Not at all...at gym...for bit...no drive to workout tho

No drive? Tired?

Yeah...beat...haven't eaten today...

Oooof...gotta do

I know...what you doing...appointments?

Nah, home.

(Later)

I wanna kiss your pink parts...nibble on tan parts...

You dooooo?

Yes...I do...so bad...

Mmmmm...was nice seeing you yesterday...

Very...very nice

Yeah...got things stirring again...

Such as

Wanted to crawl on top of your lap...

What would have happened?

Lay your seat back...unbuckle and find my favorite...parts...straddle to feel your deep penetration...while nibbling your neck...chest...lips.

Instant cream pie...

Instant...

Monday?? All morning??

What mean?

**Can I cum see you Monday...wanted today...and tomorrow...
have 4 kiddos at house...so damn...loud**

Lol, 4 is loud...

Way...loud...kinda my bad...got...each one giant packs of smarties candy...so...didn't think that the whole way through

Lol...

...so Monday...Monday...I lick you till you speak Chinese?

Chinese, huh?

**Chinese? Mandarin...your choice
Heheheh...**

I think I'm going to practice just...being quieter. I mean if you get me speaking tongues then there's a real problem...anything religious...just commit me (laughing emoji)

Ohhh...bite your lip kinda girl...me likey

Mmmmm...you do make me want to bite...

Mmmmm...and nibble...and suck

Suckkkkkkkkk

All above please

Requesting?

Yes please

Yearning...for lips and mouth around your...shaft?

Yes...you suck me dry...

January 30, 2022 12:08 PM

My apologies...crashed, woke up at 11, cocooned in a blanket, titties almost out lol...
roomies staring down saying, "Peg, you ok, girl?"
Stumbled to bed...fuck...damn ovulation coma lol...

Mmmmm...hope you can relax

Lol...yeah, hit the gym so I'm better now.
Hope you're relaxing as well...
Still on for morning...or have you changed your mind?

I'm down...you?

Mmmmm...very...

Ok...text in morning? Bout 9ish?

Save me some...

Some???

You know...that...hot...thick...

Yes...

Any requests?
(Sent pic with side-boob in lingerie)

That's perfect

Yes...you are...

Very sexxxxxy...

Mmmmm...I'm forgetting...been too many days since
you were under my hands...and wet-nessssss...

So wet...squirting wet...

Ya kinda do that to meeeeee...

Can't wait...can I stretch you in every...way?

Please? In only the ways you do...

Wow...will you let me cum in your pussy...and ass??

Have I refused you yet? Feels so good...
the way you...thrust...slow...and soooo deep...

Even anal???

Especially...so good

Mmmmm...

Have I corrupted you?

Yes...simply put...you fuck my brains out...

Really?

Totally wreck me...pulling-sheets-outta-my-ass sex

Never heard it put that way lol...
I think I'm flattered...

Good stuff...there...

The best...from my angle...

Its...been...many...angles...

Favorite yet?

All...you?

*Hmmm...I think I'd like to try them all again to make an accurate assessment LT...
over time of course...I'm not the kind thats in a hurry...*

Very true

(Later)

Ugh...

Ugh???

Roomie tested negative but her boss wants her to stay home until Wed...

Ohhhhh...ummmm...damn the world

DTW (sad face emoji)

DTW? Ohhhhh...

*Wants you...
Just so you know...*

Want you back

Mmmmm...soooooo need you...

(Later)

**Hi
What ya doin**

*Hi
Thinking of you
You?*

Same...pussy wet? Wish I was there...rubbing on you

Wet...for you...we need to meet...

Mmmmm...where...how...

Don't know...

You touching yourself??

No...but dropping an egg...need you today...

Mmmm...need my seed...swimming inside you...dripping...

I do...want you...your hands...your mouth...your cum inside me...

I want ALL of that...

Make it happen, baby...

Want you so much

Want you more...under me...on me...in my mouth...

See you suck the precum off me...

Mmmm...where can we...

Hmmmm...what you thinking?

You mentioned...getting a room?

I can't use cc

How fast can you get here? We have to be very quiet...

Don't wanna make things awkward like last massage studio?

Yep

Roomie...ok with visits?

Not sure. She knows you were here...wonders why so "absent" lol...

Don't want awkward for you...just her there?

Son lives here as well...20 yr old...

He there? Roomie...massage client?

Yes, he sleeps till 1pm. She till 10 but they don't see me most days...
No, neither are clients. Friends

January 31 2022 8:58 AM

Thinking...of your...

Ohhhhh....you really wants me...

Yes...you...change your mind?

No...just don't want you to get in trouble again...

Thank you. Don't want that either...

Wednesday?? All morning fuckapalooza? Fuck...I want you now...

Not sure

Still home Wed????
Been hard for last 30 - 45 minutes...

I would sooo enjoy...your hard...

So dreamt of that...appointments today?

Nope. Day off...

Would you be able to give me massage?

Yes. What are you thinking?

I don't know...but I want to fuck you babe...

I really want you...

Pussy throbbing...like my cock?

Been...all night...

Did you self-pleasure?

No...was saving for you...

Roomies up?

No

Will you get in trouble??

No idea lol...don't want you to be exposed...

Covid? Yeah...I forgot...gotta be careful with mom

That too...

You feel ok?

No

Exposed?? You feel sick?

No. Your identity...

Exposed???

Gonna go for a drive...missing you

You ok??...

No

Can you tell me what you are thinking?
Ok...seems like you need to be alone?

At gas station filling up. Trying not to think.
You? Alone? Lol, opposite. Wanting to be on you, around you, riding you...

Mmmmmmmm...you grind...like no other...

So...you've mentioned...

You truly do...

You make me want to...

To???

Ride...thrust...rock...kiss...suck nipples...squeeeeeze you inside me...

Ohhhhh my...nipples...
You squeeze and squirt...as you cum

Feel you deep...yezzzz...wanna feel you inside...
your warm hands on my hips...pulling me down on you...

How's drive?

Ok...Ozzy, Metallica, Disturbed...heated seats help my aching...
How are you?

Dick throbbing...

I would so help with that...love your cock...

Wish roomies were gone

Yeah...

Want your warm wetness

Mmmm...so wet...

Slide...slide right in...wet

Alwayssssss...

Ohhhh my...where did you drive to?

Milagra Coffee

Where's that

Behind Lorenzos...tucked in the shopping mall across from NMSU

Ohhhh...that one

Dark in back...no one knows me...yay lol

Good coffee?

Tea...don't do coffee anymore. Adrenal fatigue almost killed me lol...

Wearing tights??

Lol...yes,
How'd you know?...

You always wear them when pussy drips...

True, need comfort...feel good...you'd feel better tho

Mmmmmm...pussy still??

Worse now. Soooo aching...triggering me...

How...

Deprivation of being in lifeless, loveless marriage...learning a lot lately...

Like a tutor
Wanna go for a drive

I am driving lol

Where are you

Headed down Uni

Meet me?

Where?

Old Kmart...main

Cameras?

None-

Lol...

Kmart...if you can

Be there in 10?

Yes

k...

Make it Aimleys Furniture across street

Ohhhh k

Got you something...you drive slow

I like s l o w...

***

<u>Peg's Journal Entry 1/31/22:</u>

I woke excited to see him, but my roomies being quarantined put a damper on things. Gunnar's mother can't be exposed to Covid, so he couldn't come to my place and risk catching something from my roommates then taking it back to her. I totally understand, but no one told my body, and I CPTSD-relapsed into rejection trauma. I was trying and trying to process, even coach myself, but I eventually turned to flight and got in my truck for a drive to try to escape. I always did that in the past so I wouldn't turn to substances or some other addictive outlet. I took some time and processed from my subconscious mind which is easier since I drive from the subconscious mind so easily. He was texting me, which was decent, I didn't want to take him into my downward spiral as I was trying to stop from stepping backwards myself. I'd love to get a handle on this. I have to admit, I've been having a much easier time since leaving Dereck. He always made me feel horrible about my emotions and even worse about how I process. I am so proud of myself for finally breaking free.

A few hours went by. He ended up texting, "Can you meet me?" We ended up hidden out in the desert parked in his truck. I can't understand the pull towards him and the relief from feeling his hands in me, on me, and wrapped around me. He bought me a really nice aqua-colored personal vibrating massager and after seeing how wet I was for him, he used it on me, sending pleasure and sensations through my entire body! His tongue explored my mouth while his hands searched beneath my clothing. I was more and more aroused but it was my hands that found he was so incredibly hard for me, sitting in the driver's seat. I made sure to use my mouth in ways that made his breath hitch until he breathlessly admitted he wanted me.

I responded, "I want you inside me." And before we knew it we were in the backseat, me straddling him as his huge cock burrowed slowly into me.

"Babe, you're so fucking tight," was whispered in the quiet of the vehicle, and all I could do was breathlessly nod as his penetration took me to places I hadn't felt for over a week. He pumped passion and ecstasy into my body, and I met him at every move. Somehow, I ended up on my back and he on top, kissing and speaking softly to me as he does. The truck was small and cramped, but it didn't matter. Nothing seems to matter once we're united. My brain loves the pleasure!

At one point, he stopped and said, "I have to taste you!" Before I knew it, he was out of the truck with the door open, his mouth plunging between my legs, climax riveting through me! I would never have guessed car sex in the afternoon sun could be so exciting. He climbed in and was in me again, my sacredness wanting and pulling him in. I wanted him so much...he felt so good.

I asked him, "How do you want to cum baby?" To which, without a beat, he answered, "However you tell me to." So I asked, "Would you like me to swallow you." It was only fair as he always tries to please me at least once orally before all the other times. He whispered, "Do you want to?" I huffed a laugh and said, "While you decide, I'm going to turn around." I moved so I was on my hands and knees and he groaned happily finding me and thrusting deep, taking me from behind. I couldn't contain my gasps and he said softly, "I'm not going to last long this way." I smiled and said, "I know..." I pressed back to him over and over and...over just the way he likes until suddenly he grasped my hips tight and went silent as he does when the pleasure kidnaps every inch of him! I let go and came as well. It...was fire! Best car sex ever.

On the way back, we drove holding hands and he shared his story about how he had brain matter splattered on his sweat pants and was told they were needed as evidence but he had gone out to the call so abruptly that he was "commando" underneath. So in Gunnar fashion, ended up walking into Walmart with brain-splattered pants so he could buy something to wear for after he gave his clothing over to the detectives. I laughed so hard because the way he explains it is hysterical.

We drove passed the movie theater as he lowered his hand to my inner thigh. He explained how he loves the movie theater popcorn way more than he should. He remembered running into Dereck at the theater over the holidays and said the weirdest part was looking at him and thinking how fucking weird it was to bump into him when just an hour earlier "I was balls deep in your ex." I laughed even harder at that because his mind works as sarcastically as mine. There is irony and karma for Dereck...and Lordy does he deserve it. I thought then how Dereck always thought he was so sly in getting one over on me...but wow have the tables turned!

Today started out a bit challenging for me but ended up so satisfyingly fun. Great memories made!

February 1, 2022 8:20 AM

Goooooooood morning

Hope it is...you safe and warm?

I am...I am...how are you

I'm doing well...

I am soooooo...tired

Awwww...me tooooo. Feeling ok tho?

More run down than normal...but solid

Uh oh...reeeeeest. Your immune may be fighting all the gross shit floating about...

Doubled up on pre-workout...cured

Oh good
B12 shots lately?

Today

Mmmmmm...

(Later)

Hey you. Wanted to check in before I go puff puff lol...feelin' any better?
Exhaustion ever cease?

Way tired...wish I could curl up with you...relax...fall asleep...

Best..answer...ever. You know I'd so snuggle you.

I'm snugglicious...

I do agree...

Chapter 30

HATE HER

Dereck watched the house and looked over at the clock. He'd visited morning, then afternoons, and now in the evening. *She's over at his place fucking him and playing house.* His face grimaced at the thought that he'd been waiting for her all these times and she wasn't even needing to return. *Why doesn't she park in the driveway anymore? Shit! She's probably hiding the truck in the garage.*

He opened the door and started to get out, he then put his foot back in and slammed the door. Exhaling in disgust, he realized he can't just go look or ask Jan where she is. It would show desperation, and he couldn't allow that. Picking up his phone, he searched for the shitty PI he'd hired but then threw the device down, rubbing his forehead. Paying the guy two-hundred and fifty bucks for subpar work that wouldn't guarantee an answer didn't feel right.

"Damn it!" Dereck slammed the steering wheel. "Why can't you just take her out you fucking coward!" He shouted into the quiet of the cab of his small truck. He was angry at himself. He knew he could pay someone to kill Peg but a larger part wanted the significance of doing it. Then again, it had been months and he hadn't done it yet...because somehow deep down he knew a world without Peg in it would be a world...not so...right.

"Fuuuuuuuuuuck!" He turned his key in the ignition and put the truck in gear to leave. He knew he hated her, hated so much about her, how she moved, how she fucked the life into a man, how she loved love and everything he wasn't. He hated her. As he pulled out onto the main road he looked at the beauty of Las Ramas. The place he moved her to and made a life in...away from her family.

His chest hurt, a sunken feeling swallowing him up. He hated her...or at least wanted to. He turned left towards their home deciding he'd figure something else out. She'd die another day.

Peg awoke wanting Gunnar again. Both her roommates tested negative for Covid which; admittedly, annoyed the shit out of her. The truck sex was great but she wanted more of him. She had an idea and hoped he'd be willing to experience her pleasures, her way. She picked up her phone to see if he was awake.

Gunnar was texting his staff when her message flashed down from the top of his screen. A smile crept across his lips.

February 2, 2022 8:05AM

It's time...

Time??

*For you...to experience my massage..as I tongue your...a***
No stress, no performing...just pleasure...before you head to the sauna...

Wow...as fuck...

Make time for me some time?

For sure
When???
Your place?

I'm jumping in the shower...yessssss

I want your ass...is that ok

Of course...

Your pussy was amazing in truck other day...so hot...dripping wet...pussy lips swollen...

Think? You haven't said much. I don't think I've ever been that wet...

546

certainly not in a truck lol...

Was amazing...I hope cum was dripping all day

Alllll day...the pheromones of us made people linger...and say weird shit to me...

Wow...such as??

"This is a big backseat, you could live back here!"
Del said, "You look tired,
here's a shake, no nuts because you've obviously had some already today." Lol

Funny...jumping in shower

Oh yummmmmm....

(Later)

You home?

Yep

Ok to...cum by

Please do...

Speeding...

Noooooo...want you...intact...

I'm here

K

By 9:25 a.m. Peg had Gunnar lying on his stomach as she poured a massage oil on his back and slowly rubbed it into his rippled muscles taunting him to relax. Climbing up his body, she pressed her breasts into his back while whispering in his ear how beautiful she thought his body was and how desired he is. She was incredibly attracted to him and she told him so. His breath eased and although aroused he let her continue to massage and relax him as she worked her way down to his low back and glutes. She continued down the back of his overbuilt hamstrings releasing tension and stress. Gently moving in between his legs, she worked her hands up again to his tush, massaging each muscle and relaxing him until he began to exhale and moan. She slowed, working the slick oil down through his anal area and to his perineum where she spent some time causing him to press back, arching towards her fingers, his body yearning. He was so clean and smooth, his cock fully erect, begging for her touch.

Peg reached under sliding her oiled palm forward along his thick shaft to his tip feeling his warm precum slippery along the pads of her fingers. She stroked slow and long matching his breaths. Gunnar sucked air through clenched teeth, the pleasure overtaking him. He loved the sensations she invoked and arched more.

Peg continued her slow torment as she lowered her mouth to him and inserted her tongue into his gorgeously muscular ass, her tongue warm and soft. Gunnar's cock hitched in her palm, the feeling of her tongue mind-blowingly sensual. She continued her rhythmic pace, pleasuring him with her mouth as well as her palm along his shaft. Gunnar gripped the blanket loving the ecstasy but also trying not to cum beneath her magnificent tongue. He moaned and breathed aloud until he could hardly hold on then turned over onto his back.

Peg took his engorged cock into her mouth and began her slow, sensual caressing, sucking him and gliding along his shaft until he was as far as her tonsils. His body wreathed and he bucked trying not to let go too soon. His hands reached down and pulled her on top of him, his mouth on hers kissing her deep as she straddled his lap and sunk down over him, a deep moan releasing in her mouth.

Peg took her time riding him slow, feeling his girth deep inside her, loving the pleasures shooting through her body as she took all of him again, and again. As he got close, she released from him and kissed down his chest and stomach until she reached his cock and took him in her mouth again, sucking and swirling her tongue to the rhythm of his breath. He whispered how good she was and how she made him feel so wanted. Peg moaned in agreement and continued down taking each one of his balls in her mouth, sucking gently then releasing. She went back to his dick and moved her mouth over him again while finding his anal opening with two fingers, slow and easy.

Gunnar thought he'd lose his mind at how she so easily brought sensations to his body he'd never felt before. So many times he wanted to explode but fought it allowing her to do all that she wanted. She was slow and took him deeper into her throat, then released, bringing her tongue to his tip swirling around the rim as her palm slid and milked his shaft. His stomach muscles quivered, he clenched trying to stop his ejaculation. She sunk down to his base until he could take no more!

Gunnar took her gently by her shoulders turning her and placing her on her back. Before she knew what was happening, he had his mouth between her legs tasting her sweet juices and tonguing her clit until she lost her breath. He stopped to look at her beautiful face, smiled as her arms reached up over her head, then slide down onto his stomach, his mouth again on her.

Peg got close, but before she could cum, he turned her on her stomach and reached for the oil. He pushed his orgasm down while massaging her back, his hands lowering to her tush causing her to arch towards his touch. He spread her ass and pressed his tongue into her anal opening, wanting to please her just as she had him. Peg moaned, her ass and pussy pulsing beneath his mouth. He loved how her body reacted to everything he'd do, even before she knew it. Peg was the most sexually orgasmic woman he'd ever met and he loved how she surrendered beneath his touch.

Gunnar turned her over and pushed into her full and engorged. Placing her arms over her head, his mouth crashed down onto hers, muffling her sounds of overwhelming bliss. He fucked her deep and long until she started to lose control. She stopped, pushing against him until she could turn him on his back, then again took him into her mouth as she reached for his blue toy. Using lube, she gently inserted it and continued blowing him as his eyes began to roll back. He got too close and stopped looking up at her and whispering, "May I? May I have you anally?"

Peg smiled, nodding, knowing what he wanted. He moved her to her side and used lube on his shaft, spreading it all over himself and then her so sensual and slow. He lay down behind her and pressed into her the way he loved so much. She pushed back against him and relaxed, waiting until her body accepted him, allowing him in. Both exhaled, the pleasure so intense and tight. Gunnar wrapped his arms around her cupping her breasts, she clasped her palms over his, arching into him, meeting him and creating their slow rhythm that made him feel so wanted. He held her close, thrusting slow into her, so tight...and safe.

"Babe?"

Breathlessly, she answered, smiling at how he loved to whisper during sex. "Yes?"

"Did...well, did you do anal during the threesome?"

"No, sweetie."

"No?" He kept slowly caressing inside her.

"No...Dereck couldn't well...he couldn't reach in. Too...uh short? Or...well, I don't know. He just couldn't get it in...kinda gave up."

Gunnar eyebrows raised, "Ohhhhh..." He held her tighter and thrust in again and again realizing how much he enjoyed her ass and how easily she made their anal sex so enjoyable. He relaxed, realizing she was amazing and how Dereck was a complete idiot for treating her they way he did.

"Baby...you feel so...good..." she whispered, and he could hear she was as close as he.

He whispered, "Will you lie on your back? I want to kiss you...facing you."

Peg moved, answering him with her actions and a smile. He moved between her legs and entered her anally while kissing her mouth. His tongue plunged into her mouth as he engulfed her in his strong arms. Peg reached under his arms, spreading her palms along his broad back, arching into him, feeling him deep within her body. He gently thrust and thrust, feeling her tight and wanting. Peg made him feel worth and...needed in her body.

Gunnar lifted up looking down at her, "Touch yourself for me?"

She smiled bringing her fingers to her clit, rubbing slowly matching his perfect rhythm. He stared at her so turned on, he began to lose control, "Cum for me? I want you to cum for me, Peg."

She did as asked, her fingers going a bit faster, her neck arching up, her head flying back. Suddenly, a moan from the depths of her soul erupted as her body wreathed and convulsed around him. He could take it no longer and joined her, breath escaping his chest, his hands grasping at her hips as he let go releasing streams of cum inside her...pumping...and pumping...and pumping. They both fell weak. Satiated and breathless.

(Later)

I'm speechlesssssssss

Mmmmmm my legs...don't work

My everything is jelly...you...are...amazingggggg

Good luck with appts

Lol...might need a nap before. Good luck with the shift...hope you feel less stressed now...

Much less...

Ooomggg...Del just announced in front of all these guys, and my roomie, in the shop that I'm not allowed to post about vegans anymore on Instagram because I get more meat than any of them!! W...t...h...? Bahawahaaaaaa

Hehehe

February 3, 2022 4:55 PM

Hi

Hi

How are you

Well...holding up ok?

Doing ok...

Makes me happy

Sorry...was on treadmill. You finally get rest or on shift again?

(Later)

Hoping you're safe and warm...

Such a long night...cold as hell

It is baby...pls take care of you...

End of pursuit...grrrr
(Pics of smashed patrol SUV)

OMG...are you okay??????

All good

Get'em???

For sure

Fuck Yeahhhh...great job!

Jaeden Law awoke suddenly, his heart racing, the thought of his mother dead, with her eyes open, searing through his mind. A pang of guilt swarmed as he realized he hadn't texted her in weeks. He knew he had to work on his "out-of-sight-out-of-mind" bullshit and contact both his mother and sister more often. His mom was always so competent, and survived everything, that he often found he got comfort in the thought that she was just always okay. He wanted that, for her to be okay.

He threw the covers off and rolled out of bed reaching for his phone. It unnerved him at times that he escaped New Mexico and Dereck's mental imprisonment, but his little sister and mother were still there. New Jersey wasn't the best state to live in but it was what he remembered at the happiest times of his childhood...and it didn't have a Dereck Law wandering about. He dialed and waited.

"Hi..." Pegs voice cracked a bit but he knew she recognized it was him by her tone.

"Hi momma!"

"Hi son, are you okay?"

"Yep. Just checking in, I haven't heard from you in awhile. Everything going well? Oh shit! It's two hours earlier for you...crap Ma, I'm sorry."

Peg smiled, "I was awake. I don't sleep much."

"Oh okay, well...why not?"

"Age babe. I guess it's just an age thing."

"Hmmm. Are you doing well?"

Peg felt his concern, "I am. Just navigating through the day-to-day. How about you? You and my grandpuppers happy?" Peg missed them both so much.

Jaeden scoffed, "Yeah, she's over here snoring away. She has the life."

"As she should. So everything all right? You don't usually call."

"I prefer texting but I had a weird dream about you and wanted to hear your voice."

Peg frowned, "What is "weird"? Was I dead or something?" She huffed trying to be funny.

Jaeden was quiet for a moment, then asked, "Has everything been okay Mom? I mean, do you feel safe?"

"Not particularly son, but this is a new life for me. Most days I'm feeling stalked or in fear, but that's just a thing. I'm getting through."

"I don't mean to bring it up but has he...left you alone?"

Peg nodded, which he couldn't see, "I think so, I did move, and I take different ways home each time. I haven't changed my address from the house, just forwarded my mail."

"Why do you take different ways home Ma?"

"In case he were to follow me. I see him around sometimes but heard he doesn't really come out of the house. You know how he is with his paranoia and guns."

Jaeden exhaled, "Yeah. Has he followed you?"

"There was the stupid private investigator thing in October, and then one night I was followed in the dark. I recognized his truck. Nothing much lately." She was being truthful.

"Not good Mom."

"Could be worse sweetie, I could still be married."

"Do you have someone that makes you feel safe?"

Peg smiled thinking of Gunnar, "Only when he's near me...but none of this can concern him. It's not fair to bring my drama into someone else's life. Look what it did to you and Zena...and thats when I was learning about him and how much I fucked up thinking he was safe to build a family with. It took me so many years to break the trauma bond Jaeden. I'm still healing from all of it and the demise of our family. I never want to hurt you, Zena, or anyone else with this."

"I understand. I'd just feel better if..."

"Thank you. I love you...I'm doing the best I can under the circumstances. What's all this about?"

Jaeden felt uneasy about his dream, "Just wishing things were different."

"Me too. If I could do it over though, I'd still want you both. You and your sister kept me going. Thank you."

"I love you Mom."

"I love you more...*infinity*."

February 4, 2022 8:49 AM

Mmmm...dreamt of you...

I feel like hot death...I think I have flu

Uh ohhhhh...Aches? Shits? Stomach contractions yet?

Stomach...yes

Yep, it's 24 hr. Better take the weekend to recoup...Bad stomach virus in LC. If your hair follicles and skin feel sore later it's viral and you'll need to sleep to beat it. Might sweep through the PD...sooooo contagious but should only be 24-48hrs from what I'm hearing.

Yeah...started about 0300 this morning

Ugh, soooo sorry you're feeling that. Lotsa electrolytes, TV, and naps will help. Swept through my work, and also shake shop, Walmart employees too. Blows...was 2 wks back. Hear it started around New Years...

(Later)

Checkin in...between clients...shitting water yet?

All day...long

You're getting through the worst now. I'm so sorry. My guy in Albq put me on a protocol so I'd fight it like I fight covid. You'll need to sleep in order to kick it. If you can do zinc, vit C, and D under your tongue (sublingual) along with BodyArmour drinks (better than Gatorade) you'll be over it by Sunday. Promise...but your whole family might get it. Skin/hair hurt yet?

Skin yeah...achy

Ahhhh...only 12 hrs to go. Great job you!

(Later)

Covid test...neg

So happy you're kickin' viral butt now!!!

February 5, 2022 8:50 PM

Hoping your feelin' better?

Getting there...still not 100%...

February 7, 2022 8:47 AM

Hello

Hi

How are you...

Alive...you better, I hope...

Much gooooder...what you doing...hope it involves your clit

Gooooder huh?

I am...use new toy this weekend?

Once...yes and thank you. Use yours?

No...just laid in bed all weekend...was rugged

Tough to do, I know, but you needed the reset no?

I think so...

I'm happy you're well...

Wish I was being naughty with you...

Really? What's naughty to you?

Long...blow job...ass play...trading cum with deep kissing...

556

You like loooooooong blow jobs huh?

I like how you play with my balls...ass...cock...mmmmmm

Do youuuu?

I believe you have...well tasted the result...hehehe

Mmmmm...I believe I have...

My naughty dream was that...

Naughty dream? Of me...tasting?

Yes...

Oh wow...nice to hear your vivid imagination is back...

It is...it is...

Mmmm...jumping in shower...gotta shave all the...kitty parts lol...

Wow...so sexxxxxxy...

Not really...but worth the 5 mins lol...

Very sexxxxy...

Mmmmm...feels good now...

Description please

Ummmm.....silky, makes me want to touch my skin all day...

Trimmed?

Just slightly...thong trimmed...

Mmmmmmmmmm...you should use toy...

I believe you know this already lol...

Mmmmm...did you cum quick when you used...
Sure wish you were...riding...all the cum out of me

Sure wish I was toooo...

The way you move...

How's that? You likey...

Was our last anal ok...new angle.

It was...full body intense. Angle was incredible. What did you think?

Yes...you glide entire length...up...down...but also grind entire time...nipples erect...clit engaged

Mmmmmmmm...

Was amazing don't want to hurt you...was instant cream pie when you began fingering yourself...

You don't hurt me...because you're respectful and my body responds to our "slow" ways. I came hard in 3 ways, made me emotional though. Scared me...

Scared?

*Yes. Processing still...damn women stuff lol. Balances the shit out of my body*mind connection though...our uh, sessions lol. What's it like...backdoor cumming?*

Ummm...great...you allow me that trust...access...
powerful...but not greedy...

Mmmm...well, you allow me to be sexual...and myself.
Had to suppress that for so many years...felt awful...

Well you are so very sexxxxy...

You're very kind...I think you're fucking fire...

**Well...you get one last day of rest...I don't wanna give you flu...
but when I am better...**

What happens when you're better?

Black heels...on your knees...gonna fuck you till you cream, cum, squirt, and collapse...

Hmmm...persuading me a bit...

Then...on your back...legs up

*Mmmm...I do like your...
Deeeeep penetration...hmmmm persuading...*

**You use your hands...spread yourself...enjoy watching me look down...
watching me go in...out...deep...
Stupid flu...my dick is dripping for you...seriously wet cock**

*Mmmmm...can't get enough of...
Your thrustsssssss*

Baby are you rubbing your pussy?

Not yet. Be back at house in a bit...save me some...

Mmmmmmmm...wet?

Period. Soooo yep

Already??? Way cool...you know I like

Mmmmm...glad you do...

(Later)

Lol...my client just sent me this meme:
Would you kiss me on my neck and go down and grab my ass, give me a nice little spanking...

Sounds reasonable

She wants to know if she should sext it to her bf...I told her it's a great start...but give him some more visuals.
She asked if she could use stuff from my books...
I was like fuck yeah girl...

Wow...that's hot
Freaking so insane...what you tell her...

I told her "of course!" I'm flattered actually. Love when my clients read my books and she's told me often how they make her dream..and get off. Now she's got a new man she wants to try my stuff with. Well...the spankings part is all her...I knew she had a freak side. Poor gal has never had an orgasm from a man...

What...how's that possible??? I think she wants...you...
Still hot

Lol nawwwww

Sounds like...see...coach...like a dream

Oh. I hope not...need her to focus on him lol...

You tell her how to cum...cuz...you knows

I know how you make me...

Mmmm...you cum...it's explosive to watch...better to taste

Stooooop I'm trying to work and you're making me yearn for you...

You...glaze...glistens...that's why I open the blinds...

You remembers thaaaaat??? You do get me glistening...

560

Called in...just gonna relax

Aw gooood...gotta heal...

Yeah...gotta go to PHX on Friday...

Oh cool!

...wish I could bring you...

Fun stuff I hope!!
I'd go in a heartbeat.

Shooting stuff for sponsor

Love that...
The things I would do to you in that hotel room would not go well with your shooting lol...

I would bring you home...sore...still begging though

Lol...you know it. Tremblinggggg...
You'd need a sweater on your lap for the plane ride too...

Ohhhhh really...

Errrr...a blanket perhaps...

For sure...naughty girl

Is it tho? How can something that feels so good be naughty?

YES...

February 8, 2022 9:17AM

Hola...kiddo out for dentist stuff...grrrrr
Expensive braces coming up...won't be by this AM...

Yep

February 9, 2022 10:47AM

Kiddo sick now…awwwwww….

Very contagious…

You too???

Nope…still fighting it off I guess…

Yeah…my little girl…a hot mess…

Ohhhh so sorry to hear…hoping it'll only be the 24hrs…

Yeah…how you being…

Relapsed…but I'm…

Relapsed?

Steppin' foreward…stupid CPTSD crap…

Well forward is best direction…thats why windshield is bigger than rearview mirror…

Thank you…just the past. 35 years…I refuse drugs, alcohol, gambling, etc…time helps. Quantum hypnosis really helps. Got a court date finally.

When???

Seven days…

You ready???

Born ready lol…

What's attorney think???

Judge has to decide if I can move back into my home, run my massage business there, my four airbnb rooms, receive permanent alimony since he took my retirement savings...attorney is asking for everything due to the spousal abuse...see what happens. Worst case, he drags it out for years, and I have to live with my sister in NJ. Pray for meeee lol

Sister???

My bestie is my older sister in NJ...

Ohhhh....

(Later)

How you holding up?

Busy...busy...kiddo sick...work is work...usual

Excited about your sponsorship stuff?

Yeah...head to Phoenix on Friday...I enjoy...

That's awesome...gotta have things to enjoy!
It's got to feel good to be sponsored...very validating!

Yeah...it's cool...gotta do bunch for them too...win win

You will

February 10, 2022, 8:38 AM

Good morning beautiful

Hi sexy...you ok?

Way tired after sickness...can't get recharged.
Gotta travel tomorrow to PHX

I remember...

How are you...ready for court...seem anxious?

I'd like it to go really well of course...and not drag on.
Kiddo any better I hope...

Finally coming around...poor kiddo for couple days

Awww...
Tummy stuff is brutal

Very...what you doing

Shower...listen, is it easier if

If? ...mmmmmmm...shower...

Sorry, clients...what is it with suicidal ideation this week!
Yeah, shower...was quick

Ohhhh crap...it is...went to suicide yesterday...lady had two sons...each committed suicide on 30th bday. She did it on her 50th...handgun...

Jeeeeezus!!!

Yup...front yard.

Wow...

Yeah...lady across the street saw it all...ring cam recorded it...poor thing

Damn...whole family gone huh? Sad.

Yeah...poor neighbor lady...

(Later)

How you be
Psssst...I Wants U

Hiiiiii

What ya doing

Heading back to the house...you?

Gym...trying...not to think about your taste

Whyyyyy???

Cuz you should be your own food group you so damn good

Awwww, that was nice...

In a corny kinda way...

Still sweet

...hey babe????

Yep

Wanna...Let Me Lick you

Lol...only if you'll let me ride...Reverse Cow Girl...

Mmm...I'm coming over... and cumming in

We'll see

Can I come by?

Of course

Mmmm....

Here

(Later)

You get the call yet for the two fat fucks road-rage fighting at the intersection of Lohman/Telshor?

Not yet...

Hysterical...speaking of, I did an oops today...

What

After you left I, washed up and fixed my crazy hair. I get to the shop a Del gives me the eye. I just smile. She's like "You're late..." (like I have a set time lol) so she asks me to fix her neck...she slept wrong. After sassing me and making me a shake she says, "Here's your shake but with less nuts, because your hair tells me you've had enough nuts today..." So I tell her to sit in my chair so I can fix her neck...and I will try not to break it lol...

Wow...well...not wrong...

After most of the men leave to go back to work she sits and I start to fix her fucked up vertebrae and neck... she's like gushing (was embarrassing lol) then she says, "You smell really good" so I kinda smell myself... nothing, just detergent, then I smelled my hands...bam!! You and me together still all over my arms and hands...even after washing up! I was LITERALLY rubbing our sex all over my friend's ears, neck, traps, shoulders, and even fixed her jaw! Mortification much?. Lol...

Wrong...and funny

I hadn't the heart to tell her you and I...was what she was smelling lol...our pheromones are delicious...even for others...

Great day

Was...a...great...day...I'll stop bugging you now...hope you're safe...and warm...

You can rub your sex hands on me too

I loooove rubbing them on you...and sucking you...and grinding...on you...

Mmmmmm....

Mmmm...can't stop feelin your hands along may back
and holding onto my traps as you...

You came very hard

I have been huh?

Very...

I think I'm getting more comfortable...

Very...mmmmm

Peg's Journal Entry 2/10/22:

Not gonna lie, my CPTSD triggers have been running wild lately. I've had to dig deep for some healing and regulation. Thankfully, Gunnar's touch and energy help, a lot.

After he went to the gym to work out today, he wanted to come by. I really needed him. It was nice to see him in my room within thirty minutes. It was as if we started where we last left off, our bodies ready before our clothes were even off.

He started abruptly kissing me and disrobing me after pushing me down on the bed. He pulled my leggings off and was tasting and pleasuring me with his mouth right off the bat. His tenderness and want made me quiver and arch to him! I missed his desire. We somehow stood back up and made sure he was as naked as I so I could arouse him with my mouth, as I love to reciprocate.

Laying him on the bed, I taunted and teased with my fingers and tongue, making him almost explode a few times. He has such interesting control. As he got close again, I released him from my throat and climbed up his glorious frame to sink down and ride him! He looked up and commented how he's never regretted giving consent to me and how he feels every time "is as good as the first time!" I made sure to rock and sway enough to take his breath away. He couldn't speak much and grabbed my hips as if to hang on to the earth. We moved into missionary somehow, and at one point, he bear-hugged me, pulling me in and whispering, "Give me your soul."

I just looked up at him not knowing what to say. His mind truly is beautiful and complex as he is detached yet immersive. Gunnar has got to be the most intriguing human I've ever encountered.

Oddly, after a while, he wanted to get up and look out of the window! I couldn't tell if he felt he was being followed or if it was because we heard my roommate's son leaving. It didn't matter much as I felt him pull me to the bed and bend me over entering me hard and slick from behind. He felt incredible, even more so when his palms ran up my back and I heard, "Oh my god, you have no idea how beautiful you are...what I get to see."

He held my traps and grinded in me deeper! Suddenly, he pulled out and walked to the window again trying to open the curtains for more light. He returned and bent me over once more for us both to lose ourselves again in the bliss of our sex. I ended up feeling a strong climax coming on, so I reached down to caress my clit, and it made him want to go faster. I couldn't take it, so I told him, "I'm going to cum." He went harder, and I exploded. Once he heard me, he let himself go as well...it was fucking magic!

He wanted to lie on the bed and pulled me into his arms. We talked of his stomach illness, and he apologized for missing my period week. I chuckled. He said he'd been struggling to bounce back and felt he only ate once yesterday. I made a joke about how his highly active crazy mind needs only glucose to function, so eating is a must. He laughed and asked if I really just said that. I nodded and told him I felt he was incredibly intelligent, which he seemed to like.

He shared that he was concerned he may be getting "cynical" with all the stress of crime and not enough staff to help it. He mentioned a meth head was lighting up right in front of a three-year-old at Little Toad Creek in town, and he told the guy it was time to leave. He said the guy told him to "fuck off" and he laid him out on the ground after a second warning. My heart hurts as I remember the stress of the job and how it can make even very empathic officers turn short-tempered and the kindest cops appear mean. I listened and thought about how self-aware he can be. That's an excellent skill for growth, and I admire that about him.

He turned the conversation to me and asked me about court and how I'm feeling about the hearing next week. I told him I'd just really like to be back in my home, but I don't see Dereck leaving to Colorado anytime soon. I mentioned it seems like he's protected by friends here, what he would consider high-level friends. That's when Gunnar revealed he didn't believe friends would stand by him in a situation such as mine. I told him if his so-called friends ever found out what I had about the underage girl, they'd never speak to him again. Gunnar admitted he'd never heard about all Dereck had done, but he did see red flags each time he had a conversation with him. I praised him for his instincts wishing I'd had sharper ones...or didn't ignore my gut so much. I'm much better at it now. Gunnar mentioned Dereck told him he should take one of his martial art classes, and he told him he didn't look good in tights or leotards. I cracked up. He's a hoot!

Gunnar asked if I was going to keep my married name. I told him I hadn't thought too much about it. He said my maiden name was very Irish, and I got quiet. I hadn't realized he knew my maiden name, but then again, he's a cop and obviously had looked me up. When I was in law enforcement, I did the same. I wish there had been more than simple traffic violations flagged in Dereck's profile. I would have run!

We talked about our week. He said there was an interesting thirty-eight gun seizure in Dona Ina on a truck headed in the direction of the cartel. He said they didn't need to retain the driver so the guy turned and started walking down the highway. Two fifty-calibers and military-grade AR's were amongst the collection. We talked of how bad our town is getting, and I realized at that moment that I fear for his safety...and sanity with all that's going on.

We dressed. He mentioned he was heading out of town for the weekend. I missed him before he even kissed me goodbye. Not sure why...

February 11, 2022 5:27 PM

So I hear those born in November are never average but rather...s a v a g e! Wishing you winning vibes and the admiration of those who see your greatness...

Muah...

Chapter 31

IMPENDING

Peg wasn't feeling her best lately due to the impending court date with Dereck. Not seeing or thinking of him had proven to enhance life tremendously, but with an established court hearing, she couldn't escape the doom within her gut. Deep down, she did think about how lovely it would be to go and just walk out...divorced. That would be a dream come true, but knowing him, he'd either not show or pull some sort of misleading or fraudulent move as he'd always done in the past. As a coward, he was the type to focus on whatever tiny win he could create, even if it made no sense or was a complete fabrication.

Peg picked up her phone and signed into her email. The portal to her lawyer's site showed that she had nothing more to provide. She had uploaded all bank account statements, all credit card statements, and any other pertinent paperwork requested. She knew she was the only one who provided proof of their marital expenses. Dereck was the laziest person she'd ever met, so expecting him to even provide a copy of a paystub was asking a lot.

Exhaling disgust, she logged out and decided instead to see if Gunnar was logged into his phone app. Thinking of him was so much more fun and texting with him was even better. He always knew how to occupy her mind with serotonin, oxytocin, dopamine, and endorphin-filled visuals to help the anxiety cease. He wasn't available. She smiled at his icon pic and remembered he'd been away traveling so he was probably getting back on shift.

Gunnar walked out of the house trailer annoyed at another bullshit call. He waved at his officer and climbed into the patrol car while slamming the door to escape the cold. He hated the cold. For twenty-eight years, he had battled the elements while working, and it never seemed to get easier.

Putting the Tahoe in drive, he pulled away thinking of warmth, and she came to mind. He reached for the dial to turn the heat on and saw Peg's face in his mind, her smile, her skin, her swollen, wet, and wanting pussy. His cock hitched in his uniform, and a smile crept to the corner of his mouth. Turning left, he found a safe spot to park and pulled out his phone.

***

February 13, 2022 9:31 PM

Hi

Hi

How are you...I want to lick you

I'm still lickable...how are things. Sponsors happy...you happy??

Yes...good time...long weekend

Love that...

Mmmmm...how are you...ready for court?

I'm struggling lol...gonna keep my expectations neutral as everyone is advising me that it may get drug out...

How??

Obstruction. Divorcing a narcissist takes much longer than any other type of divorce because they are super defiant to anything the court requests or a judge enforces. Just a tough year but I'm making the best of each day...

Yup...what if anything can I do?

You? Thank you...just being supportive really helps...I really like that you asked that...I hear if he no-shows it gets postponed?

Just getting home...wanting to lick...fuck...please...dream of you...

571

Just now getting home??? Oh my...well, you wanting me makes me VERY happy. I'm still drooling over our last encounter...

Mmmmmmm...you need...a shot of lots of cum...

Do I?

Yes...Jedi mind trick engaged

How's that...

Mmmm...me licking you...deep...inserted...

Mmmm...saving me some?

Lots...and lots...

Makes me...happy...

Mmmmmm...don't worry about this week

Tell me it'll be okay...

It will...steps are in place...you are in better place...better mind

Thank you...

Better days

Yes...

Every day

Most days...I'd have to agree

Most???

Yes, life is ten times better this year

So glad to make you smile babe

You are very sweet tonight...

Chapter 32

VALENTINE'S DAY

Dereck threw the letter to the side and hit the keys on his laptop. Annoyed he opened his email and searched for the message from the fat manager at the bank in Florida. It was a bogus letter but enough to cause suspicion and get Peg spinning trying to defend herself. He loved how he could upset her so easily by lying about her character. Since he hadn't had the time or courage to go after her the way he wanted, and with the court date approaching, he just needed to prolong the divorce and get things postponed. The other court cases he had going hadn't come through yet and he needed that money in order to tie up loose ends before heading to the mountains after killing Peg. With her dead, the divorce wouldn't matter, and the insurance money would eventually roll his way. Once cleared as a suspect, he'd have his whole life ahead of him.

He reached for the printed letter and put it with all the other incorrect paperwork to submit to her lawyer. He decided a shower was in order since he did have a date later with Susan Jenkins, and her lovely underage daughter, who he delightfully invited along. Smiling, he made his way to the bedroom and daydreamed about the things Susan could do to him as he manipulated her into moving in and living in Peg's place for a while. He huffed thinking how nice it would be to have another teenager living in the house in his daughter or son's old room. She could have her pick as long as she continued to wear those tight tops and skinny jeans.

Touching and checking the temperature of the water, he stepped into the stream and let it run down his aching spine. Running his hands down his stomach and to his dick, he felt his balls and realized he should shave in case Susan was as freaky as she appeared. She wasn't the greatest looking, but he thought he might be able to get hard if she put her face close enough to his cock.

Peg awoke trying to gather her thoughts and get herself away from feeling sad about spending the biggest love-day of the year, alone. She turned to her side and remembered Valentine's Day when Dereck brought a huge balloon and teddy bear into the house, walking it right passed Tammy, the older ugly karate student he was fucking, and presented it to her in front of the woman. She rolled her eyes remembering the look on Tammy's face and how she should have known he was sleeping with her. At the time Peg actually thought the woman was sleeping with Jon, the other student sitting next to her on their bar stool in their kitchen. She was surprised he bought her anything, especially ridiculously large gifts, as they were separated at the time and just living in the same house. There was no doubt in Peg's mind thats how he convinced the woman to have an affair. She'd heard from various friends of his that he used to complain about his marriage, luring unsuspecting women into his drama, and creating a feeling where they thought they'd win against her.

Peg cradled her arms around her torso to stretch her back and realized how proud she was of herself. Getting away from Dereck felt like a victory every day because she'd never have to feel toxic shame again for the things he'd done to her, and others.

Twenty minutes later, she reached for a towel to dry off. Her phone dinged and she smiled grabbing it. It was him.

Gunnar woke with thoughts of her swirling around in his mind. He did pick up a gift for her for Valentine's Day and wanted them to spend some quality time together on such a neat day. The weekend had been long, and thoughts of things they'd done in previous encounters permeated his thoughts over and over. He wanted her again.

***

February 14, 2022 8:09 AM

Hi

Good mornin'!

How are you? Laying in bed?

Just out of shower...you in bed?

I am...my hard cock...would have woke you up today...

That...would have been heavenly...

Kiss your neck from behind...fingers slide in you...cock pushes in...start to thrust...you push back...no words...simultaneously cum...leave my cock inside...drain every drop of cum...

Mmmm...that deep penetration of yours is...definitely breathtaking...no words

How's...your pussy...mmmm...

Wanting...wet as usual...

Did you self-satisfy this weekend

Incredibly so...I was lonely. Tried remembering my talents and...how you feel...

Use toy???

Once, mostly just fingers...you?

Once...cum all over chest...stomach...

Yummmm...save any for me?

Sure did...

Mmmm...makes me happyyyyyy...

Was thinking about anal...as I was cumming...when you were on your back...fingering pussy...

That was incredible huh? Full body orgasms!!! You are sooooo,..
Good...sensual...hit all the right spots...

I exploded...literally 1 minute of non-stop cumming...

576

Mmmm...love that. Love that we have such amazing lingering visuals...helps for self-pleasuring laterrrr...

Cock in you completely as I was cumming

Really? That's soooo...mmmm...filling...sorry, at a loss for words...

In ass...your fingers...working clit...

Like that huh...

Yes...lots...had bout 2 hour hard on driving home...daydreaming bout you

Daydreaming of me??? That feels really nice! I looooove your hardons...

Yes, naughty thoughts...

Naughtyyyyy?

Yes...was daydreaming...

I do that allll the time...Try not to lay in my bed too much because it brings all the thoughts rushing back...

I was...

So the anal is what gets ya going huh?

You being pleased is what gets me going...

You get me going with these conversations...soooo wetttttt....

Mmmmm...wet...

Very...

What you doing?

Thinking of...

Of???

Your hands on me...your dick...

Dick...where

Pleasuring...my mouth, my kitty...my

Yes...

Tush...

Mmmmmmmmmm....

Mmmm...

How's...Your clit...

Fevered...swollen...

How can we fix that?

Any ideas?

Can I come by...

I would really like that...

Jumping in shower...

Ohhhh myyy...yummmmm...

Mmmmm...day dreaming again...

Yeah???

Yes...

Mmmm...that mind of yours is such a turn-on...

Always running...my mind...

Mmmmm...

(30 mins later)

Here

Yay!

(Later)

O...m...f...g...

Mmmmm...like???

I think I'm still cumming...

Did I leave wallet there?

No babe...want me to check outside?

Ummm...no inside

Not on or around couch and floor...

Ok.....

Park in other neighborhood?

Might be at home

I'm outside looking...

No...was across street...prob at house...

Hope so...I didn't see it with your gun...

(Later)

Pls tell me you found?

I did...was at house...thank you
How's legs

So happy you have it!
Can't...really...walk lol, knees ok?

I'm great

I agree...

Just dropped a rider off at our laundromat...mmmm...memories of when I first felt your arms around me, smelled your scent after so many years, kissed you, and felt how big your cock is...

Wow...

***

<u>**Peg's Journal Entry 2/14/22:**</u>

So I had an unexpected AMAZING Valentine's Day! I didn't think I'd see him but he did show... and with a gift for me. He stepped into my room and hugged me long. I inhaled his scent and eased. He had a pink box in his hand, his gun and phone in the other. Handing it to me I could see it was a set of four personal vibrators that were travel size. It made me smile. Throwing his items to the couch, he turned and kissed my smile away, a deep intensity in his energy. Suddenly, he was undressing us both then backing me up to the bed, opening my legs with his hips, his arms around me, entering my wanting pussy in one thrust, gasping at how it felt. "Baby, you are SO wet, god it makes me feel so wanted and desired."

I looked up at him and whispered, "Because you are. You are so wanted and desired. Feel how my body needs you?" It was so fucking hot, I wanted to cum right away, he had me so aroused so quickly. This man's energy hits me from across town! Just knowing he's on his way to come see me or driving over gets me incredibly aroused and feeling a "good" anxious. It's a nice change from all the other anxiousness I have to experience.

580

He drove in deep making us both lose our breath! I reached in and sucked his nipples which he loves. He mumbled how if I kept it up he would cum too fast. So I sucked harder lol. He stopped sliding down to torture me orally until I couldn't take it any longer and came long. He smiled then climbed on me, thrusting in again and again and again! I could barely keep myself from crying out and covered my own mouth as he took me the way he wanted! One leg up, deeper still, grabbing my hands, pushing them over my head, driving in deeper and deeper. He was intensely aggressive but never hurt me once.

He pulled me to the edge of the bed, turned me over, and entered me hard and slick from behind. It felt so good I exhaled into the sheets to muffle my pleasure. I could feel him deep inside reaching to my cervix, his balls caressing my clit from such an amazing angle. He started getting close, so I pushed back and stood to throw him on the bed. I started blowing him torturously slow and used two fingers in his ass to increase the pleasure. He was trying not to cum! He got up and bent me over again to take me from behind.

It was wildly blissful, but as he got too close to cumming he switched up and turned me over to enter me at the edge of the bed, then we went to missionary again, then I blew him again...he got too close and stopped me by asking if I would ride him. Of course I did...and slow, then fast, then slow again. We were giving so much pleasure to each other and it was amazingly slow so SOOOOOOO enjoyable. I turned around to ride him reverse cowgirl and he had such a difficult time not cumming. I told him he should. He asked me how I wanted him to cum, and I chuckled softly, "You decide, it's Valentine's Day, you should choose."

He couldn't, he said he loves me swallowing but likes to inside me...then he said he loves it in my ass, too. I could tell that's what he ultimately wanted so I moved. He got lube, pulled me to the edge of the bed on my back and eased in. OMFG he was so big but so gentle... I couldn't hold out, and I ended up cumming once by rubbing my clit, it turned him on so much and as I started to cum again he couldn't take it and exploded with me! BEST Valentine's Day EVERRRRRRRRRR...

We laughed at how we both could hardly walk, our legs were shaking. As we dressed he told me the state cop that was shot in the sternum was his buddy. I feel bad for him. There is so much going on. He shared how nine officers were shot in Albuquerque and after a six-hour standoff the shooter ends up taking his own life. I thought of Dereck and how he would do the same thing...because attention is his most important commodity. He mentioned also that he had trouble with a druggie and had to put hands on him (reluctantly). He hates the cynicism. Said the guy was like, "Don't fucking touch me!" And although he didn't want to, he had to remove him from cooking meth in front of his kid.

I worry as I see how burnt out he is, it's in his eyes. The cops are too overworked. The empathy that got them into such a thankless job ends up dissipating slowly over the years and anger prevails. He joked how his sponsors gift him so many guns, often $4,000 ones at a time that if he *gets "smashed in police work," his kids will have lots to sell for profit. This saddened me as I realized I don't want to ever see him hurt...or his kids to have to be in such a position. I'd love to see him go out on top and live an honorable and proud life of retirement, telling the stories of his life to all who will listen.*

Chapter 33

CAN YOU MEET

Aileen was a large woman of six-foot-one height with a menopausal body type five of over three-hundred-ten pounds. She walked carefully in her slippers as her feet ached from the tile floors in her home. She hadn't planned to stand so long, but admittedly, Dereck Law was becoming more and more interesting to watch through her blinds. If she weren't retired FBI from the behavioral analysis unit, she'd just think he was fucking weird, but her neighbor was beginning to exhibit dangerous sociopathic narcissistic decline. As the months went by since his wife left him, and rightfully so, he'd gotten more and more alarming. She knew it was time to inform Gunnar.

If she were a younger, she would have put a few little camera devices inside Dereck's home. For now it was easier to just hack into his emails and cell phone. He was what she liked to refer to as a "sick puppy." The kind the mother canine eats at birth to protect her offspring and also the world from her *misfit*.

Aileen scuffed along passed the living room eye-rolling the sight of the president tripping up the stairs to Airforce One on the overly large flat screen. She hobbled around to her desk and slumped down in the high-back chair to check the monitors spread out along her large desk. She clicked the mouse and changed the views to her neighborhood. She saw the ass-end of Dereck Law opening his front gate and walking up the sidewalk to his front door. No one would know he was just across the street in his pilot neighbor's garage and house doing the weird shit he does. She knows because she's followed him on days when her lupus wasn't so bad. Dereck liked to covertly terrorize those he didn't care for. His sociopathic ways were bordering on psychopathic now as he liked to move others' furniture and create a sense of fear and confusion within their safe spaces. This was more serial killer functioning and practice for something. He may be conjuring up.

She sat back exhaling. It was time to make a call to Gunnar O'Clery and warn him. She knew now he was sleeping with Peg Law, but luckily, Dereck Law hadn't figured it out yet. Normally, she wouldn't give a shit, hell she might even go after Peg if she were younger, but she always liked Gunnar, she liked working with him over the years when it was necessary. She knew he had a rough marriage, his wife had a lover and now he did. He was decent to Aileen when others were not, and because of that, she knew she wanted to warn him, but also because he seemed to care for Peg. Besides, thinking of him and Peg together kind of turned her on. Indirectly she rooted for them in a weird way. When she analyzed them they were damn-near perfect for each other. She picked up her phone and dialed.

Gunnar's phone vibrated against the console. Aileen Lauden's name shown on the screen. He hadn't talked to Lauden in years. He touched the screen to answer then returned his eyes to the road.

"Ms. Lauden, how the hell are you, ma'am?"

Aileen smiled, "Gunnar O'Clery. I'm alive. We need to share a conversation."

Gunnar's eyebrows raised, "Do we?"

"When can you meet?"

"It's a meeting thing?"

"That would be preferable sir."

Gunnar slowed and put his turn signal on to make a left into the PD back parking lot. "Well, as you know we're short-staffed, so how urgent are we talking? And...aren't you retired?"

She huffed, "Well, yeah. You know how that goes. And it's urgent, like Peg Law urgent."

Gunnar felt his gut sink. He got quiet. He thought he'd been more careful.

Aileen waited a moment then continued, "O'Clery, in all the years you've known me, have I ever crossed you?"

"Not once."

"She's a good person Gunnar, I just want..."

Gunnar pursed his lips, "Me to stay away from her..."

"The opposite actually. Let me know if you can swing by. Park down the street...you know because of these weird fuckers I live around. Won't take long."

"Affirm."

"See you soon. In a day or so?"

The line went dead.

Gunnar exhaled stress and turned off the truck. His heart pounded at the thought of he and Peg's affair being exposed. He slammed the door shut slightly pissed at himself but more so at the thought of the one thing he had that was just about him, about the intimacy of just her and him, was no longer just theirs.

Dereck smiled looking up at the ceiling fan. The evil in him enjoyed the thought of his neighbors confused and scared trying to figure out how their furniture got moved, items got placed on different surfaces, and their mutt of a chihuahua somehow got locked in the sink cabinet in the kitchen. He laughed out loud in the room. Next time he'll do away with the dog, that'll really shake them up. Maybe they'll even move. He would love to have the power to get them to go.

He turned on his side thinking about how Juan had said the pilot and his wife thought he deserved to lose his family, that he didn't appreciate what he had. It made him seethe with hate on the inside but he was feeling better. Revenge always felt better. He remembered the hearing for the divorce was the next day. A smile crept up as he thought about the sound of her voice on the conference call with the judge and her lawyer. Especially when she hears the lies.

Peg was a bit sore from the fun with Gunnar the day before, but it was a good sore. She was quite challenged during her workout at the gym. Not so much gassed just fatigued in her muscles from all they'd done and the full-body orgasms that followed. Thinking of it made her body react in a quivering, goosebump way. It amazed her that she already wanted him again just a day after.

February 15, 2022 3:00 PM

Hey you

Baby...

How you feeling...how was leg day

Lol, didn't happen until this morning at 7:30. Lil tight still...you holding up ok?

I'm good...busy at work...nonstop

I've noticed we don't talk as much...everything ok?

Great...worried about you...tomorrow

Thank you. It feels nice you remembered. I do feel a bit sick in my stomach but I keep remembering how freedom feels so...
Thank you again for yesterday...and allllll your gifts!

Mmmmm...I have never seen you cum so hard

Was phenomenal...how did it make you feel?

Like king kong

Really? That's hot!

Yup...was amazing...you kept cumming

It's worse today...literally squeezed my "stuff" on the way to the gym in the truck to reset my tantric energy...
and had what we ladies call

Call???

A "jeans-gasm" but it was more of a leggings orgasm! I think ovulating on a full moon maybe

Full moon...yes!!

Bringing out my inner wild or it's you AGAIN...just making me want more and more of you? I don't get how cumming 5 times one day can make me yearn for more lol...thanks for ravishing me...you're still sooo desired...and wanted all these months later!

Odd day, 3some guy messaged me...

Was it hot?

I didn't open the message sweetie. Not looking to go back 20 years. I did hear Dereck got a hold of him...not sure why he'd contact me. Thoughts?

Shared time and emotion...won't hurt...you holding up?

I'm trying. Tummy trouble. How are you?

Good...nerves???

Lawyer wants me at her office in AM but he knows where her office is now. They said he showed up there Monday pissed off. Haven't seen him in 9 mos...don't want to. He's supposed to call in to judge from his location...

Hmmmm...be ok...you will...

Mmmm...baby yodaaaa...

Right...I am

Thank you for talking with me about this. Best case scenario...divorced tomorrow 2-16-22!!

Strength is in the moment you took a stand...and said I am done...first step was so hard...but critical for you to grow with...and as you know...tomorrow is just documents

You...make me happy...I'll pull more strength...respond rather then react...

(Later)

Can't sleep...hoping you're safe and warm??

I'm all good...nervous?

Ugh...

I bet

Blows...
Guns drawn at Arena Dr?

Was...bullshit call

Thought so...assholes on FB said cops were training in a house.
I was thinking yea right, no time for trainings...

Nope guy with gun...suicidal

Jeeeezus...like you need more of that shit...

(Later)

Sorry...was fighting...where were we

Fighting???? Did you win?

Ummm...kinda...no one ever wins a fight...Patrick Swayze

Roadhouse?
Mouth or hands...both are your very effective weapons

Well...more of a neck crank...direct pressure to philtrum...effective

Oh yes...very effective. Great job! Kind of a turn-on visualizing that...are you ok tho?

Yeah...pursuit...meth...fight...usual

Fuckin' drugs...hate'm

Yeah...getting rugged

Lol...neck crank to cuffs?

Yes...very effective

Love it!! Good choice...

What ya doing

Layin in bed thinkin'...

Bout????

Oral...

Receive??

Swallow

Mmmmm...soooo close to that yesterday...wanted your pussy too

Sooooo good...allllll. I enjoyed so much...

You were a cumming machine...so hot

Yes...full body. My quads are killing me from...riding. You held out foreverrrrrr...

Wanted all your cum...what shop peeps say?

Bo asked Del today what she got for V-day and she said "Nothin, he wouldn't even put gas in my truck. I want what Peg got!" I didn't have to say anything, just smiled yesterday and she was like "You're late, do the Irish celebrate Valentine's Day, Peg?" She's a hoot.

Way funny

*Three of them take turns teasing...competition to make me blush.
Have you been good to your body today? Hoping you've eaten more than once?*

No...having 1 hr old hot wings...sat in my truck since 1030ish...

Ohhhh...wings are great cold...

Chapter 34
DANGER

Gunnar looked down at his phone and figured she must have fallen asleep. It wasn't like Peg to stop texting so early but with all she'd been going through with the divorce, he thought she may have crashed out. He opened the door and exited the cruiser way down the street from Aileen Lauden's house. He put his phone on silent, lowered the volume to his radio at his hip, and shut the door slowly with little noise. He looked around and scanned the neighborhood. He knew Peg's house was up the road and made note of all the street lights leading up to it. There were four to be exact and as he walked down the sidewalk to Aileen's courtyard he could see the tail ends of two trucks in Peg's driveway. He remembered Dereck's truck from seeing it parked at the gun shop then assumed the other truck was Peg's black truck that Dereck wouldn't let her have.

The gate to the courtyard was locked but it unlocked as he took his hand off the knob. He walked in and closed the gate looking around at the lawn furniture and a few solar lights illuminating the path to the door. Aileen opened her front door and met his gaze. He half-smiled not really wanting to have a discussion about he and Peg's connection with a retired behavioral analyst from the FBI.

"Lieutenant."

Gunnar reached out to hold the door she opened for him, "Agent Lauden. How are you this evening?"

She backed up letting him in, "Very well thank you. I'm glad you could stop by. I know you're very busy."

She closed the door behind him, then turned to admire his gorgeous frame and taut uniform. She was not into men but she smiled agreeing that if she were, Gunnar O'Clery would definitely be her type. He was a beautiful specimen of a man.

"We are pretty short-staffed due to this rona bullshit, so I'll need to leave my radio on."

"Not a problem. Can I get you something to drink?" Aileen scuffed slowly passed him and towards the kitchen that was lit up with way more lights than Gunnar liked.

"No thank you."

"Please make yourself comfortable." She motioned towards the bar stools on the other side of the counter from her, creating distance between them but a full view of his eyes and facial expressions.

Gunnar pulled out a tall barstool and sat down placing his elbows down on the marble counter and his hands loose and open. He knew the game and was careful not to close his body language. He took a breath and prepared himself.

"Listen O'Clery, I'm not here to do anything but merely warn you that Dereck Law up the street from me...well, that fucker is off his rocker if you know what I mean."

"Oh?"

Aileen's eyebrows raised and she watched him, "There's sociopathic narcissism and then there is sociopathic narcissism that begins to morph into secondary psychopathy. Thanks to the decline of our society's mental health and toxic food supply."

Gunnar frowned. He knows he was no expert but that didn't sound right. She watched his face remembering how he processes.

"Basically what I'm saying is Dereck Law is declining. He's lived his life as a cowardly personality disordered narcissist but he has a brain injury that is starting to present as an emotionally unstable secondary psychopath. And....there is the epilepsy crap on his mother's side. The grandfather and the mother weren't right. In fact, the grandfather was discharged from the military in just six short months of being drafted. Fucker used to talk to the air and scare the other soldiers with his paranoia. Dereck is worse."

"Okay." Gunnar did remember Peg mentioning that Dereck "went off the deep end" early on in their conversations.

"Secondary psychopaths have traits more associated with criminal behavior but you'll still find them amongst others and in the workplace per se. Mr. Law has had no criminal record but that doesn't mean he hasn't done things...he just simply hasn't been caught for yet. Or...that he'll become a problem gradually. May I ask if Mrs. Law has mentioned any crimes he's done...under the radar maybe...covertly, or that she couldn't prove?"

Gunnar pursed his lips unsure how to answer. She could sense he didn't totally trust her to comment on what Peg might have admitted to him.

"Why I ask is because I suspect he had exhibited some secondary psychopathic tendencies that were rash, impulsive, anxious, hostile, aggressive, or self-destructive in the last year of his marriage that sealed the deal for his wife to leave him."

Aileen waited but Gunnar just stared at her. She knew she'd have to give him more.

"I guess what I'm getting at is the woman probably had to put up with his fucked up narcissistic ways throughout the relationship but, when he began to get more intense, hence sliding into psychotic-ville, she got out." Aileen hesitated to go on realizing he hadn't made an indication towards any answer.

Gunnar's hands opened slightly, she noticed they were muscular, thick, and worn no doubt from his competition shooting and weightlifting.

"I don't think I know enough about it yet to comment properly Lauden. How do you know all this about Dereck Law?"

She smiled, he was very good. "You mean how do I know you're fucking Peg Law?"

His hands closed a bit then he flattened them on the cold counter and spread his fingers. He was curious but didn't respond.

"I do get out at times O'Clery. I happened to follow Dereck Law one day and parked watching him watching her."

Gunnar shifted in the chair readjusting his gun belt while half-listening to the chatter over the radio. He did not like hearing that Dereck was watching Peg. She had said she felt he was tailing her from time to time.

Aileen leaned against the counter to ease her hip, "He's a coward so he hasn't done anything but study her. He has no clue about you."

"How do you know that?"

"I've taken an interest in his texts and emails...I'm retired, I have too much time on my hands I guess."

"Okay."

"Listen, I know this is uncomfortable. Besides you and Peg, I may be the only other person in LC that knows about you both. I'm not here to judge. I get it. I understand the job and I totally get why the two of you found each other. I have no doubt you're both dealing with your PTSD shit through sexual healing. It happens..it's almost a part of the job really. I've been guilty myself."

Gunnar smirked, "Really?"

"Really. CPTSD and PTSD are no joke. At the end of the day, we all still have to meet our six human needs to survive. You and she have very similar wounding...and need each other."

Gunnar's eyes soften and he inhaled a long breath letting it go unsure if he wanted to hear more of her analysis of he and Peg. What she was explaining wasn't uncomfortable, it was just vulnerable. He was already worried about Peg going to court the next day with Dereck.

Aileen stood upright, "I guess I'm just getting at this fucker could become a real problem. This isn't a normal breakup. He's not just going to move on because he's quite disordered. If he finds out about you he may very well stay away, as he thinks highly of you, but he may not...stay away from her. If he sees things in his mind, things the two of you have done...well, he may stay quiet because of shame but if his mind is declining the way I expect, he may go after her."

"Her...or me?"

"I feel he would hurt her because she represents the deep pain of a rejective mother. His mother doesn't like him, didn't want him, and certainly didn't want him to be something other than a girl."

Gunnar's eyebrow raised, "Christ."

"It's pretty fucked up but in my experience, especially since he respects you, he's not going to come after you at first. He'll understand why you want her...because he does. He'll spiral and try to hurt her first."

Aileen canted her head and watched him. She could sense a part of him was worried about his family, most of him was worried about Peg and how he was contributing to her danger, but not enough of him cared about himself. She knew she liked that about him. He was the type to think of others first even though there was some greed within him. He was greedy when he needed intimacy...a last-ditch effort to survive a sexless marriage.

Suddenly a call went out regarding a pursuit in progress, Gunnar keyed up and gave his badge number to dispatch stating he was en route.

"I have to go, thank you, Aileen. I appreciate your information." In a matter of seconds, he was gone closing the front door behind him.

Josephine looked down at the text and smiled. She'd been waiting to talk with Aileen about her meeting with the hottie cop Peg was fucking. Peg hadn't revealed him as she's very loyal, but Aileen inadvertently did. Josephine snooped on the pad in Aileen's top desk drawer when she went to the bathroom. She never reveal their affair or say anything but damn did she rock a few orgasms to the thought of Peg Law riding Gunnar O'Clery in her mind. Her husband was quite enamored and had mentioned how "feisty" she was the other night.

Not wanting to text back, she dialed instead.

"Hey you, how are ya?"

Aileen was out of breath, "I'm well, just fat and trying to get to the couch here."

"So?"

"Oh, you sneak about and find out things you shouldn't know and now I'm supposed to elaborate?"

"Come on Ai, you know I don't say shit. Besides, doctor-client confidentiality."

Aileen laughed out loud, "She's no longer your client or even a damn patient at your clinic. She's become your good friend. If she wanted you to know, she would have revealed him."

"I meant you, smart ass. Besides, she's not like that. But, if it helps, she smiles when I ask her how she's doing in her new relationships."

"Well, I have a feeling it's more serious than we thought."

Josephine sat up, "Noooooo, did he?"

"That man was steel. He kind of always was but as I studied him, he was tight-lipped because he cares for her, not because he's worried about being revealed so much."

"Oh fuck, no way. Not gonna lie Ai, the thought of the two of them together...it damn does something to my inners."

"Christ Jo, get ahold of yourself."

Josephine smiled, giggling, "Oh shut up you hoe, you know you think about it. The two of them together, you'd be sitting in a chair diddling yourself, watching them devour each other."

Aileen laughed louder, "You're sick bitch."

"No I'm not, I just know you. So, was he as hot as when he was younger. I remember you used to comment about his arms."

"Uh, I think he's actually hotter now that he's closer to fifty. Trim, or more cut I think." Aileen thought about how he looked in his uniform.

Josephine could see Gunnar in her mind, "More cut? Damn and they aren't even fifty yet? *Babies*."

"Yeah but, healthy and sexy babies. If I weren't gay..."

"Speaking of, did he respond to how fucked up Dereck is? Did he say anything?"

Aileen shook her head, "Not so much. He was listening, he's known for that, and I could see he was not too happy. Almost like he's worried more now about Peg's safety."

"Well, I can understand that. Dereck likes Gunnar and would prefer to take Peg out...a "if I can't have her you can't either" type mentality. We can't forget his true nature."

"You're right. He needs to go bye-bye."

Josephine agreed, "So true my friend...so true."

"Wish we could help."

Chapter 35

COURT

Gunnar didn't sleep much. The things Aileen Lauden shared sounded right, but he wasn't quite sure what to do about Dereck Law. Deep down, he couldn't stand the guy even years back, now knowing how he'd treated Peg and his kids, and that he was not going to get better but rather declining, he was not so sure how to respond. He knew Peg was going to have to begin difficult divorce proceedings today and decided to see how it goes for her before telling her about his conversation with Aileen. He didn't want to keep it from Peg but not only was she not needing more stress, Aileen is monitoring Dereck which could be helpful.

He turned over, staring at his phone. He could see she was on her phone, too.

Peg was dressed and in her truck ready to drive to her lawyer's office. She took a deep breath wishing it was all over. She rubbed her temples wishing she didn't have to go through this attention-granting bullshit with Dereck. He loved suing people. He'd done it their entire marriage and now it was her turn. Of course she wanted to no longer be married to the pedophile, she just wished it was all over and a distant memory. Mostly, because Dereck loved this part. He always loved fighting, his entire family was the same, always at war over something, even suing each other. It was the most unloving family she had ever been around and she was so glad to be getting away from all of them.

Ten minutes later she was parked in the parking space facing the building. Her eyes scanned the area and she hoped Dereck wasn't around or hiding behind a tree, ready to pounce. No one really understood what a fucking weirdo he was normally, and now with his mind declining, he was a real danger. She was early so she checked to see if Gunnar was awake.

Dereck jumped up and grabbed his phone to check the time. He overslept and started cursing while racing out of bed to get to his desk. He had to dial in to the court to be connected for the hearing. He would have preferred to meet in person so he could see her again. He wanted to see her fear up close, despite her always looking pretty well put together. He wanted to gaze upon her new body he'd only seen in pictures on social media. He *wanted* to smell her again and look at the breasts he used to touch whenever he wanted.

Gone were the days she pushed him away and he took what he wanted anyway just by waiting until she fell asleep. He still had hope that she'd cave. He hadn't found a way to make her break yet but pulling the bogus embezzlement card could do it. Peg hated when he accused her of anything she wouldn't do. Oh, how he missed the fire in her when she'd defend herself. He loved the attention and how her eyes and mouth would move as she angrily cursed at him. Everyone said she changed but he was betting on showing how she hadn't. All he had to do was get her spinning in shit and distracted defending her character. He smiled walking to his office to begin a war she'd never win.

***

February 16, 2022, 9:07AM

Lost wifi...last night...

What happened...what time is mtg?

Going in now...I

You gots this

Need...

Need???

You...

(Later)

How was mtg

597

Not...good...

What happened

$500 alimony until he submits income...

House? Colorado?

Held up until he stops hiding finances...
he may move away now...

You ok?

No.

What's going on?

Not sure...

With you??

Yes...

Whats first thing on mind?

Hug...

Was he trying to be controlling?

Yes...they said he violated paperwork by locking me out of and taking money away...

Was he being antagonistic?

He cried...

Sheeeeesh...I'm sorry

Told the judge he still loves me...then unloaded lies about me...

What lies?

Told them under oath we were separated for 8 yrs, he lost custody and POA of Alzheimer's mother because of me (had no clue he lost that case), says I left him for someone in FL...my lawyer objected like 7 times to hearsay. Judge kept interrupting him. I stayed quiet, only responded when addressed. He has to take all his financials by tomorrow. They want me to walk thru my home, he said no way, he has to be present. Judge said provide a date but stay away from each other until new hearing. He's gonna drag this out...

I...so sorry

Stupid drama...

Not scared of him are you?

Yes

Don't be

I can tell he's gonna do something...

Too many eyes...he will move on...

I hope you're right. My lawyer asked if he's been evaluated...

By VA?

Lied and told them he can't provide paperwork because I have all our records. My lawyer reminded him he was under oath and he stated I haven't been in the home for over a year...where all the bills are sent. She's thinking she may request...but knows it would drag it out... Enough of my crap. Are you well?

Ohhhh...worried bout you

Trying not to relapse lol...Honestly, want to go hibernate in the movie theater in the dark and watch that new dog movie...with super unhealthy popcorn...and a blanket...

Relapse??

My CPTSD crap. He lied and told the judge I went up on instagram and told everyone he beat my daughter and that's why she moved out. He wouldn't have his micro-penis if he ever beat my kids and everyone knows that. I just stayed quiet as my lawyer objected. I asked Zena about it and she said he smacked her on the ass in the kitchen and she felt unsafe so she moved out. I was not aware. Confirmed it was true thru the soldier too. Feel like shit. Finding out so much...but "after the fact" doesn't mean I could protect her. I'm beginning to understand why my babies keep telling me they love me and are so proud I got away but also why they can't be around me now...I failed at protecting them from him.

Better place...just a rough day

Thank you...yes...just a rough day. I'm trying to remain teachable. Pushing the guilt and tears away. Please be careful today. Full moon brings out the crazier in the crazy as you know. Wishing you successful neck cranks lol...

I'm off...just me and daughter...everyone out of town...

Ohhhh...well then, I wish you relaxation...

Worried bout you...

Gonna be fine...just processing. Feeling good today...or exhausted? I miss your scent...

Session...needed???

You have no idea how bad...

Mmmmmmmm...

February 17, 2022 8:05 AM

Hi

Hi

Get any rest?

Lil bit...how are you?

I'm ok...still worried bout you

Thank you...I'm struggling on the inside...shaking...

Why?

Not sure...my body is trying to ease what my mind is telling it but still a bit disconnected. You feeling well this week?

I'm ok...disconnected?

Yeah...weird...hands are shaking...

Good if giving hand job...hehehe...JK

So true!

Did you sleep?

Off and on...woke every two hours...you?

Never sleep well...but rested

I hear that...

Appointments today?

No

I'm watching a documentary on Ayahuasca

Nice!! I've decided I need another ceremony. 10 yrs of therapy in 4 hours helped me get back to Ramas...now I need to heal this fight-flight-freeze-fawn bullshit...

I admire your strength. He was trying his control...you didn't fall for it...that was your measure of control...

Thank you, baby...It's the after affects of the PTSD I don't like. My body doesn't deserve to go through this... trying to regulate is exhausting...

601

How you regulate?

Heheheeeee...

Puff...puff?

Not lately...

How?

Weed is a tool...if I'm feeling something it can enhance it so I try to be careful not to partake if I'm super emotional. I've gone my whole life without depending on substances so I try to stay disciplined that way... since my Mom could not...

Worried bout you...

Thank you...Working out gets me through, meditation helps with sleep...YOU help me sooooo much to feel balance and pleasure.
You mentioned to me twice now about how you were feeling cynicism...or "becoming very cynical"...did you know Ayahuasca helps with that?

Yeah...tired of the system I am part of...if people get hurt...

I admire your self-awareness...and not wanting to fall further into the system. Tough...tough career. But you know you've done better than most yes?

Yeah...no train wrecks yet...

Good stuff. Great to go out of it on top...with respectful reputation...

What you wearing??

Naked...jumping in the shower after gym...you?

Jumping in shower too

Mmmmm...

(Hour Later)

Holding up ok?

Trying...

Can I help?

Have time for me?

Today???

Yes?

When??

When can you???

Bout 20 minutes...

Mmmm...yes please...

(30 minutes later)

Here

(Later)

After you left, I called lawyer as you suggested. She had him authorize release of my phone number due to it being tied to my LLC. Just left Verizon! He has no access to my phone as of 3pm. Will be deleting FB and Instagram stuff too. Thank you sooooooo much for your advice!!

FB ok though? Build for biz

I'm having it secured as we speak...feeling better today!!

Feel better???

Got a techie client who's teaching me how to secure all my stuff.

Yes, feel soooooo much better. You holding up ok?

I'm great...

Love to hear that...

Happy you feel better...

I so do. You are amazing and helped me more than you now. Thank youuuuuuuuu.
Headed to Applebees to join Gina on her date...this is a new one...

Date?

She's on a date and "SOS'd" me. Wingman err...wing-girl stuff I guess. She was shaving her crotch earlier...
then this, lol. This day is getting more and more interesting lol...

No cum girl?

?

Girl who couldn't cum from hubby?

Yes. Six years no sex, 13 years no orgasm unless self-pleasured.
Unsure as to why I'm needed lol. But, I can't leave her hanging if she feels unsafe.

New bf?

Yes...

First time she gonna...well...fuck him?

Yezzz...so exciting...unless she needs me to end it lol...

(Later)

How's wing-chic status
She excited huh...way cool

She was...I'll evaluate

Evaluation...check

I feel so bad...I showed...but he's no-showing!

Ohhhhhhhhh...he will show...tell her he needs magnum condoms...time for shots

Lol, you know I'd pick the gold ones...

Magnums! Still no show???

Right?!! Got her to eat steak dinner with me, I really want him to show...
says he's at the gym...

Hmmmmm...poor girl...

Hurtful...no gal wants to be ghosted...
oh shit, just noticed she's starting to slur...

Ohhhh my...now what??? Anything?

Gonna...take her home...make sure she's ok.
Wow. Kinda glad I showed...feel terrible...

Ohhhh...damn

Yeah. Did you enjoy lunch?
I'm sorry, totally forgot to ask. Hoping Mom loved her bday lunch!

She did...good times

Aww...such a good son!

Oral Irish guys...loyal...oral too

Mmmm...totally my favorite...

Hehehehe
Daughter fell asleep with head on my chest...who wouldn't want to be me...

That...is the best! Safe, secure, at peace in the world.
Great job, Daddy!

...I mean...we were watching Predator...but still...

Oh shittt...lol, not her vibe?

Hers? New Disney movie...Encanto

Heard about it...I only enjoy Disney now if I've Puff Puffed lol...

***

Peg's Journal Entry 2/17/22:

Yesterday was not my favorite day. I had to head to my lawyer's office to go to the first divorce hearing. It was held over a conference call due to Covid, and the only good thing about it was I didn't have to see Dereck's fat fucking face. His voice was cringy and I noticed my body was at an all-time cortisol dump for the entire two hours. I was vulnerable and exhausted by the time I left. I honestly with I'd never married him. This would all be so much easier if I hadn't signed on the dotted line.

Of course, he'd already started his obstruction crap by not providing any paperwork, pretending he can't understand what he reads, and fabricating lies about me embezzling to gaslight my lawyer and the judge. With no information on his side, we really couldn't get far, so the judge said until he provides his financials he'll have to pay $500 a month in alimony to start. Dereck cried and shouted out that he didn't have it. The judge also said he's not allowed to lock me out of my home or keep me from walking through my house and getting my things. He ordered that Dereck would have to coordinate a time where I could go to the house on my own, he objected and said he's not comfortable with that. Under oath, we both had to answer questions. Because I had bounced back and started making money, my lawyer was a bit annoyed because she wanted to maintain that he locked me out of my life and caused me hardship. I feel she was more angry with *herself for not meeting with me prior to the hearing so we could catch up. She was unaware of how I can make money through multiple streams of income through my LLC.*

The worst part was Dereck's character assassination of me, and lying under oath, that I embezzled his mother's money. Total projection for what he actually did while I was trying to make his mother money through the Airbnb at her home. He told me to pay my credit cards back for what I spent preparing her house and I had started to do so until he was caught coordinating the threesome that never happened. He turned on me and told them I was taking his mother's money to pay back my business. I did get upset at being accused of something I would never do.

I felt super vulnerable and asked Gunnar if he had time for me today. He did come over and listened to my drama before we ended up naked and pleasuring each other. We did our favorite things (missionary, oral, doggie, etc.) and his slow, sensual pace eased me. I had him stand up at the end and blew him so slow and sweet he ended up exploding in my mouth until he was weak and needing to sit down, mumbling something about his knees aching.

We dressed, and he stayed awhile to talk me through understanding "criminal intent." He said I had no criminal intent behind helping his mother, and Dereck would have to prove that I'm a criminal in a different court than a divorce court. Gunnar mentioned he feels that Dereck is going to get ugly now, and it's important for me to be safe and separate my phone and social media from him.

After he left, I called my lawyer's office and encouraged them to call Dereck to persuade him to release my cell number from his bill so I could put it in my name. By 3pm, I had my own Verizon account and was free of him in that way! I was also able to secure my social media and block him as Gunnar had suggested.

My day turned out better by the end than it had started out. I'm grateful for Gunnar, not only does he advise me well, he balances my body and emotions so I can move forward. As for Dereck, I honestly wish I'd never, EVER met the guy. I have no respect...or even an emotion left for him.

I decided to help out Gina and meet her later for dinner. I welcome the distraction.

Chapter 36
SHOULD HAVE

Dereck paced the floor fuming about the hearing yesterday. His head pounded, and he wished he'd waken up still drunk instead of with a hangover. He ran his hand through his frizzy hair, mumbling how he should have killed her last month when he had the chance. Now, it would be even harder since the court was well aware of their history. He couldn't believe she told the truth about so many things, under oath! He always hated the truth in that woman.

Opening the top drawer in the kitchen, he searched for some Ibuprofen. He needed to get rid of his headache before he made a stupid decision and drove over to her bedroom to make sure she shut up forever.

Downing the three pills with some Crown Royal, he shuffled to his recliner and slumped down, then turned on the TV to find some porn. He needed to think harder and make her death look like an accident. He smirked at how less fun that would be but so much more necessary now...and easier to get insurance money for.

***

February 18, 2022, 8:19 AM

How are you today

Doing well...happy Friday. How are you feeling?

I'm good...your friend ok?

Not so much but she's a trooper so I'll coach her. Got her home safe...

Why guy no-show?

I think he is all talk...maybe a performance issue...just ghosted her...sad...
Planned it all but couldn't follow through...not sure what that's about...

608

Damn...walked out on a sure thing...they never before...nothing?

Making out...fondling. I guess last night was supposed to be the night. She didn't mention I was there so he should have shown...or maybe he saw us laughing through the windows...and turned around and left...not sure

Poor girl...

I agree...I mean I had her cracking up and she obviously over drank to soften the blow but today could be the fallout.
Knees better?

Much gooder.....tell her she can watch us someday....watch you absolutely do what you do.... Hehehe...JK

She did want to talk about that lol. She also said one of my books is awesome and asked me to teach her about yoni eggs lol. Then she said she needs an autograph.
Was a nice feelin...said she's been self-pleasuring to some of my chapters...wahooo...

I'm down...be awesome to perform...sexy to have you explain how pleasure works

Uhhh...not sure I'd be able to formulate a damn sentence for her while with you lol...

I bet you could...would be educational...awesome

Could be fun...

...set it up...

Heheheheeee...might intimidate her...

How?

Lol...we are fire! Not like everyone else. And our...sessions are short fire! A 3 to 5 hour "connection" would intimidate any voyeur...make them want to join in for sure...have you seen you?

It would be a seminar...what did you do yesterday with your mouth...instant cumming...

Lol...seminar for sure...uhhh, tried to pleasure your overly large cock...with my mouth...

Cock covered in your cum...as it was in your mouth...instant cum shot

Tasted amazing...obviously still ovulating...was soaked...still am...

Wet...creamy...dripping...

Was soooo needed and satisfying...always is!

You self-satisfy today?

Last night...Finishing up reps at gym. You? Dream at all?

No dreams...did self-play...

Mmmm...share? I kinda squirted after remembering how you drove in deep then bit my neck...and the doggie with my hands pushing up against the wall...to push back...yummmm...

Was reliving...your swallow of my cum...

Oh yezzzz...hit roof of my...well...you know...

Waves of pleasure...

Mmmm...I like giving you pleasure...perhaps I should do more swallowing...

**Ohhhh...was amazing...but so is cumming in pussy...cumming in ass...
all waves of pleasure...**

You're soooo much fun...I enjoy it all!! Even though I get sore...

Sore????

Thought my body would acclimate by now? Lol...kinda glad things are as snug as they are tho...such a turn-on to feel everythinggggg...

Sore? Pussy? Ass?

Pleasantly so for a day after...but gets me wet every time I think of and feel the tenderness...

Mmmm...your anal orgasms are intense

So true. It's soooo good cuz it turns into full-body orgasms. And...because of trust. The more I open up...well, let's just say you may want to run as I get more comfortable lol...

How was gym?

Mmmm...tanning bed felt like your warm hands...otherwise lonely without you...

You have an amazing tan...

You make me feel good about it...

Is amazing

Who knew Irish girls could train their bodies to produce melanin lol. Experiment a success...

Total truth

Workin' those muscles out...nice!

I was...you go by the gym? How are you?

I did! I'm great. How do you feel?

I'm good...kiddo and me all week...was great...but she ran me ragged

I bet...lol. Wish we could bottle their energy.

For sure...how are you...more at ease?

Yes, thank you for asking. I'm hangin in. Able to move about the day fine, working out, and...well the "toys" help, it's just the broken sleep sucks. Toxic shame for believing in him. You sleeping these days? You seem better with some time off.

February 21, 2022 8:34 AM

Hi

Hi

How are you

Hangin in. Everything good?

Yes...kiddo home today...no school

Lol, fun! Yeah, whole neighborhood is home here

Right...no issues from attorney?

Not yet...yay!

Rubbing clit?

Walking into the gym. That might create some stares lol.
How are all your sensitive parts?

Very much needing your touch

Awwww...

Watching tv...gonna make a waffle

Nice! Love that you cook...

(Later)

Ahhhh, feel so much better now...but needing your touch! You have great talent in choosing toys by the way.
Thank you so much for the gifts. Heading to the shower...

Did you use them???

Of course...was a looooong weekend. Gotta be careful of the turbo mode...can put a girl through the ceiling! Lol. I'll share sometime...

Did you cum lots???

Uhhhh...of course! I just prefer it with you lol...

So sexxxxxy....

Ya think?

I do...I do...I want to watch you play

That might be fun!

Yup...sit on couch...watch you playing...butt plug in...vibrator going inside you...me stroking my cock...

Wow...

Did you insert?

Was just shaving my lady bits lol...
So...would the reward be...

Mmmmmmm...Reward?

Would the reward be you...at the end of my displaying?

Yes...for sure

Mmmmm...my fav, you hard, dripping, filling me...thrusting in...

See precum dripping

Yezzzzz, so warm, slick...

Are you toying pussy now?

No sorry, showering. Last night though. Helps me sleep. Thinking of you cumming in me...wanting me. On my way to shake shop, office, work crap. Maybe tonight tho-

Mmmmmmmmmmm

Are you playing?

No...

Any dreams lately?

Yes...watching you with toys

Heheheheheee

(Later)

Hi...toy time??

You're my toy, no?

Great answer

How's your Monday?

Easy...kinda quiet

Nice!

(Later)

Thinking...

Bout...

Tongue...to tip...
You safe and warm?

I am…dealing with a dip shit…

Oh no. Anything interesting???

Stolen car…foot pursuit…incarceritos…

Ugh…
Yup, definite dip shit status…

Very…
How toys???

No toy just yet…
My favorite toy is unfortunately dealing with a dip shit…lol
Muah…save me some…

February 24, 2022 9:59 PM

I was able to delete messenger messages…secure fb/insta…and of course get my phone number private/
protected. Thank you for help. Are you feeling ok?

I'm ok…tired…but good

I'm glad. Sorry so tired, long week?

It's good…what you wearing?

Silk…you?

Kevlar…

Mmmmm…yummmmmmm….I would so peel that off you…

February 25, 2022 9:44 AM

Hi

Hello...

Hoping you are feeling well. Long week?

Very...no school today...have kiddo...she is a busy body...

Yes, there are kiddos all over the shake shop. Had to come work here, no wifi at home. Dream?

Yup...woke up by your mouth...no words...no reply...cum all over tits, face...you say nothing. Went to turn on shower...walked back to me to offer towel...invited me to shower...

Whoa...quivering...wet...did you choose towel...or shower...curious...

Shower for sure...washed you...fucked you...washed you...fucked you some more...

Damn...anal?

Of course...one leg up on side step...lube on me...warm water all along your body...relaxed... guide me in...deep...

Oh myyyyyy...

You slightly bend...more access...look over shoulder...encourage me to go deeper...harder... take what's mine...tell me to cum for you...cum inside...I pull your shoulders...cock completely in you...last deep thrust...hot cum spraying inside you...
You turn...holding each other...kissing...swaying to 80-90s glam rock...till water goes cold...

Damn...that's quite a dream...thank you for sharing with me...looooove it...so much pleasure...

Did you touch today?

Did...was thinking of you holding my hands to the bed as you...penetrate...thrust deep....taking my breath. Your mouth crashing down onto mine, engulfing, taking...making me succumb to your...

617

Yes...
Toys? Fingers? Both?

Fingers...hips rocking...so sensitive...

Mmmmmm...period hormones?

Yes. Been yearning for some slow...riding...make you c o n s e n t....

Mmmmmm....I enjoy your periods...I consent...
You cum soooooo much...instantly too...

So happy you enjoy even my "icky" days...make me feel less...ickyyyyyyyy...

Not icky...hot...still want you in hot springs...would love a whiskey night...get good buzz...

Yezzzz....maybe with that Orange Jameson you told me about...I am curious...

Mmmmm...yes...and an old bar somewhere...shots...close conversation...rubbing...touching...
flirting...leave big tip...bartender knows I'm getting laid as I leave...

Wow...like a movie scene...

No movie...I would get laid...

You sure???

Yup...sure...

What's that like? Knowing someone desires you...enjoys all your pleasures...

Very...empowering...

Mmmm...you do like empowerment...

Every human does...

Meets our "significance" needs.

My dream was simpler. Somehow you needed me to meet you...out in the desert...it was dark
except for the small fire you had going. I walk to you...you bed me over your tailgate...was fucking hot!

Ohhhhhhhh myyyyy...

Lol...

Heading into movie with kiddo...msg soon...

Have fun!!

Later

Gotta lay back off phone tonight... daughter has it now...muah...

February 28, 2022 1:24 PM

Hi

Hoping you're safe...and happy...

I is...how are you?

Livin'! Anything fun in the crime-fighting world?

Same...same...same...what ya doin?

Just workin'...thinkin' bout heading home...you?

Workin...workin...no truck this week...

Truck?

Car getting fixed...grrrr

(Later)

619

Hey...

Hi. Hey, how many hours after an assault/rape is a rape kit good?
I know sperm lasts 1-5 days in the womb...

Not exactly sure...DNA lasts longer...What ya working on?

Client (18) was sexually assaulted

Where?

Saturday night...Mayfield Basketball Player (18) at a party.
She's moving from denial into anger and grief phase. Might head to PD to report?

Needs to...for sure...

I've advised. She has to make a tough decision...

Chapter 37

DISTRACT

Dereck coughed, trying to muffle his breath, his chest burning inside. He couldn't believe he relapsed and got covid a second time ruining his plans for Peg. He pulled his robe tighter around his chest and scuffled his feet along the tile floor towards the bedroom. Being in bed for days, he thought he could sit at his desk and get some work done, but that was not going to happen. He felt like death. Everything was on hold, life, his job, even his plans to rid the world of Pegasus Law.

He pulled back the blankets and crawled back into bed, hoping it wouldn't be for weeks.

Gunnar was slightly annoyed. He wanted to drive over to see Peg but was without his truck, so he was sitting around waiting until it was time for his shift. The patrol car is not one to use when going to see one's girlfriend as it can rattle the neighbors when parked in a neighborhood.

Completing another set of push-ups, he rolled over onto his back and stared at the ceiling. He had not had time to share any information with Peg about what Aileen Lauden told him about Dereck, nor did he want to. She was going through so much already with the divorce, and the thought of upsetting her further hurt his heart. He'd known men like Dereck Law his entire career. The guy was a grade-A coward. That didn't make him feel much better. He knew Dereck still loved Peg, and that was most likely why he hadn't pulled anything stupid yet. What Aileen said made too much sense though, and considering Dereck's mental decline he might actually come after her.

He rolled over and started in on another hundred push-ups uneasy with the fear that he couldn't protect Peg the way he wanted. She was the type to hold her own...she was top-notch. He lowered, placing his forehead to the floor and sinking into it, guilt coursing through him. He realized at that moment that Peg was safe now that Dereck was distracted with all that came out in the divorce hearing. His concern was more that she would be safe up only until Dereck found out who *he* was.

P eg was feeling the effects of too much stress. The divorce hearing, along with her client's rape, on top of not seeing Gunnar in two weeks was beginning to wear on her emotionally. Fatigue settled deep within her core despite how great her gym sessions were lately and knew that a hug from him, which turned into an orgasm, would be most beneficial. She wanted Gunnar. She always wanted Gunnar and couldn't understand their intense pull towards each other.

Spreading the sheet out on the massage table, Peg ruminated about what Anna had told her about the rape. She had a hard time sharing how she was married to a man who was sneaky and liked to wait until she was asleep to "have his way". Relapses lingered from time to time, but she held back on her experience, happy that she could help another with her pain. There was something liberating by explaining to Anna how Dereck could do whatever he wanted to her body, the toxic shame was on him, but he would never, *ever* be able to hurt her soul. And that was a win for her... every damn day.

Peg finished dressing the massage bed and went to greet her client in the lobby. Her body was going through the motions of working, to distract herself from the trauma she knew would visit her in her sleep. She opened the door, her smile intact, her eyes caring, but really, all she wanted to do was be in Gunnar's arms.

March 1, 2022 10:40 AM

Good morning

Hi there…

What you doing?

Nothin' much yet…you?

Same…no truck…no gym…no way to go over…leave you full of cum…

Aw, I should Uber you…

Awwwwww

(Later)

Sex assault client just asked me to come get her. She can't take it anymore…

To report sex assault?

Let ya know. Is there a particular officer you'd suggest?

No…will be secondary to investigations…address it happened at…might be DASO…

I have heard that…thank you…

What is address where crime happened…if she knows…

3600 Majestic Ridge…would DASO come to her home to take report?
Can't get her to leave house yet…it's baaaaaad…
nvm…she's regressing…sorry.

Yes…contact DASO

Ty

Chapter 38

U-TURN

Gunnar awoke with a hard-on he knew wouldn't quit. He dreamt of Peg and how wet she would get as soon as he touched her...or rather, just texted her. Her body was amazing. It had been so long since he felt her legs and arms wrapped around him. His travel, and then no vehicle, had been too long and his shifts too stressful. He needed her...

March 2, 2022 7:58 AM

Hey

Heyyyyyy...

Whatcha thinking?

Well...I know you probably haven't been appreciated lately as you function in a world where there are more withdrawals than deposits like I do...just wanted to throw out some gratitude. Let you know I appreciate you and all you contribute...thank you for making me feel wanted in a time when I didn't feel it so much...ty for helping me with my sex assault client too...

You are awesome...
You are wanted...for sure

*I enjoy our shared connections...and you're sexy as f*ck...*

Mmmmm...pussy wet?

Yep, gym, shower, getting day going...how'd ya know lol...
Sensitive tip lately?

Very...lots of precum as I masturbate...

Oh myyyyy....

How is your client...from Mayfield?

She's from Arrowlund...he's from Mayfield. Got her through enough to go back to school today. Fingers crossed but it's the coming weeks we have to watch her...thank you for asking.

What happened?

They were crushing on each other for few weeks. She set boundaries, even told 4 people at the party that she would not be with him until she consents. He waited until she was passed out drunk. She started to have flashbacks next morning driving home. Remembering his voice saying "Anna...you awake?" She's blaming herself, angry, up, down, feeling violated, responsible... Just held space with her, helped her through. Gotta full scholarship to college, bright but upset she drank knowing it could make her vulnerable. She wanted me to elaborate on my experiences (with ex) and walk her through the emotional stuff. I answered as I could. She's strong. Might go forward with paperwork might not...tough times...

Damn...

Yep...

Was she...well, was it her first time?

No...I think that would have been worse...

Yeah...not much better...but...

He apologized in a way that makes her suspicious he's done this before. She feels if she tells, others may step forward, but risks exposure and everyone from the party choosing sides...tough call...

Assuming unprotected?

Yes. Her mother put her immediately on Plan B...

Was just gonna ask...

She says it was a full-on rape. She did not consent and was incredibly angry no one at the party cared. Apathy is huge with that generation...

What part of town?

Apt on Majestic...across from the mall...

Ahhhhh....

Broke my heart to hear her say, "Peg, I'm so mad because I didn't listen to my intuition like you had taught. I felt something was going to happen...that I wasn't safe, but I didn't listen...to me."

Sorry you had to relive some of your tough times through this...

Thank you...it's healing for me to help heal others... keeps me going...

Yeah...if needed...I can come play therapist for you...I can even be your reference doll!

Oh wowwwww...I would definitely enjoy that healing session...

Hehehehe.....

What would that entail exactly?

You taking out any...and all emotions upon me...no safe words allowed...

Mmmm...more explanation please...

**Do anything you desire with...me...no boundaries
What ya doing???**

*Nothin' lol
Losing WiFi apparently*

Peg climbed up into her truck to get to the shake shop where there was better wifi. It wasn't often, but sometimes, the wifi at her roomie's house was less than stable. It would just go out here and there.

She put her sunglasses on and put the truck in gear to pull off and up to the cul-de-sac turn-around. As she turned and accelerated, she saw his truck passing her street. She pulled out and to the stop sign just in time to see him making a u-turn. She waited, wondering if he was all right. Her stomach swirled hoping he was okay and that Dereck hadn't contacted him or hurt anyone.

Gunnar pulled up opposite of her truck and rolled down his window, Peg did the same. He half-smiled, she mirrored him lowering her sunglasses.

"Wanna fuck?" His voice made her body quiver with arousal.

Peg looked him over. He was freshly showered with hunger in his eyes that made her insides tremble with want. She looked around the neighborhood, thought for a moment, and responded, "Yeah."

Gunnar nodded, rolled up his window, and accelerated to pull down her street and park. Peg followed him, parking in front of the house. She hopped down just in time to meet his stride from across the street. They both walked up the sidewalk and to the door sneaking in, careful not to wake the still sleeping second roommate.

Gunnar walked swiftly towards her couch and threw his gun and phone down. As he turned, Peg was already coming towards him. He embraced her, sure to drag her hand down his chest to his crotch. She gently gripped his engorged cock and moaned into his mouth as his tongue explored the sweetness of her he'd missed so much. He spun her around and pushed her towards the bed, laying her on her stomach as his weight came crashing down on top of her. Peg could feel his erection pressing hard into her arched tush, the thin fabric of clothes the only thing separating them. Gunnar spread his hands along hers, spreading her body beneath him as he sunk his mouth into her neck, kissing down then sucking hard on her trap. Peg cried out wanting him deep inside her, penetrating her slick, dripping womb.

"Feel how much I want your pussy, baby?"

He growled low in a deep whisper that made her body shiver beneath his hot breath. Gunnar lifted up and brought her to her feet. He grabbed the bottom corners of her scrub top and flung it over her head, moaning at the sight of her breasts plump and lifted in her bra.

"I guess I have too much clothing on."

She smiled, reaching to remove his shirt as he'd done hers. His chest was large, muscles swollen as if he'd just come from the gym. She reached out to caress down his sternum to his stomach, her touch causing his breath to hitch.

Disrobing the rest of their clothing, both stood up gazing at each other as if it had been years since they last met. Gunnar pushed Peg back against the bed, letting her fall gently so he could spread her legs and gaze upon her wet, glistening vulva. He loved to look at her and reached over to get the toy he bought her.

He handed it to her, "Please...I want to watch."

Peg smiled and obliged, her eyes on him as she began caressing her clit with the little aqua-colored massager he'd chosen for her. He was pleased and trailed her outer lips with his fingers, spreading her open then inserting two fingers to further her pleasure.

Peg stopped every so many moments to try to concentrate and catch her breath. The vibrations, mixed with his thick fingers, were almost more than she could stand, the pleasure pure bliss. Gunnar bent down and lubed up a small anal beaded butt plug, which he gently inserted before lowering his mouth and covering Peg's swollen, wanting clit. Gunnar moved his mouth and said, "I love to watch you and learn."

Peg nodded, gasping for air at how good his mouth felt on her most vulnerable and sensitive parts.

"You...you are incredible."

Gunnar stood and pulled her to the edge of the bed, entering her in one motion, filling her until she cried out. He pumped and thrust, looking down into her begging eyes, knowing he'd never felt a pussy as tight as Peg's. She was magnificent to him and the best lover he'd ever had. He watched her orgasm build, stopping to bend down and sink his mouth into her slickness, caressing and sucking with his tongue until her hands found his ears as if she were going to fall from the earth.

Her breath was labored, her stomach quivered, and she cried out almost ready to cum. Gunnar stood again and penetrated her, grabbing her hips and pulling her towards him as he thrust deep. Peg's pussy squeezed as her legs enclosed around him pulling him in. He loved when she pulled him deeper and deeper. Peg made him feel so wanted. He stopped and pulled out before getting too close.

Pulling her hand, he guided her to a stand and turned her around to bend her over onto the bed. He pushed into her and slid deep. He gasped at how wet and tight she felt. Running his hands up her back, he thrust gently and deep in unison with her breathless moans. He wanted to cum but instead turned her over and orally pleasured her again, this time making her cry out his name before he relented. Pleased with how his name rolled from her lips Gunnar laid down, but Peg was already sliding her lips down over his engorgement. Gently he swiped her hair away from her face so he could watch how slow and methodical she pleasured him. No one had ever made him feel so desired as Peg. Her oral play was like art to her. She took her time and moaned making him want to explode each time she'd slowly move down his shaft to his base, taking all of him.

Gunnar pulled her under her arms, up his body then turned her on her side until he was behind her spooning her. He wrapped his arms around her, pressing his cock into the small of her back while sinking his mouth down into her neck. Peg's lungs sucked in air quickly as his bite sent tantalizing chills up and throughout her whole body. She was about to cum from it, and he wasn't even inside her yet.

As her body arched back to him, her neck craned upwards. Gunnar groped her breasts gently, pulling her body to him and sliding long and hard into her slick, tight opening. Peg gasped again, her breath hitching. He pulled away then slid deeper, thrusting over and over and over. Peg thought she'd go mad, the ecstasy almost causing her eyes to roll back in her head. She wanted more of him, their immersion so comforting.

After a while, Peg pulled away and turned toward him to blow him again before climbing up his body to sink down on him and begin riding. Gunnar looked up smiling, whispering how beautiful he thought she looked fucking him the way she does. She smiled, placing a hand on his chest and the other behind on his thigh to brace herself for faster hip thrusting. He grabbed her hips, relenting to the pleasure, he could feel Peg caressing her clit against him and he told her it was so gorgeous to watch her.

"Baby, turn around for me. Let me see you from behind?"

Peg smiled and moved around sinking down again on him. She began rocking and moving slow against him, moaning at the pleasure his size gave her from the reverse cowgirl position. Gunnar moved his hands to her hips again and whispered, "Touch yourself, baby... I want you to pleasure your clit while you're riding me... you're so fucking hot...use me." Peg did as he wished, arousing him until he almost exploded.

The front door opened and closed making them both halt. Peg realized her roommate's son left. Gunnar whispered, "He gone?"

"Yes."

"Good." He flipped them both slowly until he was placing her on her back on the bed. "Now that we're alone I want to make you scream."

Peg smiled at the boyish grin on his face, his dimples presenting along with a gleam in his eye. He hiked up her right leg and slammed into her soaked womb. Peg gasped and cried out, Gunnar thrusting deeper and deeper until she buried her face in his chest to muffle her moans. His length and girth still too large for her, Peg's body happily accepted him anyway. She moved her mouth up and found his nipple, taking it between her lips and teeth, sucking just hard enough to drive him wild. Gunnar drew air between his teeth and thrust deeper, Peg pushed towards him meeting each and every glorious hump of his pelvis.

"I want to cum inside you, baby."

"Yes."

"May I cum in your beautiful pussy?"

"Yes baby, yessssss..." she whispered then took his other nipple into her mouth, sucking harder forcing his orgasm.

Gunnar could take no more and thrust deep, letting go as his climax overtook his entire body, an exasperated moan escaping his throat. Peg let herself go too and met his release with her own, both crashing over into pure bliss, moaning loudly in the little room!

Afterwards, Gunnar collapsed onto her, Peg wrapping her arms fully around his strong, muscular back. As they caught their breath, he slid from her and lay at her side. He turned to look at her, his eyebrows lifting, "You...are a freak."

Peg looked shocked.

"But since you are an Irish freak...then it's fracken Irish freak."

"That's not true." She frowned with a small smile.

He smirked, "No, you are definitely...a freak."

Peg looked up at the ceiling trying to think what would make him say that. They hadn't even ever gotten into any kink stuff yet. She thought to herself if enjoying all they did immensely made her a freak to him, then so be it.

Changing the subject, Gunnar mentioned plans to go shooting the next day with another officer that was shot up on the highway then joked that he told him they could go but he "better not Chris Kyle him". Peg turned to look at him realizing he didn't trust the state of mind the guy was in, she also hated thinking he might be unsafe. She tried to remove the thought from her mind, scared that she cared much more for him than she was supposed to. He saw her face and distracted her.

"I met Chris Kyle, was offered a job with his company actually but he was killed. He was a great guy...but had his demons. I mean you don't blow a hundred and fifty headshots and not have some issues...and that's just what was recorded."

Peg stared at him admiring how his mind works, especially right after sex. He said he had to get going, dressed while asking her about her day ahead, she watching how magnificent his body moved as he talked and gestured. She enjoyed seeing how well his muscles contoured to his frame. He mentioned he was always in pain and busted up so much they couldn't find spare parts for him in a junkyard...but she just smiled. He moved with grace and commanded respect just with his gait. She thought how she'd love to get him on her massage table someday and show him how well he could heal.

He bent to kiss her goodbye then was gone. She rolled over to watch him from her window, completely satiated...freakness and all.

(Later)

Mmmmmm...yes please...

Ohhhh myyyy gawwwwd...

You happy gal??

Very! Are you? With this Irish freak girl and all...

Very freakalicious...

A step up from badger? Can't really walk...

I'm gooooooood....like a penguin lol

Wtf???

Hehehe...happy feet!

You...are fire!!

(Later)

Mmmm... so I have bite marks, a hickey on my left tit, another on my right trap...and I'm a fracken Irish girl freak? Ummmm...okayyyyyy...

Yupper

Hmmmm...you had a hunger in you today that was ferocious...suits you...

You like?

No...LOVED!!
Almost lost my mind when your mouth sunk into my skin as your cock filled me all the way from behind.
What's gotten into you???

Just a frisky Irish kid...

Mmmmm...feels sooooooooooooooooo good...

Shake shop conversation?

Yup!
Del: "Peg, you're late! Where's you're eyelashes biotch??
Me: (Not answering, just smiling) "Isn't it beautiful out? Amazing hump day yes?
Christa: "Oooooh Peg got-"
Me: "Heyyyyy, what's new?!"
Del: "It's Ash-freagin' Wednesday! Whatcha gonna give up Peg? Huh?"

Funnnnnny....

Me: "I've sacrificed a lot this year..."
Del: "You've got a point! So no ashes?"
Me: "Nope. Pegs don't do organized religion."
Christa: "Nice! Hey Peg, guess what I gave up?"
Me: "Nookie with Chris?"
Del: "Better...tell her!"
Christa: "Online shopping!!"

Me: "Oh hell naw, seriously?"
Christa: "My moods are going be severe!!"
Del: "Guess what some of the guys are giving up?"
Me:"Uhhh, I give up."
Del: "Alcohol, soda...looking at our butts! Any juicy details for us Peg?"
Me: "Me? Nope."
Del: "You sure? You're late and walking slow from your truck."

They live through you...

Nah, they think you're an invisible magic dick leprechaun from my imagination lol. How are you holding up out there?

(Pic of dead guy on sidewalk)
Same ole...Fentynal OD...

Fuuuuuuuuuuuuuck...

He ain't...fuckin' no more....

Oh wow. Welp, maybe in the high he was getting laid. Damn...

Nope...flatlined...Fred dead...

My, my, myyyyy...
Gonna head to my bed...see what thoughts of you bring about for me...

Mmmmmmmmmmmauh...

Muah...

March 3, 2022 2:28 PM

How's legs????

Heyyyyyy! Leg day was fun at the gym this morning...but I'm tough...
How are my favorite pink parts?

Busy...busy night...

Were you assisting on the mess I saw up on the highway?

No...guy decided to do home invasion robbery...
Smashed head open on cell door...at hospital he barricaded using surgical knife left by his bed...
He don't like me so much anymore...

Barricaded?

In room...then bathroom...whole floor evacuation...

Jeeeeezus...kinda fun?

Meh...No one wins...

True. So was the head injury from you...not making friends? Lol...

No...he smashed his head on the wall in booking...has shredded tricep from Belgian Malinois... and jacked elbow from a forced stabilize takedown...

Dayemnnnn...homie sounds like a real pain in the ass. Fentanyl or meth?

Boff'em

Fuuuuuuuuck. Shredded tricep sounds neat...good puppers!

Very badass little dog...

Mmmm...love'm. So did you have to use negotiation tactics to get him out of the bathroom...or forced stabilized takedown?

No...Come out in 30 seconds...or you will wish your mama swallowed type negotiations...

Bahawhaaa...I'm dyin'...

Chapter 39

LULL

Dereck rounded the side of the house and crouched low. He silently moved along the stucco, careful not to make a sound in the rocks beneath his feet. His heart pounded deep within his chest, he was proud to finally be able to go forward with his plans for Peg. It had been a while, but he finally got his strategy together and got away from the damn pot gummies Todd gave him. They helped him forget all the stress with his mother and her estate, but they also made him forget to go to work...and terrorize Peg.

He looked over to see the light from the neighbors' house glowing into the dark. He had to steer clear of it and crawled on his belly to move below it. She was a nosey neighbor, as he'd seen her watching everything and everyone while watering her landscaping. She was old but in shape, so he knew she paid attention.

Dereck moved up to his hands and knees enough to peer into her window. The light was off but the door to her room was open and the hall light illuminated the room enough for him to see...it was empty!

WTF!

He lowered his head as he could see the little brat run passed the door into the living room. He waited a moment then lifted his head again, not believing what he was seeing. The room was empty! No bed, no desk, no items, and no Peg!

Fuuuuuuuuuuck!

Dereck pursed his lips, angry he'd been so preoccupied and out of it, he'd slacked off and not even realized Peg left. He was so pissed. Crouching low he crawled back the way he came and against his better judgment, decided it was time to walk right up to the front door and knock. He had to know where she went. There was a time Jan would have fucked him...if Peg hadn't read their texts.

J an jumped when the doorbell rang, it was after nine at night and she knew Alana's father wasn't supposed to come by. She pulled the blanket off of her legs and stood up in her work scrubs, her feet barking from too many hours standing. Alana came running down the hall looking f her mother for instruction.

"I'll get it, stay here on the couch with your iPad."

"But what if it's Daddy?"

Jan looked at her sternly, "On the couch please. If it's Daddy, I'll let you know but he hasn't texted."

"Okaaaaay, Mommy."

Jan turned on the hall lights and walked to the door, she opened it almost jumping at seeing Dereck Law on the other side of the glass door. She hesitated, wishing she'd locked it. He'd already had his hand on the handle and opened it but stayed, making no step forward. She closed the door a bit to peek from the side.

"You shouldn't be here."

Dereck smiled, "Just need to talk to Peg for a quick second. How are you beautiful?" He was dressed all in black with his stubby flip-flop feet peering out from black sweatpants.

"That's not gonna work this time."

"Oh, I'm not allowed to text you, call you beautiful, check up on you now?"

She looked him up and down, "Fuck off. You ghosted me, so go fuck yourself."

"That was a long time ago Jan. Don't be like that...besides, I'm free now."

"Yeah, free of intelligence maybe. Are you fucking out of your mind to come to my home?"

Dereck stepped back one step but still held the door, he looked her over and smiled, "How's your little one by the way? Daddy still stiffing you for child support?"

"She's not here."

"Like not home or not here anymore?"

Jan didn't want to admit she fucked up and Peg had moved out, "She's not here. You need to go." She started to close the door.

"It's important Jan, it's about Zena."

Jan smirked, "I texted with Zena today, she seems fine. You need to get the fuck off my property."

"Why so hostile?"

"I mean it Dereck. Don't come here. You aren't supposed to be near Peg."

He huffed, "Who told you that? Her beau?"

"Go away."

"So she does have a guy huh?"

"Goodbye, Dereck. Do yourself a favor, leave her be. For once in your life do something admirable."

Dereck laughed, "Yeah ok. Just tell me this, did she go to her sister's or is she still in town?"

"Get fucked Law." Jan closed the door and locked it.

Dereck stood on tippy-toes to look through the glass window. "She did go back east didn't she?"

"Gettttt off my front porch!"

Dereck turned half-smiling, taking his hand away from his waist and the gun hidden there under his clothing. Jan was harmless and annoying her was just as much fun as years prior. He started making his way back to his truck two blocks away, all the while trying to figure out where Peg had gone. He was pretty sure she moved back to New Jersey with her sister but there was a part of him that worried she was already moved in with a new man. He hated that everyone took to Peg. Friends, neighbors, kids, even dogs always took to her so naturally. He exhaled, thinking about someone else taking care of her, comforting her, helping her get on her feet! Squinting he could see his truck ahead, he thought about how she'd come back, got a lawyer, a new friend group, work, it pissed him off that she never showed up or even spoke to him again. Part of him wanted to kill her just for being able to stand on her own two feet without him. Opening the door and slumping down in the seat he felt conflicted. Most days he wanted her gone...dead, then others he just wanted to be near her, fuck her again, hear the soothing lull of her voice.

Driving along looking ahead to where the headlights lit up the street, Dereck decided to get back to the house and research flights to New Jersey. He needed to visit his mother and daughter anyway...and maybe while there, see how he was able to get Peg to return to her old stomping grounds with her tail between her legs...if she was in fact back home.

eg exhaled clicking the close button on her phone and throwing it to the bed. *Fuck.* She didn't know whether to be relieved that she missed Dereck's visit to Jan's door or anxious that he was looking for her. She decided on a little of both and wondered if she should tell Gunnar. Their time together was her escape...a survival, she hated to ruin it with the likes of Dereck. She'd hoped he would go away. It had been weeks and now he was surfacing again? She wondered what he could want as he was not supposed to be contacting her.

Jan said he looked terrible. Fat still, his hair overgrown, his eyes black and glazed over, that stupid antagonistic smirk on his face. Peg remembered that Jan and he had some sort of sexting affair years back when she thought Jan was a better friend. He strung her along and never chose her. Pissed her off not to win. Peg knows she's not a friend. Even now, texting and letting her know he came by, seems like a friendship thing but she could tell Jan just wanted praise and to hear her reaction to which she gave none. She just thanked her for letting her know. Peg silently praised herself for getting away from those who can't love her and especially those who'll never have her back. Her phone dinged. She turned to check it hoping it wasn't Jan again. She'd had enough reminders of the stressors she'd gotten away from.

March 4, 2022 12:45 PM

Hi...

Hi

How you be

I be well...you?

I'm good...hate wind...
Did you rub pussy today...I think you have...

Guilty!
Wind is no bueno...you? Thinking of me at all?

Yes...absolutely...

(Later)

How's your day?

Really good...you?

Little tired...but good...you working?

Nah, not today. Sleeping well?

Not really...never really do...how's shake shop???

Fun today...crowded. How was the shooting Chris Kyle Day yesterday?

Why crowded? Was really good...

Nice! Friday I think...Just breaking each other's balls lol...

Great girl chat...worse then guys!!

Yep, women are savage lol...

I hear...when is egg day...

Sunday into Monday...

Nice...

Mmmmm...

Wanna fill you...

Want...too...over...and over...and over...lol

Mmmmmm...other day was...ammmmmmazzzzziiiiing

Really was...So much more I want to do to you but...you distract me so well...

How are hickeys?

Fading...but make me wet when I see your marks in the mirror...

Replace them...thats my mission...

Yes... please...

Mmmmm much pleasure...

Pleasure heals the CPTSD/PTSD mind for sure...the other day was off the chain...

Yup...yup...

(Later)

Hi

Hi

How are you...one of my guys was just in a shooting...

Omg!!! Is he???????

He's good...
LC sux-

Are you safe?

T1000...(sent thumbs up with terminator gif)

Mmmm...T1000 huh?

Yupppppppppp....

Savage...

Every fucking day...

640

It's just part of who you've become huh? Have to admit...you are VERY good...

Very good at?

Savage traits...animalistic...force of nature traits...wolf-like...lol...

Wish peeps knew me...for being well...not sure...tired of being good at...

Yes...you ARE tired...I see you...
There's something behind your eyes when you speak...

Everyone knows me for being...headphones guy...no BS...walk into fire with smile guy...but there's more...

Much more...yes...

Only few really see...

Right...not often safe to show...

It's ok...
Legends are mostly show and tell

Hmmm...agree...

Yup...hope you sleep well...gnite

You as well...nite...

March 5, 2022 7:31 PM

Hi
Just...well...thinking of you...hi...

Hi!

Hope you are full of smiles...on Monday...will be full of cum...

641

Oh? Well, smiles now...

Hehehehehehe...

Thought about ice cube sex today...

Ohhhhhh really?

Was nice...to revisit...

Mmmm...great stuff

Great...great memories...

Hope you are well...gnite babe...

Nite...

March 7, 2022 8:04 AM

Hi

Hi

How you doing

Livin...you?

Same...how was weekend?

Started well...but anxiety visited...ugh...

Anxiety???

How'd your weekend go? Shooting cop suffering any PTSD?

Naw...he's all good...just another day at work...

Oh, nice...quick recovery...

Yeah...
Why you anxious?

Finances...hard to sleep...sometimes gets me down...

Still worried bout Florida stuff?

Not so much...

I don't have truck again...or...I would be inside you...anal day...

Anal day huh? How are your...sensitive...things?

Feeling...bigger today...like stretch you day...

Lol...every...day...is bigger day for me...

Yes...sooooooo horny...would cum in mouth...pussy...and your tight little ass today...

I'm sure...horny days...my favorite...kind of every day for me...

Wanna fuck you hard...from behind...

Mmmmm...I do likey...feels really good...makes me want to push back...hands against the wall...meet you...

feel allllll of you deep...

...and stretch you....

Hurts so good...

Yes...
Rub pussy this weekend???

Yep...thoughts of us...your whispers, your mouth on me...how you hike my leg up...drive in deep...You?

Yes...3-4 times...thinking about anal...giving...you playing with mine...

643

So happy I've made you a fan...enjoyable!

I like....will relax more...

Heheheeee...that's something not even I have mastered yet...depends on the day really...

Depends??? You...take me entirely...anytime I ask...slow...gentle...pick up pace...balls deep... cumming deeper...you are pro babe...

Nah, just enjoy us...somethin' about ya...

Dick hard again...thnx...

Lol...mmmmmmm...my fav...

(Later)

What you doing

Was showering...you resting?

Yeah...bored...wishing I had you in heels...naked...

I was going to put those on today...it's been quite a while...

Ohhhhh my...yummy...

Mmmmm...

Did you cum today?

Unfortunately no, sorry....
Was just on phone with my son...had a mini-breakdown.
Now I've got to go into the bank with swollen eyes lol..

I'm sorry

644

Ah, it's what we women do to get through...hoping your boredom ceases.

(Later)

Touch yourself?

Yes...gonna do it again too...very horny today

Mmmm...nice...save some for me...I'm throbbing ...

**Wish I was in you...woke...up...much wanting your ass...vibrator on your clit...looking down.
As I slide in and out...watch your pussy gush...as you cum...**

Mmmmm...nice visuals...drives me wild..the way you slide...in...and out...and in....

Mmmm...cock in tight ass...pleasing you...vibrator sending you over the top...rolling orgasms...

Mmmmm...full-body orgasms...we...just have that thing...

Remove vibrator...continue with fingers on clit...in pussy...

Mmmm...

**Complete surrender of your body to me...I bend you over...kiss...bite your neck...release...for
each other...throbbing cock cumming in you...your pussy explodes while squirting...legs
shaking...**

You do...make me squirt...

**Yes...you have had my cum everywhere babe
I'm stroking again...**

Mmmmm...so hot...

Gonna spray all over my chest...thinking bout you...

Love that...hope it's blisssssssssful...

Mmmm...taking to the edge...backing off...time and time again...

Edging?? Oh, hells yes!

Wishing I was in your mouth...fingers in my ass....

On the list for next time...

Yes...please...as I cum...swallow...straddle me...kiss me...share our pleasures...my cum...yours...mmmmmmmm...

So wet...

Mmmm...still hard...mouth on me...straddle me...keep me hard in wet dripping pussy...mmm

Holy helllll...you are fire today...

Mmmm...yep...thinking of pulling down on your hips...cock filling you...

Stretching me...feels good when you pull me down...

Feel tip of cock...popping against cervix...cum in your most deep part...

Yezzzzz...

Slowly pull out...leave last drops of cum on clit...you massage my seed on it...I watch...

Wow...

Bet your face is tingling...pussy throbbing...nipples sensitive as you sit there...

Might have to head home for a nap...with fingers wandering and thoughts of you. Throbbing...yearning for your touch...you deep in me...

Want to cum in....on...for you...will you touch your pussy?

Mmmmm...

Yes???

You make me really, REALLY like my body parts...and want to share them with you...
Yessssss

I love kissing every inch of you...inside and out...

I love your mouth on me...almost came Wed when you bit my neck like that...had to grab the wall to keep composure....

Super hot...leaving marks on you...
Still at shake shop? Pussy throbbing?

Yes. Gina is laughing at me smiling at my phone. She just admitted she gets butterflies in her vagina when her man sexts her. We're calling them vaginaflutters...

Tell her you will have them tomorrow...cuz I'm coming over...and will take care of them...

I get them when you sext me...every day since October 8!

Mmmmm...tomorrow...I want all of you...

I'll try to give alllllllll...

You always do...ALWAYS....

You make me...want to...

Yes?

Yes...all my parts, pleasure, ecstasy...

You dooooooo...
I so enjoy when you gush...very pleasing...

Gush huh? Lol

Yes...you do...

What else do you want to do with me...anything you desire...

Mmmmm...I have a few things on the list...never get bored with our list...

Such as? Tell me...

Mmmmm...do you know what Nutella is?

Yes

Yoni eggs?
Beads?

Yes please...

We'll explore...

Yup...yup...

Mmmmm...I know you favor...a threesome too...

No...I favor you...your pleasure...in any and as many ways possible...

Seeing you excited...cumming...makes me wild inside...

Never had threesome...most of what I know is make believe...enjoyed your story about yours... but...really like to see you pleased so...

You please me more than the threesomes honestly...

Makes me sooooo happy to hear...would love to put you in a sex swing...

That would be a first for me!! On the list for sure...
Want you on my tantra chair too...

Me too...Is that the chair in your room???

That's my chaise...kind of like that...

Rubbing yet??

No lol..at shake shop...lesbian friend just hugged me goodbye. Nice gal...

Ohhhhh my...any interest at all? You could make her scream...

Oh, fuck no...strictly dickly here...

I know you are...how wet are you???

Quivery wet...I ache. You satisfied?

**I am...very
Came lots...huge...kinda hit my chest...**

So hot...

(Later)

Hope you're safe and warm...

Yeah...easy night...

March 8, 2022 8:34 AM

Good morning

Hi

How you be...still without truck...was supposed to be fixed by last Tuesday!

Oh wow...

Pisssssssssed...

I'm sorry. Tough way to wake up on a Tuesday...

Yup...I had plans for you...grrrrrr

Mmmmm...me too...Anything I can do?

Can you replace a trunk of a Honda?

Oh um...I've got skills but not trunk fixin' skill...was it...hit?

Yeah...waited 2 months for them to fix it...

Perhaps the parts are on the convoy trucks in MD! Lol...

**Something...I think it's more lazy workers at Honda-Borman
I really...wants ya...**

Understaffed maybe...
Wants ya too...

Had plans for you...

Like?

Lots of oral...work our way to other things...anal...cum all over

650

You...looooove fluids...

Yup...enjoyed how last time we did anal...you were on your back...rubbing clit...screaming orgasm...

Mmmm...was a full-body orgasm!!
I have plans for you...with my mouth and tongue...

Yes? Such as?

Taste precum...make sure I have your attention...
have you facedown in my pillow...make sure you chant my name...

Tell me how...

Gentle massaging to help with relaxation...of things. Warm, wet tongue insertion..soft at first...increase...
match to energy and your breath...

Peg...

Caressing with long, languid tongue stroking...

Anything...for you...

This...would be all for youuuuuuu...

Nope...

You then get to pick a toy...

Nope...your choice...

Prepare you...turn you over so I can sink down on your...

Yes...

Gloriously large...manhood...

651

Make me cum for you...in you...
Are you...playing now?

Driving in tight jeans...very wet...

Mmmm...tight pussy...you rock and take me deep...

Always...
Your cock feels incredible so deep ...I love to ride and rock on you...

(Later)

(Sent article: Woman arrested in New Mexico for crash that killed 2, including officer)
Just...wow...

Yup...her hoax pursuit

What a fuckin' nipple-head...

2nd guy killed was a firefighter...

I heard...so tragic to lose two uniformed in same moment...she should fry...

(Later)

Hoping you had another "easy night" and you're safe and warm...

Easy day...how are you?

I likey when you have easy ones...

Still no fuckin car...hate in my eyes today...

Hate?

For Borman...supposed to have had it last Wednesday

Ah yes. They suck donkey dick from what my clients tell me...

**Totally...told them to give me my car back...they're like...sir, it's in pieces...
WTF?**

Ugh, pieces...no bueno...

Yup...supposed to travel to AZ on Friday...

Oh wow...

**Oh well...
Babe...how's pussy?**

(Sad face emoji)

Ummm...grumpy pussy???

Nooo...never grumpy...just...

Just???

*Just...needing.
How's your...parts?*

March 9, 2022 12:34 PM

Hi there...guess what I'm doing...

What?

Remember when you...swallowed me the first time...my hard cock in your hand?

Yes, of course...

**Thinking of...that
What you doing???**

Was fixing Del's leg here on the couch at the shake shop...
guys are staring at us of course lol...

I bet...I would too...

Feel better?

Still no truck!!

I'm sorry...that's truly frustrating.
I needs...your...healing...

Yes...
I don't...don't...don't...wanna miss your...period...

I know you're so busy and pulled in so many directions...
Needs ya...

I'm sorry

Me too

(Later)

Hey you? Holding up ok?

On fatal crash...

Omgggggg!!

Motorcycle

Oh fuck...went quick I hope?

Very...avulsion of entire face...

Oh wow...no helmet?

Had helmet...way speeding...headfirst into car...

Jeeeezus...you ok...with seeing it all?

Easy day...

Ohhhh...

March 10, 2022 1:48 PM

Hi there

Hi
Sorry, was in a meeting with the massage place owner. How are you holding up??

Good...how was mtg...all good??

Ugh...

Ugh????

Says I'm being requested. Want more days from me for less pay. Their prices not mine. Just...Thursday struggles lol...How are you?

Good...took today off...still no truck...grrrr
But, got Irish Whiskey...might dance to YouTube in my underwear...

That...sounds amazinggggg...

...everyone loves Disney songs...

Lol...Winnie-the-Pooh wears no pants...go with poooooh...

What you doing today?

Just living.
Was thinkin'...I haven't taken a minute to appreciate you lately. Wanted to thank you for making me feel desired....pleasured...seen...s a t i s f i e d...

Thank you...very...very desired...

Mmmm...

So how much less $$...

Half...Chiro doesn't want me taking on more clients but...

Grrrr....

You ok?

I'm good...just hanging with my mom...at house...guess I had to put pants on...

Lol...proud of you...

Could have been awkward...

"Awkward" everted!

(Later)

How's evening???

Hiiiii. Better. How are you feeling??

I'm good...took off...at daughter's softball practice...

Oh, fun! Glad you're getting some time off...

Yeah...how's the book cumming along?

Lol...it's so hot...

March 11, 2022 10:45 AM

How are you?

Getting ready to leave to AZ...

Right!! Hope it's some fun time for ya...
I'm well, thank you. You ok??

I'm great...

Chapter 40
RETURN

Dereck screamed into the silence of his hotel room then placed the phone back to his ear.

"Are you fuckin kidding me?" He ran his hand through his bushy long hair, frustrated at what Dean was telling him. He could have sworn Peg was back home here in Jersey, he was even on his way to go pay her and her family a visit, intimidate them a little. Since his divorce paperwork said not to see her in New Mexico, he figured seeing her in New Jersey would happen. He planned to be gone before she or her family could file anything, but now this.

"You positive you saw her D? It's not like her to go so long without seeing her sister. I was so sure she was here." His eyes tried to focus on the ugly floral wallpaper of the hotel room. Dean mumbled something and told him to look at his phone to see the pic he just forwarded.

Dereck squinted, cursing, he saw her then. A photo of her, sitting with four other women near a shake shop downtown. The pic was taken an hour earlier. She looked amazing. Smiling, being hugged by a blonde, others looking on laughing. His heart ached, his dick actually hitched, he wanted her. Seeing her might not be the best idea after all. Hating Peg was always easier if he didn't see her. There was something about how human she was with others that softened him.

"Alright, man, I'm going to finish up this shit with my mom and these fucked up cousins of mine then I'll be back. Thanks, dude. Not what I had hoped. I appreciate the info though."

Dereck listened as Dean reminded him that she's not living her best life and she'll most likely come back when she falls on her face.

"Dean! Motherfucker, you've been telling me that for the last year and now she's off somewhere in Ramas' still...making it! You even said she was having the best sex of her life. What if some rich guy is giving her everything...and getting everything in return!" His stomach churned at the thought of all that Peg gives. She was the most miraculous lover and he was almost sick with the thought of how she's pleasuring whoever she's with. He listened to Dean bitching at him and exhaled anger.

"Alright, alright...yeah, I get it. I gotta go, man. I'll hit you up when I get back this weekend. Let me know if you find out anything else."

Gunnar couldn't believe how much his body craved Peg after so long without her. Travel was nice for distraction but now that he was back he wanted to ravish her body, her mind, and immerse within her soul. She'd been so quiet lately and truth be told, he felt some guilt by not being available for her. Work seemed to be just more and more demanding leaving less time for his favorite things. Finally done the last of some legal bullshit training he picks up his phone hoping she was around.

March 14, 2022 2:21 PM

Hey you...just got out of training...legal update...woohoo

(Later)

You holding up?

(Later)

Holding up...

How you be?

I be well...You?

Busy...was nice in AZ...

Was?

This weekend...AZ State Shooting Match

I remember! Made you happy??

659

Was good...how was your weekend?

Mine? Uhhhh too many clients, too many shifts lol...but, lotsa chapters written so...positive!!

Lots of work? Work tomorrow?

Too much workieeee...Not tomorrow thank bejeezus lol. How's the shift?

Kinda easy tonight...so far...

Love that!

How's attorney with all divorce stuff?

No contact really...until taxes done. I finished mine. I'm sure he'll extend to prolong everything. Doesn't want to submit gun inventory or financials per the judge's demands.

Ohhhhh...that...
You been ok with everything?

Yes...

Ok...hope you can relax and rest...

Thanx...nite-

March 15, 2022 11:40 AM

Hola...mi amiga...mi gusta...you

Hi...how are ya?

Good...at gym...finalllllly...feel like a slug

Oh gooooood deal! Gotta get back into the groove!!

What ya doing?

Talkin' w/my girls...

Ahhhhhhhhhh...honest...wish I was cumming in you...

Wish...too...

Up to you where...just sayin'

What?

Where I would cum...up to you...

No teasing now...lol

I'm thinking...today...swallow day...

Really?? What if my mouth doesn't work...

It always...works...alwayssss....

IDK...I may have forgotten how to do uh...

Nope...and only...after you say you need a break...and pussy is sore...

Mmmm...nice plan...

What taste better...shake from shop...or my cum

Lol...

Need a myth busters...

?

Tell ya later...is funny tho

I'm sure...

How's conversations at shop?

Meh...how's the weightlifting?

Meh...cuz you daydreaming bout...
Uh...it's ok...

Well...I am now...

Mmmmmmmmmmmm....I bet...me too...

Specifics?

Take shower with you...put butt plug in ass...vibrator on clit...I shave and trim your beautiful pussy...

Wowwwwwww....

Yup...in a little diamond pattern...

Ahhh...details guy...

Yup...

Mmmmm....

(Later)

Hey

Hey
You safe?

Always...was chatting with son...rough paramedic day

Oh no...he ok??

Rough day...4 month old shot and killed...first on scene

Jeeeeeezus. That's a tough day...how does a 4 mos old get shot?

22 yr old showing off gun...side shot...through and through...

So sad. Is he...your son processing ok?

What does a 21 yr old kid do when you see that? He called..."Can I talk to Izzy?"...my 10 yr old...chatted with her for about 20 minutes...

Ahhhh...bet Izzy is the infant he held and was closest to in life thus far?
It's a thing. I used to do the same with my son when I had tough calls with kids. I know you probably still do it yes?
Tough day. I hope he...
Can understand he has a great support system in you...and a family he can call and connect with. Key elements in going the distance in such a rough, but needed, career. Great dad...great son...

Yeah...he is my hero

Love that...

March 16, 2022 11:40 AM

Hi

Hi

What you doing?

Jumping in shower...kitty shaving day lol. You rest at all?

Little bit...
Can I come by...cum by...cum in...cum on...

Mmmm...what time?

Bout 1/2 hour???

(Later)

I'm here

Mmmm...

(Later)

Lol...girls texted me from shop wondering where I am...

Smirk engaged

***

<u>*Peg's Journal Entry 3/16/22:*</u>

Gunnar finally made time for us. He got his vehicle back and drove over this morning. It was so nice to feel his embrace, our bodies fell right back into the pleasure patterns we'd developed.

I dressed in coral-colored lingerie and black heels, he thanked me with words but more so with touch and affection which I feel we were both starving of! He hugged and kissed me while backing me up towards my bed, tossing me down so he could slide his fingers inside me whispering how amazing my wetness for him felt. He moved my panties further aside and pressed into me, sliding right in as my body wanted his hard cock fully inside. My body molded perfectly to him and his slow thrusts felt incredible. I pulled him into me with my hands and legs, wanting him deeper and deeper. We realized shortly into it that we still had clothes on and had gotten ahead of ourselves, most likely because so much time and gone by. We stood and completely disrobed, then I took him in my mouth until he got close and had to stop me. We went to our favorite again, missionary, then oral for me, to doggie. It was nice to remember all the pleasurable positions. As I sunk down onto him to ride him he whispered how nice it is that I'm a Nympho and like what we do. I frowned then laughed whispering back that first I was a "Badger" then a "Freak", now I'm a "Nympho"? He chuckled realizing the progression of his compliments? Then followed it up with an admission that "No one has ever ridden me like you is all." I smiled and kissed his mouth, then I trailed kisses down his chest. He asked me to share some of my novel with him but I was getting close to another orgasm and had to tell him I couldn't concentrate. I was riding him super slow and I could feel so much energy pulsating through my body like electricity mixed with tingling.

He somehow flipped us over and wanted to be close in missionary again. I can't explain it but that position feels the most natural for us, lips caressing, whispers heard more easily. I enjoy the way his chest presses against mine and his arms wrap around me as our lower halves take over and create pleasure so easily. As he got closer and closer he started to pick up speed. As he started to release he asked me to look up at him and I obliged of course. He's beautiful at his most vulnerable times and enjoys being watched and admired. I can do that so effortlessly, he is gorgeous in my eyes. He has kinks about body fluids and being watched. I like his kinks.

Afterwards, he lay with me and mentioned he'd love to fuck me in a swing. I told him I haven't forgotten and if I get a place I'll be sure to install one for him. This made him smile, and he quickly said he's lucky to be with someone like me. That felt nice.

The mood shifted a bit when he had to tell me of upcoming travel and his daughter being on spring break. I know he was preparing me for our distance and reminding himself of his responsibilities. I'm aware we are just a "side thing" and I'm grateful for the tiny moments of pleasure. This certainly has helped my most stressful time, and I know the sex definitely helps me cope. I can't deny the intense sexual connection and would love to bottle it and sip on it anytime I want but that's never been something I could say I've had. For now, I'm simply going to continue having gratitude for our attraction and that the sex is so satisfying. I could have turned to drugs, alcohol, gambling, or shopping to deal with my CPTSD but none of that feels right. For some reason, no matter the trauma bond we have or not, this "thing" we've got going feels spectacular! The releasing into each other, the desire, the intense feelings of ecstasy and bliss lasts for days and feels somehow right. It is...what it is.

We talked for quite a while after. He admitted he didn't want to leave to go coach a suicidal cop whose career is ending. He said, "What do you say to someone about that?" And I felt for him. I mentioned sometimes nothing is okay and just "holding space" is all that's needed.

He regaled me of past Vegas trips with strippers and midget dirt bike races in the middle of $450,000.00 parties where 400 guns were given away along with a brand new truck. He said sponsor parties are events he has to go to since he was picked up by the sponsor for being a top shooter. He went on to tell me about a friend who calls him "cracker honkey white boy" and how he tried to get him a buckwheat t-shirt from the tractor store across from their hotel. I laughed so hard, admiring his good memories. He said they even convinced people his friend was Samuel L. Jackson and they were on the set of the movie "The Bodyguard". He went on to a story about the top female shooter and how everyone wanted her but he ignored her making her more interested in him. When asked why he didn't go for her, he said it just wasn't him. He then flowed into the incident about a young man being killed in a motorcycle accident earlier in the week and I could see it really got to him. His work is not something most could understand or even do, I know he is one tough guy.

As he dressed he told me of a lieutenant that my bestie was sleeping with. He mentioned she was kind of a useless cop with big fake tits. My friend told me he was hurt by her because she wanted to explore a threesome and he wasn't into it. I shared what I knew and we went on.

I started hysterically laughing when he shared a story about he and four cops riding in a pickup, before there were Ubers, and his bright idea of if they got pulled over, everyone was to run in a different direction! I enjoy how his mind works and it felt nice that we could both share some memories and reunite. Great day.

March 17, 2022 6:52 PM

Hi

Hiii

How are you?
Sorry...been at work since 11...

Figured you were super distracted. Didn't want to bug. I'm out to dinner with a client. She's gettin' the big D, Yay!

Sweeeeeeeet...

Lol...kinda is...she's 78!!! Feeling ok or super stressed?

March 18, 2022 12:45 PM

Hi

Hiii

How you be?

I be welllllll...how you holding up??

Good...how was dinner?

Entertaining. I enjoy seeing others evolve past the stuck belief systems. How are you doing during this full moon?

666

Busy...busy...

(Called a half-hour later)

<u>Peg's Journal Entry 3/18/22:</u>

So weird thing happened today (yes, it's a full moon sooooo okayyyyyy) Gunnar called me while I was at the shake shop. I went outside and sat on the wall to hear him better. He said my ex just called him! My stomach sank. My brain was like, "Peg, the last person you fucked a year ago is calling the current person you're fucking!"

I shook it off as dumb and focused on his words. He said Dereck told him his life is in shambles, his cousins kidnapped his mother from New Jersey and took her to Scottsdale, Arizona. He was asking him for legal advice on doing a police report. Gunnar said he asked him for clarification like, "You want to do a police report for something that's taken place in New Jersey, Florida, and Arizona?" I could tell Dereck only wanted his attention and Gunnar is realizing what an idiot he is. Gunnar asked me if he was the only cop Dereck knows to which I responded, you're the only one he thinks doesn't know what he's really like or he's burned bridges with. All the others figured him out. Life is so ironic sometimes. Out of an entire city full of officers, Dereck calls the one who's fucking (me) his ex-wife!

He told Gunnar he lost custody of his mother, the POA, and her house in Florida. Gunnar referred him to the attorney general. I apologized that he called him and bothered him with his drama. He said Dereck is in "a bad way" and super preoccupied with all that he's in he forgot to even mention me. I was relieved to hear that.

He changed the subject and said, "So you were quite the cum-queen the other day!" And I responded simply, "Well, that's just what you do to me." We laughed a bit and he eased me from the anxiousness of Dereck. He said he had two days off and then he was off to Colorado to teach for his LLC. I praised him and wished him well. He is definitely a go-getter. We talked a bit more and he said he likes making me laugh. Before hanging up he mentioned, "Kisses to all your pink parts." Making me chuckle more. I did appreciate him sharing with me that my ex called him, but wow, how the fuck awkward can life be?

March 21, 2022 3:49 PM

Hi

Hi

March 23, 2022 8:35 AM

Hi

Hi

How are you?

Alive...how are you?

Alive...tired...but home...last night...bout 0230....

Ohhhh myyyy. Hoping you're loving the new LLC stuff?

Its good...travel sucked...but class was good...

The travel is a bit long huh? Teaching rocked tho? Hope you're feeling proud?

Was great time...how is your???

My?

Gorgeous tight...super pink parts...

You rememberrrrr??????

Ohhhhh...I do...often...very much...

That makes me happy to hear...

Rub yourself lately?

Yes. Woke at 4, helped me get back to sleep. Thought of your thrusts, whispers, sinking your mouth in my neck. You touch and think of me at all?

Sure did...thought about you on back rubbing your clit...hard thick cock in your ass...how we came together...your deep anal orgasms made you moan...

668

Ohhhhh yes, I likey your anal...very much...been a while huh?

Yes...was gonna last time...but couldn't seem to leave your tight pussy...

Was wondering...thought we were gonna...

You were moving and fucking me soooooo great...

I wanted to do sooooo much but...

Like what else?

Well, I kept putting your hands above your head because I wanted to spread a lil Nutella on your nips and tip then taste you and suck it off...but we were rushed...

I know...I need 32 hour days...

I'd love to write your autobiography...but then I think how it could take years!

I am mostly an uninteresting guy...

We both know that's not accurate...

I'm sorry I have not had much time lately...

Your curse...I've never been an angry person but...I may have to take it out on you...with my mouth...

Yes! Very much...please know...every chance I get 1-2 hours...I force time to see you...

That feels nice to know...I appreciate you...

What you doing?

Trying to get myself moving...you?

Same...kiddo home for spring break...

Yep! All these kids are off...traffic is easier tho lol...

Right...on period this week?

Late...

Ohhhhhhh...ummmmm...

Only 6 days...

You ok??

Yes...happens...I increased my weights at the gym and supplements. I think it's more so because my hottie guy just can't dick me down as often (lol) my kitty is deprived...confused maybe...

Ohhhhhh...or...my super cum found a way...

That would be a miracle...

Use toys lately?

Yezzzzz...you think of my toys?

I do...I know you like real cock tho...but think how you please yourself...its so sexy...

Mmm...tantalizing...

Later

How are you?

Shaving...things...

Ohhhhhhh myyyyy...tell me more...

Butt, crotch, thighs, calves...feels soft when wearing scrubs at work...

Mmmmmm...rub your clit for me?

Okayyyyyyy....

Mmmmmmmmmm....wanna flick tongue along...inside...you...

I do like that...gonna go lay on my bed...are you touching for me?

I am...tip...dripping...running down shaft...

That's hot...I'm close...

Thick...clear...dripping...rubbing your clit...making you wetter...teasing...tip angles in slightly...
pull out keep rubbing tip on clit...

Teasing....

Yes...keep tickling...tip only...precum dripping from me on you...rubbing furious...you tell
me...I'm cumming...I drive deep in you...balls deep...you bite my chest...

Deep...mmmm...

As you cum...I feel your pussy pulsing...you feel my cum...I pull out...cum all over pussy and
lips...watch you rub yourself with my cum...

Building again...

Watching you...rubbing cum...all over...in you...you lay me back...take me in your mouth...
Then...straddle me...my hands on hips...you start to guide me in...your ass...using our cum as
lube...slow...relaxed...deep...you spread open glistening...rub yourself...anal-gasms come on
strong...whole body tenses...grinding deep...I now bite your chest...we cum...

Mmmmmm....

On second yet?

Done...you?

Ohhhhhh yes...clean up on aisle 3...

Lol...thats awesome! Well, hoping you're feeling good. I gotta motor, got a $120 massage scheduled at the office...

Mmmm...squeezy, squeezy...with boff hands...

Yes, will do...lol...hope your day rocks...

Chapter 41

LATE

Peg looked down at the white toilet paper not understanding what her body was doing and why she was still so late getting her period. Her mind wandered as she knew it was impossible to be knocked up. It had been twenty years since her tubal ligation and not once did she have a scare. It unnerved her how this was happening, and she tried to push it from her mind. She knew her tubes were cut and cauterized! The thought of her friend Carol came to mind where she had her tubes tied and one came undone to where she ended up pregnant with twins. Peg squeezed her eyes shut then opened them pushing away the thought, threw the paper in the toilet, and got up refusing to accept the fear.

"No! This is just because of all I've been going through." She whispered it into the hollow of the bathroom and flushed the toilet. There was no way she was going to accept or even entertain the thought of pregnancy at her late age...and she refused to add more stress to Gunnar's life. Deciding she would just ignore the fear-based thinking she readied herself for work, welcoming the distraction of healing others and forgetting about not only her body, but her brainless ex.

Dereck pulled into the driveway and turned the engine off.
Dean looked over at him, "What are you doing?"
"What do you mean?"
Dean frowned, "I thought you were going to let me drive out there, why'd you bring us back here."

Dereck smirked, his attitude making him sound like the prick he is, "It's not running right, I have to call for service on it." He opened the door to the ATV and got out.

Dean looked in the backseat towards his girlfriend Juna, "You wanna head home babe? He's..." He waved a hand towards Dereck's back as he walked away and headed towards the house.

"Well, this was a waste of our time. Why is he like this?" Juna squinted, annoyed yet again at the summoning of Dereck for them to come spend time with him because his wife left. She knows he thinks somehow the three of them will end up in bed together to help him erase the memories of Peg. She's still not interested. Juna half-smiled knowing it was because of Dean that Peg left Dereck and wondered what would happen if Dereck ever found out that they told her about the threesome he coordinated with them while she was in Florida.

"I have no clue. He's getting worse and quite honestly, I'm tired of this shit."

Dereck came around and out of the gate, he leaned forward and threw the keys on the driver's side seat, "Here, do what you want, I don't fucking care." He stomps away in his tantrum state and slams the gate.

Dean looked at her and rolled his eyes, "Okay, I'm done. I'm going to bring these keys in the house to him and meet you in the car. His immaturity is more than I can stand."

"Okay, babe."

Gunnar laid his head back against the recliner and wiped his head with his hand. He wanted to relax but felt a tightness inside at the thought that Peg could be with child. Truth be told, he wanted to trust her but couldn't completely, since most of his life involved people and deception. Admittedly, he did not feel she was the type to trap him, he didn't even want to think of that, but he just wasn't sure.

His daughter, noticing her father trying to relax, came over and leaned in to hug him close. He wrapped his arms around her, squeezing just enough, then placed a kiss on her freshly washed wet hair, "Thank you, baby girl, I needed that."

He knew, feeling her in his embrace, that another child would make him the happiest father ever in one way but, in another way it would reveal more than he's ready for. He couldn't understand why deep down he'd want Peg to bare his child. He exhaled trying to remove the thought and relax.

March 24, 2022 9:31 AM

How's your today?

Hi there...doing well...you?

I ok...just hanging with kiddo...

Glad you're relaxing!

Period???

Sorry no...not yet...

Preggie??

No preggie...unless you keep manifesting it!! I'm going to be
a grandmother in July...I'm just a week late...

Right...how is daughter?

So cute! Feeling good now that she's in 2nd trimester...(Pic sent) miss her tho...

Wow...she looks amazing...

I agree...I tell her daily...thank you for asking...

What you doing?

Sipping dandelion coffee...being lazy...you?

Just hanging out with little troll...work at 300...

Ah yes, gotta watch the trolls when not in school. Can't have them running amuck, they're everywhere
during the day...I had to swerve a few times this week while driving...

Speedbumps...

675

I stay away from the bip-crunch speedbumps lol...

Good plan...hard to clean off white truck...

Lol...so you may find this interesting, the guy that stood my friend up at Applebee's is driving over to her right now to...well...

Wow...now?

(32 minutes later)

Ohhhhh myyyyy....

He no show again??

Uhhhh....he showed...

Shots of whiskey time? Celebration?

Not exactly...

Why?????

She hasn't had sex in six years! I asked, "Was it like tequila or..." She says, "Peg is as more like ice tea... unsweetened...with nooooo fucking sugar."

Ohhhhhhhhhhhhhh...nooooooo....

I feel so bad for her...was in then back out the door in 18 mins. Didn't even take his jacket off. She said, "I'm going to go to bed to finish myself off...talk tomorrow."

Ouch...bad ouch...

Truth...

(Later)

How's shift?

It's ok...just booking trips for shooting matches...

Ooooh fun...go on with ya bad self...out of country or surrounding states...

All over US...

Nice!! So Gunnar?

Yep...

*What's worse? Two girls running with scissors...
Or two girls scissoring with the runs?*

Well...

Lol...

How is your night?

Meh...anything exciting out there?

Not much...

Finally...lol. I mean I know you like adrenaline but this town has been a bit much lately no?

Been...crazy...crazy...

Yeah...hoping it shifts...

It won't...will get worse...much...

Why do you say that?

I can be a prophet in my own land...I just know...it will get worse...legislation all failed for felons staying in jail...dope is out of control. And people have free pass to pass on cops...it's a perfect storm...

Ohhhh...

We're down 70 cops...ones we are hiring can't even function without adult diapers...

I see what you mean. Welp...I was...going to retire here...but...

Its...well...rugged...

Yeah...

How you doing tonight?

I'm well...you?

Little tired...worried bout your period...

Ohhhh, I'm sorry. No need to worry baby...my body gets off whack sometimes. I can't have babies. I'm trying to regulate and balance as much as I can through this divorce...but my cycle gets wonky. I didn't mean to stress you more...

Why no babies???? Worried for you too...

Tubal ligation in 2001. Why worried?

It's not normal girl stuff...just worried...

Don't want you to worry...

Just what I do...

I've noticed...we should figure out how to make this easier then...are you thinking...

How?

Are you thinking...

Well, we went from things being super fucking hot, cumming 3 times each time, seeing each other twice a week, then down to once a week, to hardly texting, then now to worry? Ugh, I'm not finding the words well...

Tell me...

I want us to be able to be real...with each other...

Yes...for certain...tell me...

Listen...I've been with only a few men. I've blamed myself for things only to have them tell me years later it wasn't me, I was the best they ever had, or I was a reminder of their weaknesses, they wished they had understood me more, etc. I remember the whole cop thing, if you need easier...we can do easier. I just can't blame myself at this juncture in my life if I'm not the reason for this amazing "Situationship" slowing. If I am, please teach me so I can grow forward. What makes something so pleasurable fade for...well, you?

Not you...never...
My life has always been...zero time allowed for kids, work, shooting, swat...all of it...still a cop at almost 28 years...every friend has left...feel like I haven't done what I started out to do...not you at all...time is still my issue...

I can hear that...I see you...don't want to be a one of those friends that leave...ok

Really...it is just time...

Yeah...time-

March 25, 2022 10:12 AM

Hello?

Hiya, sorry...no period yet but probably this weekend. No more worry. Will text as soon as I get. Why up so early?

Have to go do quals...worried bout this...

Focus on quals...I'll text as soon as I see pink...no worrying today...muah!

Are you sure?

Yes...it's just from emotion...

Why emotional?

Feeling alone...undesirable...CPTSD relapse stuff...tryin'

Undesirable???

Happens...

By me?

Yes...

How?

No time...

No time...just my life...

Yeah...

I'm sorry...you don't deserve that...you are desired...

You are as well...very, VERY much...

I'm sorry...

Me too...

(Later)

Still...desired

Always...

Feel ok?

Trying...you? How are quals?

Was good...nice day finally...

Great weather...

Home with kiddo now...

Awww...I'm home too, had to clear my head. Dinner with Gina later discuss sex encounter with accidental anal guy...

Accidental? 78 year old?

No, 78-year-old can't get her man to do anal, he's strictly missionary guy. Gina is the "Unsweetened tea" gal.

Ohhhhh, guy who didn't even take off jacket? Accidental anal?

Yeah...vaginal, oral, turn over, oops in anal...no climax...for either...ugh...

In under 20 minutes? Sounds like jail sex...neither came?

Nope...quandary...lol, jail sex, that's hysterical-

Hmmmm....condom? Bare?

No protection...went for the risk...

Well...

Yeah...

Bummer...where's dinner?

Her house...olive garden takeout and girl chat...she came to see me at the shake shop today...her body is all fucked up...not my best day to help but a good distraction...

Cuz...of me?

No baby...Cuz of me...

Anal can be traumatizing if not properly done...I don't want her to create a mental block...pleasure is essential in my world and the basis of what I teach...she needs to experience a full-body orgasm from anal... just hoping he's the guy that can help with that...

Too big?

No. She said he is average. He went too fast, too rough, no lube, no consent. I'm wondering if he even knew he was in her ass. I need to ascertain where she's at and evaluate if she's disassociating her mind from her body. She says she wants him again...so there's that...

(Audio call)

***

Peg's Journal Entry 3/25/22:

Gunnar admitted my being 9 days late on my period is worrying him. I reminded him I can't get pregnant but I'm sure he has trouble trusting, I know it's a side-effect of my CPTSD and childhood, I can only imagine what his mind may be doing. All I can do is continue to be honest and let life unfold. I have no need or want to hurt him, just wish my body would stop fucking around. He ended up calling me so we could discuss it more.

I reminded him that I am going through a tremendous time in my life and my emotions may be messing up my cycle. I also told him at my age I am closer to peri-menopausal issues than ever having a viable egg if one could ever get through my tied tubes. He agreed but said this "stuff" has him stressed. I apologized letting him know that's not what I wanted for him.

He went on to apologize for not being around much and said, "This is my life. It's been this way since I was twenty-three years old." I could tell he wanted me to understand his absence. I told him he didn't have to explain it and he cut me off saying, "No, I do need to explain, you shared your body with me, I need to explain it." He went on to clarify that he does in fact desire me he just has no time to show me. He admitted he sometimes wants to see me but worries that stopping to give me only thirty minutes would dis-satisfy me and he doesn't want to disappoint me so seeing me only once every two weeks or so is what's happening. He then said he knows it may seem I am dismissed or ignored but that's not his intention. He apologized and although the information was difficult to accept, I did and appreciated our open communication about it. I told him he didn't have to keep apologizing and he said, "Yes I do, it's the little Irish kid in me." I understood what that meant because I was raised similar. We have common CPTSD processing and I was reminded of how this whole thing got started!

I did admit to him that I hadn't expected this to be so pleasurable and for us to be so intensely sexually compatible to each other. He agreed then cracked a joke saying, "Are you saying you like my penis?" I laughed and responded, "I do...a little more than I expected." He laughed and I know he felt good about that.

After we hung up I processed a bit more while watching meaningless television. I honestly don't know what to do about our "situationship" now that we're six months in. Not sure if I have to do anything really. Neither of us knew what this would be, nor that it would be so satisfying. I ended up just giving it over to the universe and allowing it to be what it must. I fell asleep thinking about how he said everyone leaves...and I know exactly how that feels and realized abandonment and rejection trauma is still very much present in us both. Ugh...

March 26, 2022 10:04 AM

FYI...woke up on pink...all good...

Ohhhhh ok...ummmm....
how was dinner?

Entertaining...thank you for asking...holding up ok?

I'm pretty tired...no gas in tank...

I hear you...rest...

How was conversation...solve problems?

Yes. I love solution-based convo...she wants to try again and build. There's no trauma so it looks promising...

she likes anal!

Her first time?

Yes...rough but pleasurable enough to want a full-body anal-gasm...said she was so wet it went right in...

Wow...good...
What ya doing?

683

Uhhhhh...

You make me so hard...just saying...huge hard on...cock in hand now...thinking about...you having last anal-gasm...

Oh?

Yup...I initially thought you only did anal...for me...now I realize it was for us...and you truly enjoy it...makes me so hard...

It took me a lil bit to trust you...but it was for us...I loved being your first...

Yes! And when you cum...you explode...so great to watch...feel...you taste amazing....

Mmmmm...I love pleasure...it heals all the fucked up parts lol...so happy you're a fan now...

Never hurt you...all pleasure...

All pleasure so far...love, LOVE our pleasures...

You make me cum...desire...need you...

Quite satisfying...even in your truck!

That was hot...huge cock in hand right now...wish it was your mouth...your hands stroking me...

Yes...been a while since I've been able to explore you fully with my mouth...and lips...and fingers...and...

Mmmm...so nice...

Cum yet?

Yes...
Exploded...cum all over stomach...chest...lots...warm...dripping...

Mmmm...honored you thought of me...love to know you are pleasured...

684

When can I bury myself in you?

Whoa...just got me wetter...

Want a 3 orgasm marathon...
In mouth, in pussy, in your beautiful ass...completely covered in sweat, legs shaking...cum everywhere...

Sounds amazing...

You biting my chest...sucking my nipples...

Yummmmm....

Very...very yummm....
Hope you have a great day...

You as well...

March 27, 2022 9:57 PM

Desired...you are...

I...wants you...

...as I bite your neck...

Mmmm...just got...

Wet?

Yezzzzz....wants to touch your...

Yes...

Hard...warm...c o c k

Yup...thats meeee...

Mmmm...I likey...

You're gonna...as I fill your tight ass tomorrow with my hot cum...just sayin...

Mmmm...wanna play?

Yup...tomorrow...I will fuck you...in every way until your legs quiver...

Wow...what's gotten into you?

You

Not sure I remember...how things work...

I'll remind you...you will suck me...fuck me...I'll cum in my baby's ass...as she claws and bites at me...

Did I do something? To warrant all this?

Yes...being you...needing me...to fuck you...in every position and direction...

Kinda need...

Good...
So 930ish

Mmmm...sounds good...

Done...mmmmm period...

Yeah...

March 28, 2022 8:05 AM

686

Hi

Good morning!

How are you?

Well...you? Have you changed your mind?

Not at all...
Can I please...please...please...come fuck you?

Hmmm....

Will you suck my cock?

Of course...it pleases you...

Will you ride my cock?

Happily...

May I fuck your...gorgeous tight ass?

Yessssss

I am so hard...

So hot...save me someeeee...well you know...

Every drop is for you...

Mmmm...what's gotten into you?

Uhhh....I'm getting in you...in every way

Hmmm...not an answer...

It turned me on to think how you were telling your friend about anal...

We did discuss how sensual and scrumptious your movements are...the full-body orgasms. I gave her tips...
wish people understood pleasure better...

Did you get wet thinking about...me?

The...entire time...my kitty really likes you...pulses and aches thinking of the ecstasy we share...

Wet now?

Of course...every damn time you text!

I would have woke you with three fingers...caressed you to orgasm

Mmmm...that's the way to wake!
I would be so sleep deprived...

Yes...yes we would...
Answer door in only heels...please...

Will try...

Jumping in shower...

Mmm...would love to wash you...

All of me?

Every...glorious inch...

Pussy throbbing?

You know it...wet...wet...wet...

Wow...almost there

Hope sooooooo....

Mmmmmmmmmmmmmmmm......

Later

Mmmm...felt amazing...

Agreed....walked into shop and:
Del: "You're walking slow and your hair is all fucked up, you get a visit?"
Me: Smile
Del: "Seriously? How many times?"
Me: "Ummm...kinda lost count, maybe 5 or 6? And aftershocks...so..."
Del: "Oh my god Peg, that's a lot!"
Me: "Yeah...but sooo good, I may have a slight addiction."
Del: "Best kind girl."

Naughty girl...

Me?

Your lips...and those hips...mmmmmm....

I feel...I can barely function or keep my eyes open...done feel I've been hit by an O'Clery truck...

You is funnnnnnyyy...

Muy muy cardio...
Soooo...deep. Magic dick sorcery!

Sorcery...wow...made me giggle...

Chapter 42

TIMES 10

Gunnar couldn't explain why he had such a hunger for her lately. There was just something about her responses to him, her desire, the way she made him feel like the only man she could see. Peg was so much woman, the kind dreams are made of.

As soon as he pulled up and parked across from her truck he was rock hard. He could hardly wait to be inside her.

Peg watched as he slammed his door and briskly walked across the road towards her house. There was something a bit intense about him, his lips were pursed with a tiny smile at the corners. She lunged up in her pink lingerie teddy and black heels to unlock the door and feel him close. It was only a Monday but, she knew any week that started out with Gunnar O'Clery was going to be a great week.

***

<u>Peg's Journal Entry 3/28/22:</u>

Gunnar looked me over as he breezed by, heading straight for my futon couch where he threw his hat and gun down then turned and grabbed me in an embrace with his tongue plunging into my mouth! I reached for his cock and he was rock hard! Before I could break our kiss to say hello he pushed us to the bed and fell on top of me, his body and dick pressing into me making my body ache and yearn for him deep inside. His hand wandered and he found my wanting pussy, wet and begging, he sunk his fingers in then finally spoke, "Oh baby, you are soaked!"

"I am...for you."

He moaned, moving down my body. His other hand moved my g-string aside and his mouth lowered, kissing and caressing me making me quiver. He whispered, "I've missed this."

He backed up then, staring, removing his shirt. I stepped to him smiling and looking him up and down telling him he had too much clothing on, then helping him remove them before kneeling and sliding him hard and thick in my mouth. He was intensely engorged and sucked air through his teeth at the feel of me moist around his shaft. I like to hear his pleasure and slowly caressed my tongue along his glorious length until he placed his hand on my head and begged me not to stop. He quivered every so often trying not to cum and as he got too close he pulled me up to take off my teddy. I let him as I like the feel of his strong hands on me but as he threw my clothes to the floor I turned him and pushed him down on the bed. He exhaled into my pillow and I climbed on his waist sinking my wetness into his back. He moaned and I leaned forward to nibble his ear then down to his neck, I kissed down his spine to his amazingly muscular ass and slid my tongue into him making him grip the sheets in pleasure! He sunk his face deeper into my pillow as I reached gently under him and stroked his dick in unison with my tonguing rhythm. Truth be told, Gunnar has the greatest ass, hairless, smelling of fresh soap, and tight! He moaned into my pillow until he could take it no more, then turned over pulling me onto him.

"Ride me, baby, ride me with your tight, wet pussy. You make me feel so wanted."

"I do want you..." is all I whispered as I put his hands over his head and then asked him, "Do you consent?"

He smiled up at me as I sunk down over his huge shaft and he plunged his tongue in my mouth while exhaling long. I enjoy hearing and feeling what I do to him makes him happy.

I had a little trouble fitting him inside right away, my body had to ease to his size as it had been twelve days and I get tighter the longer he is away. I still had his arms pinned down and noticed he was trying to move. I commented on how it seems he doesn't like to be confined, he just looked into my eyes and was quiet. Next, he changed the subject and asked me about my period. I asked who had traumatized him and he got quiet again. I realized he's been lied to by everyone and his job is mostly dealing with deceitfulness and liars. I dropped it and rode him a lil' faster to distract us both. He reached up caressing my tits and said, "You are so tan, how did I get so lucky to be able to see such a beautiful body." That felt amazing to hear and I found my mouth exploring down his chest, nipples, and stomach. I let go of his hands and drug my chest down his body until his hard cock was in between my tits. He grabbed them and caressed them around his shaft then whispered, "Would you...suck my cock again?"

I smiled up at him nodding and slid him hard and full in my mouth while sliding my two fingers in him. He moaned and I could hear he was losing control as his dick kept hitching then releasing, hitching again, then releasing. I was driving him mad and soon he pulled me up his body to kiss my mouth and tell me he was getting too close. He slid himself into me again and gasped at how it felt saying, "Jeezus your pussy is so tight." I smiled and he admitted, "I have NEVER been ridden like you baby."

An hour went by and I almost lost count of all the pleasureous positions. He pleased me orally, moved to missionary, then doggie, on my side, missionary again, he held my hands down while sucking my skin until a hickey formed on my left trap, he pulled me to the edge of the bed, turned me over, entered me pulling my legs up to his chest, then open wide while fucking me deep, he moved his mouth down and orally pleased me until I came so hard saying, "I think I might die." He commented, "Well, this is a good way to die." He slid deep inside me again and said, "I love to watch you cum." A smile grazed his lips and he teased and tantalized my pussy more looking down at me in awe. I tried to recover but ended up cumming again! This made him very happy. He moved us to our sides and sunk into my pussy again as his mouth sunk into my neck giving me the best goosebumps I had to gasp. His hands cupped my breasts and I felt my eyes rolling back into my head at how much ecstasy he was giving.

He got up to get lube and stated, "I want your ass baby." He laid down and slid his dick between my tush, slowly entered me, waiting and allowing my body to acclimate around his large size. He was gentle and patient, which I have to admit it a huge reason why I enjoy him so much anally. We went for some time and then he got up and pulled me to the edge of the bed saying he wanted it that way. He entered slow and kept a steady pace that felt so damn good I couldn't help but reach down and rub my clit to his rhythm. We both ended up cumming so damn hard we moaned loudly in unison! WAS FULL BODY ORGASM times 10!!!!

Chapter 43

MATTHEW GANTRY

Matthew Gantry stared out the window towards Peg's front room across the street. Gunnar O'Clery exited as he did, locking her front metal screen door and gliding along gracefully in his two-hundred and twenty pounds of rock-solid muscle. His eyes scanned left and right throughout the entire neighborhood, his face non-expressive beneath his Baretta ball cap.

He crossed the street, opened his truck door, climbed in, and drove off. Matt could see Peg through her curtains watching as he left her. No doubt, she was completely satisfied in a way only Matt could imagine. Paralyzed from the waist down since a four-wheeler accident at nine, Matthew Gantry could only dream and imagine the pleasures Pegasus Law and Gunnar O'Clery exchanged on their once, sometimes twice-a-week rendezvous. He looked more forward to the visits then they did, if that's possible.

He glared down at his skinny legs, only a quarter of the size of his overbuilt chest, which he worked hard on to look like Gunnar's. He'd been watching their affair for the last few months, monitoring Peg for the last nine on social media since she got back to town. She'd always been a favorite of his in Las Ramas, he loved her books, her social media, and now her secret sex life.

To him, she was not only a beautiful woman but a beautiful soul, too. He was really happy to hear that she was divorcing her abusive husband after that year away. Las Ramas wasn't as fun when she'd left but Matthew and his two buddies talked about how they couldn't blame her. Dereck Law was the biggest piece of shit ex-martial art teacher in town. Peg really dodged a bullet by getting away from him. Even some of the girls on the college campus had told Matt about how sleazy Dereck, and his bromance friend Jude were, when they'd show up at parties and harass girls like they weren't in their fifties and hard up for young pussy. He remembered laughing because his friends would say half the time the two old dudes acted gay, then the other half of the time, they were trying to buy their way into drunk girls' pants.

Matt watched Peg exit the front door and walk to her truck freshly done up looking gorgeous as ever in her scrub top and leggings. Divorce never looked so good on a lady and whatever Gunnar O'Clery did to her in that little front room, Matt thought must have been magic by the looks of the smile on her face as she held her phone to her ear.

Matt decided to roll his wheelchair to the front door and go out to get the mail so he could wave at her as she drove away. He hated to admit it but seeing Peg smile at him was the highlight of his day. One day soon, he hoped to get up enough nerve to talk with her.

Chapter 44

PACKING UP

Aileen dialed his number wondering if a text would be better. Gunnar was the busiest cop in the city but what she had to say she didn't want to put into a text. The times she had texted since their meeting in her kitchen had only been met with one-word responses.

"Yes ma'am?"

"Ah, O'Clery, I didn't think you'd answer on the second ring." Aileen half-choked on her pizza pocket.

"Right."

"Listen, I don't want to keep you too long I just wanted to catch up on the uh, Dereck Law thing for a minute."

"Okay."

Aileen rolled her eyes at his responses, he still didn't trust her or want to offer too much information. She normally wouldn't bother but she's seen how crazy evolves and a large part of her was still worried about Dereck Law's *crazy*.

"Well, he left to the East coast looking for Peg and came back a bit peeved that she's still here."

"Oh?"

"Yeah, he thought she had moved back east to be with her sister. I mean he had to see his mother and daughter too but, he was more interested in Peg being there. When he found out she's still here, and doing well, he came back pretty pissed."

"I really wish this asshole would drop this."

Aileen was surprised Gunnar said anything showeing emotion, "Right. He's an idiot. Still doing stupid shit but the one thing I wanted to mention is that he appears to be packing slowly...a little each day."

"As in moving?" Gunnar sounded hopeful.

"Not that I can say for sure, more like a camping trip."

"Camping?"

"Yes. Portable grill, some guns, linens, and household items for say a...cabin? Or hunting? Do you know if he hunts?"

Gunnar huffs, "I doubt it." He hunts men for a living so he knows hunting. The only thing Dereck seemed to hunt was fast food.

"How about friends or maybe a cabin somewhere?"

"I can't be sure but I could ask."

"Has Peg mentioned him at all? Has he harassed her? I don't have him really leaving the house too much."

"Not that she's mentioned. You still tracking him?"

Aileen smiled, "Of course, I'm telling you O'Clery, the guy isn't right. He needs to be monitored, even if only by an old washed-up agent like me."

Gunnar smirked, "Well, it's appreciated. I'll see what I can find out. His leaving wouldn't be a sad event."

"So true, this town has enough going on. Okay, sounds good. I'll be in touch."

"Out-"

"Uh yeah, bye." She looked at her cell and shook her head. Gunnar was known as one of the top cops in the state, with a huge sense of humor but, he could be all business sometimes. She laughed and headed back to her desk to see what Mr. Idiot Law was up to.

Dereck had to take a seat on the outside couch cushion to rest a moment. He hated packing and lifting heavy items because of how it so easily got him out of breath. He looked around, his hand on his knee, neck craning to see all the beauty in the courtyard Peg had started. She and her son planted an amazing vegetable and herb garden and it smelled incredible. He wanted to hate the entire setup but if anyone could make a home feel like home it was Peg.

He looked over at his truck and the few items that filled the back. He wanted to make the cabin look as good as their home. He didn't know how he was going to force her, but whatever it took, he would make her want to be there. Make her be his again...away from Las Ramas, tucked away in the mountains like he'd always told her he wanted. All his, where no one could hear her...or see them.

unnar felt uneasy every time he talked with Aileen Lauden. It reminded him that he was being watched. She was helpful but he had to be in her debt, and that made him uncomfortable. He thought about Dereck leaving and how nice it would be if he just moved the fuck out of state like he'd planned early on. Not having to worry so much about Peg would make life easier. He hated thinking she was in danger.

Pulling his patrol car over he put it in park and dialed her number.

"Hiiiiiiii, you."

"Hey, beautiful. Got a second?"

Peg smiled, his voice making her crotch moisten, "For you, of course. What's up?"

"Well, A. I want you...but B. You heard from your ex?"

Peg giggled then her smile faded, "Well, I like A. Much more than B. Has he called you again?" She hated that her past somehow reached Gunnar's busy day.

"He hasn't no, just checking in on you."

"He's left me alone thankfully. I honestly don't even know if he is still alive."

Gunnar smiled, "If he wanted to depart...it wouldn't bother me so much."

"Right?" She giggled. He loved to hear her giggle.

"So not sure if he'd head to Colorado, or did you say he had a cabin?"

Peg frowned, surprised at the memory Gunnar had sometimes, "I was hoping he would move to Colorado, but it seems he's not going to give up the house here. He always wanted a cabin in Ruidoso...like for years, so that would be more likely than moving out of state now. Why babe?"

"Looks like he's packing up his truck a bit, wondering what's going on."

"Oh really? I could only hope! Did he pretend to be your best friend? You know he's always wanted you right?"

Gunnar's nose scrunched, "Ugh, not that again. The only one I want to want me is you, babe."

"And wow do I..."

"Hope so. Maybe Thursday."

"Mmmm...that sounds perfect."

Gunnar's radio blared loudly as the dispatcher announced a call across town, "Shit, I've gotta go, babe, talk soon?"

"You got it. Be safe."

March 31, 2022 8:15 AM

Hi

Mmmm...was just dreaming' of...

Of? Are you touching?

Our truck quickie...you deep...inside...

Oh my...yes...cum dripping everywhere...

Mmmm...

**I am gonna grab a nap...got off late...took kiddo to school at 7...
Can you have a visitor today?**

Yes...slide you in my door...let me know but rest now...headed to gym...always wanting you...

Later

How was gym?

Mmmm...was a good leg day...how was nap?

Was good...how are those legs...can I get between them?

Always...I'm at shake shop...when were you thinking?

Roomy home?

Both are but hibernating in rooms...

You sure? Don't want to make awkward...

Just can't make me...noisy lol...church mouse status...

Ok...quick shower...then head over...

698

Later

Mmmm...MDS...

MDS?

Magic Dick Syndrome...

Snort laughed...

Mmmm...I'm Incurable...

Later

How you be?

Wet...how ya holding up?

Soooooooper dooooooooper

Why???

Catching bad guys...fun!

Mmmm...I likey!! Anything neat?

Same old same...drugs...guns...crooks...

Yeah but...you love it, makes it awesome! Makes the streets safer, you're fuckin' hot babe...top cop status-

Thank you

***

<u>**Peg's Journal Entry 3/31/22:**</u>

Gunnar mentioned a quickie but we ended up spending much more time than usual. My roomies were home, but hibernating, so he silently slid right in my door and locked it. His eyes were bloodshot from fatigue, but one would never know it from how the man moved inside me.

He was already hard by the time he walked in and pressed against me. My body missed his touch. He kissed me long and deep backing me up and pushing me down on the bed. I tugged and pulled at the instructor's shirt that pulled tight across his chest as he spread my legs open and pressed deeper causing surges of arousal to flash through my body. We were clawing at each other and he began cracking jokes and making me laugh while covering my mouth to kiss me again and again. He lowered his mouth to suck on my chest while searching with his hand for how wet I was. He moaned realizing how much I wanted him and briskly got up pulling me to my feet saying, "Please take your clothes off!"

We disrobed quickly and he tackled me gently to the bed penetrating me until I gasped in his ear. He went so deep so quickly whispering, "Oh my god...I slid right in your beautiful pussy, you have no idea how good and wanted that makes me feel." I whispered back, "You are SO wanted... and very desired! I love how good this feels EVERY time!"

He liked what he heard and rewarded me for it with deep, tantalizing thrusts that took my air away. He knew I was trying to be quiet since my roommates were home, but the more I tried to muffle my pleasure, the more he gave me. He likes when I cry out and made sure to use the head of his penis to caress my cervix deep and mercilessly. It took all my strength not to yell.

"Can you imagine an entire weekend of this? I can't wait to take you to the hot springs...fucking, showering, eating, fucking more, shots of whiskey, hiking, fucking again..." He smiled down as his pelvis lulled me into a deeper ecstasy. I whispered, "I'll meet you, just tell me when." He liked that and kissed me hard, his tongue plunging into my breathless mouth. Before I could catch my breath he got up and pulled me to the edge of the bed, entering me long and hard again. He whispered, "I so want you like this way in our sex swing. I'd restrain you, tie you down, and fuck you so good you'd never forget it."

I smiled and replied that the first thing I'll install in my new place is a swing for him right in the beam. He smiled replying, "Yesssssss." I like his imagination and how he can share his fantasies and wishes with me. I do want to make them come true, his happiness pleases me...and the fact that he likes the same things I do!

He was very intense and began grabbing hungrily at my breasts before kneeling down to please me orally. He was incredible and I came so hard I had to climb away, he was intense! He stepped in then and took the head of his dick flicking my clit. I love that he is a freak Scorpio and a beautiful lover to my body.

He pulled me up and swung around to lay on the bed, patting the space next to him saying, "Lay with me?" I took the opportunity to nod yes but not before I slid him full and deep into my mouth and sucked all along his shaft gently. He quivered trying not to release and said, "You are amazing...can't believe how you do that to me after I've just been inside you." I smiled and said quickly, "We taste incredible together." Then slid him back down my throat. He clenched and almost came, stopping himself with his awesome cock control.

Pulling up he placed me on my side and from behind he hiked my leg up and entered me deep. I love the feel of his embrace around my body as he thrusts deeper and deeper inside. Everything we do is so pleasurable and passionately slow, I can feel all of him!

He wanted me to ride him so I did and he looked up at me his eyes half-rolling back. He tried to focus and said, "Can I ask? With the other men you had, did they think you were tight too? Did they mention how tight your pussy is?"

I could tell he was genuinely curious and it was quite flattering. I replied honestly, "Yes, the few I've been with mentioned it here and there." He nodded then said, "Am I...well, the biggest you've had?" And with eyebrows raised, I admitted it by nodding vigorously. I made him feel good and he knows if he were average I would have made a joke but he is honestly the largest cock I have ever had and wow do I like him! I leaned up and he felt so good I had to close my eyes, gliding my hips and swaying to our combined rhythm. He pulled my hips down and ground my clit. He wanted to talk more which means he wanted to prolong his orgasm.

He asked, "So how did your girlfriend end up accidentally having anal with her guy that time?"

I found this amusing as his mind is so detail-oriented. I replied, "Well, they were going at it, he groping her tits, pumping inside her then suddenly he flipped her over to take her from behind."

He said, "Really?" His teeth slightly clenching.

I nodded, "When he entered her, things were so wet, it slid right into her ass...and he didn't even know....but she did!"

Gunnar's eyebrows raised in shock. So I continued, "But she said it felt good so she went with it...it was only after they compared notes at work that she mentioned he was in her backdoor. He was like, "I was?" I about died laughing!"

He said, "How did he not know babe?"

I said, "Right!?" He shook his head in disbelief then grabbed my hips again and started to concentrate.

"Can we turn over? I want to look down at you?"

Of course I agreed as he feels so good pressed against my body and his cock so deep. He moved and as he entered me I asked if he had decided how he wanted to cum today. He replied, "However you tell me baby." I smiled. I always find that funny since he could choose any position or any way he wants to release but he wants me to pick his pleasure.

He smiled and took my hand to place it on my clit as he was thrusting, putting pressure on my hand with his pelvis. I felt extreme bliss and said, "You've got me so swollen and ready."

He looked at me and said, "You were swollen and ready when I got here babe."

"You do that to me."

He started going harder and groping at my chest, I could tell he liked what I said and was getting close. As he increased his movements I matched them and synced our breathing. Seeing him begin to lose control made me want to go faster and I grabbed at his back pulling him deeper and deeper until he could take no more. His body released and he fell silent into his cumming euphoria pumping...and pumping...and p u m p i n g...and I had to remind him to breathe by saying, "Breathe....breathe baby..." and finally...he did!

He rolled to the side and I noticed I'd soaked him! I asked if he would mind if I cleaned him and he smiled saying, "Sure." I do like to clean him and watch his huge dick begin to go back to a satisfied, flaccid cock laying full and relaxed on his leg...knowing I did that. I gazed down at his body and told him how "fucking hot" he is. He gets quiet when I say so but I want him to know how attracted I am to him and he needs to hear my truth. He looked up and said he had to go because when he was leaving his mother showed up to do her laundry and asked where he was going so he told her the gym and that he would bring her back lunch.

I got up and helped him up, we both started dressing and he regaled me with details about a motorcycle pursuit a few nights prior where they chased a guy for assaulting his wife. As he bent down to put his gym pants on he looked at me and said he has absolutely no empathy for a man that puts his hands on a woman. His eyes glazed over and I got the chills at the depths of his sincere opinion. At that moment I thought about how he's only ever touched me with extreme tenderness and passion all the times we've been together, even when we were at our most hungry for each other. I wondered where he learned the belief he had about women and remembered how much he respects his mother. I found this so attractive especially after remembering how horrible my mother-in-law and my ex are to each other. I have concluded that a man who loathes his mother will most certainly treat all women in his life worse.

He continued about how he had "words" with the guy and he was not very nice to him. The guy mouthed off to him and he told him he had no problem "going up against his 140lbs with his 220lbs". I remembered seeing him race down Vully Drive and asked if he'd been in pursuit passed the Sonic. He nodded and I knew it had been him I saw in a Tahoe. He said our town is getting out of hand. I guess the guy threatened Gunnar's life and I got an eerie feeling when he told the guy that he could "try to take him out but if he won his family would hold a fundraiser for his funeral", if the guy killed him...he would "fill a stadium!". I had a vision of the funeral in American Sniper and my gut sank. I remembered how hard I cried at that movie and how people come together to honor a fallen officer or soldier when their life is taken in the line of duty. I realized that I am the lover, the secret lover, of a very well-liked "top cop", known for his intense, honorable nature and very popular. Fear took me over and I looked at him in a way to where I knew I'd rather die than see him hurt. I'm scared of how fragile life is and his even more so since he puts on a uniform daily that's more a target for those who will never value his life. This shook me a bit, and my mind wandered to how he and I ever came to be...and that I wouldn't ever have NOT wanted to experience him. I tried to remove the dark thoughts from my mind not wanting to trigger my CPTSD. I know me and I would have run from him in the past so I wouldn't have to think of him getting hurt. Now, after Ayahuasca, I want to experience every pleasure life can offer.

He saw my quietness and stood bringing up my ex so that I'd come back around. I told him I'm nervous because his family started calling me recently. They want something but I don't want anything to do with such horrible people, especially if they want me to speak against him. As much as I disdain the man I don't want any part in being used against him for someone else's gain. Gunnar nodded then said he was shocked that Dereck called him and did not once mention me or the divorce. I did think that odd as well. He said he used words like "FBI" and "Kidnapping" and needing legal advice. He said he told him the FBI wouldn't get involved because it was already a civil case. Then he said he can't imagine what Dereck does all day thinking about it. He said, "Does he sit in a $400,000 house all day thinking of revenge?" I told him, "Yes, Dereck only thinks about winning. Instead of selling the sauna, hot tub, or the ATV and paying his mother back the money he used he'd rather play the victim and tell everyone it was because of me."

Gunnar said, "Yeah, get rid of the ATV that never works." This surprised me because I knew the ATV was always breaking down but I didn't know Dereck had told Gunnar that. He said Dereck told him he'd take him out in it for a ride which is how Dereck tries to get people to hang out with him. I told him it's not a good idea, that he'd run him right into a boulder. He chuckled, and I said that's how Dereck is. One of his biggest phrases was, "If I'm going down, I'm taking everyone with me." Gunnar shook his head saying, "Standup guy" with a smirk on his face. I ended with, 'Yeah, not the kind of husband to be proud of."

So today was absolutely incredible and there was intense pleasure, but I also realized I need to be okay with my journey and what's in store for me. I do have fears surrounding how I feel about this wild man who entered my life at a time I really needed him. Not sure why or how...I think I'm still processing it all...and I will NEVER FORGET this...nor do I want to-

April 1, 2022 4:36 PM

How are you

Well! How's your Friday turning out?

Good...wanting to find...more of your...

My???

Slick wanting acceptance...needing cream pie...

Mmmm...wanting again?

Mmmmmm....

April 4, 2022 2:34 PM

Hi

Hiiiiiii...

How are you?

Well! Setting up a second office...how are you holding up?

Good...not too bad today...

Yay!

Egg day???

Is it obvious? Can. You feel me summoning your magic?

Yes...yes I can...
How's moving?

Oh, didn't move, just expanded to second office, three jobs now lol. How's the shift?

Holding up...

April 5, 2022 9:28 AM

Hola

Hey...

April 6, 2022 9:30 AM

How are you?

Holding up, are you okay?

Tired...allergies killing me...you fingering?

Sure did, you?

I will now...for sure...how was ovulation?

App recalculated...starts tomorrow now...

Ahhh...I want your...ass...

Oh?

On your back...buried deep...your pussy filled with 3 fingers...

Wow...3?

I'm ambitious...

Mmmm...aroused?

Mmmm...you home??? Rubbing??

Mayyyyybe...

Want to spread my precum on your clit baby...

Mmmmm...so silky and slick...

Salty...as I lick your clit...feel you cum in my mouth...

705

Wow...what's that like?

Amazing...your pussy starts to quiver...as you cum...creamy juices release...you throb in throes of orgasm...suck my fingers deep...

You can feel...my convulsing?

Yes...then I drive my cock in you...deep strokes...then rub tip on g-spot...help you release... more...

Mmmmm...yes...you do...

Warm...runs down legs...ass...sooooooo hot babe...

Ecstasy...

Are you rubbing?

Done. Gonna shower...shave my kitty parts and legs...you?

Done...big...mess. Going in late tomorrow...can I???

Can...you?

Fuck your beautiful tight ass?

Mmmm...I do likey you...

Mmmmm....

Later

Headed to gym to work out this...horny...so I can sleep...your magic is too far away tonight...

Ahhhhh...you mean my magic...cock...

Mmmm....

Later

How was workout? Looooooong day for me...kinda beat...

Was good! You guys seemed to be getting slammed out there...too much for us manyana?

I will be there...super busy...but need you...to be...well you...

Sorry, you're so busy...I needs you toooooo....

I wants you...gonna let sperm swim in ya!

I wantsssssss youuuuuuuu...

How's egg factory...gonna pump twins into you...

Triplets...making me wet...

Woozy....

Wanna attack ya...

Mmmm...like how?

Like...throw ya down and ride you "attacks"...

Wow...baby needs cock...

What did you call it? My inner Nympho?

Our nympho...

You've brought her to the surface...guess I had her hidden for many years...summoned by your pelvic sorcery and magic dick...

Really? You hid her...I just said...hi

I had to hide her...until deserved...

Best...answer ever...

Just...honest...

I like that...

Same...

So fukn hot babe...

Yes...yes you are...

I'm sorry...been so busy...I do think of you often...

Was hoping...

About???

That you...think of...us...

Ummm...yup I do...

Later
(4/7/22 12:02 AM)

How's pussy?

Wet...wanting...aching...yearning...calling to you...

Mmmmm....

How's my favorite sensitive tip?

Needing...well...your wetness...
How are you? Fingering?

Lol...no, in the living room...not sure that would go over well with roomies...on an interesting note...

Ohhhh...note? Go...

Roomie flattered me...says I look "cute" in my scrubs...and she thinks I have a great ass...

I wanna lick that great ass...so true...you do...

Thank you! Her kid looked at me slightly appalled lol. Roomie said she's not into chics but just had to "put it out there" I was like "thanks". I do like how you lick...me...

Yes? I would rub your clit even in public...till you take me to the dark...

In public?

Yup...bar...dancing...fuck it even...Walmart...

Really? I guess I should wear more skirts...

Yup...yup! Free finger zone...

You...like risk...and being watched...Scorpio trait?

And you like being admired...my baby girl's trait...

Do I?

Ummm...thinking yes...3some was performing aspect...love your confidence...that allows for that...

Oh, I don't remember thinking I was admired at first...stepped out of shower and looked up to see Dan across the bedroom smiling...taking shirt off...said, "Hey Peg"

What did you think? Honest...

Saw hunger in his eyes...

Then you moved to him? Wanting? You needed?

They both went to my bed...

And???

I could have walked passed them and out of the room...or...surrender...lay between them...

But?? It was okay...to desire yes?

True. I wasn't thinking I was admired...was trying to shut my brain off...allow my nature to take over...siren nature...

Then...accepted and enjoyed? I sooo seek your pleasure....

Admiration wasn't expressed...until ...after...

I know he did...you know it led to great...pleasures...

He seemed shocked...in awe...after...I was struggling for balance...because well, my ex was there...

Yes...you do struggle...pleasure...well...the first couple times with me you felt that...

I struggle daily for balance...for the calm...you somehow calm all of me. I'd love an entire weekend of our calm...but I worry...

Worry??

Worry...I would want more...I feel pleasure is a drug for me...eases my CPTSD...

Good drug...

I crave pleasure...

Crave...how?

Orgasm...pleasure...I feel high and balanced after...like I can finally be me, solve problems, write, be authentic, accepted, heal trauma...the pain goes away...kind of how you explained going on a call is part of being the solution...make sense?

Very much...for sure...

Well...rest...so I can put your high heels next to my shoulders...

Lol...yes! Hoping you have a safe shift and well...and you're smiling...

Super tired...but motivated...needing your well...taste...

Always here...for tasting...nite

Later 4/7/22 8:49 AM

How's throbbing? Level 1-10?

Uhhh...just woke, is 25 an option?

Wow...motivation...like the movie Rudy...but with your clit

Lol...love that movie!

You home???

Yep

Baby???

Yes?

Can I come...fuck you?

Can you?

May...I?

Mmmm...please?

Jumping in shower...give me 30...gonna shave cock for you...

Chapter 45

THE DAY

Dereck stared up at the ceiling. Everything hurt but he ignored all the body aches and pounding in his warped mind. He knew today could be the day he dies but then again it could just be the day meant for he and Peg to reunite. For her to be his again. All the divorce stuff could end, whoever she's fucking could disappear, she could be all his again, or she could...*die.*

Peg turned off the water and opened the shower curtain. The cool air felt good on her skin, the excitement in her low belly even better. He still gave her butterflies. Anytime she knew they could be together her body reacted in the most exciting ways. He aroused her like no other.

Running the towel along her thigh she smiled at how pleasurable his hand would feel caressing her freshly shaved skin. She loved the way he touched her, his hands course from the gun range yet so tender for her.

Making her way back to her room, she decided on black lingerie and heels as Gunnar seems to smile the widest upon seeing her in them. The lace felt lovely near her most sensitive parts, she bent down to fasten the straps of her heels and heard the handle of the screen door turn. He was early! She forgot to unlock it for him. She got up excitedly and bounded toward the front door to let him in...and then into her!

Matt heard a car door slam and picked his head up. He could see the silhouette of a larger person exit a red truck and realized it must be Gunnar O'Clery. He seemed bigger somehow and had the only red truck out of everyone who parked in the neighborhood, except for Mable Hinley who lived down the opposite street.

He sat up adjusting his legs off the side of the bed and reached for the armrest of his wheelchair to pull it close. Lifting up he heaved his body into the chair and leaned to the nightstand to grab his glasses to see better. He wondered if today would be only an hour visit for Gunnar and Peg or one of their longer escapades. He knew it was wrong to monitor and stare at them, trying to imagine what was going on through that front window to her room, but he couldn't help it. They were a gorgeous couple.

He thought about calling his buddies Kris and Landry over, they always loved watching her house while playing video games. They'd stare waiting for O'Clery to exit and then Peg shortly after, all smiles, headed to the shake shop to coach clients or hang with her friends. If she waved at him, when he pretended to get the mail, both Landry and Kris had to buy him lunch. He smiled and picked up his phone to text them. He looked up but the smile faded from his face when he saw a short, fat, frizzy long-haired man bending into the front of Peg's truck, a set of keys in his left hand, her gun from her truck in his right! He closed the door and walked up the driveway and to her door!

Gunnar hopped in his truck and slammed the door quickly. He hated being late and mumbled a few curse words at taking a call from the Chief so early. He decided it was not going to ruin his time with Peg. Crime would still be there later, on his shift, as would getting his ass chewed by his boss. He texted her quick that he was leaving and he'd be *in her* shortly.

Chapter 46

BANG

Peg flung the door open, her smile faded, her heart sank, her body ceased! A wave of flight-fight-freeze hormone washed over her entire body making her shiver, her vision tunneled, and her ears began to buzz in a high-pitched frequency. He'd found her!

Dereck looked her in the eyes then his gaze moved down her body to her gorgeous frame, black lingerie, heels, then back up to her terrified eyes. "Well, hello beautiful. Dressed up for me huh?" A sneer moved across his face, his lips pursed knowing she was expecting someone else.

"Leave Dereck, now!" Her voice was smooth despite the fear that washed through her, only the metal screen door between them. She saw him lift his hand up to draw on her! As soon as she turned to lunge she heard the bang ring out and felt the breath leave her body! It felt as if a truck hit her. She flew back, her eyes squinting as the room moved up on her. Her head crashed hard against the carpeted floor. The last thing she saw was the ceiling above her. The darkness closed in as her eyelids shut, she exhaled his name, *"Gunnar..."*

Dereck opened the door, proud of the hole he'd just put through it and through Peg. Her word didn't register yet. He stepped in, looked around realizing no one else was there, gazed down at the blood spilling from her and reached for the blanket draped on the couch. He threw it over her half naked body and picked her up. Her body lifeless, arms and legs hanging, he heaved her over his shoulder, proud he could do exactly what he came to do...*take her*. And...he did.

Chapter 47

TOOK HER

Gunnar turned down her street and smiled seeing her truck parked in it's usual spot. He went to the end cul-de-sac and made a u-turn to drive up and park across from her. He sighed as he saw a handicapped college kid come out of his house and roll his wheelchair quickly down his driveway waving and flailing his arms. Gunnar really didn't want to have to be friendly so early in the day. He just wanted to breeze into Peg's door and slide into her glorious body.

"He took her!" Matt screamed while rushing towards the curb near his truck. His voice cracked as he shouted again.

Gunnar frowned, his hand reaching near his waist reflexively. He couldn't understand what the kid was yelling about but could see he was desperate. He opened the door and heard what he said.

"He took her...he took Peg!!" Matt raised his overbuilt bicep and pointed toward Pcg's front door that was open.

Gunnar's head moved in the direction of where Matt was pointing. Suddenly two other males Matt's age came running from their parked car towards him.

Gunnar drew his gun keeping it low and crouching as he ran across the street and in between Peg's two roommates cars, up to the garage door, and along the stucco wall. He peeked around, his heart racing, he knew exactly who Matt was talking about. He scanned the doorway and saw blood drops down the sidewalk. His heart sunk. *Fuck no. No Peg no.*

He continued slowly knowing he needed to secure the scene but make sure Peg's roommates hadn't been hurt. Sadly, he knew the blood was Peg's but he'd hoped she fought Dereck...hoped it was his mother-fucking blood too, as she gave him the fight of his life.

Aileen came to mind, he knew she'd been tracking Dereck's phone and vehicle, and with any luck could help him with which direction he'd taken Peg. He had a pretty good idea of where he was headed, stupid ass that he was.

M att's hands shook. He looked down at his phone and chanted the tag
number over and over as he tried to type it in the notes section for when
Gunnar came back out of the house.

He hadn't called 911 yet. He wasn't sure if he should. A patrol car came abruptly around the corner with lights on but no siren. It blocked the entrance to the street and a younger officer jumped out, a scowl affixed to his face.

"Sgt. O'Clery is inside that house. The women's ex shot her and then took her in his truck!" Matt's voice cracked again and the officer ran towards the house and his boss.

Gunnar, careful not to step in the blood, hopped over the doorstep and alongside the sidewalk, half in the rocks. He looked up and saw Officer Jon Reyan.

"I can't find the two roommates that live here, apparently he took the third one."

Jon nodded, "The wheelie kid across the street seems to have witnessed what happened...you want me to talk-"

Gunnar stepped passed him, his gun close to his body and pointed to the ground, "No. I'll interview him. Find out where the owner and her kid are. There cars are here, but they're not inside the house or garage. Not sure if they fled or aren't home. Looks like one round was fired. 9mm casing there. Same blood, one trail."

"Yes sir." Jon did as instructed. Gunnar briskly walked back to the three guys across the street.

Matt pushed his phone towards Gunnar, "This is the license plate sir!"

Gunnar squinted and committed the disabled veteran tag to memory. He couldn't believe Dereck could be so stupid. "Okay, thank you. Tell me what you can, quick."

Matt threw his phone on his skinny, paralyzed legs then swiped his hands through his hair, "Okay, so I was waking up..."

"Which way did he turn out of the street?!"

"Uh, left then right, like farther into the development!"

Gunnar threw his business card at Matt's lap, "Call my cell phone in a minute. I'm going after her! You can fill me in as I drive."

Matt picked up the card and nodded, "Okay sir. I mean I thought it was your truck. If I had known....oh and he went into her truck with keys...and got *her* gun!"

Gunnar holstered his gun and walked backwards towards his truck, "Don't talk to anyone but me! Call that number in one minute Bud, I'll answer in my truck. And tell your friend's to keep their mouths shut until I say otherwise."

"Uh...okay Lieutenant. I'll call you!"

Gunnar flew around his truck and got into the driver's seat tearing off after Peg. He remembered she said Dereck would do this, and he slammed his hand on the dashboard wishing he'd had headed her warning. He remembered then that Aileen had told him days ago that Dereck was packing up for a trip or something. *Damn it!*

His stomach tightened knowing that Peg was shot and really hurt otherwise she would have fought him to the death...and he prayed she was only hurt.............

Chapter 48

RAGDOLLED

Gunnar accelerated and drove through the main street into the back of the development using his instincts as to where Dereck Law would have driven with Peg. He knew if he continued on in the direction of the mountains, he was going the right way.

He called into dispatch and reported he was in pursuit of a Chevrolet Colorado pickup, red in color, with the license plate tag number of (DV) XTG-L8R, suspect Dereck Law kidnapped his ex-wife Pegasus Law, possible gunshot wound to the female. The dispatcher confirmed that tag was registered to that vehicle and Gunnar shook his head and sighed at how idiotic Dereck was. He didn't care if he was identified by neighbors, he didn't care it was broad daylight, he didn't even care about shooting her in front of witnesses.

He accelerated realizing Aileen warning should have been followed up on, he cursed his busy schedule. He knew he really should have listened to Peg months ago. The asshole was batshit crazy. He knew he had to catch up to them before he let her bleed out or worse, if she survived, he knew the fucker would torture her.

Gunnar notified dispatch that he was in his personal vehicle and off duty but pursuing the suspect vehicle based on witnesses at the scene where Officer Jon Reyan is now securing. He knew they were aware already but he wanted to put it out over the radio in case Aileen was monitoring. He continued giving suspect description of a 275lb hispanic male, long frizzy salt-n-pepper hair, matching beard possible destination Ruidoso, New Mexico.

Gunnar's phone rang. He hung up with dispatch and accepted the call, "Wheelchair guy?"

"Yes sir."

"Sorry, I don't mean to be disrespectful, I didn't get your name." Gunnar accelerated and swerved around a few drivers wishing he had lights and sirens for safety. Matt could hear the engine through he phone.

"I'm Matt Gandry. I live across the street from Ms. Law."

"Matt, it's very important that you tell me what you witnessed but Matt…it's also important that you only talk to me right now."

"I understand Lieutenant but other officers are arriving."

Gunnar had to think quickly in how he could protect Peg. He wasn't so worried about himself but she wouldn't need the publicity if the nature of their relationship got out, "Thats okay, I don't want you or your friends involving my staff in our personal relationship unless it has to come out. Peg doesn't deserve the backlash. I'll take the heat if I have to. Right now this is a kidnapping and domestic situation…and shooting. Gonna be a real shit show but right now I just need to find her…she's wounded."

"Yes sir, he raised his right hand up, she lunged to her right and he shot her in her left shoulder…or upper lung."

"Fuck!!!!" Gunnar's stomach surged with ache. He knows what she felt and how Dereck was able to take her so easily.

"I think it was just her shoulder though, but she flew back hard, her body went back and then down against the floor. He shot her through the metal screen door so it could have been worse. I'm hoping it slowed the bullet."

Gunnar's lips pursed, he felt rage, "Yeah I saw that. Can you tell me what happened next. Was she fighting?"

"No sir, she was on her back…and sir?"

"Yeah Matt."

"She was in black lingerie…and heels….sorry. Totally rag-dolled, knocked out."

Gunnar ran his hand up his forehead and threw his hat on the seat next to him. He felt responsible and worse, Dereck probably shot her because he knew she wasn't dressed like that for him.

"That's okay, the important part is we have a direction to go in to find her. You're a big help Matt."

"I don't think he got any vital organs but he did shoot her in her left shoulder for sure, her shooting arm. It was like he knew if she was going for her gun…and she would have got him. When he bent down over her I was hoping she would hit him with he right hook…but she was unconscious."

"No doubt." Gunnar agreed. He'd heard about Peg's abilities and remembered she was right handed but left-eye dominant so she had dead-aim when shooting with her left hand. As for her right hook, he wondered how Matt knew about that. He knows Dereck is aware. "Okay, what else do you remember?"

"Uh...well, he had trouble opening the door which was weird because Peg always keeps that metal door locked...it took some violent yanking..."

"Yeah, yeah I know. So it may have been unlocked and what, he stepped in then?"

Matt's voice quivered, Gunnar caught on that this kid was quite fond of Peg, "Yes, he stepped in kind of putting the gun in his waist and craned his head to look around. Peg's roommates aren't home, I saw them leaving in an SUV that the boyfriend of the son picked them up in."

"Okay, what else."

"He did a double take towards the couch and reached for a blanket. He threw it on Peg then bent down and picked her up over his shoulder. The blanket is light blue and really large...it covered all of her...and her blood dripped from under it."

Gunnar hated thinking she was wrapped in that blanket unconscious in Dereck's truck, unable to breathe. He squeezed his eyes trying to erase the visual. "So he only took that...I mean her in the blanket? Did you see if he touched anything...or had gloves on?"

"No sir, he turned and walked fast to his truck. I could see blood on the floor where she was and the trail of drops coming from her swaying arm and dripping from her fingers under the blanket. He didn't even care. His prints are on the door, no gloves. He's a real douchebag sir."

Gunnar nodded, "Yeah."

"That Glock 40 from her truck is powerful."

"Matt, how'd you know what gun she had in her truck dude?"

Matt thought for a moment, "I- I'm into guns sir. She had it holstered down by her calf on the driver's side and when she opened her door I could see it sometimes. It has an extended mag and also a light laser on the bottom of the barrel because her ex modifies all his shit. I'm sure it's his gun by the way he knew exactly where to grab it. He also had keys to get into her truck."

Gunnar knew that was true as Peg had mentioned early on Dereck wanted his gun from her truck but her lawyers said no exchanging of possessions. He also knew Dereck was trying to sell off some guns at the gun shop but the owners didn't prefer how he modified all his stuff for "attention". Peg had told him Dereck was all about "bells and whistles" because it got him narcissistic supply and attention.

"Okay. Do you remember how he put Peg in his truck. Is she in the passenger seat?"

"No, he opened the back door and heaved her in on her side...like in a fetal position. He shoved her heels in under the blanket and slammed the door then trotted around to the driver's side and sped out as fast as he could, kind of looking around to see if anyone noticed him. He never saw me through my window. My Mom has these shear curtains. I can see a lot though."

"Great. How old are you Matt?"

"Twenty-two."

"Okay.

"Sir?"

"Yeah."

"What are you going to do about...well, you know, you and Peg's secret."

Gunnar was uncomfortable with the question but knew it could always come up, "Right now, I just want to find Peg and make sure she's safe. I also want to protect her reputation. I can handle mine. If you could just...basically, at this point it would just be that she's his ex, a local massage business owner, and in very real danger. I just want her safe...all right?"

Matt nodded, "No I get it."

"If I go down for whatever, I go down, it's part of the job, but no need for her to...lose her reputation and business."

Matt knew he liked Gunnar, whether they were wrong for being together, they were still real people with real feelings and problems. He could tell that Gunnar was deeply concerned about her safety first and doing as much as he could at the moment to find her. "Do you see them at all?"

"No I don't but I have a general idea where he's headed. I'm going to hang up now Matt. I've got to see if I can track her somehow. Thank you man, you've been very helpful.

"Absolutely Sir. Peg is amazing...a really great neighbor. I'll help the officers here as best I can."

"Thanks. Much appreciated. Out-" Gunnar hung up and Matt looked at his phone seeing it disconnected.

Chapter 49
TRACKING

Gunnar scrolled through his phone driving at a high rate of speed. He couldn't believe he hadn't caught sight of Dereck's truck. He couldn't imagine he'd gotten such a big head start. He needed to think.

He found Aileen Lauden's number and pressed call. She picked up on the second ring.

"He got to her didn't he? I see his truck is headed toward the mountains!"

Gunnar was annoyed, "He shot her and I'm in pursuit. I need-"

"You're about four miles behind."

"Lovely. A witness said she was unconscious when put in his truck. Are you tracking his phone or vehicle?"

"Yep, both. He's desperate, doesn't care about getting caught. She's in real danger O'Clery." Aileen clicked away on her keyboard and looked between monitors.

"Right." Gunnar knew the behavior and that his window of opportunity to get Peg was narrowing. Luckily, Dereck wanted her, might even feel love for her. That may give them time. He started texting his boss who'd called four times and sent him three texts demanding to know what's going on.

Aileen clicked a few more keys and zoned in, "Okay, how far are you from San Augesten Pass?"

"Not there just yet."

"Okay, so he's passed there. He's only a few miles ahead of you."

Gunnar felt some relief as his heartbeat calmed in heightened situations, "Thank you Aileen. Can you tell me his speed?"

"Hey, you need me to smooth things over with your boss?"

Gunnar huffed, "What are you going to tell him?"

"Well, that you were in the area for your shoulder therapy, realized your massage therapist was kidnapped, and now you're in pursuit and he needs to send backup."

"Clever Lauden, but I think I'm fucked on this one. I don't care. I just want Peg safe. He shot her and we both know if he's driving he's not holding pressure on her wound. I don't want to think about her bleeding out in his backseat."

Aileen could tell he cared deeply about Peg, "Okay, listen. I'll make a few calls and continue to watch the screen. Pick up if I call. Oh wait..."

"Tell me."

"He's slowing Gunnar...he's turning off an exit...shit..."

"Tell me!"

Aileen was clicking away zooming in on the location. She squinted and moved her face closer to the monitor.

"Lauden!"

"Okay, Gunnar are you familiar with that old truck stop after the Love's one, I think it's got some weird woman's name."

"Sunny's?"

"Yes! Sunny's Stop and-"

"Got it." Gunnar pushed the pedal to the floor.

"Looks like he's driving around back...near some low hanging trees. I'm trying to zoom in. He's trying to hide his truck under there."

Gunnar moved the phone to his mouth, "Thank you Lauden. Send backup."

The line went dead and Aileen did as he asked. Deep down she felt more emotion than she wanted to for both Gunnar and Peg, and secretly hoped Gunnar would be able to put a bullet between Dereck Law's eyes and rid the world of the psycho.

Chapter 50
DISGRACE

Gunnar felt the sweat covering his body beneath his t-shirt and gym pants. He pushed the pedal more towards the floor, his truck engine whining from the high rate of speed. Both hands were firmly on the wheel as he passed car after car, tractor trailer after tractor trailer, risking his life to get to her and save hers. He only knew he had to get to her quick.

His mind raced as he thought of what he would do to Dereck once he caught him. He had to keep his rage tucked deep and feared with all the stress of the Jon recently that he might lose his temper. Peg, admittedly, helped. Not just with her passion and amazing sexual prowess but also, with her connection and deep friendship. His heart calmed in the odd way that it would when he raced to a call, it was just his mind this time. He cared too much, he knew he was too close and also feeling guilt for not doing more sooner. *Fuccccccccccck*

Dereck placed her in the passenger seat he had laid all the way back. He looked down at her beautiful skin, blood contrasting against the new tan she had. He didn't ever remember Peg looking this good.

The black lingerie was gorgeous but infuriated him mostly as he knew it was not for him. His eyes gazed down her perfect breasts, her tummy, then to her legs that had fallen to the side as she lay unconscious. He wanted her. He'd always wanted her. Peg was a goddess and he knows he should have told her so.

He took rags from the back and pressed them down and into her bullet hole. He needed to get back on the road and knew he had to move her to the front seat so he could hold pressure on her wound. He had her all set in the seat, and even put the seatbelt on her, but he was still nervous at the thought of her waking. If she regained consciousness while he was driving she would beat the shit out of him. Peg was a fighter. He knew he'd have to knock her out which was easier to do if she were sitting next to him.

Dereck lifted the rags, the bleeding wasn't as bad as he thought but she had soaked some, his backseat, and the blanket. He knew he needed to get to the cabin and take care of her. Bunching up the blanket he was able to tie a knot around the rags and pull the seatbelt taut against them. For a moment he felt bad for how he shot her and very obviously broke her clavicle with the bullet going through then out but, the feeling passed and he remembered he had to get going. He stepped back and closed her door quietly. He looked around from the trees he had parked in and ducked to walk around to the driver's side.

"Don't fucking move Law!" Gunnar's voice was deep, clear, and scary.

Dereck froze, fear washing over him. He couldn't believe he was found already and knew it was him? He spread his hands out showing he had no weapon. His eyes went to the sight of his wife inside the window. *Fuck.*

"Turn the fuck around slow...if you reach for that gun I'm going to make sure you never walk again." Gunnar sneered, the sight of Dereck's fat, dumpy frame making him feel disgust. He remembered how Peg said she would wake up and he was fucking her, or how he manipulated a sixteen-year-old to blow him in the parking lot of his martial art school.

Dereck turned towards his right in the direction of the voice, very slowly realizing it had come from inside the trees. As he brought his eyes around to focus, his eyebrows raised, shame washed over him, he could not believe who it was! A cold sweat followed and his heart began to race. He was shocked Gunnar could be so stern. He looked him up and down realizing he was in street clothes, his lips pursed and rage seared through him as he connected that Peg's last word before she went out was *his* name.!!!!!!!

He faced his palms out wanting to reach for the gun but, Gunnar had his pointed right at his head and Dereck knew he wouldn't miss. Gunnar O'Clery was known for head shots.

"You mean the gun I left in the console of my truck O'Clery? So it was you all this time huh?" Dereck didn't move his body, just his lips. He knew if he even flinched, he'd feel the wrath of O'Clery's double-tap. He looked him over in disbelief that he and Peg were fucking and he never figured it out!

"We both know that's a lie. I'm okay with that. I'd prefer you reach for that piece...make my life easier."

Dereck stared into Gunnar's eyes trying to mask his rage at what he was seeing in his mind between his wife and Gunnar.

"Bet you wouldn't be saying such things if you had a body-cam on. It's obvious you're off duty. Wouldn't have anything to do with why my wife is dressed in lingerie and heels would it Gunnar?"

"Wife? Asshole, everyone knows you lost her...and rightfully so, that woman stayed longer than anyone should." Gunnar was fine with the bullshit banter if it passed the time until backup arrived. He'd prefer to put Dereck down, especially now that he shot the woman who'd shown him the greatest passion he'd ever known.

"Speaking of, your wife still work in Downing?"

"That's not gonna work."

Dereck smirked, "How about your daughters? The female O'Clery clan still virgins?"

Gunnar remembered what Peg told him about Dereck's affinity for young girls and big dick dudes.

"Oh, Peg mentioned your sick preferences. Still not gonna work. I can do this all day."

"She's bleeding out O'Clery."

"No she's not. But just for shits-n-giggles, lets have you take a few steps towards me in case your fat ass falls."

"I'm not going down as suicide-by-cop Gunnar."

Gunnar watched his black, glazed eyes. Peg was right and so was Aileen. He wasn't right. "Oh I'm aware. Narcissists don't commit suicide, not even by cop."

Dereck rolled his eyes, his palms still open. "Sounds like you guys have spent enough time together for you to absorb her life coaching crap."

He wondered how long they'd been fucking, the visuals in his mind half making him want to rush and tackle Gunnar, the other half turning him on. Watching Peg in a threesome was mind-blowing so he knew seeing her with Gunnar would be just as fulfilling. He wished he'd approached him years ago about joining him and Peg. He frowned wondering how long the two have been together.

"Peg needn't say a word Dereck. I had your number years back when I would try to have a conversation with your father and you would keep interjecting like some little kindergartner." He watched Dereck's face. He knew he hit a nerve.

"Leave him out of it!"

"You're a disgrace to his memory. If he were here he'd have you shunned from the Mason's even."

"Shut your fucking face."

Gunnar still had his gun pointed straight at Dereck's face. Admittedly, he'd love to rearrange his facial bone structure with one bullet.

"You didn't think I knew about your 32nd degree huh? There's no way you'd get to 33rd, especially if your father was here and knew who you truly are. They let pedophiles in Law?"

"She fucked you so good you even believe her lies."

"Peg has no reason to lie."

"So she did fuck you. Isn't she the best O'Clery?" Dereck nodded his head back towards the truck. "That's grade-A, prime choice pussy."

Gunnar hated how he referred to her, "You did not deserve her."

"Oh really? And you do? How well do you really know her Gunnar? You've been fucking her what? A few months since she got back?"

Gunnar smiled. Dereck's lips pursed, fear washed over him thinking she may have been in love with him for years. He tried to think back to when he met Gunnar and introduced Peg to him. He hated that she never would have known him if it weren't for him.

"You really fucked up Dereck."

"You've got some really fucked up negotiating skills man."

Gunnar canted his head slightly, "I'm not negotiating with you."

"Oh? Just biding time?"

"This is exactly how I'd talk to you over shots of whiskey...right before I put you down you fat fuck."

Dereck smiled, "Oh my, if your Chief could hear you now. And I thought we were friends."

"My friends don't hurt women."

"Well, my friends don't fuck my wife."

"She was never your wife Dereck, all of Ramas knew you didn't deserve her. In my book, she was never your wife."

"You have no idea what you're talking about. So tell me, how would you feel if I went to visit your wife at her job? Maybe fuck her on her desk during her lunch break?" Dereck smiled.

"You're one sick motherfucker. Peg was right on every level about you."

Sirens sounded in the distance. Multiple vehicles began closing in, the sound coming closer. Dereck eyed Gunnar up and down noticing how muscular and fit he kept himself even all these years later. He knew Peg devoured every inch of the man and gave herself fully to him. Thats the kind of woman she was when she really cherished someone. It made him feel a seething jealousy that started to make his body shake with rage. So much of him wanted to rush Gunnar and snap his neck.

Chapter 51

TRULY

Gunnar stood against the wall, one leg up, his hands in the front pockets of his jeans. He stared over at her happy the bullet was a through-n-through and not lodged in her body. She looked peaceful but he hurt deep down knowing she could have died if she hadn't lunged when Dereck aimed and pulled the trigger. He was for sure aiming for her heart. She was lucky to only have the clavicle and shoulder injury. He knows she wouldn't be here if the bullet had reached his target.

The monitors beeped, he could see she was breathing well. Her body lay relaxed and gorgeous under the hospital blankets and knowing how sexual she was, he had racy thoughts about what he'd love to do to her. He knew she would wake soon, and he wanted to be there when she did.

The shift changed and a new nurse entered while half-knocking. He stopped, noticing Gunnar across the room watching her. Curious as to why an officer was outside the door sitting in a chair, he half-whispered.

"Oh, I'm sorry. I need to do vitals." The tall, slender nurse looked Gunnar up and down, impressed with his physique. He smiled slightly then went to Peg's side.

"Do your thing dude, I'm just waiting for her to wake."

"She will baby, just gonna take a little bit. Her surgery went smooth, it's the recovery that may take some time." He went back to checking monitors then writing things down on Peg's chart.

"Right."

Clarence White, RN, as his name-tag read, walked around the bed looking over Gunnar once more then averting his eyes,

"You the hubby"?"

"Uh no, just the guy who put her in the ambulance."

"Mmmm huh." Clarence did not believe that at all, as good samaritans who help the injured aren't often granted access to a patient's room that needs an officer sitting outside.

"Thats not because you were the guy who put the bullet through her right?" He could tell by the firearm on Gunnar's hip, he was not a paramedic, but didn't know if she was a criminal he shot and he was waiting to interview her when she woke.

Gunnar squinted slightly annoyed, "I did not."

"She a criminal?"

Gunnar felt even more annoyed, "No. She's the victim of a domestic si... situation."

"Oh don't you worry. She'll be well taken care of. And she'll be staying until we know there's no infection. So far so good. She did lose a lil' too much blood."

"Like I said, I'm just waiting for her to wake."

Clarence smiled seeing the deep worry in his eyes, "We can call you if..."

"I'll stay. She'll have questions and I don't want her to wake alone..."

Clarence nodded, finished writing a few updates on the clipboard and walked to the wall to use a dry erase marker on the board. He put the cap back on and returned the marker.

"Well, feel free to use that loveseat for a nap. You look like you could use one."

Gunnar looked over at the little couch and considered it for a moment. The day was one of his longest and anytime he could lay down and think of he and Peg together was a good day. He nodded at Clarence and walked towards the seat. As soon as he stretched out he could feel deep slumber creeping in and thought he'd just catch a nap. At least he was near her.

Peg fluttered her eyes a bit, opening them, closing them, opening them again. She could see the ugly mauve paint on the wall with an equally ugly design painted near the top. She realized she was in a hospital but felt too groggy to keep her eyes open. She rested them closed again, sensing and feeling him near. She fell back into a deep sleep.

admus Aoife Merch or "Cady" for short, rolled her suitcase along the pavement and pushed the key fob for the Hyundai. The taillights flashed for the white one. She pushed the trunk button and it opened so she could toss her bag in. Already annoyed with the dry New Mexico heat, the wait she endured trying to get her rental car was worsened with the size of the tiny car. It was already noon, the heat creeping in, she turned on the air conditioning and exhaled trying to will her stomach to ease. She's wanted to throw up since the day before when she got the call about Peg being in surgery for a bullet wound. All her relief from Peg finally getting away from Dereck escaped her body the second she heard the stranger's voice say, "She's okay, Peg is okay but....". She frowned remembering the officer's name. Gunnar O'Clery...Lieutenant Gunnar O'Clery. He sounded calm and very familiar with her sister.

Cady typed in the address for the hospital, and groaned at the two hour drive, wishing Peg was closer or at least in her own town. Why Dereck kidnapped her and tried to run to the mountains is not a shock. He was always such an ass. She couldn't be happier that he was finally in jail, hoping he stays there for good.

unnar looked down at her right hand, her fingers limp and intertwined with his. He was so tired. His head was laying on his forearm, eyes trailing along her sleeping frame. The monitors beeped, her heart rate increased. He raised his eyebrows hoping she was ready to wake. It felt like forever since he'd seen her eyes. She moaned, he lifted his head forcing a smile.

Peg's eyes opened, her hand squeezed his, a faint whisper. "Ouch."

Gunnar stood up slow, looking down at her. She'd never seen him look so tired. He smiled, "Hey you."

"Ugh, what the fuck." She tried to smile but her left shoulder felt so sore and she couldn't move.

"Try not to move."

Peg's eyes gazed around the room but she kept coming back to his, confusion taking over. Gunnar watched her, waiting for her to fully wake.

"Water?" She half-whispered, her eyebrows furrowing.

He let go of her hand and poured her water from the tray near by. She took it with a shaky right hand and despite wanting to gulp it, she sipped it feeling a bit queasy.

"Thank you." She handed it back to him. "Okay, give it to me." She tried to smile but he could tell she was bracing herself. He thought about cracking a joke but decided to save it for another time.

Peering into her eyes he gave her a moment to focus. She looked up at him frail, it broke his heart to see her weak. Peg was the least weak person he knew.

"You were shot, kidnapped, rescued, and now you're safe and resting after surgery to fix your upper shoulder there...clavicle was shattered so don't try to use that arm. Open reduction and internal fixation stuff. Gonna be good as new."

She watched his face remembering how attracted she is to him while processing all that he just told her. She could feel her body reacting to the stress, her heart beginning to race. Suddenly she remembered Dereck, the look in his black demon eyes, him raising the gun...

"Oh fuck." Her eyes searched his, water filling them as she was overwhelmed with her body's reaction to the memory.

Gunnar wanted to take it away, he could see what was happening in her body as her chest started rise and fall with panic, the little heart on the machine blinking faster. He knew Peg had worked so hard in the last year to get away from Dereck and ease her CPTSD symptoms. He didn't want this to be a huge step backwards.

"You're safe babe. He's detained."

Her eyes went from the wall to his face, "He won't allow that. He'll get out and..."

"I don't want you to worry about that right-"

"He saw me! He saw me in...our lingerie, the heels!" She looked around, lifting her head trying to see where her clothes were in the room. Her shoulder was sore and she winced.

Gunnar smiled, "Yes he did...and you looked amazing." He took her hand, she was warm and it pleased him.

"Oh no, oh I'm so sorry Gunnar I-"

"Stop, don't worry about me. Things will blow over. They always do. The important thing is he didn't get far...and you are going to make a full recovery." Gunnar was very happy about that.

Peg's eyes softened, "I didn't want this drama to impede into your life, I am so sorry."

"Don't do that. You were right about him. I'm sorry I didn't listen to you...he is not well."

She looked desperate, "He won't be detained. He'll hurt people, injure guards...he's not-"

"It's being taken care of as we speak baby. You're right, he wouldn't do well in jail so I've arranged for him to be uh...evaluated and highly medicated. He spoke calmly, happy he could pull some strings and put Dereck away...with the help of his higher ups and Aileen Lauden.

Peg tried to smile, "Ohhhhh? Medication would help. He was always so sensitive to medicine. This is...good news." She felt relief and exhaled. "I feel..."

"You lost a good amount of blood but should start feeling less weak now, then you can go home."

Peg's eyebrows raised, "Oh my gosh, are my roomies okay!?"

He smiled, "They were out so they came back to a mess but are happy you're safe. My officers calmed them and the neighbors. It's just being explained as a domestic situation and that your ex was mentally unstable and shot and kidnapped you.

"And you saved me?"

"That...*I did*. I'm so happy you're okay."

"My magic dick top cop hero." She smiled.

He laughed, relieved her sense of humor was returning, "It went smooth. Slapping those cuffs on him was so satisfying babe."

She searched his eyes, "I wish I'd seen that!"

"He's not very happy."

"He never is. He's a horrible human. Did you both have words or just took him into custody?"

Gunnar moved to sit on the bed next to her, "Oh we had words baby. There was time while I was waiting for backup...I was kinda of hoping he reached for that gun, I even let him keep it in his waistband for some time but-"

"Yeah, he's psychotic...not suicidal."

"True."

"How...how did you find me? Was I on the floor?"

Gunnar realized he needed to walk her through everything, "We can go through it all when you're feeling stronger...but no, you were on your way to the mountains in his truck. I uh...ruined his plans for you."

Peg's eyes watered a second time. "Thank you. I don't know what to say...or how to thank you. What he would have done to me up there-"

Gunnar stroked her face, "You don't have to think of such things. He didn't win. You won baby. You're finally free from him." He could see she was overwhelmed. He leaned forward and kissed her on her forehead. He then looked her in the eyes and leaned into her lips, his body reacting to the feel of them on his. The woman affected him I every cell of his being, even injured in a hospital bed.

Gunnar's phone vibrated and he checked his texts. Moving to stand, he smiled and kissed her again excited to have arranged for her sister Cady to be with her, "I've got to go. You have a special visitor. I'll be back when I can okay?"

Peg hated when he left but never protested, "Okay, be safe...and Gunnar?"

"Yes?"

"Thank you...*truly.* I-"

"I...love you Peg...I'll be seeing you..."

Her eyes searched his, her heart aching deep inside because she couldn't ascertain by his gaze if it was the last time she'd ever see him. It felt like he was for some reason. Leaving for good, maybe to protect her? And his words, it was as if...for the first time in her life, she could believe.

She whispered them back, "I love you..."

Gunnar smiled, turned

and

was

gone.................

DEZI GOLDEN is an American Author from Las Cruces, New Mexico. This is her eighth novel. Find Dezi online or write to her at dezigolden@gmail.com. Autographed copies are available.

The author would like to acknowledge:

That the characters, plot, places, timing, and intimacy in this novel are fictitious. It is not to offend anyone's personal preferences, culture, or history.

Gratitude to those who shared their experiences and time while research for the story's characters, scenarios, plot, and careers was being developed.

Thank you for purchasing this book published by Author, Dezi Golden.

To receive an autographed copy for your collection. Contact the author at dezigolden.com or dezigolden@gmail.com.